Praise for *After the Fall*

'Original, wonderfully written and utterly gripping, this is a corker of a tale.' *The Sun*

'A page turning book to while away a winter's evening.' *Red*

'If you enjoy reading family sagas involving current, edgy dilemmas I really recommend it.' Judy Finnigan

'Jodi Picoult had better look over her shoulder – she's got a new contender by the name of Charity Norman.'
Sydney Morning Herald

'A gripping story, which touches on the fragility of trust, the strength of love and, of course, second chances.'
Sunday Canberra Times

Praise for *Freeing Grace*

'Will appeal to devotees of Joanna Trollope and Jodi Picoult... [Norman] is hot on their heels.' *Daily Mail*

'Easy to read, hard to put down, it'll move you to tears.'
Easy Living

'Intelligent and warm.' *Sunday Age*

'This is a compelling, accomplished and often dark debut.'
West Australian

'Last month I heralded *Room* as the best novel in a decade, but hot on its heels – as strong a contender – is this wonderful story... the tale is satisfyingly complex and involving.'
Australian Country Style

Also by Charity Norman

Freeing Grace

After the Fall
(published as Second Chances in Australia)

The SON-in-LAW

CHARITY NORMAN

First published in Great Britain in 2013 by Allen & Unwin

First published in Australia in 2013 by Allen & Unwin

Allen & Unwin
c/o Atlantic Books
Ormond House
26–27 Boswell Street
London WC1N 3JZ
Phone: 020 7269 1610
Fax: 020 7430 0916
Email: UK@allenandunwin.com
Web: www.atlantic-books.co.uk

A CIP catalogue record for this book is available from the British Library.

ISBN 978 1 74331 668 9

Set in 11.5/15.5pt Sabon by Post Pre-press Group, Australia
Printed and bound by CPI Group (UK) Ltd, Croydon, CR0 4YY

10 9 8 7 6 5 4 3 2 1

For Tim

Thanks for all the banana cake.

In the Leeds Crown Court

REGINA
V
Joseph William Scott

Exhibit 53: Transcript of 999 call made by Scarlet Scott

Operator: Hello, ambulance emergency.
SS: Um, can you please help? My mum's lying on the ground.
Op: She's lying on the ground? Is she conscious?
SS: We can't wake her up.
Op: Is she breathing?
SS: Dad, is she breathing?
Joseph Scott (in background): No, she's not breathing, she's not breathing . . . Christ. Tell them there's no pulse!
SS: She isn't breathing, she hasn't got a pulse.
Op: Okay, help's on its way now.
SS (crying): Please tell them to hurry, she looks wrong.
Op: Who have you got with you?
SS: My dad and my brothers.
Joseph Scott (shouts): Help her, please! Her heart's stopped.
Op: Okay, I heard that. Help's on its way, lights and sirens. I'm going to tell you exactly what to do, okay?
SS: Okay.
Op: Listen to me carefully and tell your dad.
SS: Okay.
Op: Is she flat on her back?
SS: No, she's—
Op: Tell your dad she has to be flat on her back.
SS: Dad, she says to get her flat on her back. Okay, he's done that.
Op: No pillows?
SS: No, there aren't any. We're in the living room.
Op: Tell him to check her mouth . . . Is there anything in there, like food or vomit?

SS: Dad, is there anything in her mouth? . . . No, there isn't.

Op: Tell him to put the heel of his hand on her breastbone.

SS: She says put the heel of your hand on her breastbone.

Op: Put his other hand on top of that hand.

SS: Put your other hand on top of that one.

Op: Okay? He's doing that? Now press down, pump her chest about twice a second.

SS: She says pump her chest about twice a second.

Joseph Scott: Twice a second, okay . . . Oh my God, oh my God.

Op: Is he pumping her chest now?

SS: Yes, but she isn't . . . why isn't she waking up?

Op: You're doing really well, really well. What's your name?

SS: Scarlet.

Op: How old are you, Scarlet?

SS: Ten.

Op: You're doing so well. That music's very loud, isn't it? Could you turn it off?

SS: Um . . . no, I can't reach the knob.

Op: That's okay, don't worry. Your dad needs to pump rapidly, tell him just to keep going, I'll let him know when it's time to stop.

SS: She says you have to pump rapidly, keep going till she says to stop.

Op: Good girl. You're doing so well. How old is your mum, Scarlet?

SS: I don't know . . . um, thirty-three I think.

Op: What's her name?

SS (long pause): She's gone a funny colour.

Op: I need you to listen to me, Scarlet. Is your dad still pumping her chest?

SS: Oh no—I think she's dead! I think she's dead!

Op: Scarlet, listen, I need you to stay calm for me. Is he still doing it?

SS: Yes, but she isn't waking up.

Op: Okay. Your dad needs to keep going. How old are your brothers?

SS: Theo's seven and Ben is a baby.

Op: I can hear the baby crying. He's not hurt is he? No? Did your mum have a fit, or . . .

SS: No, she didn't.

Op: So what's actually happened to her?

SS: My dad . . . (crying) . . . my dad hit her.

Op: He hit her?

SS: And then she fell over and now she's . . . (screams) There's blood on the floor!

Op: You're doing such a great job. Do you think Theo could go to the door and look out for the ambulance?

SS: Theo—no, he can't go because he's hiding, he's scared.

Op: Okay. Are you in the front room? Can you see into the road?

SS: Yes I can.

Op: Is the front door locked?

SS: No it won't be . . . Please, could you tell them to hurry?

Op: The ambulance is almost there, and the police, okay? Is your dad still doing the compressions?

SS: The . . .

Op: Is he still pumping her chest rapidly?

SS: Yes he is, but he's crying and crying.

Op: Help should be with you any minute now.

SS: My dad's crying and Ben's crying.

Op: You're being very brave, you can be proud of yourself.

SS: They're here! I can see the lights outside.

Op: Can you go and let them in, Scarlet?

SS: Okay . . . (to paramedic) In here, quick, she's in here. (Voices in background, unintelligible)

Op: Scarlet? The crew are with you are they?

SS: And some police.

Op: You've done really well.

SS (crying): Is my mum going to be all right?

One

Scarlet

My mother used to say her wedding day was like a fairytale. It was a blue and gold morning, and a million daffodils rippled beneath the city walls. She and my father were young, beautiful and crazy about each other.

'Don't let people tell you love isn't like in the films, Scarlet,' she said. It was one of those moments when she seemed to be surfing right on top of a foaming, frothing wave of happiness. 'Why on earth shouldn't it be? There *is* such a thing as happy ever after. People think it's cool to scoff.' She gave a little laugh, humming along to the jazz music she had playing on the stereo. 'Miserable sods, I say.'

For some reason, that evening is one of my clearest memories of Mum. She smelled of . . . well, of Mum; her special sandalwood scent, and coffee and maybe wine. I've got one of her soft cardigans under my bed, and it still smells like her. If I press my face into it and shut my eyes, I can pretend it *is* her. I must have been about eight because Flotsam and Jetsam were kittens then, fluffy white pom-poms galloping across the bed. Ben wasn't even born. Theo was lying on the floor, trying to read a baby book from the new entrants' class at school. His tongue was sticking out.

Our parents were getting ready to go somewhere for the evening. Mum seemed thin and quick, like an elf, with her red-gold hair cut short and chic and a shining sweep of fringe to one side. When she was happy, as she was that night, she seemed to light everyone up. The music went right through her like an electric current. It made her dance, and her dress sparkled and flashed as she moved. When she sparkled her way past Dad, he pulled her into his arms—*gotcha!* he said—and they danced together. I thought they looked like film stars. Their legs moved at the same time, in the same direction, and they looked into one another's eyes. Then he kissed her.

'Do you believe in love at first sight?' I asked when she sat down at the dressing table.

'Absodiddly! It was love at first sight for Dad and me. He was my knight in shining armour, did you know that? He rescued me from a wicked knave, fought for my honour and carried me away.'

'A wicked knave?'

She laughed into the mirror as she stroked on her dark pink lipstick. It was as though she had a secret joke with the lady reflected there. I could see that mirror lady's eyes. They were all colour, like glowing green glass in a pale face. 'I was having a little trouble with a guy at a party.'

'And Dad carried you away?'

'Well, in a manner of speaking.'

'Like Prince Charming?'

Dad was listening to all this, chuckling as he laced up his shoes. Mum reached out and touched his face with her long fingers. 'Charming shmarming! Your dad was *much* more glamorous than that big girl's blouse! Hang on.' She danced over to the cupboard and found her photo album. Then she made room at the dressing table, patting the chair beside her. Dad rumpled Theo's messy hair and said he'd read him a story before the babysitter arrived, and the two of them pottered off. Theo was a miniature Dad, really, except that he had a button nose where Dad's was heavy and strong. They both looked old-fashioned, with slate-coloured eyes and serious expressions that seemed to burst into sunshine when they smiled.

Mum and I looked through her album, though I'd seen it many times before. In my favourite picture, my parents were standing by a fountain. They'd just got married.

'See?' she said, smiling at it. 'Look at him! I still think he might turn out to be a lost Russian prince, only he doesn't know it yet.'

I agreed, because I loved her. But I remember thinking that Dad looked just like Dad, even dressed in a posh tailcoat which I've never seen him wear in real life. He was gazing at her as the photo was taken. She was talking, and whatever she'd said was making him laugh. He was pushing his glasses up his nose and looked like a nice, very handsome history teacher and not like a murderer at all. Mum's wedding dress clung to her body and gathered in white folds around her feet, like double cream when you pour it out of a jug. She wore a lace veil with a circle of flowers. This had been my grandmother Hannah's, and Great-Gran's before her, and I could wear it one day.

I ran to my bedroom and fetched my library book, *Maid of Sherwood*. The illustration on the jacket was of Maid Marion riding into the forest to look for Robin. She was wearing a blue gown and a white cloth over her head, held on by a circlet of gold. She had huge eyes and a thin face.

'Maid Marion's you,' I said.

Mum clutched me to her chest. Actually, it was a bit too tight. 'Oh, Scarlet.' She sounded as though she was running out of breath. 'Don't you ever change. Don't ever be horrid and sulky like I was. You absolutely have to stay just the way you are right now.' Then she kissed both my cheeks—*mwah, mwah*—quite hard, almost angrily. It gave me dark pink kiss marks.

I later wondered whether that was why she let him kill her. Perhaps she didn't want to see us three grow up. I thought if she'd really wanted to be with us she would have found a way to stay alive. Then we wouldn't have had to live with Hannah and Gramps. Now, of course, I realise this is nonsense. Mum couldn't help dying. Her brain was flooded with blood which made it swell up.

I never did take that book back to the library. Eventually they sent a grumpy letter and I paid the fine out of my Christmas money. So *Maid of Sherwood* was my Christmas present to myself. I've still got it under my bed. I've got the photo album too, but I've made a few changes there.

Two

Joseph

The prison was carefully designed to look grim, dwarfing the streets as a dour warning. On a bitter December day, when gusts knifed in from the Pennines, it could have been the brooding castle in a horror film.

It was on such a morning that a metal door swung quietly open. It led into an open area festooned with yellow signs announcing that this was *HMP Leeds,* as though Armley Jail was a jolly tourist attraction. A man in his thirties stepped out into a world that whipped and churned with icy particles. He wasn't dressed for the Yorkshire winter; a lightweight cotton suit hung, crumpled, from broad shoulders. The fingers of one hand were rapidly turning red as they gripped the handle of a plastic bag, and round-rimmed glasses disappeared beneath a film of sleety particles.

The door banged behind him, shutting him out. For a second or two he seemed unable to move. He turned his head and watched a prison van as it swept towards massive vehicle gates. Then he raised a forefinger, pushed his glasses up his nose, and set off past the yellow signs, past the eyeless walls and into the city's streets. A car honked and swerved as he seemed about to step out in front of it. An elderly woman edged past with her eyes averted. Finally he crossed the road and took refuge in a bus shelter.

Four schoolgirls in uniform perched on the narrow seat, smoking and gossiping. They cast sidelong smirks at the stranger as he stood examining a timetable on the wall. One of them—obviously the clown of the group, a ponytail sprouting from the side of her head—whispered something, and the others erupted into giggles.

As time passed, the smoking girls began to stare openly at the newcomer. He looked vampire-pale and faintly exotic. His cheekbones were high and Slavic, tinged blue in the bitter air. After much nudging, Ponytail spoke up.

'Want one?' she offered, holding out a packet of cigarettes.

His eyes were blue-grey, bloodshot under heavy brows. 'I don't smoke. Thanks.'

''Scuse me,' she persisted, with a do-or-die glance at her fellows. 'We've got a bet on about you. Not being funny or anything.'

'Not being funny,' echoed the stranger dryly. His voice carried a hint of Geordie. 'Go on then.'

'Did you just get out of jail?'

'Been a free man for . . . ooh, twenty minutes?'

'Thought so!' she screamed. 'Whassit like? My boyfriend's uncle was in there. He reckons the food's terrible, worse than bloody Hull and that's saying something.'

The newcomer shrugged discouragingly, and turned back to the timetable.

The girls were not put off. *You ask . . . No you ask . . . I asked last time . . . Go on, Karin.* Ponytail stepped closer, wrapping her striped school scarf across her mouth.

''Scuse me . . . erm, look don't take this the wrong way or anything, but my mates want to know what you was in for.'

He was shivering now, shoulders hunched, forcing his hands into his trouser pockets.

'*She* reckons you're a nonce,' said his interrogator, pointing at one of her cronies. 'But I reckon—'

The stranger never heard what she reckoned. Her voice was drowned out by the furious blast of a car's horn as a black four-wheel drive mounted the pavement.

'Scott!' yelled the driver, leaning across to open the passenger door. 'Scott, you fuckin' tosshead, where d'you think you're going?'

The tosshead managed a strained smile. 'Akash, where'd you get the wheels? Tell me you didn't pinch it.'

'Company car. Now stop asking bloody stupid questions and get in. You must be freezing your tiny bollocks off out there.'

The girls had watched this exchange with fascination. Ponytail had one last shot. 'C'mon! Can't have been that bad. Bet you didn't kill nobody.'

The stranger looked over his shoulder, one foot in the car. 'You bet I didn't?'

'I've just bet two quid you didn't.'

'Then you're two quid out of pocket,' he announced calmly, before ducking inside.

The four truants stood watching as the heavy vehicle lurched off towards the dual carriageway. There was a thoughtful silence. Eventually, Ponytail ground her cigarette stub out on the pavement. 'What a load of shite. I reckon he was in for something really boring. Looked like a friggin' undertaker.'

'Sexy eyes though,' said the smallest one, fanning herself comically. 'Whew! I've just been smouldered at by a murderer.'

Ponytail made an obscene gesture. 'People with little round specs don't do murders.'

•

Joseph Scott huddled in the passenger seat, blowing on his numb hands.

'You're as pig-ugly as ever, Scott,' remarked his companion affably. He was young, white-toothed and hair-gelled. 'Let's turn up the heating . . . That better? Fuck's sake, tell me those aren't the only clothes you've got?'

'The suit I wore to court when I got sent away. Symbolic.' Joseph looked out of the window, flinching as cars flashed past, dazed by the sheer speed of the outside world.

Akash smiled at the back of his friend's head. 'Crazy, isn't it? You think you're going to be all woo*hoo*! You fantasise for months about chasing skirt and getting totally ratted and filling your face with Mum's home cooking. Then you step out that gate and . . . what next?'

'Feels like a foreign country.' Joseph rubbed his face. 'How did you know I was coming out today?'

'I phoned your solicitor. Got to the gate complex, they said you'd already gone. I've been driving around bloody Armley looking for you, silly prick.'

'Thanks.'

'You're welcome.'

Joseph turned away from the window. 'You rescued me from some monstrous ladettes. Shouldn't they be in school?'

Akash put on a plummy accent, which seemed to come easily to him. 'That's modern gals for you. Country's going to the dogs . . . It's the parents I blame. Anyway, where to, mate? Pubs are open, barmaids are lined up and waiting.'

Joseph imagined the taste of a pint. 'You're on.' He hesitated. 'In a bit. I need to get to York first and see my solicitor. I was planning on catching a bus. I've got a travel warrant.'

'You're out of your tree! You don't want to spend your first hours of freedom sitting in some lawyer's office. Me, I never want to see another one again as long as I live. Look, there's the Prince Albert. Shall we—'

'After I've paid a visit to my solicitor,' Joseph insisted. 'He's expecting me.'

'Is this about the kids?'

'Of course it's about the kids.'

'Mate, is this a good idea? You're on licence, right? I bet you've got a condition on there about not contacting your family.'

'True.' Joseph had a copy of his licence conditions in his pocket. 'I'm not supposed to go anywhere near their house—which is in York, admittedly. But nobody said I couldn't visit my solicitor.'

'Let's get some decent food and a pint down you. You need to think this through.'

'You can feed me caviar and champagne if you like. Bathe me in ass's milk, I won't change my mind.'

'You've waited all this time, Scottie. Another couple of days won't hurt.'

Joseph's jaw tensed dangerously. 'I've been counting down the hours until I can walk into that solicitor's office. It's all that's kept me going. Come on, Akash, you know what it's like in there—nothing to do but think. If you don't want to nip across to York, fine—I'll catch a bus.'

Akash capitulated. 'Okay. York, here we come. Where are you staying tonight?'

'I told the probation guy I was planning to look up my sister in Gateshead,' said Joseph unenthusiastically. 'He wants to know my new address by Friday.'

'Have you phoned her?'

'No. She'd dance on my grave, given half a chance.'

'Any other family?'

'Just my old man. Last I heard he was living it up on the Costa Blanca.'

'I've got a sofa. You're welcome to it for as long as you need.'

'Thanks,' muttered Joseph. 'That would be . . . Thanks.' He stared down at his hands, and after a moment Akash turned on the radio. A boy band was playing.

They'd reached the outskirts of York before Joseph spoke again. 'Sorry. Sorry. Thanks for picking me up. I've got a discharge payment of sod-all, so we'll blow it on a pint.' He pulled some notes from his pocket. 'So, is this your car?'

'Yeah . . . well, technically it's Dad's. He set me up in a business. You're looking at the managing director of Squeaky Clean Offices and Domestic. The good news is, I've got a load of women to boss about. The bad news is I work half the night.' The young man forced his way into the overtaking lane between two cars, gesticulating when one of them flashed its lights.

The wind had dropped by the time they arrived in York. So had the temperature. 'I'll wait for you in the pub over there.' Akash blew out his cheeks, rubbing his hands together. 'Fuck, it's brass monkeys.'

Joseph looked around, getting his bearings, still disoriented. The air seemed oddly opaque.

'I think it's going to snow,' he said.

Three

Hannah

I don't know where to begin. Not with him, that's for sure. How can he be the beginning, when he destroyed everything that gave my life meaning?

She was our only child, you see. There was no understudy. Joseph Scott brought down the curtain forever. She was extraordinary from the moment she was born—a delicate creature with the brightest eyes the midwife had ever seen. I was twenty-six years old, and euphoric. My baby was a crumpled thing of wonder, an alien creature from outer space, the most precious object in the universe. Things that seemed vital a week before had become irrelevant. The skiing holiday? Ridiculous—of course we couldn't go, not until Zoe was old enough to join us. My battle for promotion to departmental head? Who cared? My alcoholic sister Eliza wanted to stay for a few days? No, she bloody well couldn't. Nobody could. We had a new baby.

Zoe was born in a cottage hospital, near where we were living at the time. In the next bed a girl called Jennifer nursed her eye-watering eleven-pounder, Bradley. Jennifer had pink cheeks and a pinker towelling bathrobe, and her bedside cabinet was covered with cards screaming *It's a boy!* As though she didn't know.

'What you calling yours?' she asked, eyeing the scrap of life in the cot by my bed.

'Zoe,' I said. 'Zoe Eliza.'

'S'nice. This your first?'

I nodded, a grin of idiocy plastered across my face.

'Bradley's my third,' she said. 'And believe me, he's my last!'

Freddie held Zoe as though she was made of crystal, his foolish smile his matching mine. His hair was already in retreat, leaving shiny temples. I thought it looked distinguished, with his long face and fine bones.

'Is that the granddad?' whispered one of Jennifer's visitors.

Freddie and I pretended not to hear, while Jennifer shushed and the visitor giggled.

Jennifer's husband came to take her home the next morning. I watched as she organised her things, chattering amiably. Minutes later, she had gone. The midwife came to make her bed. Funny thing: I missed her terribly. In fact, that was the day I began to cry, for no reason at all. Freddie found me snivelling in the nursing chair. Zoe had fallen asleep in my arms, heart-shaped mouth open, dribbling milk onto my blouse.

'It's not getting her,' I sobbed, as Frederick patted and soothed.

'What's not getting her?' He touched the whorl of copper hair on Zoe's mushroom-soft head. Her veins pulsed beneath the fontanel.

'Life,' I said. 'Death.'

But it did.

•

I think I shall start with the letter.

It arrived the day they let him go. It lay there, making the kitchen table filthy with its very presence, with a rash of purple stamps from the censors. Perhaps we'd dropped off the list of forbidden correspondents, or perhaps the authorities had slipped up. We'd already had two from his solicitor, so I had a fair idea what this one was about.

I wouldn't open it. The thing could go in the bin. *There!* I cast it into that dark pit and heard the satisfying click-clack of the plastic lid. It would be sinking helplessly into a glob of leftover porridge. *That's what I think of you!*

It had been snowing since lunchtime, and the garden was already a white wilderness. The heaviest fall had passed, but miniature wagon wheels of lace still waltzed and swirled. Frederick and Ben were out there, trying to make a snowman. I could see them through the kitchen window. Ben took three steps to each one of his Gramps' as he shovelled snow into the tiny wooden wheelbarrow. Frederick made that barrow for Zoe, when she was small. He and she used to weed the flower beds together. I'd hear her chattering—yabber yabber yabber, without a pause for breath—and his delighted laughter. We wanted more children, expected more, but after three excruciating miscarriages I got the message and poor old Frederick got the snip.

I opened the oven to find my scones smoking merrily. Damn and blast Joseph Scott, he even made me burn the scones. I rescued the best of them before tapping on the window. Frederick and Ben were bent low over the winter-bare cabbage patch—examining some life form, for sure. Frederick would be speaking in rich, enthusiastic tones like David Attenborough, and Ben would be staring up into his grandfather's face with a look of total absorption. Four years old, and seventy-six. Those two had a love affair going on.

I opened the kitchen door, warbling names to the tune of 'Waltzing Matilda'. 'Frederick Ben, Frederick Ben, would you like some tea and scones?'

The warmth of the kitchen billowed out, hanging like a heavy eiderdown in the frozen wastes. Freddie took his grandson's hand and the two figures headed towards me—one tall and too thin, each step taken cautiously for fear of a slip on the icy path; the other small, plump, with a jerky quick-walk. Flotsam, one of Zoe's Birman cats, pattered behind, tail high.

They were letting him out today. He'd probably be free by now. We'd had a letter from the authorities to tell us so. Nice of them, I suppose. I certainly didn't want to meet him face to face with no warning. I didn't want to meet him face to face at all; but one day I would turn a corner in the supermarket and there he'd be, bold as brass, leering at me like the psychopath in a bad film. I could feel the familiar hatred stirring inside me. It burned. What would I do, when confronted by my daughter's killer? Perhaps I'd find his car and cut the brake cable. Nobody would blame me.

Ben and Frederick burst into the house in a flurry of slush and Tarzan calls, hanging up their coats on pegs, peeling off wet woollen gloves and—in Ben's case—plonking down onto the doormat and tugging at his wellingtons. His right foot was by his nose. I don't remember ever having that India-rubber flexibility.

'Put your gloves on the radiator,' I ordered. 'And your horrid wet socks.'

They weren't listening. They were two artists, planning an installation. 'So we're agreed on bottle tops for buttons, and . . . What about eyes, do you think?' asked Freddie.

Ben pulled the boot off his other foot. He had a revolting running nose, and squirmed as I wiped it.

'Here—give that snowman one of Gramps' caps,' I suggested, taking down an old one from a peg. It was a tweed flat cap, and the silk lining was torn.

'It's a snow*lady*,' cried Ben, guffawing indulgently at my density. 'Not a *man*! Can we have one of your great big wedding hats?'

'I'm surprised at you, Hannah,' added Frederick, white brows twitching. 'Making assumptions based on gender stereotypes.'

'Oh, shut up.' I stuck out my tongue, and Freddie put his arm around my shoulder, as he must have done a million times over the past forty years.

I was twenty-four when I met and married Frederick Wilde. I had no intention of falling in love—not then, not ever. I was absorbed in my doctorate in York, and Not the Marrying Type.

One evening, a fellow postgrad called Laura talked me into going to the last night of *The Caretaker*. Apparently the production had garnered rave reviews (*in Frederick Wilde's hands, humour and darkness intertwine with shocking sensitivity*). I sat through the play, thought it ugly and didn't care two hoots whether the director was Frederick Wilde or Donald Duck.

Laura was having a fling with the stage manager, so we were invited to a last-night bash afterwards. They were an entertaining lot, I had to admit, and I began to enjoy myself. A lanky, tweed-jacketed chap seemed to be the centre of attention.

'Who's that?' I asked Laura's boyfriend.

He glanced around. 'That's Freddie Wilde!'

'Who?'

'C'mon, I'll introduce you. You're going to love him.' And with those unwittingly prophetic words, he led me to my destiny.

It was Frederick's humility that struck me first. People in the theatre hung on his every word, yet he always seemed to regard their stories as more interesting than his own. I found in him everything I admired, perhaps everything I lacked—creativity and humour and forgiveness of human nature. God knows what he found in me. He was twelve years my senior, though that seemed ludicrously irrelevant. My parents fretted and fussed about the age gap but they soon fell under his spell. We married within a year, and were still married forty years on. Laura and her stage manager parted company a week after *The Caretaker* closed.

That wretched letter. The lid of the bin seemed agitated, as though some animal was scavenging in there. Who knew? Perhaps Scott was writing to say he'd never trouble us again. Perhaps the letter was a suicide note—just the kind of thing he'd do, try and load his guilt onto us.

Flotsam settled in the armchair in the corner, close beside his sleeping twin sister. Ben climbed up onto his tall stool at the table and grabbed a scone, legs swinging. Frederick sat opposite. 'Scones! How lovely,' he declared, tactfully ignoring the whiff of incineration.

'There's a review of Scarlet's play in the local,' I said, passing him a copy of the *Yorkshire Post*. 'Take a look.'

He put down his cup, lifted his glasses onto his nose and studied the paper. *The Bootham amateur dramatic society's production has much to delight . . . lighting, music . . .* I watched him read, knowing that he was getting to the best bit. 'Oho!' He cried in trumph. '*Scarlet Scott has commanding presence as Puck, and steals every scene she is in.* Oh, that's marvellous. Well played, Scarletta!'

'I'm not surprised,' I said, rereading it over his shoulder. 'She lights up any stage. So did her mother. So do you, when you act.'

'Are we going to see Scarlet's play, Hannah?' asked Ben.

'Of course!'

'Hm.' He considered this information as he reached for more jam. 'Will Theo come too?'

'Definitely! It's just the sort of play he'll like.'

'Will it be boring?'

'No, it's wonderful. It's about fairies.'

'More to the point,' added Freddie, 'if you sit still and keep quiet, we'll take the three of you out for pizza afterwards. And ice-cream.'

'Okay then. Gramps, d'you think tee-ran-a-saw-us ate pizza?' asked Ben, whose twin preoccupations were food and dinosaurs.

'Meatlovers was his favourite,' Freddie replied seriously.

The pair of them began to witter absurdly about prehistoric pizza while I wandered in aimless little circles, fretting about that envelope in the bin.

'All right, my darling?' asked Freddie. 'You're not eating.'

'I'm watching my weight . . . trying to keep the rate of inflation under control.'

He knew me so well. 'It's today, isn't it?' he asked quietly. When I nodded, he seemed to age another ten years. He looked like what he was—an elderly man who would never stop grieving. He reached out and rubbed my arm. His own hand was crisscrossed, indigo rivers under the thin skin. 'They have to let him out. He's served his time.'

'If I see him anywhere near here . . .' I muttered.

'He won't come here.'

'Who?' asked Ben, scraping his knife around in the jam. 'Who won't come here?'

'Nobody you know, sweetheart,' I said. And it was true. Ben hadn't seen his father since he was a year old.

'Shall we go back outside now, Gramps? Let's get it finished before Theo and Scarlet come home.' Cramming the rest of the scone into his mouth, Ben slid from his stool.

I dug out a straw sunhat for their snowlady and promised to pay a state visit as soon as she was ready. 'I'll bring the camera,' I said, as they pulled on their boots.

'And a woolly scarf?' wheedled Ben. 'Even snowladies wear scarves.'

'What are you calling her?'

As Ben tugged at the door, winter swirled in with a long, cold gasp. 'Snowmummy,' he replied without hesitation, and I could have wept for him.

Once they'd gone, I cleared the table and poured myself another cup of tea. It was still there, fossicking around in the filthy depths. I couldn't stand it. So I reached into the bin—tea bags, porridge, revolting sticky bits of toast—and lifted out the envelope between finger and thumb. It oozed menace.

I ripped the thing open and read the letter fast as I could, feeling polluted.

Dear Hannah and Frederick,

Already, four words in, I was disgusted. *Dear*?

I don't know whether you've received my solicitor's letters, but as he has had no reply I thought I would send one of my own. I expect to be released very soon now. As you know, I haven't seen the children for over three years and I've missed them more than I can say. I didn't ask, and you didn't bring them. The visiting area isn't a great place for families. I didn't like the idea of them being searched and prodded, and anyway it wasn't how I wanted them to think of me.

But soon I'll be out, and that's very different, as I hope you'll agree. So I was wondering, where could I see them and when?

'You'll see them over my dead body,' I said aloud.

They need to know me. They need to know that their father is a human being, not a devil, and that I am bitterly sorry for what I did. If wishing would change things, Zoe would be alive and I'd be the one dead.

At least we could agree on that. In a perfect world, he'd be the dead one—or, better still, expunged from history.

Please write to me at this address, but put my prison number on the envelope or it won't get here. Or else to my solicitor, Richard O'Brien in York. If I don't hear from you, I'll have to apply to the court. I hope it won't come to that.

With my genuine best wishes,
Joseph Scott

The letter was dated two weeks previously. It must have taken some time to get through those useless censors, out of Armley and into the postal system. Didn't matter. I wouldn't be replying to him or his blasted solicitor. The mere sight of his handwriting—the image of his murdering hand holding the pen—made my knees shake. Letter and envelope were hurled back into the bin.

Then I sat at the table and pressed my hands against my mouth. I wouldn't cry. Joseph Scott wouldn't make me cry, not ever again. I'd cried gallons of tears; I'd wept until my eyes were bruised. I'd lived in darkness, even flirted with the idea of ending my life. All because of him.

More than anything else in the world, I longed for Joseph Scott to disappear forever.

Four

Scarlet

I hope to be an actor when I'm older. It's my greatest ambition. A lot of girls say they want to be actors, and most never make it. But I'm different. It's in my blood.

We've got videos of Mum on the stage and even on the telly. The most famous thing she did was playing the anti-heroine, Melinda, in a mini-series called *The Last Postman in Bosnia*. Girls at school haven't heard of it because it was on years ago. My English teacher, Mrs May, saw it when it first screened and she says my mum's portrayal of her character was superb. She actually said Mum was 'the best thing about that production'. I think she was trying to tell me she hated the rest but loved Mum's acting.

People say I look a lot like her. On my thirteenth birthday, I had all my hair chopped off. Gramps was horrified because he used to love brushing my hair. He and Hannah and the hairdresser all went on about how it was such a glorious colour, all the way to my waist, and it was a crime to cut it off. They made a monumental fuss, but Hannah had always promised I could have a haircut once I was thirteen, and I held her to it. I got a pixie cut like Mum's, with a longer fringe and little triangles in front of my ears. It was much easier to keep tidy.

I've also got green eyes, and people say I've inherited Mum's sharp chin, so in some ways I really do look like her. There's one big problem: she was very, *very* slim. There wasn't a bit of anything saggy about her. All her ribs showed. When she wore hipster jeans, her hipbones showed too. She didn't look like other people's mothers. Other mothers are mother-shaped. Some have massive bums, and most have stomachs that stick out no matter how much they wear Spanx or try to suck them in. My mum looked young and skinny enough to be their daughter. People used to tell her she needed feeding up, and that really pissed her off. 'What right have they got?' she complained. 'It's so rude. I don't comment on their bloody great bingo wings.'

Anyway, I seem to have quite a different sort of body and no matter how little I eat, how much exercise I do, I just keep swelling and growing taller and taller, like Alice in Wonderland after she's nibbled the mushroom. I'm not plump, but I'm a different shape from Mum. I've even got a bust. I hate it. I really do.

The week it snowed, Ben and Gramps made a snowlady in the garden and I was Puck at the Little Theatre. Our last performance was a Sunday matinee, and the family came to watch. Gramps and Hannah sent a mega bunch of flowers to the stage door. The creepy old guy who called himself 'stage manager' brought it in, leering in his pervy way.

'Got an admirer,' he said, and rolled his eyes as though I was sleeping with whoever had sent the flowers. I felt like kicking him in the goolies.

The play went brilliantly that afternoon. I'd spent all day thinking myself into the part and it paid off because I really felt like a mischievous, slightly cruel sprite who thinks human beings are fools. I don't want to sound too smug, but I definitely got the most cheers and whoops at the end. I was still buzzing when I left the theatre. Gramps was waiting for me at the stage door, while Hannah took the boys to fetch the car. He stood tall among a crowd of parents, wearing his tweed overcoat and flat cap like something out of a spy film. He's a celebrity at the Little Theatre, being a well-known director. I was proud to be met by him. He held both his hands out to me with the palms up, and I laid mine on his.

'You brought the house down,' he said. I saw tears welling in his eyes, but he wiped them and smiled. 'And I'm a silly old twit.'

I guessed he was thinking about Mum, and hugged him. Hannah arrived in the car, honking, while Theo hung out of his window yelling to us to *hurry up, slowpokes!* because they were parked on a red line.

Hannah and Gramps took us to Antonio's restaurant. Hannah was looking lovely. She's still pretty, considering her age. She has blue eyes and a swishy bob haircut that makes her seem a lot younger than sixty-four; and she's nuts about Gramps, absolutely nuts. He only has to stand near her and she looks happy. Her earrings were twinkling in the candlelight. Gramps gave them to her for her sixtieth birthday. They had emeralds to match her engagement ring, and she only wore them on the most special occasions.

Everyone was jolly until Ben had to go and say something stupid. What is it with four-year-olds? Personally, I think he didn't like me being the centre of attention for once. Ben was a premature baby, and Mum wasn't well after he was born. Now he's cute and freckled with fluffy fair hair, and looks more like a two- or three-year-old than four. People always fuss over him. Gramps was talking to me about the costumes and I could tell Ben was getting more and more agitated. Then he thought of a way to get the spotlight back onto himself.

'Hannah?' he began, in his most annoying wheedly-whine.

Hannah was asking the waitress for more water. She didn't hear him, so he started yelling, 'Hannah, Hannah, Hannah!'

'Mmm, poppet?' She looked a bit hassled. 'No need to shout.'

Ben had just taken a massive mouthful of pizza and he was spluttering bits of cheese as he talked. 'Um, Hannah, um, are we allowed to talk to strangers?'

'Shut up, Ben,' hissed Theo. He'd gone pillar-box red.

And of course Hannah was all lovey-dovey because she doted on Ben. That wasn't surprising, since she and Gramps brought him up from the age of one. They're like his parents. He's *their* baby.

'No. It's not a good idea to talk to strangers, unless there's somebody nearby who can protect you. They may be perfectly kind, and you shouldn't be rude to them, but some people are not good people, I'm afraid. So no—don't talk to a stranger, and especially never accept sweets or get into their car.'

It was a long answer to a short question, and Ben didn't listen to a single word. His head was rocking backwards and forwards impatiently. I knew he was planning to cause trouble. I just *knew* it. 'So that means we shouldn't talk to strangers?' he persisted.

'Why do you ask?'

Theo dropped his fork and ducked under the table. Ben frowned and pretended to look worried. 'Because Theo talked to a stranger today.'

'Really?' Hannah wasn't anxious. Not yet.

'Theo talked to a strange man in the park. I told him we're not allowed. "We're not allowed, Theo!" That's what I said.'

The park is at the end of Faith Lane, where we live, close to the city wall. It has swings, a roundabout and a miniature football goal, and because it's only a few yards away from our front door the boys are allowed to play there on their own.

Gramps and Hannah looked at each other, then at the chair Theo should have been sitting in, then back to Ben.

'Tell me more,' growled Gramps, making a pretend fierce face.

'Well.' Ben put on his goody-goody expression. 'I was on the swings, but they were wet from the snow so it was yuk, and I asked Theo to wipe the seat with his scarf and he wouldn't because he was too busy kicking his ball at the goal, and this man got out of a big . . .' He paused for breath, and we all watched him. It takes Ben ages to tell a story. 'Um, he got out of a big, um, big black car and sat on the wall.' Another breath. Chewed-up pizza flying everywhere. 'He was watching us for hours and hours.'

'Liar! We weren't even there for hours!' came a muffled voice from under the table.

'Maybe the poor fellow was minding his own business,' suggested Gramps. 'He could have been waiting for somebody.'

Ben scowled. 'He might have been waiting for somebody, but he was watching *us*. When Theo dribbled the ball near the wall, he said hello to Theo and then, *then* . . .'

'Shut up, Ben!' yelped Theo.

'Then Theo said hi back.'

'I did not!'

Gramps lifted up the tablecloth and peered under the table. 'It's all right, Theo,' he said. 'It's not a crime to say hi to someone.'

'Yes, because it *is* a crime to say hi to a stranger.' Ben was looking very pleased with himself. 'Anyway, that wasn't all. The man said, "That's some pretty fancy footwork you've got there." And Theo said . . .'

'I'm going to kill you, Ben Scott!'

'Theo said, "Thanks, I've been practising." And he showed off some of his tricky moves. And then they both started going on and on about football. Which is *definitely* talking to a stranger! Then I went over there and I said . . .' Ben puffed out his chest. '*I* said, we're not allowed to talk to strangers, we're not allowed at all, and *you* are a stranger, and if you don't stop talking to us and go away right this minute I'm going to go home and get my grandma, she lives in that house there, and she will come running out here and tell you off, and she will call the police. Then the man looked a bit scared and he said, "Well we wouldn't want that, would we?" And he drove away in the black car.'

'Well done, Ben,' said Hannah, mussing his curls. 'You did the right thing.'

Ben hadn't finished yet, though. 'But I don't know if the man *was* a stranger, really. Maybe he was a . . . a *not* stranger person.'

'Why?' asked Hannah. 'Have you seen him before?'

'No, but I think he'd seed us before.'

'Why do you think that?'

'Because he said, "Bye, Ben! Bye, Theo!" Then he got in his car. Then he started up the engine. And then he *still* didn't go, he opened the window and leaned out, and *then* he said. . .' Ben stopped for another breath. He had his audience spellbound. 'Then he said, "How's Scarlet?"'

'Did he?' I was rather chuffed. 'I expect it was someone from the theatre, then.'

'Theo asked him how he knew Scarlet, but he just smiled and drove away.'

'Oh my God,' whispered Hannah. She looked angry, but somehow I didn't think she was angry. I'd seen that look before, when Theo didn't come home from school one time. She almost called the police, but it turned out Theo had been invited to a friend's house and had forgotten to tell her, so it's lucky she didn't.

'Don't worry, Hannah,' I said, trying to cheer her up. 'It was just someone from the theatre, or school, or . . . I dunno. Could have been lots of people.'

'What did this man look like, Ben?' she asked.

Ben couldn't answer because his mouth was bulging with pizza.

'You're a greedy little pig, Ben,' I said. His face fell, and I felt guilty. I don't like to hurt his feelings even though he is a spoiled brat. We three have to stick together.

Gramps leaned under the table again. 'Come on out, young man. It's all right. You're not in hot water.' Once Theo was back in his chair, Gramps turned to face him. 'Now tell me. Did you know this man?'

'No,' mumbled Theo. 'I dunno. Anyway, shut up, Ben. I didn't do anything. I didn't get in his car or take any sweets. He said I had fancy footwork and it would have been rude not to say something back, wouldn't it? You do want us to have good manners, don't you, Gramps?'

Gramps blinked. 'Er, we don't want you to be rude. That's quite right.'

'What if he was a talent scout? 'Cos if he was, Bigmouth Ben ruined my big chance.'

'You're our champ,' said Gramps, putting his arm around Theo's shoulders. 'But perhaps you could describe this talent scout for me?'

Theo looked even more shifty. 'Oh, I dunno. I think I've seen him around somewhere. He looked a bit like, um, like that man over there, cooking the pizzas.'

We all looked. Antonio's chef was slaving away by the big oven. He looked about as old as Hannah—sixty-something—and he was completely bald under a chef's hat. He never stopped smiling, as though he loved playing with pizza dough. Actually, he looked as though he was made of pizza dough.

'No, he didn't! He wasn't at all like that!' scoffed Ben. 'He was much much *much* thinner and *much* younger. That over there is an old fat man!'

'Shush,' I muttered. I could feel myself blushing.

'He was *thinner*,' screeched Ben. 'And he had lots of black hair. And he had round glasses like Harry Potter.'

Hannah stared at Gramps. Gramps stared at Hannah. Then Gramps did something really strange. Without a word he got up out of his chair, made his way around the table with his old man's walk and knelt on the floor beside Hannah. He took her hands in both of his and pressed them to his cheek.

'I think we should call the police,' whispered Hannah. I wasn't supposed to hear, so I pretended I hadn't.

'Less aggressive to write to his solicitor,' said Gramps. 'Warn him off.'

'I hardly think he's in a position to accuse *us* of aggression.'

She added something about someone having to go back and finish their sentence. I wondered if she meant Ben, who's always stopping halfway through his sentences, but that didn't seem to fit the conversation.

Suddenly, Gramps leaned forward and wrapped his arms right around Hannah's chest, which was seriously humiliating because a waitress arrived at that moment to take our plates. I hadn't seen her before, but like all Antonio's waitresses she was (a) very pretty and (b) totally dressed in black.

'Gramps!' I hissed. I was totally mortified, but the waitress didn't seem bothered at all.

'Gran and Grandad taking you out are they?' she asked. 'Birthday treat?'

'Er, no,' I said. 'I was in a play and—'

Ben was fluttering his long eyelashes at her. 'I'm four and a half,' he squeaked. 'Four years and a . . . half one!'

'Four and a half!' She pretended to be flabbergasted, the way adults always do, which is feeble because there's nothing clever about it. We've all been four and a half. If Ben had been a hundred and four and a half, *that* would have been worth bragging about. 'Wow, what a grown-up boy! You'll be at school soon, then.'

'In January,' I said. 'And I hope they teach him some manners.'

She took my plate. 'Nice, though, your grandparents taking you kids out for dinner. Giving Mum and Dad a night off, are they?'

'Mm,' I said.

'Yeah,' agreed Theo, nodding furiously. 'Night off.'

'We don't have a mum,' declared Ben. 'She's in heaven. And my dad's a very, very bad man. He's been locked up for years and years because he killeded her.'

Theo and I were cringing. We never, ever tell the truth about our parents. People don't want to know. They can't handle it. Ben will learn that.

Sure enough, the waitress looked as though she wished the earth would swallow her up. 'Oh dear,' she gabbled. 'That's a shame isn't it? Um. Well, lovely. Any desserts?'

That night, Theo wet his bed. He'd started doing it after Mum died, but it hadn't happened for over a year. We truly thought he had grown out of it. Well, obviously not.

Five

Joseph

'Mate, I told you it was a really dumb idea.' Akash slapped a packet of cornflakes in front of his guest. 'That's the last time I lend you my wheels. You've only been out three days and it's fuckin' lucky you've not been locked up again already.'

'Sorry,' muttered Joseph, pouring himself a mug of black coffee. It was Monday morning. He felt ropey and dishevelled. Akash and he had shared a few pints last night, after his vigil in Faith Lane. Even a drunken haze hadn't given him peace, though. He didn't deserve peace. Zoe haunted him, dying again and again, her eyes like green fire in a drawn face.

'I've found you a car,' said Akash, changing the subject. 'Fiesta, a million miles on the clock. They want five hundred for it.'

'Is it legal?'

'Is it legal?' Akash radiated injured dignity. 'I'm wounded, mate. *Wounded!*'

'With your track record it's probably ten different cars all welded together, given new plates and a beautiful paint job.'

'No, it really is legit actually.' Akash looked vaguely surprised at himself. 'They've got all the documents. One of my cleaning girls says her sister's selling it because she's having twins and they need something bigger. We can go and have a look tonight, if you're interested.'

'I'm keen,' said Joseph. 'Thanks.'

Akash began to eat cereal with one hand while opening his post with the other. Joseph had heard him leaping blithely out of bed and heading off to work at three that morning, and gathered he'd had spent the next six hours directing an army of employees while wielding a vacuum cleaner himself. Every movement was effective; his clothes were ironed, black hair immaculate. He was on the short side—five foot six, he'd once told Joseph—but indefatigable.

'Daylight robbery,' he complained. 'Look at this—electricity companies take the piss, don't they? Best thing about being inside is never having to open a bill. So what did your probation fella say on the phone?'

Joseph shrugged. 'Warned me to stay away from their house. Wants me to go through the *proper channels* when it comes to seeing the children. I told him I *am* going through the proper channels, painfully bloody slow channels, but I had to check they're okay in the meantime.'

'Which involved hanging around a kids' playground like a nonce.'

'I wanted to catch a glimpse, that's all. Just a glimpse.' Joseph shook his head. 'I've waited so long, and it was like a miracle. Theo I'd know anywhere, with his hair sticking straight up like he's had a fright. Genius with a football. Well, I taught him to kick a ball before he could walk. He had a little guy with him, a little blondie, had to be Ben. My boys, Akash. My *boys*!'

'Your in-laws will be bricking it. They probably think you're planning to abduct the kids.'

Which might be true, thought Joseph as he scanned the jobs column in a newspaper. Young Akash had a knack for getting straight to the nub of things. His acuity had taken him to the top of his profession—handling stolen cars—at the tender age of twenty-one. He came from a family of high-flying doctors, and nobody had ever doubted that he would follow suit. At first he obliged, and was a star pupil at his grammar school; a prefect and cricketing legend. Then he fell out with his father, fell in with a new crowd and rebelled spectacularly. He had a few run-ins with the police and his offending escalated until he was the mastermind of a team of car ringers. Then a tip-off landed him in Armley.

'What are they like?' Akash asked now. 'Your in-laws?'

'Zoe had 'em wrapped around her little finger—can't blame them, I was wrapped around it too. Hannah's a scary intellectual, lectures in physics at the university. What she doesn't know about quantum theory isn't worth knowing. She never liked me. We got off on the wrong foot.'

'Why?'

'Nobody could be good enough for her daughter, but I must have been her worst nightmare—a butcher's son from Tyneside. I was young, I was nervous, I was way out of my depth, and I had a bit of a chip on my shoulder. She got my hackles up.'

Akash raised an eyebrow. 'You were rude to her, weren't you, Scottie?'

'Mm.' Joseph looked embarrassed at the memory. 'It was all unspoken; she was polite on the surface. She asked me about myself, but in this pained sort of way. It brought out the worst in me. I acted a bit yobbish, talked big about a fight I'd been in. I still had a massive shiner of a black eye, so I must have looked like a low-life.'

Akash smacked his palm across his forehead. 'Doh!'

'Freddie did his best, though.' Joseph smiled. 'He'd just directed some play in Leeds. It was a sell-out. Hannah and Zoe were gloating over the reviews, but old Freddie didn't give a toss. He spent the afternoon digging away in his garden, covered in mud, waffling on about insects.'

'Insects.'

Joseph chuckled into his coffee. 'He fixed me with his glittering eye like the ancient bloody mariner and spent ten minutes going on about how a teaspoon of soil contains millions of organisms.'

'That's true!' exclaimed Akash delightedly. 'Teeming with 'em.'

'Well . . .' Joseph closed the paper. 'Unless I want to be a pole dancer, there's nothing for me in here.'

'You're pretty enough to be a pole dancer.' Akash's mobile phone rang. 'Bit of lippy, you'll be a real pouting beauty. You do pout a lot. Hello? . . . Yes, mate. Yes, not a problem, I can sort that out . . .'

While his friend talked, Joseph tried to consider his future and got nowhere. His mind seemed to be locked on a set of rails that inexorably led back to Zoe. Her eyes haunted him, bright with wild energy even in death. From her his thoughts led to the children; and when he was thinking about them, nothing else seemed relevant.

Akash flipped his phone shut. 'So what are you planning to live on?' he asked bluntly.

'I've got a bit of cash in the bank. I'll be okay for a while.'

'Did you own a house before you got sent away?'

'Signed everything over to the in-laws, including responsibility for my children. I didn't have any choice, nobody else volunteered. They sold the house and put the money into some kind of trust for the kids. Didn't fetch very much.' Joseph gave a bitter half-smile. 'Apparently buyers were put off by what had happened in the living room.'

'What about all your stuff?'

'Got rid of everything. I knew I was going away for a long time.'

'Mate.' Akash looked slightly embarrassed, rubbing his nose. 'Um, if you need work while you get back on your feet, I can give you some hours, no problem.'

Joseph stood up and clapped his friend on the back. 'Thanks. I might just take you up on that.'

'Where are you off to this morning? Got a date?'

'Not exactly,' said Joseph.

•

Although this *was* a bit like a blind date, he reflected as he sat opposite the starchy woman at the employment agency. He'd finally had enough of being cold, and had paid a visit to a charity shop. Now he was bundled into a long black overcoat and paisley scarf, both with that charity-shop smell.

The starchy woman was fiftyish, greyish and bored. 'Snowing again out there?' she asked absently as they both took seats.

'Thinking about it.'

She was reading through the form he'd just filled in. 'Now, Mr Scott . . .' Her brow furrowed in mild surprise. 'Degree in history, MA in European history, PGCE, secondary school teacher for um, eleven years. Oh.' She blinked. 'You were head of department at Tetlow High? I know people who've moved house to get their children in there. That's impressive.'

'Also irrelevant.'

'I'm sorry, but . . . why are you here? Surely you have better channels? Education sector magazines, websites, specialist agencies—the broadsheets have employment sections. Really, this isn't the right agency for you at all.'

'Keep reading.'

She obeyed, her eyes skimming down the page. 'Then a gap, I see. Three years. No employment at all during that time?'

'Not really.'

'Any reason?'

'Keep going.'

She turned the sheet, hunching over as she read. It was several seconds before she looked up and met his gaze.

'I don't think I'm going to be top candidate for a teaching post, do you?' Joseph's voice was even. 'School boards might run a little shy of people with convictions for manslaughter. Makes the parents jumpy.'

He saw her eyes flicker towards the door, as though measuring how fast she could get to it. Then she seemed to pull herself together, grabbing her computer mouse and squinting at the screen.

'Um . . .' She cleared her throat. 'Yes, I think we can assume that positions involving work with children are definitely closed to you.'

'Forever,' said Joseph.

'Probably. And I don't think you'll get far applying for bartending work, anything involving alcohol or vulnerable people—people at all, in fact. So caring for the elderly is out . . . ditto security . . . Um, let's see what we've got.'

Joseph waited as she clicked, sighed, and clicked again. Eventually she wrote a couple of notes on her pad. 'Your qualifications don't count for much in this economic climate, especially not with that particular blot on your copybook. All I've got at the moment is a window-cleaning firm. They have a high turnover so they might give you a go.'

'Offices?'

'And schools. Including . . .' She checked her screen. 'Oh. Perhaps not, after all.'

'Including Tetlow High.'

She nodded, watching him. She seemed fascinated.

'I really appreciate your help,' said Joseph, pressing both hands on the table as he got to his feet, 'but I think that gazing through the window at my old swivel chair would probably finish me off.'

She saw him to the street door. 'Good luck,' she said as she opened it. 'Really, I mean that. Good luck.'

Joseph paused on the threshold. 'I never thought I'd miss the place.'

'Tetlow High?'

'Armley Jail. Three days ago, I knew who I was. I knew what was going to happen every second of every day. They had me teaching literacy. I was useful. I was even respected. I actually had a positive impact on men's lives.'

A chill seeped into the office, laden with exhaust fumes. The girl on the front desk answered the phone.

Joseph smiled ruefully. 'Not useful out here, am I?'

•

He bought coffee and found a quiet seat in the window of a proper greasy caff—one of many institutions he'd been surprised to find himself missing over the past three years, with its moulded plastic seats and air permeated by the fug of fat frying. The place was heaving with people in woollen hats and anoraks; a haven from the cheerlessness of the street. Outside, snow had turned to sleet and then to rain. The odds on a white Christmas had just lengthened.

Sitting unnoticed in the crowd, Joseph took off his coat and scarf before pulling a phone from his pocket. It had been held in storage by the prison authorities and looked comically clunky compared to the slim-line gadgets he saw around him. He had a call to make, and he was dreading it.

He tried her mobile number first, but there was no answer. Scrolling through his contacts, he found *Marie work*. He pressed *call* and waited, staring through the steamed-up window at the road. Three workmen in shiny wet-weather jackets were lifting a manhole cover.

On the eighth ring, someone answered. It wasn't Marie. Far too gentle.

'Women's refuge?'

'Hi.' Joseph's throat seemed cluttered. He had to clear it. 'Um, is Marie Scott still the manager there?'

A distinct hesitation. Then the soft voice again. 'I'm sorry, but would you mind telling me the nature of your call?'

I'm calling because I've got nobody else. 'I'm her brother,' he said. 'Joseph Scott.'

'You're *who*?'

He repeated his name patiently. This time there was an even longer pause, with scandalised whispers in the background. Joseph could imagine the effect of his name uttered in a women's refuge. He was, after all, the poster boy for everything they most reviled. He was a man who killed women.

In the end he caught a muffled 'Oh, for God's sake.' This was followed by a thud, as though the phone had been knocked against something; then a stronger voice.

'Joe?'

Joseph's lips curved wistfully. Ah, now. Here was his sister, her speech still rich with the music of Tyneside. She'd always called him Joe, somehow managing to give the name more than one syllable.

'Hi.' He closed his eyes. 'It's me.'

She sounded impatient. 'So I gather. You're out, then.'

'Yes. I'm out . . . Um, how are you?'

'I'm fine.'

'That's good.'

'What d'you want?'

I want you to forgive. I want you to love me again.

'I don't know,' he said, despising the pleading jocularity in his own voice. 'I just thought I'd get in touch, see how you're doing. Maybe I could come up and visit you?'

'Have you dealt with your anger issues?'

'I don't think I really have a problem with anger.'

'Ha!' He'd forgotten that mirthless bark. 'Have you not? I very much doubt whether Zoe would agree.'

'Come on. You've known me all my life. You, of all people, know who and what I am.'

'No, Joe. I don't know who you are.'

He imagined her in the kitchen of the refuge, perhaps carrying out the bin bags or counselling some downtrodden girl with a miserable baby; he could picture his sister's careworn face and frizzy hair. He longed to reach out to her down the line. 'Please, sis. Nobody hates me more than I do myself.'

'I doubt that.'

'What do you want me to do—crawl away and die?'

Her accent broadened. 'I'm surprised you can joke about death, in view of your history.'

'You *know* I'm not a monster. Was I a budding psycho as a child? No. Did I fry ants under a magnifying glass, or kick our cat? No. Did I pull girls' pigtails? Never, as far as I recall, though I do remember getting myself beaten up savagely that time Matthew Brown called you a fat slag and I stood up for you even though I was half his size. Now, Matty Brown actually *was* a bully. And then there was Jared, who—'

'Never mind all that. I'll admit you didn't display any of the classic signs. But you've made up for that royally.'

The trio of workmen were sliding barriers around their open manhole.

'Please,' begged Joseph. 'If you could just take the time to hear my side—'

'Oh, I've heard your side of the story, Joe. I went along to your sentencing, and I sat there open-bloody-mouthed as I listened to what that poor female barrister had to say on your behalf. I hope they paid her lavishly for the public humiliation. I heard what you told your probation officer. I heard an awful lot of snivelling about life with Zoe, I heard shitloads of self-justification and self-pity. It's Zoe's side of the story we never heard! The judge might have been taken in but, believe me, I wasn't. I've come across a thousand men exactly like you, violent men who think their women deserve everything they get. So let me tell you this, Joseph Scott: until you take responsibility and accept it was entirely your fault—not Zoe's, not Hannah's, not Frederick's—until then, you needn't even bother applying for membership of the human race, so far as I'm concerned.'

'Look, Marie—'

'Oh, piss off.' A click, then a continuous tone. As rejections go, this one was pretty unequivocal.

•

Even the rain spat in his face as he stepped into the street. Passing cars seemed to scream, so that he actually ducked and pressed his hands to his ears. The pavement was coated in de-icing grit. It crunched under his feet.

A bus lumbered around the workmen's barrier. The sign on its broad crimson forehead read YORK. When it pulled ponderously into a stop and disgorged a mother with a pushchair, Joseph began to sprint down the gritty pavement.

Just a glimpse, he told himself as he found a seat; just one sight of his beautiful daughter. He'd make sure he wasn't spotted this time.

The bus stopped at every village on the way to York and became mired in traffic on the inner ring road. Joseph jumped off and ran the last half-mile, arriving gasping at the school gates with three minutes to spare. He knew it was the right place, because he'd used Akash's computer to search for Scarlet's name and found her among other award winners on a school website. Someone had left a property magazine on the bench outside the gates; he sat down and pretended to be absorbed in a selection of three-bedroomed semis in Tadcaster.

When the school bell rang, it seemed to be hooked up to an electrical circuit that ran right through his body. He jerked to his feet. A door banged, followed by the thunder of five hundred pairs of shoes as girls began to stampede down a path and through the gates. Joseph forced himself to sit down again. Any minute now. He hadn't clapped eyes on Scarlet since she was ten, but he'd know her anywhere: a skinny pixie with long legs and a wild mane of reddish hair. She used to sit on his lap and wrap thin arms around his neck. Lovely Daddy, she used to say, when she wanted to get around him. Dad-*ee*. She'd smack kisses onto his nose, and pat his cheek with her palm. He'd always given in.

The pupils were a spring tide, hugging and texting and gossiping and promising to phone. Some pushed bicycles, others ran for buses. Traffic was gridlocked as parents in cars tried to inch closer. Gradually, though, the tide slowed to a steady stream, then to a trickle. By three thirty the street was quiet. The Minster bells began to ring.

Joseph leaned forward to stare at the pavement, resting his elbows on his knees and his mouth in his hands. He'd missed her. She must have walked right past. He hadn't even recognised his own daughter—what kind of a father was he? Useless. He was useless, and he needn't bother applying for membership of the human race so far as Marie was concerned. He shut his eyes.

It was dusk when he raised his head. A small sound had disturbed him. Not five yards away, frozen in mid-stride and staring at him in horrified fascination, stood a ghost.

Six

Scarlet

Oh my God. I honestly thought my heart was going to smash through my ribs and go bouncing along the pavement like a rubber ball.

I was supposed to have violin on Monday, but the lesson got cancelled. Violin bitch was ill. I hoped it was something really serious, like cholera. Music teachers get shirty if you don't turn up for your lesson, but they don't practise what they preach. To add insult to injury, I'd waited nearly twenty minutes before anyone bothered to tell me. I normally walk home with a sixth-former called Rhiannon on Mondays. She lives in Faith Lane, and has judo. So I waved to her through the door of the gym, and set off alone.

Evening was falling already. The streetlights had come on, and the Minster bell ringers were practising when I walked past the tennis courts and out through the school gates. I love the feeling of a winter afternoon, when it's frosty and clear and the sky turns mauve as day slides into night. There's nowhere more Christmassy than York in winter. It's like a postcard come alive: lights in the old shops, and narrow streets, and the smell of roasting chestnuts from the man with his cart. The air felt like icy glass, as though it might shatter.

There were the usual lost tourists wandering around, talking in French or German or Cantonese. A party of choristers from the Minster school passed in a crocodile, on their way to Evensong. I knew some of the older ones because our two schools do stuff together. They're great singers but, believe me, they're not as angelic as they look. Especially Zac. He's hot and he knows it: tall and blond. He wolf-whistled quietly. I put up a finger, but I couldn't help smiling.

The pavement's very wide just there. Once the boys had gone I began to play hopscotch along the paving stones. Not so that anyone would notice; I was playing it in my head. Suddenly I got this feeling that there was something absolutely crucial nearby, something I *had* to see. So I stopped counting stones and looked around.

There's a bench beside the pavement, where the lost tourists stop to peer at their maps. A man was sitting on this bench. He didn't look like a tourist. He was wearing a black overcoat that fell almost to his ankles, and a satiny scarf, and he had a lot of dark hair falling across his face. His mouth was pressed into his hands and his eyes were closed. I couldn't stop staring. It wasn't that I recognised him; it was just that this person seemed really, *really* important.

Then his eyes opened. He looked straight at me, and I was as scared as I've ever been since the day Mum died. In fact, it was as though Mum was dying all over again. I couldn't scream. I couldn't even breathe. It seemed as though I was going to catch on fire, the way he was staring with those crazy eyes.

Then he whispered something: *Zoe.*

That did it. I was running even before I'd told my legs to run. I rocketed down a snickelway that I often use as a shortcut, and I was sure I could hear his footsteps thudding along behind me. I didn't stop running until I was in the middle of town, among shops and bright lights. I was gasping for breath as I dodged between the Christmas market stalls and shot down Coppergate. I looked back to see if he'd followed, and I'm sure I glimpsed that long coat in the crowd. I bumped into lots of people on the narrow pavement across the bridge, and kept having to say sorry. A really ugly woman wagged her finger and told me to watch where I was going, but I didn't even answer. I just needed to be home.

The scariest part was Faith Lane. It was very dark there, under the city wall. I was afraid he might have overtaken me somehow and be lying in wait. I knew it was stupid, but I started thinking perhaps he planned to kidnap me and smuggle me away. I'd just disappear. Children do disappear. I mean, what was he doing waiting outside my school?

It wasn't until I opened our front door, called out and heard Gramps reply, that I felt even half safe. I started to sniffle with fright, so I charged straight upstairs to my room. Flotsam and Jetsam were curled on my rug in a snowy heap of softness. Two pairs of doll-blue eyes looked up at me as I rushed in. Flotsam yawned, and Jetsam squeaked a contented 'hello'. Mum's cats. I didn't stop to stroke them, though. I pushed a wedge against my bedroom door, rolled into bed and pulled the duvet over my head.

The music was playing in my head; the music that means death is coming. It has surround sound and built-in fear, and it always makes me want to scream. The man with a very deep voice was singing, though I can never quite make out the words or even the tune. Instead of words or a tune, his singing brings me terror.

Everything had gone terribly wrong. The air was about to explode. Mum was laughing too much, and Theo ran to hide behind the sofa. Dad was shouting: *Jesus Christ, Zoe, I can't go on.*

I didn't know why he hit her. I didn't know why. I didn't know why. I screamed and he hit her again and she just went down, really fast and really hard. There was a horrible clunking sound. That was the sound of my mum dying. And the man kept on singing.

Later, once the ambulance had come, a policewoman took us children around to a neighbour's house. The neighbour told us they'd taken Dad away and he'd never trouble us again. Those were her exact words, as she squinted out from behind her lace curtains at the police cars in the road: *Don't you worry. He'll never trouble you again.*

'But he'll be coming to collect us soon, won't he?' I asked her.

She dropped the lace and went to make the policewoman a cup of tea.

I remembered what that woman said as I lay shivering under my duvet. *He'll never trouble you again.* Well, she was wrong because he was troubling me now. Suddenly, I understood something else: the man who talked to Theo and Ben in the park. He knew all our names. He had dark hair and round glasses like Harry Potter.

Dad was stalking us.

In films and books, the murderer is the last person you expect it to be. Normally it's the motherly cook or the shy young vicar. It's never the creepy guy with the weird laugh who's always sharpening knives. It was like that with Mum being killed. Until then, I used to think my dad was the best. He was a fun person who wore cuddly jerseys, took us to feed the ducks and read bedtime stories. He looked after us. He kept us safe. I thought I was very lucky, because in my eyes my dad was much more handsome and kind than other people's.

The kitchen door creaked. Gramps' voice. 'Scarlet! Please come down. Sca-ar-letta!'

I crept along to the bathroom, locked the door and faced myself in the mirror. I didn't look too good. I had little piggy eyes from crying, so I filled a basin with warm water and splashed it over my face. That helped. I ran a comb through my fringe, exhaled loudly—I learned that in drama, it's good for managing nerves—and forced myself down the stairs and into the kitchen.

Gramps had his arm around Hannah, and she was leaning her face against his shoulder. They weren't speaking, and there was a terrible sadness hanging about them. It made me feel dark. He kissed the top of her head.

'We have to play this absolutely straight,' he murmured into her hair.

'Play what absolutely straight?' I asked.

•

Hannah

Freddie was playing his harpsichord as I stepped into the hall that Monday morning. Complex cadences permeated the air with calm, like a lavender candle.

'Hello, Freddie?' I called, stopping by the mirror to pat my hair. More grey than fair now, but the hairdresser did wonders and it was cut in quite a youthful bob. I liked the way it swung.

Mondays were oases in the pandemonium of our lives. Ben went to nursery school, and I had only one lecture. Freddie and I had developed a small, contented ritual: I always visited the delicatessen on Micklegate and came home with French bread, brie and a salad. We'd have lunch at the kitchen table. This was how I used to imagine our autumn years would be: just the two of us, talking and reading and loving our way into a mellow old age, visited by our grandchildren at the weekends and spoiling them rotten. We'd begun saving for a cruise to Alaska and an adventure on the Trans-Siberian railway. I never in my wildest nightmares imagined we might become our grandchildren's only guardians, agonising over every decision, our lives entirely subsumed by their needs. So I looked forward to Monday lunchtimes.

I was warming my hands on the Aga when the music stopped. Frederick appeared in the doorway. He lit up at the sight of me—literally, as though a torch had switched on behind the fading honey-brown of his eyes. I felt my own face lift in response.

'Hello!' he cried, with the emphasis on the second syllable. Hel-*lo*! He always managed to make it sound as though my arrival was a delightful surprise. He came over to kiss me. 'I didn't hear you. How were your undergrads?'

'Two were actually asleep, one played games on his phone, and one was grinning at her laptop—I'm fairly sure she was watching cute cat videos on YouTube.'

Frederick had opened the fridge door and was peering at the shelves. 'I'm not sure what we're having for lunch.'

I felt a twinge of irritation at his scattiness. He knew perfectly well what we were having! I'd bought brie and baguettes and other goodies, as I had done every Monday for years. It was waiting on the table. I could smell warm crust, faintly yeasty.

'It's all here,' I said briskly, taking a seat. 'You ready to eat?'

No, he wasn't ready. He stooped over a chair back, gripping it. There were age spots on his knuckles. 'A letter came this morning.'

I sat with a baguette in my hand and a rictus smile on my face, looking up at him. For some reason, I was thinking of the moment we heard Zoe had been murdered. We were sitting at that same table; we were happy, laughing, hosting a dinner party for good friends.

It was murder, you know. The lawyers did a little pleasant plea-bargaining over a cup of coffee (they denied it, but I'm sure that's what happened) tipped sweet-smelling scent all over the crime and rechristened it manslaughter. But I know what it was, all right, and so did the judge and the police and the ushers and the woman from the CPS and all those wigged barristers who wouldn't meet my eye.

Frederick pushed an envelope across the table. 'He wants to see them.'

'They don't want to see him.'

'He warned us he'd go to court.'

I read through the papers with a sense of disbelief. It was an application on a standard form. It sounded innocuous enough: *Joseph William Scott applies for contact with the children Scarlet Zoe Scott, Theodore Marcus Scott and Benjamin Frederick Scott.*

'Will we never have peace?' I whispered.

'I don't think so.'

'If anyone else had killed our daughter right in front of her own children, we'd never have to see him again! Yet this monster can walk into a court and ask—no, not ask, *demand*—that we offer them up like sacrificial lambs!' I took a long breath. 'It's not happening, Frederick. Last time they clapped eyes on that man . . .'

I didn't need to finish the sentence. We both knew what had happened the last time the children saw Joseph Scott. That was the moment when the world came to an end.

Freddie looked weary. 'I think we'd better phone Jane.'

'I'll do it.' As I picked up the phone to call our solicitor, Freddie wandered to a shelf beside the Aga upon which we'd arranged photographs of Zoe. This was instigated by Nanette, a bereavement specialist we brought in to help us in those early days. According to her, in some families there was an unhealthy conspiracy of silence and the dead person was never mentioned; others went to the opposite extreme and made the entire house a sort of shrine, with memorabilia everywhere so that the past was revered more than the present. Instead, Nanette suggested the photo shelf.

'It's to acknowledge Zoe,' she said. 'They need to make new relationships rather than fixating on loss; but let her be a part of family chat around the table, if you can. Share your memories. Don't let her become a taboo subject.' Our kitchen was the hub of our world, so that's where we put most of the pictures.

Frederick put on the glasses he wore on a chain around his neck and picked up a framed photograph. Zoe, thirty-three years old, cross-legged on the bonnet of her beloved old MG. She was wearing jeans and a tiny scrap of a T-shirt, head poised on a dancer's neck. You wouldn't believe she'd given birth to three children. She was so slim. Thin, actually. I used to fuss about it. Her eyes dominated the picture—those luminous eyes that turned heads in the street. You could almost hear her laughter.

Scarlet was pressing her own soft cheek to her mother's, while Theo had squashed himself half onto Zoe's lap. He'd just had an appalling haircut, a black pudding basin, and was scowling at baby Ben, who'd taken prime position in his mother's arms. Midsummer light glanced off their faces, dappled through the umbrella of the lime tree in their garden. The photograph was taken by Freddie, just days before she died. That was the last time we saw Zoe. She seemed so happy.

Too happy. We knew that.

Frederick stood looking down at the picture of his daughter. I saw him touch his forefinger to his mouth, and to her smiling face. He stood for a moment, head bowed. Then he quietly returned the photograph to its place.

•

By four o'clock my grandsons were home and lolling in various states of scruffiness on beanbags in the sitting room, watching television. I checked that the front door was locked. With Scott prowling around, it was best to be on the safe side. Scarlet had a violin lesson after school on Mondays. She'd be walking home with a very sensible sixth former, so I had no concerns there. I'd begun making a fish pie when I heard her key in the lock.

Freddie heard it too. He put down his *Guardian* with an expectant smile. 'Aha. Miss Scarlet.'

''Lo?' That was Scarlet's voice.

'Greetings, Scarletta!' called Freddie.

The front door shut with a bang. Scarlet had always done that, ever since her mother died. Always, always. She never shut the door until she was sure there was somebody in the house. Perhaps she didn't trust people to be alive. I heard the violin being dumped by the harpsichord in the bay window and waited for my granddaughter to come and share her day with us, warming her shapely hands on the Aga and complaining that the violin teacher was a witch. I could tell she really wanted to say *bitch*.

This time, she didn't appear in the kitchen. I heard light footsteps running up the stairs. Freddie levered himself up and stepped out into the hall. 'Hey! Aren't you coming to say hello?'

Her voice sounded faint, as though she had a sore throat. 'In a minute. Just got to do some homework.'

'There's chocolate biscuits.'

'In a *minute*, Gramps!' Her door slammed shut, and I flinched. Her bedroom used to be Zoe's. I knew exactly how that door sounded when it was slammed.

Freddie reappeared, shrugging. 'Busy, busy,' he muttered unhappily. 'Can I help with anything?'

'You could stir the white sauce. Tedious job.'

He took the wooden spoon out of my hand, stirring distractedly and much too fast.

I touched his arm. 'Stop, Freddie. Stop fretting.'

'She slammed her door.'

'I know.'

He stirred faster still. Sauce slopped out, sizzling and smoking on the hot plate.

'She isn't Zoe,' I said desperately.

'I dread it.' He turned around and leaned against the Aga rail. 'It was at this age, wasn't it, that it first showed itself?'

Signs. Signs ignored, written off as adolescent hormones. Screams. Mugs smashed, doors slammed. Soft young arms pocked with crescent nail-scissor cuts. An adored face pinched with fury as she swept her arm along the sitting-room mantelpiece, hurling china and vases and an antique clock to the floor.

'No,' I said firmly, as I began to lay the table. 'Scarlet's her own woman. She has many of her mother's qualities—talent, for example; brains, looks, a sense of humour and a strong character—but none to be feared.'

Freddie wandered away, shaking his head. He'd completely forgotten about the white sauce. I caught it just as it was rising up the saucepan. He was back in the doorway, calling her.

'Scarlet! Please come down. Sca-ar-letta!'

'Freddie,' I hissed. 'Should we tell her about this?' I jerked my head at the court papers, jammed haphazardly into their envelope.

'No.' He hid them away in a drawer. 'Scare her half to death.'

'I agree, but if we don't warn them, it might come as a ghastly shock.'

He stood with his hands straight down by his sides, swaying a little like a tired soldier. Freddie seemed to need more time to gather his thoughts as he'd grown older, but his words were worth waiting for. They were never empty.

'I think it would be best to wait until after we've discussed it with Jane,' he decided. 'Taken some legal advice. There's no point in upsetting the children unnecessarily. Scott may give up. He may move away.'

'He may get run over by a bus,' I suggested hopefully. 'Or perhaps we could pay someone to send him for a swim in the Ouse.'

'Hannah!' Tut-tutting gently, Freddie dropped his arm around my shoulder. 'We have to play this absolutely straight.'

'Play what absolutely straight?' asked Scarlet. She was standing in the doorway, green eyes burning in a bloodless face, glaring at us.

•

Scarlet

The pair of them jumped like I'd caught them snogging. Hannah ducked out from under Gramps' arm. She was looking pretty shifty.

'How was violin?' she asked, pretending to be jolly.

'Cancelled.'

'Did you get your homework done?'

'I've still got more to do.'

'How about a cuddle for your old ancestor?' pleaded Gramps. 'I haven't seen you all this livelong day.'

He enveloped me in a bear hug, but I wasn't going to be distracted so easily. 'Play what absolutely straight? I'll keep asking until you spill the beans.'

They looked at one another.

'I'll keep asking,' I warned them.

'Biscuit?' suggested Hannah. There was a burst of activity as they fussed around, force-feeding me lemon squash and Hobnobs. When they shut the kitchen door and both stood awkwardly by the table, I knew for sure that something was going on.

Hannah spoke first. 'Your father is out of prison.'

I know, I thought. *I've just seen him.* I didn't tell them, though. I knew they'd be absolutely terrified. Anyway, my dad was never mentioned in our family. I'd sooner say a really bad swear word in front of my grandparents—even the 'f' word, even the 'c' word—than my dad's name.

'He wants to see you,' said Hannah. She pulled something out of a drawer. 'He's made this application to the court.'

I stared. 'No! No *way*.'

'We thought so too. And that's exactly what we're going to tell Jane Whistler.'

Gramps was standing behind my chair. I could feel his fingers spiking up my hair. 'But it's your choice, Scarletta. If you choose to see him, we'll respect your wish.'

Hannah looked as though he'd stuck a fork into her backside. I mean, my father is just like the devil in our house. Gramps might as well have said, 'Go on, smoke a cigarette,' or, 'Hey, why don't you nip out and shoot up heroin and maybe sleep with some random guy in the street?'

I didn't stop to think. I didn't *want* to think. I ran around the table and grabbed that envelope out of Hannah's hand. I ripped it in half, then quarters—which wasn't easy, because there were a few sheets in there. 'Here's what I think of his application,' I yelled, tossing the bits all over the floor. Then I stamped on them. 'And *here's* what I think of him!'

'Shh,' said Gramps, looking upset. 'Calm down. You'll make yourself ill, flying into such a rage.'

That just made me even wilder. I wanted to shake him, but even thinking such a horrible thought made me feel guilty. One of the most annoying things about being brought up by grandparents is their old-fashioned ideas. Sometimes it feels like living in the Dark Ages. For instance, the idea that you can make yourself ill just by getting angry. The idea that you can catch a chill from having wet hair. And the idea that eating the disgusting cold jelly off a roast chicken is 'excellent for invalids'. I love Gramps and Hannah but they drive me up the wall sometimes.

Hannah began picking up the pieces from the floor. Her mouth was as straight as a ruler. 'Don't you worry,' she said. 'We'll see him off. Don't tell the boys, will you, Scarlet? There's absolutely no need to be frightening them. This may come to nothing.'

All through dinner the three of us tried to behave as though everything was normal. Theo had some good news about becoming class prefect at school. Ben was being a little twerp, winding Theo up by calling him Ferret Face.

'C'mon, Ben—you too, Theo,' said Gramps, after we'd eaten. 'The girls have homework to do. Let's us lads do the washing-up, then get yourselves ready for bed and I'll tell you a story. What shall it be about?'

The bribe worked. He soon had Theo and Ben lined up with tea towels, and I laid out my homework on the kitchen table while Hannah disappeared off to her computer. Gramps' stories are legendary in our family. You can give him any subject, anything at all.

'A great big, um . . . a big hairy caveman,' suggested Ben.

'A spoon,' said Theo, who was drying one.

'A wee!' screeched Ben, sniggering with his hand over his mouth. He thinks anything to do with toilets is hilarious.

'Hmm . . .' Gramps thought for a while, swishing the water around with his yellow rubber gloves. 'Yes, well, I think this evening we'll hear the story of three Neanderthal children, and how they invented the very first spoon. Of course, wee is an important part of the plot.'

'What are they called?' asked Theo.

'Wo, Wa and Wee. You see? Two boys and a girl with flaming red hair.'

'Strawberry blonde, actually,' I piped up.

'Flaming strawberry blonde. Sorry. These three children are your ancestors, and you each have a little bit of them in you. Did you know that we all have Neanderthal DNA in us? Especially Ben. I suspect he has more than most.'

Theo started doing his sabre-toothed tiger impersonation with two kitchen knives. I tried to get on with my science homework, but drawing a diagram of an amoeba really didn't interest me that evening. I suppose we share DNA with an amoeba. I started doodling on the cover of my book. I drew lots of vertical lines, darker and darker and then extremely dark, until my biro went right through the paper. Then I sketched a person behind them. He had scribbly hair, and round glasses, and mad staring eyes.

•

I couldn't get to sleep that night. I hate those lonely hours.

My bedroom used to be Mum's when she was a child. Her costume dolls still sit along the windowsill and some of her books are on the shelves. You'd think this would make her feel closer, but it doesn't. The singing man seems much closer than she does. He visits all the time. I'll hear his song, and know that death is coming. I'll gather all my breath and try to force out a scream, but all I can ever manage is a tweeting sound, like a trapped bird. Then I wake up crying.

I used to beg Mum to give me a sign that she was there. Anything at all—even a whiff of her special scent. She never answered. Eventually I faced facts: she was well and truly gone. I didn't tell Ben or Theo, though. It would have broken their hearts. They believe she's watching over them, like Mufasa in *The Lion King*.

On this particular night I'd been lying awake for hours when I heard a floorboard creak. I was pleased to think someone else was up, so I got out of bed and crept to my door. Theo was just leaving the bathroom, carrying a big towel. He saw me and stopped on the landing, trying to hide the towel behind his back.

'Wet bed?' I whispered.

He was awfully embarrassed, bent over and shivering. Poor thing, he'd taken off his pyjamas and was wearing nothing but underpants. He looked little and knock-kneed and spindly.

'It's all right,' I said. 'Don't worry. Nobody will be cross.'

'I don't know why it's starting up again.' His mouth was turned down, his nose running.

I felt very adult. It was a whole lot better than feeling young and lonely. 'Were you going to try and sleep on that towel? C'mon, let's get you some clean stuff. I'll fetch it—you go and pop on some nice dry pyjamas. Put on a sweatshirt as well. We don't want you getting cold, might set off your asthma.'

I tiptoed to the linen cupboard and pulled out clean sheets and things. They felt warm after being near the hot-water tank. Then I took off Theo's soaking sheet and mattress saver and duvet cover and put new ones on. Theo stood watching with chattering teeth and his arms tightly wrapped around his chest. Finally he hopped into bed, and I covered him up. He reached down to the floor and picked up Bigwig, his rabbit.

'Thanks,' he said, as Bigwig disappeared under the duvet with just the tips of his ears sticking out.

I bent and kissed him on the forehead. Gramps often did that. 'You're welcome.'

'You know Dad?' he said.

It was a shock, coming out of the blue. 'No, I don't,' I said. 'Not anymore.'

'Remember how he used to play football with us?'

'No.'

'Remember how he always used to carry us on his shoulders? I remember looking down at people's hair. You must remember that.'

'So?'

Theo squirmed deeper under the duvet. 'Nothing.'

I sat on the end of his bed, trying to work out what was in my brother's head. He's a mystery sometimes.

'You know Neanderthal man?' he asked suddenly.

'Not personally.'

'We all have a little bit of Neanderthal man in us. They lived thousands and thousands of years ago, didn't they?'

'That's right.'

'Gramps said we all have some of their, um . . .'

'DNA.'

'DNA. Anyway, a bit of them. Right?'

'Right.'

Theo was quiet for a few seconds. Then he said, 'So we must have a *lot* of Dad.'

'You're mad. Shut up and go to sleep.' Feeling cross and twitchy, I turned off the lamp and burrowed under the duvet at the opposite end, so that we were topping and tailing. There was plenty of room. I meant to go back to my own bed, I really did, but I thought Theo might drift off if I was nearby. His duvet cover was warm and smelled of Persil, and I didn't want to be alone again. So I decided to stay for a minute or two. Or ten.

Sleep was settling all over me in a purple cloud when Theo broke into my cloud-drift. He'd been thinking. He does *far* too much of that.

'Scarlet?' he whispered.

'Shh. Go to sleep.'

'I can't.'

'Try counting sheep.'

I could hear his breathing, just a little wheezy, and wondered whether he was going to have an asthma attack. He could only have counted about twenty sheep before he piped up again. 'I'm scared.'

I sighed. 'Why're you scared?'

'I think I've got the nasty part of Dad in me.'

Seven

Joseph

'You're a bloody genius, Scott,' groaned Akash. 'Not *again*! Less than four days out of rock college and you're begging to get sent straight back. What's your problem?'

Joseph shrugged. 'I just wanted to . . .'

'Yeah, yeah. I know, spare me. You just wanted to see your daughter. Couldn't you have waited? You've applied, right? You've got a date for court? So do yourself a favour and stop trying to get yourself locked up again. She'll have run straight home and told your in-laws. Might be a warrant out for you already.'

They were on their way to look at the car for Joseph. Akash was driving.

'I called her Zoe,' Joseph confessed wretchedly.

'What the hell did you do that for?'

It had looked so like Zoe, silhouetted against the Minster's windows; as though he'd met a wraith in the icy dusk. After her death, his shock and grief were bound up with arrest and interview and criminal charges. He'd been forbidden to contact his children or anyone connected to the family—that was a condition of his bail. Turning up at Zoe's funeral had been impossible, though he later discovered that she'd been cremated and her ashes scattered into Lake Windermere, a place she'd always loved. He had pleaded guilty to killing her, but a part of him didn't believe that she was dead at all.

Even as he spoke her name, he'd realised his mistake. Scarlet was off, fast as a fox, darting down the alleyways of the old city with her violin case swinging. He was left sitting stunned on the bench.

Idiot, he had told himself furiously. *You've blown it.*

All he'd wanted was to see his girl. Well, now he had seen her and terrified the poor child into the bargain.

Akash was still ranting as they pulled in behind an elderly blue Fiesta. The pregnant-with-twins sister came to the door of her flat and handed over a set of keys. After a lot of fumbling with a rusty catch, Joseph lifted the car's bonnet.

His friend watched proceedings with a sardonic smile. 'You don't know one end from the other, do you Scott?'

'Nope.'

'Stand aside,' Akash ordered, pulling a small torch from his pocket. Joseph watched as his former cellmate revved the engine and fiddled with spark plugs, finally slamming the bonnet shut. 'We can take it out for a spin, if you like. But it's exactly what it looks like—bloody old and battle-scarred, like you. But honest, like me.'

Joseph had already been to the bank. Within ten minutes he was the owner of a battle-scarred, but honest, blue Fiesta.

'So what next?' Akash asked later, as they celebrated in the Prince Albert.

'You mean assuming they don't send me back inside for breaching my licence?'

'Yeah. Assuming that.'

Joseph downed half his pint. 'I appreciate your sofa, I really do, but it's time I got on my own two feet. I'll be off first thing tomorrow.'

'Oh yeah?' Akash looked doubtful. 'Off where? To see your fairy godmother?'

'You could say that.'

•

To a man who'd spent three years locked in a small cell, the North Yorkshire Moors felt surreally limitless. They stretched into hazy oblivion; bleak undulations, brooding in crystalline winter light. There were no walls here on the tops; no fences, no boundaries at all except the thin ribbon of the road. Sheep grazed freely, and once, Joseph was forced to stop and wait for an ambling pair to cross. On the seat behind him lay a kitbag with enough clothes to see him through the winter.

Several miles north of Helmsley a turn-off led into a steep valley, whose shadowed verges glittered under a layer of frost. The road twisted, slick with mud, and narrowed until it seemed no more than a farm track. Eventually it forded a beck before turning uphill again. Joseph negotiated a flock of hens as he turned through an open gate and into a farmyard. A sign hung lopsidedly from the bare branches of a tree: *Brandsmoor Camping and Caravans.*

As he climbed out, a collie arrived growling by his knee. She had opaque eyes, and walked with the stiff care of the arthritic. Joseph reached to let her sniff his hand. 'Jess, Jessy,' he said quietly, and her tail waved its white-flag tip.

The house had stood for two hundred years, weathered and stoic, mellow sandstone worn smooth at the corners. The roof was in trouble, the ridgepole hunchbacked and missing several slates. An iron boot scraper cluttered the front doorstep alongside a pair of tartan slippers, and herbs slept through the winter in pots and watering-cans. Joseph was caressing the collie's ears when the door opened, and someone spoke.

'Who is it, Jess?'

She was old; distinctly, decidedly old. She'd probably never been tall, but the years had shrunk her to hobbit proportions. Sturdy, though. She stood squarely in brown lace-up shoes and army surplus trousers, peering courageously through blue-rimmed glasses.

Joseph smiled. 'Hello, Abigail.'

'Who?'

'It's me,' called Joseph, stepping closer. He felt about twice her height. 'Joseph Scott.'

She hadn't changed much since he'd last seen her. Her hair had been wiry white then, as it was now, her skin crazily creased. She was a little more bent, perhaps, and he thought she'd lost another inch or two.

'Aha,' she said calmly. 'The wife killer. Come on in, come on in.'

The kitchen hadn't changed either: the same warm clutter, the rose-patterned plastic tablecloth, the overriding smell of farmyard muck and smouldering coal and strong tea. An airer hung from the ceiling, bedecked with several pairs of Abigail's trademark army trousers. The room was pleasantly gloomy, its windows set two feet deep. They looked across the yard towards the steep rise of the moors.

'It's so good to see you,' said Joseph. Surprised by his own emotion, he took the old woman's gnarled hands and squeezed them in his own. 'You look marvellous.'

'I doubt it,' she declared tartly, disengaging her hands to lift a kettle from the range. Abigail had run the farm and campsite alone since her brother's death thirty years earlier, and Joseph had never known her to take a holiday.

'Everything's just the same here,' he said. 'I'm just so . . .' He shook his head, laughing bemusedly. 'So bloody grateful.'

'How long's it been?'

'Not far off four years.'

'Sit here.' She pulled out a chair from the table, shooing a prosperous-looking tabby from the faded cushion. When Joseph sat, the animal immediately sprang onto his lap.

'Digby!' cried Joseph. 'He's not wasting away, is he?'

'Look at the soppy bastard, sucking up to you.' Abigail put a mug of tea in front of Joseph. 'It's still there. The Scott family caravan. Sounds like a stately home. Your sister stayed last summer with a, um, friend.'

'Male?'

'More or less. Hard to tell, with all that hair. Nobody's been since then, but Marie's kept up the ground rent.'

'Is there still a rope swing in that massive oak tree?'

'Lightning got that tree.'

Joseph let his hand rest on Digby's back, feeling the deep vibration of a purr. 'I've just got out of prison.'

'Did you knot your sheets into a rope and escape?'

'Nope. I did half my sentence. I'm on licence.'

Deep canyons radiated from the corners of Abigail's mouth. 'You're a celebrity. I hate to think how much forest was cut down just to plaster your name across the *Yorkshire Post*.' She disappeared into the larder and came back with fruit cake in a tin. Joseph watched her wield a knife, while Digby stretched luxuriously.

'This a social call?' she asked, handing him a plate.

'Thanks—lovely. Yes, a social call.'

'I wasn't born yesterday.'

'You weren't,' admitted Joseph, smiling. 'I want to live in the caravan for a while.'

'Heck, you'll freeze.'

'I'll be fine.'

She considered him for a moment, chewing the side of her mouth. 'I hope that sister of yours did the washing-up before she left.'

They crossed the farmyard with Jessy padding alongside them. A red Ferguson tractor was delivering bales of hay to cattle in an open-sided barn. At the wheel sat a burly man in overalls.

'I see Gus is still here,' remarked Joseph.

'Not so much, nowadays. His father had a heart bypass, so he's been doing most of the running of their place as well. When he is here he spends more time on the campsite than he does on the stock. It's the only thing that pays its way.'

'Farm not doing well?'

'Nah, hardly worth the bother. Moorland farms are dying.' A kissing gate in a dry stone wall opened onto the first of a series of broad terraces leading down to a beck. Campervans were parked at the top, and a group of teenagers played with a Frisbee. Abigail and Joseph strolled together to the lowest tier. It was muddier here, the grass thick and rank. Gus had evidently been neglecting his mowing duties; or perhaps there simply wasn't enough of Gus to go around. Several static caravans lay among twisted trees overlooking the beck. Abigail and Joseph headed for the last of the row.

'Huzzah,' grunted Joseph, lifting a lichen-encrusted rock. 'Marie left the key.'

He climbed two steps to unlock the door, standing back to let Abigail enter first. Their footsteps made the structure shake. The place smelled of damp, so Joseph propped the door open.

'Well, she did the washing-up,' said Abigail grimly, looking around. 'But—silly girl—it wasn't right clever to leave elderflowers in a marmalade jar!'

A galley kitchen ran beside a built-in table and seats. One sliding door led into a bedroom only just large enough to fit its double bed; another door led into a tiny bathroom. The far end opened out into a living area with covered benches and windows along three sides.

'Bingo!' cried Joseph, peering into a cupboard. 'It's all still here. Duvets, linen, blankets, towels . . . I'd forgotten we even owned the gas heater. Zoe bought this stuff. She decided the caravan was manky, drove all the way to York and came back with brand-new everything. See? Some of these are still in their packaging. Cost a bloody fortune.'

Without comment, Abigail moved to a window and stood looking down at the beck.

Joseph was caught up in the excitement of the past-made-present. 'Aha, yes! I remember her buying these, too. The kids loved 'em.' He pulled out a packet. 'Glow sticks. Little plastic tubes that glow in the dark. Zoe said no camping expedition was complete without glow sticks. We spent hours twirling them, throwing them, making bracelets . . . and at bedtime the kids each had their own personal light source. Brilliant!'

Noticing Abigail's silence, Joseph realised that he'd spoken of Zoe as though she was alive and well and about to arrive for a week's holiday. He closed the cupboard doors and joined Abigail at the window, hands pushed deep into the pockets of his coat. The valley was already full of shadow; he could scarcely see the beck. Patches of grass by the water hadn't been touched by sunlight at all that day. The frost had never melted, and now another layer would form.

'I forget,' he said.

'Forget?'

'I still can't imagine a world without her. That sounds ridiculous. *Can't imagine a world without her* . . . Pretty crazy, coming from the idiot who killed her. Marie would have a field day with that. She'd say it proves I've got a narcissistic personality disorder, or something.'

Abigail fiddled with the window's catch and slid it open. Clean air rolled in, carrying the tang of peat and bracken. 'Doesn't seem more than a week ago that your parents bought this caravan. State-of-the-art it was, then. You took your first steps out by that tree—see? The knotted old bugger there. All the mothers fussed over you, little curly head. Your big sister's nose went out of joint. I caught her prodding you to make you cry.'

A muscle contracted beside Joseph's mouth. It wasn't quite a smile. 'She still does that.'

'You spent most of your summers here.'

'Poor Mum was only too happy to bring us. She'd sit around with the other mothers and drink cider and laugh all day every day, while twenty kids ran riot and dammed the beck. I never once saw her laugh like that at home.'

A pool glinted in the beck below, mirroring the pale sky. Joseph remembered lying there on summer days. He could still feel the eddying water as he submerged himself, tea-coloured ice that forced the breath from his lungs.

'So,' said Abigail briskly. 'What are your plans?'

'Bloody Nora! Give me time.'

'You've had plenty of time. About three years, I should imagine.'

He looked up towards the moor. 'First thing I plan to do is get myself up there,' he said. 'Just because I can.'

Once Abigail had left, Joseph made his way downhill to where stepping stones lay half-submerged among glassy rapids. Somebody was coming towards him across the stones; he dimly registered walking boots and a swirl of claret skirt. Some part of his brain appreciated the supple ease of her movements, but he desperately didn't want to speak to anyone, so was relieved when she merely smiled and passed by.

He barely hesitated, gauging distances before leaping from one rock to another with sure-footed certainty. After all, he and Marie were the architects of this bridge; it had taken them a whole day. Once across, he struck up the hillside with long strides. Evening was overtaking the moors now, and the temperature had dropped still further. Sheep lifted their heads to watch him pass, mildly curious about the dogless human.

Joseph had climbed for twenty minutes by the time he pushed his way through a patch of tangled bracken and breasted the last ridge, to be greeted by a knife-edged wind. High above him two curlews twisted and soared in the emptiness, spotlit by the last rays of sun. He could neither see nor hear any other sign of life. Even Abigail's farmhouse was hidden from view. He revelled in the solitude.

Spreading his hands wide, he let himself drop straight back like a doll tumbling off a shelf. Or perhaps a mother falling to her death; there was no marble fender, up there on the moor. He dropped onto a cushion of skeletal heather, and bounced.

Hours later, he made up the bed he'd last shared with Zoe. He used the turquoise sheets she'd chosen and which cost a bloody fortune. Pressing his face into them, he caught the lingering breath of her perfume. He added every duvet he could find. Then he dug out a book and read until long after midnight, in the hope that he might then be able to sleep. It didn't work. Sleep was a luxury.

He'd been woken by a glowing sunrise, last time he'd slept in that bed. Zoe was pressed very close, her cheek on his shoulder, elegant fingers tangled in his hair. She'd seemed so well during that last holiday. They'd been happy—though they knew their happiness was fragile, like thin sunshine. Joseph remembered tracing the line of her face with his forefinger, adoring the high cheekbones and elfin features. He'd inhaled the warm scent of her and watched as the growing day crept up her body, gilding each contour. He had wished with all his soul that the precious moment could go on forever. He'd known it would not.

Rain was chattering quietly outside. He lifted his wrist to check the luminous dial of his watch. Almost two in the morning. He was drifting at last. He was drifting in the darkness, between Zoe-scented sheets. The rain whispered to him.

At two nineteen, he woke with a yell of horror. He'd just killed Zoe. She was lying on the hearthrug, her green-glass eyes wide open. Dropping to his knees, he began to pump her chest—trying to start her heart, frantically shouting her name. He knew her life was over. So was his.

The rain was tapping on the window, tap-tappety-tap, asking to come in. It took a long time for his racing heart to slow.

At two thirty-eight he sat bolt upright, sweating with panic. He'd just killed Zoe. Her eyes were wide open. He was on his knees. His life was over.

He woke at three, because he'd just killed Zoe.

And three eleven.

And three thirty.

He was in his bunk in a cell, suffocated by blackness. He must have gone blind because it was never completely dark in prison. He heard a gentle bleat, and wondered what the hell a sheep was doing in Armley.

Or perhaps he wasn't in Armley.

The rain had ceased, leaving complete stillness save for an almost imperceptible trickling of the stream. He'd forgotten how deafening silence could be. He'd spent the past three years as a captive audience, forced to listen to the snoring and rambling and cursing of other men. He'd longed for peace; yet now, in the icy night, it blared between his ears like an alarm. He lay with his eyes open, assaulted by the silence. He was profoundly tired. He'd been tired for three years, because Zoe was dead.

•

Zoe was alive—gloriously, vibrantly alive.

She dominated the dusty stage of a South London school. Pocket Shakespeare, they were called. Three actors and a box of props, standing in front of a bloodthirsty mob of fifth and sixth formers. In an hour they whipped through *Hamlet*, *Othello* and *Romeo and Juliet*. The bedroom scene in *Romeo and Juliet* triggered catcalls and ribald slurpings—Joseph collared the ringleaders and handed out detentions—but mad Ophelia had the teenage monsters eating out of her hands. Perhaps they recognised themselves. Joseph was a new teacher, roped in for crowd control. He leaned against the wall, goggling helplessly at the redhead with green eyes and a ringing voice.

She must have been half the weight of the two male actors; there wasn't an ounce to spare. Cheekbones, shoulders, hips—all sharp, defined, like an active child's. Energy radiated out of her, bewitching the cynically gum-chewing audience. Poor Desdemona was about to die. She was pleading for a little more time. Joseph wished she didn't have to die. He wished he could change the ending.

The school's head of drama collared him as the students were filing out of the hall. She was called Henrietta. Posh Hetty. It was she who'd invited the group to perform; their manager was a friend of hers.

'Talented, aren't they?' she demanded.

'Very.'

'Party. Tonight. My place.' She scribbled an address. 'It's my birthday. Be there or be square.'

Joseph was surprised to be asked, and knew he wouldn't go. He'd only been at the school six weeks, shunned staffroom politics and could think of nothing less appealing than a stand-up-and-shout birthday bash.

'Happy Birthday, Hetty, but I'm afraid—'

'They'll be there too.'

'Who?'

Hetty's smile was arch. 'Pocket Shakespeare. All of them.'

'I think I can make it,' said Joseph.

He spotted Desdemona as soon as he walked in. She was wearing an emerald green shift dress, swaying fluidly to the rhythm as Leonard Cohen murmured 'Hallelujah' through a pair of retro speakers. A couple of pinstriped suits were all over her. Joseph was on his way over when he was hailed by Posh Hetty, three sheets to the wind. As soon as she'd sailed on, one of the school's secretaries buttonholed him. She had sharp blue eyes and an English-rose complexion, and seemed determined to take him home with her that night. On any other evening he would have been delighted to oblige, but not this one. He kept scanning the crowd for an emerald dress. Perhaps she was in the kitchen. Perhaps she'd gone.

'You're distracted,' yelled the secretary above the din.

'Sorry.'

She touched his hand. 'My glass is empty.'

Joseph picked up their glasses and began to shoulder his way through the throng towards the makeshift bar. There she was, perched on a sofa and edging away from one of the suits. He was leaning right over her, though she'd put a hand on his chest to ward him off. She caught Joseph's eye, mimed an expression of horror and mouthed *help!*

Joseph dumped the glasses on a table and was charging to the rescue when Pinstripe pounced. He slumped like a great blubbery sea lion, simultaneously tearing down the dress and trying to kiss Desdemona. Joseph grabbed him by the back of his shirt and hauled him onto the floor. The guy was drunk, so it wasn't difficult. He sprawled red-faced, gawping up at Joseph.

'What the fuck're you doing?' he yelled. Public-school accent. 'Are you off your head? That girl's mine.'

She was laughing. She was laughing so much that she couldn't speak.

'I don't think she likes you,' said Joseph.

'You cunt,' screamed Pinstripe, staggering to his feet and lunging.

Joseph shouldn't have done it. Really, he shouldn't. He knew he ought to walk away but the temptation was just irresistible. The guy was legless, and there was a dazzling girl with green eyes to impress. He only hit him once, though

'I think we'd better leave now,' gasped the girl, as blood fountained from Pinstripe's nose. She grabbed Joseph's arm and pulled him into the hall. She was still laughing as they scuttled into the lift. 'D'you know who that was?'

'Nope.'

'Neither do I. But according to him, he's an up-and-coming barrister and London's most eligible bachelor.'

The lift was very old, and very slow. The girl smelled of sandalwood. Her green dress clung to her. 'I know you,' she said. 'You're the Russian prince.'

Joseph smiled. He felt very commonplace beside her. 'Sorry. Wrong bloke.'

'Right bloke. I spotted you at Parkway High. You were leaning against the wall with your arms folded.'

'True.'

'You looked bored out of your brain.'

'Not true.'

'And there was a monster right in front of you who was texting. I could see the little bastard fiddling with his phone the whole way through Desdemona's murder.'

'Sorry. I didn't spot him.'

'I made sure you were invited tonight.'

'You did?'

She laid her mouth at the side of his throat. The touch burned him; warm breath and coconut oil. 'You've gallantly rescued me from death by boredom at the hands of London's most eligible bachelor. Let's go and celebrate.'

It was like a night out with a hurricane. Hurricane Zoe. He was a night owl, but he couldn't keep up with her. She danced him off his feet, she drank him under the table. In the pearly dawn they found themselves strolling along the embankment. His jersey was draped over her shoulders, and she carried a pair of gold sandals in one hand. She seemed as alert as she had hours before, and voracious for his story. She asked a question, listened acutely, asked another. He'd never felt so understood.

They were crossing Waterloo Bridge when she broke away from his side. The next second she was perched on the handrail, legs dangling over the mud-brown expanse of the Thames. The tide sprinted below, murderous currents crisscrossing and swirling.

'Hop down,' begged Joseph. 'Just to please me. If you go in there, you won't come up.'

She laughed, took both her hands off the rail and stretched her arms wide, *Titanic*-style. A passing car honked. Joseph stopped breathing.

'Get down,' he said quietly. 'Please.'

'Shall I dive?' She sounded cheerful, as though deciding whether to be sinful and have a chocolate fudge sundae for dessert or not. 'It'd be fun. I'm a very good swimmer.'

Joseph edged closer, ready to grab her if she fell. Suddenly she looked at her watch.

'Oh *no*!' she moaned. 'Bugger bugger bugger.'

'You're meant to be somewhere?'

She swung her legs back over the handrail, landing lightly on the pavement. 'Screen test at nine o'clock. Gotta go. Taxi!'

Even the black cabs were in her thrall. The second she raised a slender arm, two of them appeared out of nowhere.

'Phone number?' shouted Joseph.

She slid a biro out of his pocket, pushed back his sleeve and scribbled on his wrist. 'Don't wash it off,' she warned, kissing the place where she'd written. As her lips touched his wrist, a rooster crowed.

He stood watching until the taxi disappeared across the bridge. She'd left with his jersey over her shoulders and his pen in her handbag. He didn't mind at all. He'd be seeing her again. He knew that for sure.

The rooster crowed twice more, and shattered everything.

He was lying between turquoise sheets that smelled of Zoe, but she wasn't pressed close beside him. Her number was not on his wrist, and he would never see her again.

He wasn't sure whether he could bear another day.

Eight

Hannah

Freddie was up, sidling around the room and bumping into things in the dark.

I turned on the lamp. He was sitting on the end of the bed in his camel-coloured dressing gown, unrolling a pair of socks.

'So sorry,' he whispered. He pulled a sock carefully up his calf. 'Kept thinking we were already in Jane's office. What time are we due there?'

'Not till ten.' I checked the clock. Five fifteen. Not too bad, really. For a year after Zoe's death we were routinely up by four, drooping over tea in the kitchen while the world slumbered untroubled around us. My mind lost its sharp edge, clouded in tiredness. I don't think it ever quite recovered.

Our bedroom door inched open, and Scarlet's face appeared around it. She was sheet-white, her eyes unfocused.

'That you, Dad?' she said loudly.

Frederick was the first to recover. 'Scarletta!' he cried, swiftly retying his dressing-gown cord. He'd been terrified of accidentally exposing himself ever since an old friend was disgraced for flashing on Hampstead Heath.

Bottle-green eyes swivelled from him to me. 'I heard noises.'

'That was Gramps,' I announced cheerily, 'bumping his shin against the drawer. That's what shins are for—finding things in the dark.'

'Make him stop singing.'

'Nobody was singing, poppet.'

She pressed her hands to her ears. 'Make him stop.'

Then she walked further into the room, lay down on the floor and closed her eyes. We were used to this. When she first came to live with us Scarlet used to get up nightly, roam the house and sleep in odd places. We had to barricade the outside doors and windows. She seemed to be trying to escape some ghastly music that she alone could hear.

'Scarlet,' I whispered, leaning down beside her. 'You can't sleep on the floor. Get into our bed.'

She was quite suggestible in this state. Between us, Frederick and I managed to coax her under the covers.

'Two more hours before she has to get up for school,' I whispered, as we padded down the stairs. 'Sometimes she seems almost a normal girl. Then she does this, and she's like something off one of those absurd zombie films.'

Freddie shrugged sadly. 'Sometimes she *is* a normal girl, but deep inside her head it's all waiting for her. It's the same for you and me, isn't it? Time passes, you re-establish some kind of life, even smile again. But it's always there.'

I found the teapot and rinsed it out. Freddie was searching in the pantry. 'Where's the tea caddy?' he asked irritably. 'Why must people keep moving things?'

'Here on top of the dishwasher, same as it's always been.' I picked up the tin and shook it. 'Goodness me, Frederick.'

For an instant, he looked perplexed. Then he slapped a hand to his brow. 'Silly old git.'

'You're getting worse,' I teased, and immediately wished I hadn't.

'I think I'm going a bit gaga,' he said ruefully.

I took his face between my hands and kissed him. 'Rubbish!

You're the best-looking, most distinguished man in Yorkshire and nobody can fathom why on earth you put up with me.'

'I'm ancient, compared to you. Soon I'll be dribbling in my bathchair, ringing a little bell and calling querulously for you to come and change my catheter.'

'You certainly won't. I'll have wheeled you off Beachy Head by then.'

He struck a dramatic pose. 'O! Let me not be mad, not mad, sweet heaven.'

'You're not King Lear,' I said firmly. 'You're Frederick Wilde, the sanest person I've ever met.'

And with those words, I forced the incident to the back of my mind. After all, what's a lost tea caddy between soulmates?

•

Jane Whistler was one of those friends you find by a lucky chance.

It was an end-of-year award ceremony at Zoe's secondary school. In the finest tradition of such occasions, the evening seemed especially designed to make the parents suffer. We were squashed like battery hens into intolerably uncomfortable seating, clutching programs which promised hours of exquisite dullness. The blonde mother next to me swore under her breath. She had the sexy kind of haircut that costs a fortune and looks as though you've just got out of bed. She and I exchanged weary smiles.

'My idea of hell,' I whispered.

She looked agonised. 'I think I have a school phobia.'

There were endless prizes to be dished out, interspersed with the inevitable self-congratulatory speeches from staff. Zoe was fourteen at the time, and she picked up cups for drama and debating as the temperature in the hall soared higher and higher. When the chair of the governors waddled over to take his place at the podium, the blonde mother lost her composure altogether.

'God almighty!' she hissed. 'Take a look at his notes. That's a bloody novel. Shall we make a run for it?'

'This year has been a remarkable one for our school,' the chair began in a ponderous monotone. 'Before I move on to the achievements and vision of the board, I would like to begin by expressing my profound thanks to . . .'

We pushed our way along the seats—*sorry, sorry*—and forced the fire doors at the back. Seconds later we'd fallen out onto the netball court, giggling. My co-conspirator lit a cigarette.

'I think we were spotted,' I said uneasily. 'You realise we've just ruined our daughters' chances of becoming prefects?'

'Not mine.'

'Why not?'

'Never was any chance. Verity came within a whisker of expulsion this term.'

'Hang on, this rings a bell . . . Verity's the Goth? Lip piercing?'

'That's the one. Luckily, they haven't spotted the skull tattoo yet.' She looked at her watch. 'Drink?'

We'd reached the nearest pub before we introduced ourselves.

'Jane Whistler,' said my new friend, handing me a gin and tonic. Once I heard the name, the penny dropped. Whistler, White and Young, solicitors. I'd seen Jane in the local paper, saying clever things about high-profile clients. She told me she was divorced, with a feckless ex-husband of whom she seemed surprisingly fond.

'What's yours like?' she asked.

I mentioned Frederick's name, and her eyebrows rose. 'No! I saw *She Stoops to Conquer* at the Playhouse last week. No, really—it was inspired.'

Eventually we hurried to collect our daughters, promising to meet for coffee. We were both working full-time, though, and raising teenagers. Coffee never happened. I forgot about Jane until the day I knocked over a cyclist. I'd been distracted by Zoe, who was screaming at me from the passenger seat, and didn't even notice the poor man. He was unhurt, but Big Brother—in the form of two coppers in a panda car across the road—took a dim view. I was furious when the summons arrived in the post.

'Careless driving! You'd think there were more dangerous villains at large,' I snorted.

Freddie was spreading marmalade on his toast. 'A criminal in the family! Grounds for divorce. What do you think, Zoe?'

Zoe was having a good week. The storm that had made her shriek in the car had blown itself out. 'I think you shouldn't tease poor Mum,' she scolded. 'It's no joking matter. I mean, what if the papers got hold of the story? *Professor in motoring outrage*. Her reputation would be in tatters.'

'You could call it research,' suggested Freddie. 'Mass times velocity equals a cross cyclist plus a summons.'

'Shut up, both of you,' I said. 'I can see I'll get no support here. I'm going to talk to Jane Whistler.'

Zoe looked impressed. 'That Verity is such a rebel. They'd love to expel her, but she's too clever. Makes them look good in the league table.'

'Never mind the clever daughter. The mother's a clever solicitor, which is what I need right now.'

Jane was in her element in the magistrate's court. They moved her to the top of the list since she was so frightfully busy and important. I walked out with a fine and three points on my licence, which was exactly what she'd predicted.

The years passed. I became a grandmother; Verity tired of rebelling and signed up as a doctor with Médecins Sans Frontières. Jane gave up smoking with the help of a hypnotist. She supported us through the tornado of Zoe's illness, learning the Mental Health Act like the back of her hand. So when Joseph Scott came out of prison and demanded to see his children, of course we turned to her. When we walked into Whistler, White and Young at ten o'clock sharp, she was waiting for us.

'Hannah,' she cried, embracing me warmly. I'd lost the fight with gravity and no longer had a waist to speak of, but her figure was youthful. She'd refused to accept greying hair either, and her ash blonde was perfectly credible. For Jane Whistler, sixty-something really was the new fifty.

'I see the first appointment is on the seventh of January,' she said, once we were in her office. 'We've only been given a half-hour slot, but perhaps we'll make some progress.'

'What sort of progress?' asked Frederick.

'It's listed before Judge Cornwell. I know Oliver Cornwell—he's sharp, but he has a reputation for shooting from the hip. It can be infuriating. In this case, though, it might work in our favour. I'm hoping he'll tell Scott to back off.'

'Scott will be there?' I asked, horrified. I hadn't even considered the possibility.

'Yes. The first appointment is generally used for the parties to meet a family court adviser—a sort of social worker. He or she then works with the families to try and reach an agreement. They're extremely powerful.'

'We don't have to sit round a table, do we?' I asked. 'We don't have to negotiate? Because I won't.'

'The last time we saw Joseph was when he was sentenced,' Freddie explained to Jane. 'It will be difficult to face him again. Very difficult indeed.'

'I can still see him in the dock at Leeds Crown Court,' I raged. 'Looking sensitive and . . . romantic, for heaven's sake! Like a tragic hero. The terrible things his barrister said, Jane. The *filth* she threw at Zoe.'

'Nobody will have believed it.' Jane was handing out coffee from a tray.

'Oh, but they did! You must have read the newspapers? She had the judge thinking Joseph was a saint to put up with such a harpy.'

The hearing had made me sick—literally, physically sick, as soon as Scott was taken away to the cells. He'd slaughtered my beautiful girl, and then blackened her name for all the world to hear. I barged into the ladies', retching and ranting while a kind but ineffectual woman from Victim Support made comforting noises.

Jane took off her jacket, draping it over the back of her chair. I sensed she was giving herself time to think. 'These are extraordinary circumstances. I've appeared in thousands of Children Act disputes over the years. This is the first I've ever been in where the father has actually . . . well.'

'Where the father has actually killed the mother,' I said, helping her out. 'It's all right, Jane, you can say it. This isn't the time for euphemisms. And please remember—*please* make sure the judge understands—he didn't only kill her. He did it while his children screamed and begged him not to hit her again. She was actually holding Ben! It was a mercy he wasn't hurt.' I put down my cup. 'You say this judge may intervene?'

'Maybe.'

'And if he doesn't?'

'If he doesn't, or if Scott chooses to ignore him, he'll have no choice but to list the case for a full hearing.'

Freddie shook his head. 'It seems hard, Jane, after the struggles we've had. We were grieving ourselves. Scarlet was . . . it was as though she'd gone to another planet, and for a long time she couldn't come back. Theo was biting other kids at school. Perhaps the saddest to watch was little Ben. He kept waiting, hoping, looking for his mum.' He reached out to take my hand. 'We've pulled out every stop to give them a childhood.'

Jane came around her desk and perched on the edge. 'Let's see what happens at the first appointment, shall we? All we can do is get our ducks in a row and be ready to fight it out.'

'I don't know whether he's doing this just to torture us,' I fumed, 'or whether he's looking for some kind of redemption. If it's redemption he's after, he can go and feed starving orphans in Somalia, or join the Sally Army, or jump off a cliff.'

Jane began to take statements from us. It was a long meeting, and Frederick looked pale by the time she showed us out. He seemed bowed under the weight of this new worry. I watched covertly as he pulled his cap out of his pocket and carefully smoothed it onto his head. He was my brilliant, beloved man, and his heart had been broken.

Hatred rose into my mouth. It tasted metallic. I halted beside Jane, who was holding the street door open for us.

'Make Joseph Scott go away,' I muttered. 'I don't care how you do it. We need him out of our lives.'

Nine

Joseph

Jack Frost had paid a visit in the pre-dawn hours; a forest of crystal ferns decorated the insides of the caravan's windows.

He took a shower in the toy bathroom, which was when he discovered he'd left his razor in Akash's flat. His towel was frozen solid; it was like trying to dry himself with a surfboard. He dressed in clean jeans, two jerseys and his thickest socks, pulled on a woollen beanie and carried his kitbag towards Abigail's laundry block. The moors lay still as ice, and his breath frosted in plumes. The sun wasn't far away: shafts of brilliance shot from behind the horizon, and the grass was tinged with silvery translucence. He could see no sign of life from the campervan families at the top end of the site, but Jessy was sniffing myopically along the beck. When he whistled, she padded up the hill to join him.

'Hello, old girl,' he murmured, tipping most of the contents of his bag into a giant washing machine. 'Looking for rabbits, eh? Good lass.'

The sun was rising when he emerged. Stepping out into its light, he heard the metallic rasp of a van door sliding shut. It sounded smooth and careful; whoever was up and about was trying not to draw attention to themselves. Glancing towards the sound, he saw a woman leave a white VW kombi and head towards the shower block. He recognised the flowing skirt and wild curls. Anxious to avoid conversation, he strode away in the opposite direction.

Jessy trailed him back to the caravan, plodding close beside his legs. He invited her in, and she stood watching as he switched on the heater and made himself a cup of instant coffee.

'Well,' he said. 'You and me, Jessy. What shall us two daredevils get up to now?'

The old dog regarded him for a time, her brow furrowed. She seemed faintly disapproving. Then she gave a weary sigh and lay down with her nose along her paws.

'Yeah, I'm pretty knackered too,' agreed Joseph, reaching to stroke her ears. 'Had a fuckin' awful night.'

Still, he felt the need of some action; the restoration of a vestige of order in his life. He lifted one of the squabs that ran around the living area. They doubled as beds, and underneath were storage lockers. He began to sort through them, constantly distracted by the discovery of childhood treasures. Here was the dog-eared set of Monopoly that he and Marie used to play on wet days; and—ah! *Twister.* Great game—he'd been far better at that than Marie, which used to annoy the hell out of her. Scarlet and Theo had played with this very set too. He lifted out a shoebox full of jumbled packs of cards. At the bottom of one of the lockers lay a stash of his mother's magazines. She used to read the horoscopes. They gave her hope.

He sank onto a seat, leafing through a thirty-year-old copy of *Woman's Own.* There was a brown ring on the front cover, and he smiled. His mother's coffee mug. On page ten a crossword had been completed in her firm, square capitals. He imagined Irene sitting heavily on the caravan steps with a cigarette in one hand, racing through the clues. She used to keep up with all Joseph's schoolwork, and if she couldn't answer a question she took him to the library and they researched together. He'd often thought she could have been a match for Hannah Wilde, given the same advantages. Instead, she'd fallen pregnant with Marie and done what was expected of her: married a crashing bore.

Joseph ran his fingertips over the blue letters, feeling the indentations made by her pen. They brought bittersweet comfort; an echo of Irene's presence, as though the years were telescoping inwards. His mother had never rejected him. She'd come to all the court appearances and faced the blank-eyed lenses of the press. Time after time, she'd taken a train to Leeds and queued up to visit him. He saw her there three days before she died, and had thought she looked terribly tired. He missed her.

Placing the magazine on the table, he turned to the nearest bookcase. On top lay a jumble of thrillers by Dick Francis—his mother again. The next shelf held books that he remembered reading to Scarlet and Theo when they were last there: Roald Dahl and *Horrible Histories*. Stashed among these he spotted a thin, faded hardback. He lifted it out and held it up to a shaft of pale sunshine. Its cover was cinnamon and gold, slightly torn: an antique copy of Kahlil Gibran's *The Prophet*. He knew it almost by heart.

For some minutes, Joseph held the little book between his hands. Finally he opened it, knowing what he would find on the flyleaf.

Happy Birthday to my Russian Prince.
You have given me life.
With my love forever,
Z x

He sank to his knees on the caravan's thin carpet. A sound escaped him; a heaving, agonised yelp that made the dog lift her head and squint through rheumy eyes.

'I'm sorry,' he cried, and his voice broke on the words.

Jessy watched as tears sank into the fabric of the squab. After a time she crawled forward and nudged her face against Joseph's foot. He felt the pressure, and reached down to caress her head. The tears kept coming.

'I'm a wimp,' he told the dog. 'They should shoot me.'

Someone was coming. The caravan's flimsy structure trembled, followed by a rapping on the door. Joseph reached into his pocket to pull out a tangled rag of tissue, and was blowing his nose when Abigail stepped in.

'Now then,' she remarked unemotionally, taking in the scene.

'Now then, Abigail.'

'Cleaning the floor?' She didn't wait for him to reply. 'I thought you might like some breakfast in a nice warm kitchen.'

Joseph got to his feet, certain she knew he'd been crying like a baby. He caught a glimpse of himself in the bedroom mirror as he laid the book on his pillow. He looked like a rough bastard, the kind that used to come in off the merchant ships when he was a child: gaunt and shadowed, with dark stubble and desperate eyes. He'd aged a decade in the past three years.

'Sorry,' he said as they walked up the hill together. 'I don't look respectable. I'd better drive into Helmsley and buy a razor today.'

'You'll do,' Abigail replied evenly. 'What you need is proper food and a bit of mollycoddling. Unfortunately I'm no good at the mollycoddling part, never have been, but I can put a meal on the table.'

Which was true, thought Joseph as she filled his plate with home-grown bacon and sausages and scrambled eggs. Gus sat at the other end of the table, tucking into a feast of his own. He was forty or so, ruddy and solid, a man of few words. A blue beanie lay beside his plate.

'Hi Gus,' said Joseph.

The farm worker cast a glance in the direction of Joseph's left ear. 'Now then.'

'Cold morning for it?' Joseph persisted.

'Aye.'

'Still. It isn't snowing.'

'True.'

Gus seemed to think this was quite enough wild socialising. His gaze returned to his plate. Joseph wasn't offended by the monosyllabic response. He'd expected it. He knew the man of old, and suspected some undiagnosed syndrome.

Zoe, of course, had managed to make a friend of Gus. She'd done that with people, with a gift for drawing out their stories and making them feel valued. She'd known more about Gus's life than Abigail did.

'There's no syndrome,' she'd once told Joseph. 'Just isolation. Gus was brought up on a moorland farm, no playmates but the farmyard cats, snowed in for months of the year. He never saw anyone but his parents from one week to the next.'

'School?'

'An ordeal. He left as soon as possible.'

Zoe and Joseph were out walking with the children. The moors were a purple haze, laced with the tang of heather. Bees flickered in the shimmering air. She carried baby Theo in a sling across her front while Scarlet rode, singing, on Joseph's shoulders.

'I like the idea of an isolated farmhouse,' mused Joseph. 'Way up here, with just the children and you. Our own private world.'

'Me too! Let's pull up the drawbridge and be happy.'

'I'm already happy,' he protested truthfully, putting his arm around her. Zoe had been well for months, despite Theo's arrival. He hoped they'd turned a corner.

'I wish I could always feel like this,' she said wistfully. 'It's not much fun sometimes, living inside my head.' She took his hand and held it to her cheek. They walked side by side, joined at the hip, perfectly in step.

Abigail was looking at him. Digby had leaped onto her lap and was kneading her trousers. 'All right?' she asked.

'Fine,' he replied absently.

'I hear your dad's living abroad.'

'Um . . .' Joseph was mesmerised. He could feel the warmth of Zoe's cheek, the swing of her strides alongside his own, the light pressure of her hipbone. She seemed more real than Abigail did. He made an effort to pull himself together. 'Dad used to buy a lottery ticket every single week. It was his only hobby, watching those bloody numbers come up on the telly. A week after mum divorced him, he hit the jackpot.'

'So he's a millionaire?'

'Dunno about that, but he raked in enough to retire to the Costa Blanca. We're not close. He's hardly ever met his grandchildren.'

Abigail ran her knuckles down Digby's stripy back. 'Silly fool,' she said, with unexpected vehemence. 'Always was. Not bad, just soft in the head. You off now, Gus?'

Gus was zipping up his overalls, mumbling about having a look at a trough. He left without further discussion.

'Mum died,' said Joseph. 'Did Marie tell you?'

'She did. In your sister's opinion, poor Irene died of a broken heart. It was the shame that finished her off. She couldn't stand the shame of being your mother.'

Joseph's hunger abruptly dissipated. He dropped his knife and fork. 'That's *exactly* what Marie said at the funeral! Her very words. They let me out for the day so I could bury my mother, and my lovely sister told me I'd killed another woman.'

'And what did you reply?'

'Nothing. I had nothing to say. I thought she was probably right.'

'Pig's trotters,' retorted Abigail. 'Your mum was a good lass, don't get me wrong, but anyone who liked their fish and chips and cider and smoked as many fags as Irene Scott did was asking for heart disease somewhere along the line. You could see it coming. If anyone's to blame, it's your dad for making her so bloody miserable she gave up on herself. He's neither use nor ornament, that fella.'

'Maybe shame was the last straw.'

'Maybe that final packet of Benson and Hedges was the last straw! There's nothing to be gained by blaming yourself for all the ills of the world, Joseph Scott, and your sister ought to have more sense than to go scattering nasty accusations like confetti.'

Joseph picked up the knife and fork again, but he didn't eat. 'Marie and I both wanted to be pallbearers, and the undertaker put me at the front with her right behind me. It felt like a bloody long way from the chapel to the grave, I can tell you. She kept spitting insults out of the corner of her mouth as we sweated our way across the cemetery, followed by all those solemn mourners. My cousin Eric was opposite and he almost dropped his handle, he was laughing so much.'

'Ah, poor Irene. Her last journey, and her kids bickering all the way.'

'*I* wasn't bickering! I never said a word. Marie completely lost it over the tea and scones, started screaming at me, made a hell of a scene. Luckily my minders from the prison saw my predicament and galloped to the rescue. I was bloody pleased to get myself back behind bars.'

'No screaming women in Armley?'

'Well . . . no female ones.'

Abigail let out a throaty guffaw, while Digby ducked for cover.

Joseph was washing up at the sink when Abigail asked, 'Will you be seeing those poor little ones?'

'I hope so. I never got to comfort them, never got to tell them I was sorry, never even said goodbye. The Wildes don't want me in their lives, so it looks like I'm going to have to go to court.'

'You're determined, are you?'

'Just hanging on until the first court date.'

'And then what?'

'My solicitor's hoping the judge will let me see them, maybe supervised by someone at first.'

'Mm-hm. And then what?'

'Then . . . well, I hope I get to see them a lot more.'

Abigail's lips almost disappeared as she worked. Joseph kept casting covert glances at her. Finally, he couldn't stand it. 'What?' he demanded.

'Nothing.'

'Abigail, I can tell you disapprove.'

She turned her back to let down the airer—wheels squeaking on the pulley—and began to fold clothes. 'They've been through the mill, those kids.'

'I know that.'

'I trust you aren't going to charge in there, kicking up trouble like a bull in a china shop.'

Joseph had washed the last plate, but he stood with his hands in the cooling water. 'You think I'm irredeemable?'

'That's a long word.'

'Am I, though? You've known me since I was a crawler. I care about what you think.'

Abigail shook out each garment with a cross little snap. 'It isn't for me to make judgements. All I know is that some kids lost their mother thanks to you, and some people lost their daughter. And some kinds of damage aren't easily mended.'

Joseph pulled out the plug, and watched the soapsuds as they were dragged down the vortex.

'I can't give them up,' he said.

Ten

Scarlet

If you Google my dad's name, you'll come up with pages and pages of websites. There are newspaper articles and blogs and radio station sites and women's right's sites and sites for people who think sentences aren't long enough. There are sites about bipolar and sites about domestic violence. Everyone has an opinion about my dad.

When Mum died, Gramps and Hannah took Theo and I out of our primary school in Tadcaster, where we lived, and moved us to a new one in York. I think the teachers had told the other kids who we were, and banned them from asking questions. It didn't work, though. Theo and I were celebrities—and not in a good way. A group of boys bullied Theo about his dad being a 'psycho'. Theo was only seven at the time. I found him in the bushes at the end of the playground, gasping for breath. That was his first ever asthma attack, and I bet it was the upset that caused it. We didn't go to the teachers. We felt mortified, as though it was us who were the psychos.

The following week, I opened my lunchbox to find that someone had left a piece of paper in there. It was a news story, printed off the internet. I just glanced down at it, and then I felt my breakfast coming up into my throat.

> SCHOOLTEACHER ON WIFE MURDER CHARGE
>
> Joseph Scott was remanded in custody today, charged with the slaying of his wife Zoe. Scott, who headed the history department at prestigious Tetlow High School, is alleged to have attacked Zoe in a fit of rage at their Tadcaster home last month.

The article went on and on, but I didn't read any more. There was a lovely picture of Mum. It was one of her wedding photos, but the journalist had cut Dad out of it so it only showed Mum's face.

Someone had scribbled all across the top of the paper in bright orange highlighter: UR DAD IS SICK SICK SICK.

When I didn't go back to class, my teacher sent a girl called Liz to find me. Liz was the kind of girl who always has a sharpened pencil and gets to be class leader because she is so responsible. She found me blubbing in the girls' toilets, but I refused to say why.

'Come on,' she said kindly, and put her arm around my shoulder. 'We're just about to have a story. You don't want to miss that.'

The next day, there was a note in my school bag. Another article, from another website. And the day after that. It went on for months. Sometimes it was in my bag, sometimes in my desk, sometimes in my coat pocket or my violin case. There were articles about the court hearings, and about Dad pleading guilty to manslaughter, and about him getting six years; and always a message in the orange highlighter.

I dreaded going to school.

One day, I nipped out of the classroom to get my violin. Liz was standing with her hand in my coat pocket. She looked at me. I looked at her.

'Hi, Scarlet!' she sang, cool as a cucumber. 'Looking for my wallet. Someone's swiped it. Mum said to check all the pockets.' Then she turned around and walked away, with a piece of paper in one hand and her long hair swinging. I never got any more notes after that.

People aren't always nice, I can tell you that for free.

So that's why I made friends with Vienna, and only Vienna, though to be honest I probably wouldn't have chosen her as a friend if my mum hadn't died. She's not the sharpest knife in the box, but what you see is what you get. There's no way she'd have bitched behind my back or left horrible notes in my bag. She has mousy-brown hair which she wears in a fountain ponytail, and a freckly face. She eats too much chocolate and I'm afraid it's starting to show on her bum. She lives with her mother and stepdad on an estate near the ring road, and she has a TV *and* an Xbox 360 *and* a computer in her bedroom. Oh—*and* an ensuite *and* a king-sized bed with a pretend fur cover, like something off a James Bond film.

Hannah disapproves. I once heard her say that Vienna's parents are 'criminally negligent of that child's intellect, such as it is'. Hannah thinks young people shouldn't be encouraged to live in a virtual world, because the real world is jam-packed with magic. According to her, there are whole universes in a single atom. She's published papers about that kind of thing.

I often go to Vienna's house after school. We let ourselves in with a key they keep hidden in the garden wall. We tell our families it's to do homework together, but actually we Facebook and watch TV. I was there just before the Christmas holidays began. We were watching *The Vampire Diaries*, lazing on the James Bond bed.

'My dad's taking my grandparents to court,' I blurted.

'Bunty did that,' Vienna replied casually, eyes glued to the TV screen. Somebody was about to get their blood sucked. 'Mum's boss. Sued the council because she slipped on a pavement.'

I didn't care about this woman Bunty, who really should have looked where she was going 'My dad wants to see us,' I said.

'Is he out, then?'

'Yep. He only had to do half his sentence. Some stupid judge might make us go and see him. If that happens, I'm running away.'

Vienna turned the TV down. This was more interesting even than a blood-sucking. 'They can't make you—he's a murderer!'

'I know he's a murderer.'

'Are you scared?'

I thought about just how scared I was. Ever since I'd seen that man outside my school, something had been living in my stomach. It seemed to have tentacles that spread all through me. 'Nah,' I said.

'I'd be *sooo* scared.'

'Well, I'm not. If I get the chance I'll tell him to sod off, and good riddance to bad rubbish.' As soon as those words were out of my mouth I felt even worse. I burst into tears.

Vienna is a good friend, really. She grabbed the remote and turned the TV off. Then she sat there looking awkward and muttering 'cheer up' while she patted my back.

'It won't be much of a Christmas with *this* hanging over us,' I wailed. 'Why can't he leave us alone?'

'I know what *you* need!' cried Vienna. She dashed over to her fridge (yes, she actually has a fridge in her room) and dug out a bar of Caramello. She believes everything can be cured by chocolate. Actually, it wasn't a bad idea. I had to stop blubbing so that I could eat it.

'What's your dad like?' she asked, once I'd calmed down. 'Do you remember much about him?'

I did. I did. I didn't. I had about a million memories, all swirling around in tiny pieces in my head like a cloud of ashes above a bonfire. I had pictures and sounds and feelings. The soapy smell of him; a greeny-blue jersey; his voice with the soft accent; the fun of being high up above the world when I rode on his shoulders, strong hands holding on to my shins to stop me from toppling off. I had feelings of total adoration and also of being so scared I wet myself.

'Not really,' I fibbed.

'You were ten, weren't you? I can remember loads of things from when I was ten.'

'I remember him punching my mum,' I said.

'You mustn't ever forget *her.*'

I lay back on the pretend fur cover and looked up at the ceiling. I had this fear that I was already forgetting Mum. It was as though she was standing on a boat, sailing away. I could still see her waving, but her face was blurred.

'Um . . . my Auntie Carolyn was over last night.' For some reason, Vienna's voice had dropped to a whisper. 'She brought her new boyfriend.'

'Really?' I wasn't remotely interested in Vienna's aunt.

'Mm. They all drank a lot of wine, and . . . well, Carolyn started talking about your mum. It turns out she knew her. They worked together in a bar next to the river.'

Now I was interested. 'What did she say?'

'She said Zoe—your mum—was fun to be around. Charismatic, she said. Loads of friends. People just couldn't get enough of her.'

'Charismatic.' I shut my eyes, feeling much happier.

'She also . . . um . . .' Vienna stopped. I heard her scratching her leg. 'Um, no. That's all, really.'

I opened my eyes again. 'She also what?'

'Nothing.'

'Vienna!'

She stretched herself out next to me, with her head propped on her hand. 'The truth is, I don't think Carolyn got on with your mum. She said some things that weren't so nice.'

'Like what?'

'Not very kind things.'

'Yeah? Like what?'

'I just don't think they got on. Don't worry about it. Forget I said anything.'

I sat up. 'It's too late to be tactful. The cat's out of the bag.'

'You'll be angry.'

'I won't.'

'Promise you won't shout?'

'I promise.'

'Okay.' She was biting her lower lip. 'Auntie Carolyn said that underneath all the razzle-dazzle your mum was actually a total bitch who always had to be the centre of attention. Erm, she said most people didn't get that, especially men. She slept with the customers—with "anything in trousers". Carolyn said she went nuts in the end and started smashing glasses. They had to call the police. The last she heard, your mum was in the bin.'

'The what?'

'The bin. And she read in the papers that your mum was totally rat-arsed the night she died, which was probably why a couple of punches killed her. If she'd been sober, she mightn't have died. It's something to do with the brain.'

I'd promised, but I was furious. I felt like screaming at the top of my voice, spitting and swearing and tearing up that stupid fur cover.

'It sounds as though it's your Auntie Carolyn who's the complete bitch,' I snapped, jumping off the bed.

Vienna's face crumpled. 'You promised,' she sobbed. 'I knew you'd do this.'

I *had* promised; and I knew it wasn't Vienna's fault her aunt was a slithery, fork-tongued snake in the grass. All the same, I wanted to hurt somebody. So I dug the fingernails of one hand into the back of my other wrist until I felt one of the nails go through the skin. It really hurt. It made my eyes water, and I felt sick.

'Didn't you stick up for my mum?' I shouted.

Vienna wasn't really crying. She was hamming it up. 'They didn't even realise I was listening. I was playing Minecraft in the living room with my headphones on. I just stared at the screen with my mouth hanging open. Adults think you can't hear them when you do that.'

I sat down again. 'What did she mean by "in the bin"?'

'Prison, maybe? You know, sin bin.'

'Anything in trousers?' It sounded so ugly.

Vienna covered up her legs with the fake fur. 'She did admit that your mum was beautiful . . . no, that wasn't the word . . . *attractive*. She said, "Zoe was certainly attractive, can't be denied. Just like a Venus flytrap".'

'A Venus flytrap? That's horrible! They eat the flies alive.'

'Sorry. It's just what she said.'

I took a minute to think about all this. 'Sounds like your aunt's a small, mean person and she was jealous of Mum.'

'My stepdad can't stand her,' agreed Vienna. 'Even though she's his sister. When she rang to say she was coming round, he slammed down the phone and said to my mum, 'Christ almighty, Val! Hide me! Motormouth's on her way over."

'So did he hide?'

'Mum wouldn't let him. She said he could entertain his own flipping family, they're all morons and she married him, not the whole flipping tribe.'

We shared another bar of chocolate while Vienna listed all the things that most annoyed her about Carolyn. I probably seemed back to normal by the time I stood up to leave.

'You okay now?' Vienna eyed me uncertainly, as we waited for Gramps at the gate.

''Course I am! Gotta run—here he is.' We did hugs, and I dashed off to get into the car.

'Good day at school?' asked Gramps, once we were on the road. He was wearing his tweedy cap and leather driving gloves.

'Fine, thanks.' I was daydreaming about walking up to Auntie Carolyn and smacking her right on her ugly gossipy mouth.

He wanted to chat. 'Did you have drama?'

'No.'

'Music?'

'Yes. Gramps, what does it mean if you say someone is in "the bin"?'

He slowed down for a set of traffic lights. 'Well, that depends on the context.'

'If someone's gone nuts and started throwing things, and ended up in the bin.'

'Ah. In that case, they're probably talking about a hospital for people with, um, mental health problems.'

'Oh my God! So they mean the loony bin?' I couldn't imagine my mother having anything to do with a place like that.

'Well, yes, I believe that's the expression. I don't like it much.' Gramps sounded calm, but his hands were shaking on the wheel. In fact they were shaking so badly that I wondered if it was safe for him to drive. 'You know, Scarlet, a lot of people have mental health problems at one time or another. An awful lot. A person might have an episode, and then never be troubled again their whole lives.'

'So you mean I could get ill like that?'

'You?' He actually took his eyes off the road to glance round at me. 'Why ever do you ask such a strange thing?'

'No reason. Just wondered.'

'In the bad old days,' said Gramps, 'society locked people up and threw away the key. Terrible things were done to them—and I suspect that most were as sane as you or I. Saner, probably. Nowadays we know better. Really, with a lot of these problems it's just like having a broken leg, or maybe measles. People get help and then they're quite well again.'

'I see.' I didn't see at all.

Another set of traffic lights, this time the slow ones near Bootham Bar.

'Rush hour,' grumbled Gramps. 'The sheer weight of humanity.'

I watched his fingers in the brown driving gloves, tapping the wheel. I had to ask. I just had to. I needed to hear that the answer was no. 'Mum was never ill like that, was she?'

The fingers stopped tapping.

'Gramps?' I felt panicky.

'Yes,' he said quietly. 'She was. For a time. But she got better.'

My heart began pumping too fast. The other things Carolyn had said flew screaming into my head like rockets. *A total bitch . . . slept with anything in trousers . . . Venus flytrap.* Perhaps they were true as well.

'Why didn't you tell me?' I asked.

'Because it isn't important.'

'Of course it's important!'

'No, Scarlet, it isn't. It is just a tiny part of your mother's story. She was so much more than that . . . *so* much more.'

As soon as Gramps had parked outside our house, I ran up to my room and shoved the wedge under the door. It was dark outside, but I didn't turn on the light. I dragged my duvet with me under the bed, burrowed into it and curled up.

When Hannah arrived home from work she came upstairs and knocked, then tried the door. It wouldn't open more than half an inch. 'Scarlet?' she called through the crack. 'Are you in there?' You'd never guess she has an IQ of about a million. Of course I was in there—how else did she think a wedge got under the door?

'Yes,' I said.

'Gramps told me about your conversation in the car,' she said. 'I know you were upset to hear that Zoe needed hospital care.'

'I don't want to talk about it.'

'Who's been gossiping?'

'Hannah, can we please not talk about this?'

'You just come down when you're ready, then,' she said, and I heard her walking away. I don't know how many hours I hid in the dark. Time seemed to stop. I smelled supper and later I heard the boys shouting as they were on their way to bed, but it was as though all these familiar sounds and smells weren't anything to do with me. I needed to be in the dark. I needed to hide.

My beautiful memories of Mum were melting, like Ben's snowlady did when the sun came out. Nothing was what I'd thought. My memories were all wrong. Yet at the same time a nasty, wormy voice somewhere deep in my brain was whispering that I'd known it all along. I remembered her squeezing me too hard. I remembered the time she painted the whole house a really bright orange colour. I remembered her yelling at Dad, and how loud and harsh her voice could suddenly sound. I remembered the worried, tight feeling I used to get when she seemed too happy to be true, or when she went into her bedroom and the door was locked for days. I remembered listening to her footsteps as she came up to the front door, and knowing what kind of a mood she'd be in just from the way she walked, and if it was the wrong kind of mood I'd wish she hadn't come home.

I had a thought. I wriggled out from under the bed and switched on the lamp. Then I reached far under the bed and pulled out a big cardboard box. It was my precious memories box, given to me by Nanette, a counsellor who helped us after Mum died. She'd suggested I decorate it, so I'd covered it in wrapping paper and painted *Precious Memories* on the lid. I was ten at the time, which is why I used such girly handwriting. It also explains why I stuck pink silk roses all over it. Ten-year-old girls do not have good taste.

The first thing inside the box was Mum's green cardigan. It was tiny, and she only ever did up one button. It looked really great on her. I pressed my nose into the wool; I could still catch her scent, though it was fading. The cardigan was made of cashmere and felt kitten-soft.

There was *Maid of Sherwood.* There were crumpled train tickets from our last trip to London, and a leaflet from the Science Museum with the dark pink kiss of Mum's mouth on it from where she'd blotted her lipstick. It looked like something Marilyn Monroe might have done. There was also a postcard she'd sent from Brighton, where she'd gone to be in a pantomime. The card had a picture of a pier, and her handwriting in gold pen.

I miss you, my gorgeous Scarlet! Is Dad looking after you? Has he made his famous pasta every night? I'm counting down the days. One more week and I'll be home.

It's a blast to be an ugly sister. Every afternoon I have to stick on a giglinormous fake nose. It looks crazily evil, like a shark's fin. The other ugly sister has to wear a fat suit under her dress! She gets very hot.

Here's a hundred kisses and hugs from me,
Mummy

All over the card she had drawn Xs and Os. I'd counted them. There were exactly one hundred, and they hardly left enough room for the stamp. I kissed the card and put it on top of the other things.

Next, there was a note from the tooth fairy. Mum had tried to disguise her handwriting, but it was obviously hers because she'd used the same gold pen:

Thank you for this beautiful tooth. I can tell you brush and floss! We use only the very cleanest teeth to make our palace, and this one will be the cornerstone of a dazzling white colonnade. In payment, here is a golden pound of your mortal money. With love, T.F.

There were also three paper napkins from a restaurant. I was bored at Gramps' birthday meal out, so Mum got a pen from her bag and suggested we play head-body-legs. We came up with three absolutely hilarious creatures. Dad said we should sell them to the Tate Modern and get paid fifty thousand pounds each.

Mum died a few days after that. I found the pictures still in my pocket. So I kept them, because they were the last things that were made by me and her together.

At the bottom of the box was her photo album. My favourite was one taken on holiday at our caravan on the moors. She and I were sitting by the beck with our feet in the water and sunlight on our faces. She had both her arms around me, I had both mine around her and our cheeks were pressed together. She looked very, very happy. I was grinning from ear to ear. It was such a lovely picture.

I felt better after looking through the box. It didn't matter what anyone said, especially Vienna's Auntie Motormouth, who I hoped would be run over by a double-decker bus. My mother wasn't a total bitch and she wasn't a Venus flytrap. She played head-body-legs, and she loved us all.

One more thing I should mention: the album looked a bit weird. Actually, it looked very weird, and I never showed it to anybody. That's because lots of the photos had big holes cut out of them, all jagged around the edges. Some were only about half a photo.

That was me. I did it. I cut out all the pictures of Dad.

Eleven

Joseph

Christmas morning on the moors. He imagined his children waking, and fretted about them. He hoped they had stockings at the ends of their beds. He hoped they'd left mince pies for Santa Claus. He hoped they were happy.

Christmas with Zoe had always seemed enchanted. She filled their house with spice-scented candles, clouds of fairy lights and treasure troves in stockings. One Christmas morning Scarlet and Theo—creeping from their beds at five—found two outrageously fluffy kittens playing with the baubles on the tree. They were miniature cats, with creamy bodies and velvet-coffee faces and tails, scampering across the children's feet. It was Zoe's doing, of course; Zoe radiated magic. When she was around, nothing was ordinary.

The caravan had no Zoe. No magic. Joseph hauled himself out of bed and tried reading a thriller from the shelf. The bank statement he'd used as a bookmark caught his eye, and he began to worry about his joblessness. He'd trawled employment websites and searched the local paper in vain; a vague promise of summer washing-up work at one of the pubs was as close as he'd come to gainful employment.

At six, he realised he was going stir-crazy. It was Christmas Day; he couldn't spend it reading a very bad novel and pining for his children. He opened a drawer and leafed through a pile of tourist brochures. Castle Howard, Duncombe Park . . . ah, Pickering Church, with its fifteenth-century frescos. That would be open.

Dawn arrived in grey anticlimax. Pulling on wellingtons, Joseph set off across the beck and climbed to the uplands where—if he held his arm straight up in the air—he had a phone signal. He sent a text to Marie.

Happy Christmas Sis. Love J

It was a mild morning. Mist hung above the beck. He could see smoke rising from the farmhouse chimney and Abigail's compact figure lugging a bucket towards the pigpen. She'd invited him for breakfast, and at eight he fronted up in her kitchen. Abigail stood at the range, stirring mushrooms. She had the radio on; a choirboy was piping 'Once in Royal David's City'.

'Now then,' she said laconically.

Joseph felt a surge of affection, and bent to kiss her wrinkled cheek. 'Happy Christmas.'

'Get away wi' you,' she snapped. 'Make yourself useful and clear a space at the table.'

Joseph obeyed. 'I thought I'd go to Pickering today,' he said. 'Take a look at the wall paintings. Haven't seen them for years.'

Abigail didn't seem to have heard. She threw bacon in with her mushrooms before announcing abruptly: 'Gus's father had a collapse yesterday.'

'Oh no! How's he doing?'

Abigail looked grim. 'He'll live, but they reckon he's a write-off. Gus has given notice here.'

'Can you replace him?'

'Maybe.' She looked Joseph in the eye. 'Would you give it a go?'

'Me?'

'Four days a week or thereabouts, depending on how busy we are. Winter's quiet but in the summer holidays I'm flat tacks. Minimum wage, but I'll waive your ground rent and power and supply some food. I know you're a bit high and mighty to be a labourer.'

'I'm not too high and mighty to be anything anymore,' said Joseph. 'Thank you, I'm grateful for the offer, but . . .'

'But?'

'I don't know the first thing about farming. I could probably drive the tractor but I can't fix it when it breaks down. I don't know one end of a sheep from the other. I can't deliver a lamb, or—'

'Never to worry. I can. It's mostly the campsite that needs managing. I've got Rosie doing the cleaning, which is a big help.'

'Rosie?'

'You haven't met her?' Abigail seemed to be suppressing a smile. 'That's a treat in store for you. She's been away for a week or so, but she's back now. She's a vit . . . hang on . . . viticulturist, by trade. Not much call for them around here.'

Her words slid over Joseph, whose mind was taken up by the offer of work. 'Can I think about this for a day or two?'

'If you must.'

And why not? Joseph thought later, as he followed Jessy's waving tail through the kissing gate. He didn't want to struggle through life in a city, knowing that people were whispering. Perhaps what Abigail was offering him was a little peace in this ancient landscape. He walked slowly, too deep in thought to notice the person emerging from the laundry block and making her way along a sheep trail. He saw movement out of the corner of his eye and halted in mid-stride, only just in time to avoid collision.

'Sorry.' The voice was female; resonant and amused. 'I wasn't watching where I was going.'

Joseph blinked. It was the woman he'd seen crossing the beck that first night, and later in a dove-grey dawn. He remembered the claret skirt and sumptuous head of hair that seemed to twist out at every angle. A shapeless jersey was frayed at the sleeves.

'My fault,' he muttered.

'You'd think, with all this space, we'd manage not to bump into each other.'

'You would.'

She was carrying a basket full of clothes. Joseph wondered uneasily whether she was expecting him to make some kind of overture, perhaps invite her down to his caravan for coffee. The thought made him blanch. He could imagine precisely how the conversation would go. She'd ask him about himself and he'd be forced to tell his story. She would finish her coffee very quickly and leave.

'Happy Christmas,' she said.

'Er, yes. Happy Christmas.'

They each smiled with faint embarrassment, and passed on; though she flickered through his thoughts as he made his way down the valley. *Nice smile . . . a young smile . . . not skinny, not like Zoe, curvy . . . Not from round here, definitely a southerner . . . How old? Thirties? Older? Couple of strands of silver in that hair. No attempt to dye them out. Funny combination, heavy boots and a long skirt and grey in her hair. A tree-hugger, obviously. Ageing hippie. The sort of burn-the-bra merchant Marie hangs out with.*

Ah, yes. That had her nicely categorised. Satisfied, Joseph put her from his mind.

•

He felt self-conscious as he wandered around Pickering Church, conspicuously solo on a day of happy families. Yet there were worse things for a pariah to do than gape at the imaginings of artists who'd been dead five hundred years. Plastered walls glowed with martyred saints, with wicked torturers and executioners. Joseph sat down to gaze at the terrible mother-and-daughter act of Herodias and Salome, who demanded John the Baptist's head on a plate. To the medieval artist there were no grey areas, it seemed. Haloed saint or evil persecutor: that was the choice. Joseph had a fairly shrewd idea of how they would have depicted him.

He tried—really, he tried—to concentrate, to be a historian; but his children nagged and tugged until he physically ached. On a whim, he took out his phone and scrolled through the contacts list until he found the Wildes' number. It would be so easy to press *call*; he imagined hearing Scarlet's voice. Then he jammed the phone back into his pocket.

•

Abigail's farmhouse lay gilded in evening light as he splashed through the ford and into the yard. Jessy met him at the car. His caravan had become her second home, and she hauled herself inside without waiting for an invitation. He was glad of the company.

'Beer?' he offered, opening his shoebox of a fridge. 'No? Well, suit yourself. You won't mind if I do?'

The collie yawned, showing yellowed teeth. Joseph held up the bottle in salute to her, and was about to drink when footsteps shook the caravan. The next moment, a female voice called, 'Hello?'

He froze with the bottle held to his lips and his mind working fast. *Hell! It's the tree-hugger. I don't need this . . . Any chance I could hide? No, don't be bloody daft, Scott, she knows you're in here . . . What if I just keep very still and hope she gets the hint and sods off? No, that's just rude. I'll have to open the door and tell her I'm busy.*

She'd turned while she waited, and was facing away towards the beck. An unruly plait hung between her shoulder blades. As he opened the door, she swung round to face him with a smile on her lips and a wine bottle in her hands. 'I've got a deal for you,' she announced, before he could speak. 'I won't ask what you think you're doing alone on a campsite on the moors at Christmas, if you'll promise not to ask me the same question.'

Joseph hesitated; loneliness jostled with his desire to hide.

She held out her offering. 'This stuff's Australian. Not bad.'

'Thanks, but—'

'Not a single string attached, I assure you. I haven't come to seduce you or cry on your shoulder or even ask for a cup of sugar.'

Joseph took the bottle out of her hands. 'It's a hell of a mess in here,' he protested desperately, jerking his head towards the inside of the caravan. *Keep out, keep out! Hell of a mess in my life.*

'Thank heavens for that. In my book, tidiness is the first sign of madness.'

First sign of madness. Zoe at four in the morning, scrubbing every shelf in their kitchen with bleach. She was wearing nothing but an apron over a lacy bra and thong, but there was nothing erotic about the scene. The room was trashed, chairs up on the table, black and white tiles ankle deep in tins and jars and black bin bags. The chemical reek of bleach stung his nostrils. 'Disgusting,' Zoe yelped, rubber-gloved arms working frenziedly. 'Gotta get control of this place!' Back in their bedroom, the newborn Scarlet wailed with hunger.

Joseph hadn't understood what it meant. He hadn't known what was coming.

'If you're right,' he said now, standing back to let his visitor in, 'I must be awfully sane.'

She swung confidently past him, arms folded in the ragged sweater. 'Luxury!' she cried, as she reached the sitting area. 'Bloomin' luxury! I'm frozen to death in a VW kombi, and you're down here with sofas and rugs and bookcases and'—she opened the bathroom door—'I don't believe it. A cute little shower!'

'I live in a palace.'

'Does this palace come equipped with a corkscrew?'

'Sorry. Just a minute . . .' Joseph pulled open the cutlery drawer and held up a rusty corkscrew. 'All mod cons.'

He was beginning to enjoy himself, though he wouldn't have believed it possible ten minutes earlier. It had been years since he'd had a normal conversation with a woman under eighty. He hastily washed two glasses (pesky mice—they got everywhere) and splashed wine into them.

'Rosemary Sutton,' she said as she took one. 'Rosie will do.'

'Aha! The viticulturist.'

'No, the cleaner.' She moved to look out of a window, and Joseph joined her. The beck was submerged in violet shadow, but the moors blazed in the last fire of the day.

'I feel like running up there to stand in the sunlight,' said Rosie, with a touch of melancholy. 'I never want the day to end. But it would be gone by the time I arrived.'

'Have you seen this place in midsummer?' asked Joseph. 'No? Well, come back then, if you don't want the day to end. There's still a gleam in the sky at eleven, and the dawn chorus starts tuning up at two.'

Even as they watched, the brilliance faded. Joseph switched on a lamp.

'So . . .' Rosie turned away from the window. 'Generally we'd start with "What brings you here?" and "Where are you from?"—because we're human beings so we're incurably curious and intrusive. But you and I have banned ourselves from all that.'

Joseph smiled. 'We could play cards,' he suggested, half joking.

'Why not?'

He lifted a squab. 'Blackjack? Whist?'

'Your choice. But you'll have to teach me the rules. I haven't played cards since . . . hmm, not for a long time.'

Joseph heard the hesitation, and felt a twinge of curiosity; but they had a deal, and he wasn't going to be the first to break it. He lifted out a deck of cards and dropped it on the little dining table. 'Okay.' He felt flustered; he'd forgotten how to behave. 'Sorry, um . . . I'm not very civilised. I've got some crisps here. Hang on . . . salt and vinegar?'

Sliding onto the built-in seat, she picked up a pack and tried to shuffle them. 'It's like riding a bike, I expect. Playing cards. You never forget.'

Over the next few hours they played whist, and rummy, and then discovered they both knew a fast and furious game called

Spit. The wine bottle gradually emptied, so they opened another that they found in the cupboard. Joseph reheated some Chinese takeaway, and they ate forkfuls as they played. The caravan felt warm and bright. Jessy lay at their feet.

'Gotcha,' crowed Rosemary, slamming down her last card. 'Again!'

Joseph stuck out his lower lip. 'And you'd have me believe you haven't played this game since you were a kid?'

'Absolutely. I used to beat my brother. Drove him nuts. It's all come back to me.'

'Hmm. So where were you brought up, then? I can ask that, can't I?'

'Devon,' she replied promptly. 'My father owned a club in Exeter.'

'A club . . . Bowling? Croquet? Trainspotting? '

'Lap dancing.'

'Seriously?'

'Seriously.'

'Was it respectable?'

Her cheeks dimpled. 'Well . . . let's just say that the mayor swore to run my father out of town and on more than one occasion dead rats were posted through our letterbox. And now, I think I have the right to ask you the same question; though I can guess where you hail from. It's still there, in your voice.'

'You've a good ear. Gateshead. Born, bred and buggered off to London half a lifetime ago.'

Much of her hair had broken free from the plait. It was a gypsy's face, Joseph decided, with a wide mouth and untidy eyebrows. Her smile was open and youthful, revealing slightly crooked teeth. She was animated, and yet in some way she had an engaging tranquillity. He found himself guessing at her past. *Okay, environmental activist with overtones of feminist. Must nip up and see if there's a sticker on her kombi. I bet it says 'Stop the Bloody Whaling'. Single mother? Maybe, fits the image . . . but where's the kid? With its dad? Maybe she's hiding from a violent man? Probably. Christ, she'll run a mile when she finds out who I am.*

'So,' he said casually, 'you got children?'

Rosie let her mouth drop open in a pantomime of shock. 'Breaching our agreement already? I don't believe it! Heavens, men are so *nosy*.'

Joseph smiled sheepishly.

'I'll answer that one,' conceded Rosie, 'but as a penalty you have to answer two of mine.'

'Two? Okay.'

'No kids. Not a single one. Now it's my turn.'

'Fire away.'

She let her gaze travel over him. 'I see you're wearing a wedding ring. How long have you owned that?'

'Fifteen years,' Joseph replied. He fiddled briefly with the gold band on his finger. He'd first worn it when Zoe slipped it onto his finger in the church, and there it stayed until it was taken from him and dropped into a named bag.

'I'm so sorry.' Rosie was watching his face. 'That was a stupid question.'

'Not at all. And the second one?'

'Far tougher.' A roguish smile. 'Any chance of a cup of tea?'

Twelve

Hannah

Every year, the children decorated the Christmas tree, and I filled stockings which we successfully spirited into bedrooms—though we knew that Scarlet and Theo were suspending their disbelief about Father Christmas. Freddie and I did our best, but we were dismally conscious that we hadn't Zoe's flair for celebration; and this year the impending court hearing was a sheer, jagged cliff that blocked our light and robbed us of sleep.

On Christmas Eve, the whole family ventured out to the Minster for Carols by Candlelight. It was not what I'd call a success. Theo tipped scalding wax all over his hand while Ben kept up a banal stream-of-consciousness in an echoing stage whisper—'When can we go home, Hannah? When, when, *when*? This is boring . . . Yeuch, there's a big blob of chewing gum under this seat.' Eventually he began to pick his nose. It kept him occupied, so I pretended not to notice.

Scarlet wasn't bored, though. Quite the contrary. She amused herself by making eyes at one of the older choristers each time he processed past her. He was an ectomorph with fair hair, and he drew a sultry gaze from under her lashes and a wicked grin after he'd passed. Scarlet thinks I don't notice these things. She forgets that I was thirteen-going-on-fourteen, once upon a time.

We managed to keep smiling all through Christmas, but then we had the New Year celebrations to face. It was no longer a matter of fireworks and Auld Lang Syne for us. It hurt. It hurt terribly every year, while all the world celebrated, because Zoe was born on 31 December. People still say to me, 'It will be easier next year,' but it never is. We tried to make it a celebration of her life and do something special—a winter picnic or a boat ride on the Ouse. This time the children asked to be taken ice skating at the temporary rink under Clifford's Tower. Frederick and I drank mulled wine in the café and watched people zipping and twirling past under frosty lights, within jeering distance of the spot where—not so long ago—public hangings were held.

For a little while we almost forgot that we were grandparents, or that in a few days we would be facing Joseph Scott across a courtroom. We held hands, and remembered our girl.

•

We hadn't time to catch our breath before the new school term began. Sometimes I felt I was too old for lunchboxes and playground arguments and stationery lists. The term was Ben's first in the reception class, which had a January intake. That fact alone—our baby Ben, a schoolboy!—was enough to make quivering jellies of his adoring grandparents.

We needn't have fretted; Ben took to school like an old hand. It was Theo who struggled. On the second morning he failed to come down for breakfast at all, and I found a small lump under his duvet.

'What's up?' I asked, sitting by the lump. 'Has something happened?'

No answer.

'Theo, why are you hiding under there?'

'I just want to stay at home with you,' he moaned.

'I won't be here. I have to go to work this morning.'

'I want to stay with Gramps. Please? Please, Hannah?'

So we gave him the day off school. That was a first. I have never, ever let a child truant before. Freddie reported that he hung around him like a wet dishcloth. Several times that evening I saw him peering out of the sitting-room window—surreptitiously, as though afraid of being seen. He was doing that when I had a call from his class teacher, an inspiring Irish girl called Nuala Brennan. She was ringing, she explained, because Theo wasn't himself.

'I agree,' I said gratefully, and confessed the true reason for his day off school.

'That's interesting, because I feel he's been disengaged from his friends since last term,' she said. 'Sits alone, doesn't join in.'

'He's never been very social though, has he?'

'He's also been rising to the bait in the playground. There were a couple of fights just before Christmas, and I'm afraid he pushed another child right over. I was waiting to see whether he'd be better this term, but it hasn't been a promising start.'

'Oh dear.' My anxiety doubled.

'Yesterday I asked them all to do some creative writing, but ten minutes later Theo was still looking out of the window. He jumped a mile when I tapped on his desk. He hadn't even opened the work book.'

'I'll speak to him.'

'No, I wouldn't do that at this stage. I'm not calling to complain. I just wondered whether there might be something going on at home?'

'There is,' I said, and described Scott's application. 'But we haven't even told Theo.'

There was a short silence. 'Well, I'm picking that's behind all this,' Nuala said thoughtfully. 'Maybe he's overheard something, or maybe he's simply aware of your tension. How about we just support him for a little while? He's a bright student; he'll catch up in a jiffy.'

•

The last day before court was hideous. I had a departmental meeting, and I honestly don't know whether I spoke sense or not. Behind my mask of normality I was obsessing, stressing, going over and over the possible outcomes until my head felt ready to erupt with the pressure. Meanwhile, Frederick tried to bury himself in a project with the local amateur dramatic society. He'd agreed to direct a play by one of their stalwarts, and was reading through it. By seven o'clock he seemed dazed. He marched into the kitchen, staring fixedly ahead, so completely lost in thought that he stumbled into the table.

'Stupid,' he growled, angry with himself.

I poured us both a stiff gin, and handed one to him. 'It's the thought of him that's stirring us up.'

'Hatred and fear,' proclaimed Frederick, with a self-deprecating curl of his lip. 'Fear and hatred. They're brothers, my love. No, not just brothers! They're twins. Unholy twins.' He knocked back half the glass as he sank down at the table. 'This business certainly opens the wounds.'

Ben hurtled in, skidding across the floor and coming to rest with his fluffy head jammed into Freddie's stomach. 'Will you tell us one of your stories, Gramps?'

'Well, young man,' said Freddie, tweaking his grandson's ear, 'I think that's on the cards. I know a good one about three children who live on the planet Gob.'

'The planet Gob!' giggled Ben, putting a small hand across his mouth.

'It's a lovely place, Gob. An exclusive holiday destination for the rich and famous of the galaxy of Bogbrush. Where's your brother?'

Ben stuck his finger up his nose. 'He's standing at the sitting-room window, watching people walk up and down the street. He's being really boring and he told me to go away and then he pushed me into the wall and I hate his bloody guts.'

'No! Don't hate his guts, they haven't done anything to you—*ahem*! A gentleman does not pick his nose. Go and fetch Theo for me. Tell him we'll have hot chocolate and a story before bed.'

While Frederick weaved his nonsense magic for the boys, I nipped upstairs to change Theo's sheets. The poor child's bed had been saturated again. I was turning the mattress when Scarlet wandered in. She was wearing an old blue nightshirt that declared *I'm cute,* with a cartoon of a baby monkey. This childish garment stopped six inches short of her knees, but she no longer looked like a child. Her legs were long and slender in quite an adult way. This seemed a startling juxtaposition, and it occurred to me—not for the first time—that Scarlet was growing up to be a real beauty.

'Want a hand?' she asked. Without waiting for a reply, she picked up a plastic mattress protector and unfurled it competently across the bed. We stretched it out, tucking in a side each.

'Theo nearly stopped doing this,' she said.

'I know. It's a great shame.'

'He *hates* it. He got invited to a birthday sleepover at Dillon's house last weekend. He pretended he wasn't allowed to go, but really he was scared he'd wet the bed.'

'Oh, no! I could have explained to Dillon's mother, couldn't I? She seems a sensible person. Plenty of boys have accidents.'

'It's not Dillon's mother that's the problem,' explained Scarlet, forcing Theo's pillow into a case. 'It's the other boys. Can you imagine how embarrassed he'd be?'

I began to wrestle with the duvet. Scarlet stood and watched me with round, fearful eyes. She was hugging the pillow in front of her. 'It's tomorrow, isn't it?'

I felt my mouth go dry. 'Yes. Yes, it is.'

'It'll be all right, though?'

'I'm sure it will.'

She punched the pillow. 'I'll tell the judge. He'll have to listen to me.'

'You know you aren't allowed to come. You don't want to run into your father, do you?'

She didn't answer the question. 'Dick Turpin's buried just outside.'

I blinked. 'What *are* you talking about?'

'Dick Turpin, the highwayman. He's buried around the back of the county court building. Didn't you know that? He and his horse have a grave there. After he was hanged, people kept digging him up—I suppose because they hated him so much. In the end they put his body in this stuff that made it dissolve, and buried him in that graveyard. Mind you, the truth is he never had a horse called Black Bess, and he was really ugly, and he was actually a total psychopath. He was finally arrested for shooting a chicken.'

'Good heavens. How d'you know all this? Do they teach you these savoury facts at school?'

She shrugged. Her expression was studiedly blank, a sure sign that she was hiding something. It only took me a couple of seconds to work it out. Of course. Joseph Scott had a flair for the human side of history, peopling his lessons with the most vibrant and notorious characters. In conversation around the lunch table he'd been far more interested in what made Wellington tick than in the minutiae of his battles. It was one of the things Frederick used to like so much about the man; they both found humanity in the driest of topics. Of course Scott would have regaled ten-year-old Scarlet with the real tale of Dick Turpin.

'I won't see him,' she said abruptly. 'Whatever the judge says, I won't go. Full stop. End of story.'

I sat down on Theo's bed and patted it. She joined me stiffly, leaving a space between us. 'It's all right, sweetheart,' I said. 'Gramps and I will keep you safe.'

'Think you can?'

'Of course! You just let us do the worrying.'

She brushed the heel of her hand across her eyes. 'Other kids think adults are in control of things. Even *adults* think they are in control of things. But I know for a fact that they aren't. No matter how hard they try, adults can't keep us safe. They can't even keep *themselves* safe.'

I had no argument. After all, Scarlet knew. The myth of her parents' invulnerability and goodness had been crushed at the age of ten. She knew that adults were neither perfect, nor omnipotent, nor immortal.

She bent over her knees, hands clasped. I sat beside her, feeling helpless. I wasn't a tactile person, as Frederick was. I was not a natural earth-granny; I had no instinctive urge to hold and hug children. Perhaps that was a fault in me. I sometimes tortured myself with the thought that Zoe's problems were caused by my being so painfully undemonstrative. My grandchildren taught me to cuddle—especially Ben, the baby who I raised—but still I preferred to let them process their thoughts without my smothering.

'I just wish it hadn't happened,' said Scarlet flatly. 'I wish I still had my family like it was. I wish I could wake up and find it was all a dream, and Mum is still alive.'

'Me too,' I said. 'Oh, my little one. Me too.'

•

We had friends for dinner, the night the world stopped turning. I remember it all with cinematic clarity. I remember every face, every word, everything we ate. It was June, but too cool to sit outside. There were eight of us squeezed around the kitchen table: Jane, her man of the moment, and a quartet of eccentric theatre friends.

I'd taken a tutorial that day, in which we'd discussed Schrödinger's cat.

'Ah,' said Jane's latest squeeze. He was a gynaecologist, and also a know-all. 'Now. This is the one that's both dead *and* alive in the box, until it's observed. I've always found the concept intriguing.'

'Schrödinger didn't,' I retorted, a little starchily. 'Apparently he later said he wished he'd never met that cat.'

'Wanted, dead *and* alive!' Freddie was on the verge of tipsy, chuckling as he refilled glasses. The phone rang, and he yelled over his shoulder as he strode across to answer it. 'That's me before my first cup of coffee—dead and alive!'

'If it's one of my students, tell 'em I'm off duty,' I called as he lifted the receiver. He smiled broadly and blew me a theatrical kiss. I remember that so very, very clearly. Freddie smiled, and he blew a kiss. His happiness had twenty seconds left to live.

I turned my attention to Jane. 'Any news of Verity?' I asked.

She leaned closer, and told me she suspected her daughter might be in love at last. This was news indeed, because Verity was thirty-five and married to her work.

'Who is this superhero?' I asked.

'The father of my future grandchildren, I sincerely hope,' said Jane.

I was laughing. God help me, I was actually laughing when I became aware of Freddie's hand resting on my shoulder. I reached back and touched his fingers with mine. 'Verity's in love, Freddie!' I exclaimed merrily. 'Must be quite a guy. Is he another doctor, Jane?'

My old friend didn't reply. She wasn't even listening to me. She was looking over my shoulder; looking at Freddie. Everyone had stopped talking. Every face around the table was turned towards his. I felt the weight of his hand, sinking into my collarbone.

'Bad news,' he said.

'Bad news?' I echoed blankly.

When he didn't reply, I turned around in my seat to look at him. His face seemed carved out of white marble. Then he said three words, and my life shattered into splinters.

'Zoe is dead.'

Five seconds of disbelief; of knowing for certain that this was a mistake. It was not possible. It was not thinkable. It was not bearable.

Five seconds of willing myself to wake up from the appalling dream.

Five seconds of silent-screaming terror.

And then the pain began.

I sometimes wonder what would have happened if Freddie hadn't answered the telephone that night. Some part of me believes that when he lifted that receiver, he also lifted the lid on the cat. If we had never learned of it, Zoe's death would simply not have happened. She would have dropped round on Sunday with the children, as usual. Our faces would have lit with pleasure, as usual. And the world would still be turning.

If Freddie hadn't answered the phone, we might not have found ourselves in York County Court one dismal January morning. Neither of us had slept much, but we'd overdosed on adrenaline and were jangling and alert. The uniformed man at the desk downstairs pointed to a lift, but we had a terror of doors sliding open to reveal Joseph Scott. The stairs seemed safer.

We found ourselves in a bluish carpeted waiting area with sickly artificial lighting. A handful of people sat silently, in attitudes of tension and misery. Frederick and I swiftly checked each face.

No Scott. Thank God. No Scott.

A door opened nearby. Jane appeared, regal in a dark grey suit and pearls. 'Hannah!' she hissed, and beckoned. We followed her into a tiny room with an oblong table and four chairs. Frederick immediately crossed to the narrow window and stood, hands clasped behind his back, looking out across the jumbled roofs of York. He was wearing his smartest jacket and tie, immaculately knotted. I'd found him in the kitchen at four that morning. He was cleaning his shoes, and my heart ached at the sight of his dignified distress.

'How are you both?' Jane asked solicitously.

'Fine,' I croaked.

'Bloody awful,' said Freddie. 'Is he here?'

'Not yet. I've asked Malcolm—the security man downstairs—to tip me off when he arrives.' She was magnificently unflustered, just as she'd been in the magistrate's court more than twenty years earlier.

I repeated what Scarlet had told me the night before. 'She says to tell the judge that she won't see Scott under any circumstances. He may as well give up today.'

Jane opened her hands. 'I sent one final letter last week, suggesting that he do just that. I haven't had a reply.'

She asked if we wanted coffee from the machine. We didn't.

'So this is your world, Jane,' observed Frederick, who still stood sentinel by the window.

'This is my world.'

He nodded. 'Extraordinary. I've never quite understood until now: your bread and butter is conflict, isn't it? Those folk sitting on the seats out there, all immersed in their own personal nightmares. Conflict is what you do.'

Jane didn't look offended. 'It can be rewarding, believe it or not.' She glanced at her watch. 'He should be here by now . . . I'll just nip out and see if there's any word.'

Once we were alone, Frederick lifted a hand as though he was stroking the atmosphere. 'Can you feel that, Hannah? It's in the air. Churches and monasteries have a patina of prayer, I think, built up over the years. Theatres have their own atmosphere also; but this place is ghastly. There's a patina of . . . yes, of hatred.'

'Silly goose,' I said, but I knew exactly what he meant. I could feel it too.

Jane was back, shaking her head in frustration. 'His solicitor's here, but no sign of Scott. It's now ten o'clock. Wretched man.'

After another fifteen minutes she'd finished talking us through the procedure and jotting last-minute notes. She and I began to make half-hearted small talk until Freddie could take no more.

'Is the bloody man coming?' he snapped.

Jane closed her notebook. 'Well, we're second in the list and it's nearly time for kick-off.'

'What happens if he doesn't show up?' I asked.

'We ask for his application to be dismissed.'

'And that would be that?'

'Possibly. It would depend on his excuse. People do launch these applications only to baulk at the first fence. They don't care as much as they thought they did.'

It was too much to hope for. I exhaled carefully, as though sudden movement might scare away this piece of luck, and I crossed my fingers for the first time in my adult life.

As the minutes ticked by, our optimism began to take root. We discussed the possibilities. Perhaps it was all over! Perhaps Scott couldn't face his victim's parents after all. Perhaps he'd had an attack of remorse and realised that the only honourable course of action was to dive off the top of a multi-storey car park, or possibly into the Ouse.

At half past ten, Jane gathered her papers. 'Well, he's out of time. Better be ready to move as soon as we're called. Let's see if we can get this thing thrown out.'

I reached for my handbag. Frederick straightened his tie. Jane was shrugging into her jacket when the door opened. It startled me, and I swung around to see who'd come in.

The man from the desk downstairs was standing there. He had a closely-shaved head and a sergeant-major's moustache, and he beamed cheerfully at Jane.

'I've got some good news, Mrs Whistler, and some bad news,' he announced.

Thirteen

Joseph

The Ouse swarmed around the stone pillars of the bridge, forming a deep-standing wave. Mounds of debris had become imprisoned in its embrace, branches and plastic bottles forced helplessly against the stonework and dancing a macabre, never-ending jig.

Joseph sat on the wide flight of steps that rowers used to carry their boats down to the water. It was snowing again, half-heartedly, as though the sky had accidentally spilled a handful of ice crystals. He held the letter in both hands, folded and creased. He didn't need to look at it. He knew every word.

The river was narrower here. It sped silently past, eager to escape the confines of the city and rush back to the gentle fields of the Vale of York. The smooth surface glinted dully, like gunmetal.

'Jesus,' whispered Joseph. It was both prayer and oath. 'What do I do?'

RE: THE SCOTT CHILDREN
Dear Mr O'Brien,

Thank you for your letter of the 20th December. I agree with your time estimate of half an hour, and enclose draft directions for your consideration. As you see, they include an order that all documents in the criminal proceedings be released into these. Clearly, the circumstances of your client's conviction for manslaughter are highly relevant.

We do, however, question whether Mr Scott has fully considered the impact of his application. Your client must remember that his children witnessed the death of their mother at his hands; it is hardly surprising that this experience left them with severe emotional damage akin to post-traumatic stress disorder. It has taken three years, consistent care from their grandparents and considerable professional input to restore any semblance of normality to their lives. Their stability is still extremely fragile.

Mr Scott's application has already caused immense distress. Despite their best efforts, Mr and Dr Wilde have not been able to shield the children completely and are concerned for their emotional health. The situation has not been helped by your client's ill-judged appearance in the park near the children's home shortly after his release.

It is of course generally in the best interests of children to have a continuing relationship with their parents. However, in exceptional circumstances this principle may be outweighed by other needs. It is difficult to imagine a more extreme instance than one in which children have observed the unlawful killing of their mother at the hands of their father. I am instructed that Scarlet actually tried to intervene to save Zoe Scott in the moments before her death, while Theo hid behind the sofa. Both children are burdened with guilt at their failure to protect their mother. If your client would take a moment to think about the implications of this, I am sure he will accept that in asking them to rebuild a warm and loving relationship with him—their mother's killer—he is simply asking too much.

I should be grateful if you would discuss this matter again with your client. I hope that he will reconsider his application, and conclude that his children's wellbeing far outweighs his own need to establish contact with them. My clients appeal to him as the children's father, and ask him to accept the following offer:

1. *Your client's application is to be withdrawn, and he undertakes not to seek further direct contact with any of the children until Ben has attained the age of 18.*
2. *My clients agree to provide your client with annual school photographs of each of the children, together with a brief update on their progress. They suggest that this should begin immediately.*
3. *No order for costs.*

Please give this matter your urgent attention. I look forward to hearing from you.

Yours sincerely,
Jane Whistler

Joseph slid the letter into the pocket of his overcoat. He'd been paralysed by indecision ever since it reached him, via his own solicitor. He never heard the cries of his own son and daughter—what kind of a father was he? People talked about blinding rage. His had been not blinding but deafening, roaring like fire in his head, obliterating all sound or rational thought. Far from being their protector, he had become the monster under his children's beds.

Across the city, church clocks began to strike the hour. Ten o'clock. Richard O'Brien would be waiting for him at the court. Just below Joseph, a mallard slipped onto the water with quiet quacks of contentment.

He often used to bring the children to this very spot, if they happened to be in York. They'd feed the ducks. It was a happy place for them all when things were wild at home, and when Joseph himself was exhausted and strained. They came here the evening before Zoe died. Scarlet and Theo, aged ten and seven, had stood *right there*, side by side on the water's edge, yanking slices from a bag and throwing them to a feathery rabble. Ben clung to Joseph's hip, brandishing his own crust in a fist. With a yell of effort, he managed to propel his offering a full three inches. It landed on Scarlet's foot, and an audacious duck leaped screeching from the water to snatch it up. Scarlet squealed with surprise and laughter as the emerald head skittered away across the ripples. Then she reached up and slipped her hand into Joseph's free one; she did it casually, with the certainty of a much-loved child. He was Dad, after all. He was always there. He would always be there.

Or not.

Twenty-four hours later, everything had changed.

Joseph hunched on the steps, reliving that last scene. He wanted to be caught in time, suspended in a moment when his family were still together. They'd never really been a normal family, of course. He knew that. He was overcome by a numbing sensation. Existence was deathly cold. Zoe was gone. His mother, too. His sister loathed him. Worst of all, he could no longer be a father to his children because he was the stuff of their nightmares. His life seemed utterly pointless.

The alien buzzing of his phone shocked him into consciousness. He still wasn't used to having the thing on him—or any communication with the outside world.

His caller didn't bother with the niceties. 'Scott?'

'Hi, Akash.'

'What the fuck's going on?'

'Nothing.'

'Nothing?' Akash sounded as though he wanted to leap out of the phone and head-butt his friend. 'Yeah, nothing; that's the fucking point! I've just had your solicitor on my back and he's doing his nut down at the court. Seems you gave him my number when you first came out. What are you playing at, mate?'

'I'm sitting by the river.'

'Sitting by the . . .? What the frigging hell are you sitting by the river for? Having a little picnic?'

'I'm thinking.'

'Well stop thinking, Scott. Stop fucking thinking, get off your fat arse and get yourself down to the court. They're all waiting for you.'

'I think I'll have to let the kids go.'

Akash let fly with a long, loud and colourful string of expletives. 'You've been reading that bloody woman's letter again, haven't you?'

'Yes.'

'Look, you stupid jerk. You spent three years planning this day, right? You came out of Armley and you went straight to your solicitor, right? I tried to talk you out of it because I thought you were totally off your head but no, you weren't even going to stop for a pint before you'd seen that bloody solicitor. You couldn't wait a single hour longer, because you knew how much your kids needed their dad. Okay! And finally you've got your day in court. Today's the day, the big day, your one and only chance. Don't you fucking dare walk away!'

'I don't know what to do.'

'Frigging hell, I can't believe I'm hearing this. You live for your rugrats. I ought to know! I had to listen to you banging on about them twenty-three hours a day for nine hellish months. You even talked about them in your sleep.'

'They're scared of me.'

Akash changed tack. 'What right have you got to abandon those kids?'

'I'm not abandoning them. I'm—'

'You bloody well will be if you don't get down there and fight for the poor little sods.'

'No, I—'

'Your girl—Scarlet—she never grassed you up for waiting outside her school, did she? Why not? Ever think it might be because she actually *wants* to see her old dad?'

That pulled Joseph up short. It was a good point.

'Christ almighty, mate,' roared Akash. 'Stop fannying around! You've come this far, you've stirred up a hornet's nest—the least you can do is see it through. If the judge tells you to fuck off—well, then you can fuck off. But if you don't get down there and have a go, your kids will know that you just walked away. Is that what you want them to think, that you walked away from them? No it isn't! So grow a backbone, you piss-poor apology for a dad! Get yourself down there on the fucking double!'

A young mother appeared at the top of the steps. She was talking animated nonsense to her toddler as she knelt to unstrap him from his pushchair. The little boy could have been Ben, three years earlier. His cheeks were obscured by a multi-coloured hat, and he wore tiny wellington boots. A bag of bread was tucked beside him. As if at the sound of a dinner gong, ducks appeared from every side. Some hopped onto the steps, tapping the ground with rounded bills and waggling their tail feathers.

Akash was still bellowing. 'Scott, you daft bastard! D'you hear me?'

Joseph's coat flapped around his calves as he leaped up the steps. 'Okay. Okay. I'm running. Can you phone Richard O'Brien back?'

'Fuck off! So I'm your PA now?'

'Thanks. Tell him five minutes.'

Fourteen

Scarlet

Oh my God. Oh . . . my . . . God. It was court day. He sang all night in my head, that devil. I woke up in a pile of towels on the bathroom floor, freezing cold and knowing this was the day. I could still hear his voice. Not the tune, not the words, just the voice. It brought me terror and darkness all rolled together. It made me feel as though the world was about to end.

When Hannah wasn't looking I dumped my breakfast cereal in the bin. There was something wrong with my stomach: worse than a pain, more like strangling. Like when you twist a rubber band.

Gramps and Hannah were freaking out. First Flotsam threw up cat food on the kitchen floor. Then Theo couldn't find his gym kit, and his shoelace broke. Hannah coped with all that, but when Ben spilled a whole bowl of cereal down his front I honestly thought she was going to cry. Gramps got Ben a new shirt, but he was trembling more than usual. Even his poor face seemed to be shaking. They were short of time, so they asked me to walk the boys to their school on the way to mine. I was doing this more and more often.

'Good luck,' I said to Hannah as I left. 'I've got my phone—let me know as soon as you can.'

She'd messed up her lipstick and was wiping it off again, blinking and twitching in the hall mirror. Gramps saw us to the door and hugged each of us in turn. I felt shivery.

'Don't worry, my little Scarletta,' he said. 'Everything will come out in the wash.'

It was another almost-snowing morning, white and sunless and aching-fingers cold, and my brothers were especially annoying. The pair of them argued all the way to school.

'I can start going there soon,' boasted Ben, when we were walking past the building where Theo goes to gymnastics club. 'I'll be with Theo.'

Theo looked very sulky. 'You won't, because you can't even do a forward roll. You'll have to learn for years and years before you can be in my group, and by then I'll be with the seniors.'

'I bet I learn really fast,' crowed Ben.

'Let's not worry about that now,' I said cheerfully. 'Let's count all the red things that we see.'

That worked for a while. We yelled every time we saw a red postbox, or a red car, or someone wearing anything red. It kept the boys distracted. Then, just as we were arriving at the school, everything went wrong.

'Red nose!' yelped Ben, pointing at Theo's face. 'Theo the red-nosed reindeer!'

'Shut up, you little knob.' Theo's nose *had* turned a shiny cherry colour in the cold.

Ben didn't shut up. 'Your ears are red too, and they stick out like Dumbo's.' To demonstrate, he held his own little ears out on each side.

'Stop it now,' I warned him.

'Jumbo dumbo with a big bumbo,' he giggled, flapping his ears.

'I hate you, Ben,' shouted Theo. 'I really, really hate you! I wish I didn't even have a brother.'

'Theo, the red-eared bumbo!' sang Ben.

Theo completely lost it. He screamed, 'I'll kill you,' rushed across the pavement and clobbered Ben on the shoulder. It was an awful thing to do because Ben was half his size and it almost knocked him over. Before I could stop Theo, he'd done it twice more, shouting, 'I'll effing kill you!' Then he grabbed hold of Ben by his anorak and shook him. I saw Ben's head going backwards and forwards. His eyes and mouth were wide open.

I rushed over and grabbed hold of Theo's arms. 'What are you doing?' I yelled. 'He's only four years old! He's tiny! You should be ashamed of yourself.'

Theo's face had turned a strange colour, and he looked like an adult, not my little brother. He pulled away from me, stormed off and sat on a wall further up the street. Meanwhile, Ben was screaming so loudly that passers-by turned to look. Even my cuddles couldn't calm him down. In the end I had a brainwave—I offered him the cake from my school lunch, which magically turned down the volume. Then I carried him into school and delivered him to a big bosomy teacher.

'He's had a tiff with his brother,' I explained, and she made kind, bosomy-teacher noises.

I gave Theo a real bollocking once I got outside again. He didn't say anything, but I saw him rub his sleeve across his eyes.

'What's up?' I asked.

'Nothing,' he gulped. 'Just . . . nothing.'

I asked if he felt sick, but he shook his head. I asked if he was scared of somebody at school, and he shook his head harder. I asked if it was to do with Dad, and he ran away from me and into the school.

Because of all the drama with my brothers, I was late myself. The first lesson was French, which started at nine o'clock. I rushed into the classroom at five past and Madame Girard looked around from the whiteboard with her pencilled eyebrows all elegant and murmured, ''Ow kind of you to join us, Mademoiselle.' She's a *vache*. Someone should explain to her that sarcasm is the lowest form of wit.

I couldn't concentrate on irregular verbs. I kept thinking about Hannah and Gramps, and what they'd be doing at that moment.

It was time to set out for court. Gramps would be giving his shoes a last-minute polish. Hannah would be clipping on her earrings. Then she'd get out her compact and dab on another bit of powder (she called it 'putting on her face'), and straighten Gramps' collar. They'd be scared and trying to reassure one another. It was a sad thing to imagine. The rubber band in my stomach tightened another ten turns.

Our second lesson was maths. It began at nine forty-five, and I knew Hannah and Gramps would be meeting their lawyer at the court around then. I pictured them parking the car and making their way there together. I thought about my dad, who would be parking his car too and walking over to court, and all because he wanted to see us. I wondered what expression he might have on his face. I wondered whether he was hopeful or worried, and whether he cared about the fact that he was ruining our lives. The rubber band twisted again. My maths teacher gave me a detention because I hadn't even begun the work she'd set us. I'd never been given a detention before, and I would have been mortified if my mind hadn't been on more important things.

At ten thirty we had break. I knew they were due to go into the actual courtroom. I tried texting Hannah, but she didn't reply. Eating was out of the question, so I gave everything in my lunch-box to Vienna, which made her day.

Vienna had just got back from a holiday in Lanzarote, with her real dad. She showed me the photos on a flashy iPhone he'd given her for Christmas.

'What did you get?' she asked me, as an afterthought.

'A violin.'

'Cool,' she murmured, sounding unimpressed. 'Here's one of me waterskiing.'

It was a beautiful antique violin, which must have been very expensive. I knew Hannah and Gramps had done their very, very best. All the same, it wasn't what I'd have been getting if Mum had been in charge.

We had music after break, which should be fun but generally

isn't because Mrs Hague is in league with violin bitch. I call her Mrs Hag. I'm prepared to bet they're in the same coven, since they both wear the same kind of trendy over-the-top clothes, with long hair like ancient Barbie dolls. Hannah says they are mutton dressed as lamb. I feel sorry for Mr Hag, if there is one.

On court day, Mrs Hag was wearing a charcoal tunic and thigh-high boots—a combination which did her no favours whatsoever—and what looked suspiciously like a string of orange ping-pong balls around her neck. She had us playing a freaky version of 'Yellow Submarine' that she'd adapted herself. It sounded truly terrible, because she insisted even people who didn't play an instrument must do what she called 'having a go', and the result was that people squawked away on recorders—which sounded like an alley full of tortured cats—and bashed cymbals and triangles. I was playing my beautiful new violin and she had the nerve to stop the class and suggest that I was out of tune. Me!

I didn't argue the first time. I just raised my eyebrows to show I thought she was off her head. Teachers hate that. She tapped with her baton, and away we went again. While we played I looked at the clock and saw it was after eleven fifteen. It might be all over by now. My insides felt so tight that I could hardly breathe. One more turn, and the rubber band was going to snap.

The next moment I realised that everyone was looking at me. Mrs Hag had stopped us all again. 'Scarlet,' she said in her witchy voice, 'you're still a little flat, darling.'

I lowered the violin and narrowed my eyes at her. '*What?*'

'Let's try it again from the beginning.' She smiled. 'And Scarlet, darling, do try to listen to what you're playing.'

'I'm not flat.'

'Just a touch.' She has a fake posh accent. Her smile looks fake too, as though she's painted it on.

I raised my voice. 'No, not even a touch.'

'Don't worry, you'll get a more musical ear if you practise. Rome wasn't built in a day!'

That did it.

'Excuse me,' I said. 'I'm actually the only person in this room who can play in tune. It sounds awful because it's a stupid piece, and this class is full of people who are tone deaf and know nothing about music. And that includes you, Mrs Hag.'

She exploded, of course. I ended up in the head's office for the first time ever, and I'd been given my second detention of the day.

The head's name is Gilda Grayson. When she sits on the stage during assembly she has a calm, cold voice and looks very impressive. She has big blow-dried hair and wears silky blouses and very boring shoes. The school has nicknamed her 'Maggie', because she looks like a painting we have in the hall of Mrs Thatcher who was the prime minister once. Apparently Mrs Thatcher wasn't scared of anybody, whereas Mrs Grayson hardly ever ventures from her office because she has a phobia of girls.

'Pull your socks up, er . . . Scarlet,' she said. She hasn't been at our school long, and she had to look at the note from Mrs Hag to find my name.

'Mrs Hague kept telling me I was playing flat,' I said. 'I wasn't playing flat, so she was actually libelling me.'

'Slandering.'

I gaped at her.

'Libel would be in writing,' she explained.

'Oh. Whatever. I've been learning the violin since I was five years old. Most of the class don't even know what "flat" means. Or "sharp". Or "music", for that matter.'

Maggie looked shifty. I could see she didn't want to get involved. 'Never mind the ins and outs,' she said. 'I have two detention forms on my desk, and they both have your name on them. If you get into any more trouble I shall have to contact your parents.'

'Good luck with that.'

She did a double take. 'Why will I need luck?'

'Well, to contact my mum you'll need to hold a séance. And if you want to contact my dad you'll have to ask the police for his address.'

'Wait here, Scarlet.' She nipped out of the office, and I heard her talking to the school secretary, who is the person who really runs the school. I took the opportunity to sneak my phone out and send Hannah another text. It was eleven fifty, so I was sure there must be some news.

When Maggie returned, she was carrying a cardboard file. She sat down, opened it and quickly flicked through the pages. I sat and watched her. I didn't mind. It was better than being in PE, which was where my class would be right then. I had my phone on vibrate in my pocket, and I secretly checked the screen twice, but there was still no reply from Hannah.

Finally, she closed the file. 'I owe you an apology,' she said. 'I should have been aware of your story. There are five hundred and thirty-two girls in this school, and I haven't yet got to know you all.'

'And you have a phobia of girls.'

She blinked. 'Is that what they're saying?'

''Fraid so.'

'Goodness. I'm the headmistress of a girls' school, and I have a phobia of . . .' She took a sip from the coffee mug on her desk, with a snorting little laugh. 'Extraordinary. However, we're getting off the point. Two detentions in one day! You've never been in trouble before. You're said to be very able. This isn't your normal behaviour, is it?'

I shrugged.

'So tell me. Why today?'

'Everyone calls her Mrs Hag, not just me. I honestly don't know how she got the job.'

I knew I was behaving badly, but I didn't care. All that mattered was what was going on in the county court at that very moment. That was my past, my present and my future.

'Why all this trouble today?' Maggie persisted. 'What's happening in your life?'

'Stuff,' I muttered. 'Just . . . stuff.'

'Would you like to speak to the school counsellor?'

I shook my head. My nose was running, and I rubbed it with my sleeve. 'I can't handle it.'

'What can't you handle?'

'My stupid father.'

My phone vibrated in my pocket. We aren't allowed to have our phones on at school. We're supposed to turn them off when we arrive, and not look at them all day. This is a ridiculous rule and of course we all break it. The teachers turn a blind eye, but I had a dilemma now because to get out my phone and read a text when sitting right in front of the headmistress was asking for trouble.

But I had to. I just had to.

'I've got a message,' I said desperately, pulling it out. 'It's life or death. Please can I look at it?' I didn't wait for her to reply.

The text was from Hannah.

Fifteen

Hannah

'Go ahead,' said Jane to the security man. 'Give us the good news first.'

He obviously had a soft spot for her. If he'd had a tail, it would have been wagging. 'The good news is that Joseph Scott is here! Came dashing in off the street three minutes ago.'

'Oh *no*,' I whispered.

Jane touched my arm before turning back to him. 'And the bad?'

'The bad news is that you won't have time to talk, because His Honour wants to see all parties in court immediately.'

'Isn't there another case in there at the moment?'

'They're negotiating. They want more time.'

Jane sailed towards the door. 'Thank you, Malcolm. Come along then, Hannah, Frederick—let's go!'

We followed her out and across the lobby. I heard another door open behind us, followed by the rumble of male voices. I didn't look back. Freddie took my arm, and we almost ran into the courtroom. It was a modern space; windows ran along one side, overlooked by the skeletons of leafless trees under a colourless winter sky. The electric lighting seemed gaudy.

Jane led us to the far side of the room, parking us in a row of seats while she set up shop directly in front of us. There was a raised area at the front, upon which stood the judge's bench. No judge.

Frederick squinted up at the royal coat of arms. '*Dieu et mon droit*,' he murmured. 'Quite a claim.'

I sensed Scott's presence nearby. Any second now, and he'd be in the room with us. 'I can't do it,' I whispered to Frederick. 'I can't sit here when he comes in.'

Jane turned around and met my eye. 'Yes you can. Hannah, you are better than him. Stand your ground.'

The words weren't out of her mouth before the door from the lobby clunked open, and Frederick's fingers tightened around mine. I didn't look. I wouldn't look. I stared rigidly ahead, listening to their footsteps.

Then there was someone else at the far end of our row. Frederick sat to my left, and now there was someone to my right. I heard the seats creak, saw a shadow. It was as though someone had dropped a tarantula beside me. It took all my will just to sit still.

By turning my head very slightly I could watch his solicitor, who was at the other end of Jane's row of seats. The man was middle-aged, tall, with a square forehead. He wasn't quite ugly and yet he reminded me irresistibly of Frankenstein's monster.

He cleared his throat and took a pen from his breast pocket. 'Do we need to ask for more time, Mrs Whistler?'

'You tell me,' replied Jane tartly. 'It's your client who arrived late.'

'Anything we can agree?'

She flapped a hand. 'You've got my draft directions, Richard. If you're really going ahead with this it will have to be set down for final hearing. I want the criminal papers and a report from Nanette Marsden. We'll probably be calling schoolteachers. Time estimate of two days.'

'That can all be agreed.' He leaned closer and dropped his voice. 'But what about interim contact?'

'*No*,' I bellowed. The word erupted from me, echoing around the big room. I felt my face flaming.

O'Brien cast a startled glance over his shoulder before subsiding into his seat. Perhaps it was fortunate that a woman chose that moment to burst in as though she owned the place. Jane told me later that this was Vera Taylor, court clerk and supreme Ruler of the List. She was voluptuously overblown, sporting a winter tan.

'Everybody ready? I'll wheel him in,' she promised brightly, and banged her way through a door behind the judge's bench.

The next minute passed in grim silence. We sat rigidly in our tableau, aware of every sniff, every movement in the room. It was a strange suspension of time, an echoing last breath before battle was to be joined. Then the buxom clerk reappeared, calling to us to rise. She was followed by a man who strode in, nodded to us all and sat down at the bench. I was reminded of an elegant Siberian husky my sister Eliza used to keep: dapper but shrewd, with oddly pale eyes. I never trusted that dog.

'Mr O'Brien,' he said briskly. 'Mrs Whistler. I've read the papers. Any agreement on contact? No?'

Jane hadn't sat down. 'If Mr Scott cannot be persuaded to withdraw his application, we'll have to have a full hearing. I do hope that won't be necessary because of the destabilising effect this is already having on the children. If I could describe—'

The judge held up a hand. 'It would be disingenuous of me to pretend I'm not aware of the background to this matter, Mrs Whistler. The criminal proceedings were reported in minute detail in the press. You can ask me to disqualify myself if you like, but I doubt you'll find a judge on this circuit who doesn't remember the case.'

Jane pressed on. 'Indeed, Your Honour. So you will understand that these children witnessed the violent death of their mother at the hands—'

He interrupted her again. 'We don't need that kind of emotive language, do we? It really doesn't help.'

'I'm simply outlining the unpalatable facts,' retorted Jane. 'It's difficult to describe the manslaughter of a woman without using words such as *death* and *violent*.'

He regarded her with those lupine eyes. 'It strikes me that what we have to focus on is whether it is in these children's best interests to have a relationship with their father. Now, I read in the application—and I doubt whether you can gainsay this—that he had a close bond with all three, and there is no suggestion he was ever violent towards any one of them. Nor, indeed, that he'd ever raised a hand against the mother before that fateful moment.'

Jane was obviously riled. 'He certainly made up for that, didn't he?'

The judge sighed and turned to Scott's solicitor. 'Mr O'Brien, what's the applicant actually wanting?'

It was like a children's game. Jane sat down, O'Brien stood up. See Saw, Margery Daw. O'Brien had an irritating habit of buttoning and unbuttoning his jacket while he talked.

'At this stage, he merely seeks to re-establish contact. Otherwise the children will effectively be orphaned—another tragedy for them.'

Jane was back on her feet. 'What does Mr O'Brien mean by *at this stage*? Are we to understand that the father's true agenda is to seek a change of residence?'

'I never said that,' protested O'Brien.

Jane cast him a sceptical glance. 'These children want nothing to do with Joseph Scott. Scarlet declares quite categorically that she will not see him—no matter what the court decides.'

The judge grinned at her, his head to one side. It occurred to me that he liked Jane. He'd probably crossed swords with her hundreds of times. 'Come, Mrs Whistler. You and I know that children are routinely said to be reluctant to see their absent parent. I'd say I encounter it in—ooh, fifty per cent of contact applications? And generally, their reluctance is easy to overcome. *Sometimes*'—he emphasised the word, blinking innocently—'they're merely reflecting the negative feelings of whoever is taking care of them.'

I really thought Jane was going to bang her fist on the desk. Her voice rose by several decibels. 'But not in this case! It's hardly run-of-the-mill when the father has just served three years for manslaughter.'

'All right. Thank you. You've made your point.' He motioned to her to sit down, and she did so with a huff of exasperation. Then he leaned over his desk and stage-whispered to Vera, 'Is Mr Hardy still here? Could you get him in? I'd like to know how quickly he can file a report.'

As Vera bustled out, he said, 'I'm going to ask for a report from the family court adviser. Now, let me make this very clear: it is my expectation that Mr Hardy will observe one or more contact visits between these children and their father. More, I hope.'

The floor fell away, and I felt Frederick clutching at my arm.

Jane shot to her feet. 'Then I insist upon your hearing evidence today!'

'And raise the emotional temperature even further? No, Mrs Whistler, I'm against you. If Mr Hardy has concerns, I have no doubt he will have the matter relisted before me.'

'You cannot properly make such a decision without—'

'Mrs Whistler!' There was an edge to the judge's voice now. He wanted all the nastiness brushed under the carpet, nice and tidy. 'How can these children's fear of their father be assuaged if they do not meet him?'

That did it. I could feel my heart thumping. 'This is simply crass,' I cried, in my lecture-hall voice. 'You don't know me, you don't know Frederick and you've no intention of meeting three very intelligent children. They went through hell when Joseph Scott murdered our daughter, and they'll be back there again when your namby-pamby social experiment goes wrong!'

'Shh, Hannah,' murmured Jane, leaning over the back of her seat. 'You can't do this.'

'The man's an idiot,' I argued loudly.

'Indeed; but it doesn't help to tell him so.'

At that moment, the door to the lobby opened. I glanced around—and found myself staring straight at Joseph Scott, sitting not four feet away from me, looking truculent. He was wearing a dark coat and those round-rimmed glasses I remembered so loathsomely well. I had to summon every ounce of self-control not to spit at him. I forced myself to turn away. There was some kind of conversation going on between the judge and a bearded man in his fifties, but I was past caring.

Suddenly, it was all over. The judge had gone; the clerk was getting ready to call on the next case, and Jane was guiding us back into our horrible hen coop of a room.

'Outrageous!' she exploded. 'I'm tempted to appeal, but it won't get us anywhere. We'll have to wait and see what line Lester Hardy takes.'

I looked at Frederick, who was shaking his head in utter bewilderment. 'This adviser,' I said, 'what if we refuse to talk to him?'

'You'd shoot your own feet right off.' Jane held up warning hands. 'That's the worst thing you could do. The family court adviser is the oracle. You need to get him on your side.'

It wasn't a tactful moment for Richard O'Brien to intrude: Frankenstein's monster, his square face looming up at the glass panel in our door. Jane quickly stepped out to meet him, pulling the door shut behind her. She was fast, but not fast enough. I heard his opening gambit, and it drove me right over the edge.

'Ah, Jane!' he exclaimed jauntily. 'Progress at last! *Now* can we talk about contact?'

Sixteen

I, Lester Brian Hardy, was appointed family court adviser in this matter on 7 January by His Honour Judge Cornwell sitting at York County Court. The children are Scarlet Scott, aged thirteen years and ten months; Theodore Scott, aged ten years and six months; and Benjamin Scott, aged four years and seven months. I was asked to report on the issue of contact between the children and their father, Joseph Scott. Judge Cornwell expressed the view that interim contact should take place, supervised by myself, unless there were very pressing reasons to militate against such contact.

I met Joseph Scott in the court building directly after the hearing. As he lives some distance away, I took the practical step of having a detailed discussion with him on that day.

Mr Scott is thirty-seven years old. He told me that he was born in Tyneside. His father, John Scott, was a butcher; his mother Irene worked part time in a fish and chip shop throughout his childhood. He reports that the marriage was not a happy one and his parents separated once he and his sister had left home. Mr Scott was close to his mother, and she represented a very significant figure in his early life. He describes his father as 'pathologically selfish' and 'a man with zero imagination or humour'. Perhaps unsurprisingly, Joseph Scott is estranged from his father, who now lives in Spain.

Irene Scott died suddenly, eighteen months ago. This is a great sadness to Joseph, especially as she appears to have been his only family support. He fears that she died 'of shame' due to his conviction and incarceration. He has an older sister, Marie, who currently manages a women's refuge in Gateshead. She has cut all ties with her brother since the death of Zoe Scott, and is thought to be unaware of the present application. I have not made contact with her.

Joseph Scott has recently been released from HM Prison Leeds, having served three years of a six-year sentence for the manslaughter of the children's mother, Zoe Scott. He is therefore on licence. Mr Scott described Zoe's death as 'the greatest regret any man could ever have'. During our conversation, he appeared acutely aware of the distress he has caused his children. He expressed his fear that the present application may be damaging for them. However, he fervently hopes to re-establish a relationship with them that will be healing for all concerned.

I have had access to the papers in the criminal proceedings against Mr Scott. In his police interview he candidly admitted striking Zoe Scott two blows. He expressed deep remorse. Zoe Scott suffered a bleed to the brain and was pronounced dead upon arrival at York District Hospital. Mr Scott was initially charged with murder. Shortly before trial, a guilty plea to manslaughter was accepted by the prosecution. Medical evidence indicated that the bleed was caused when Zoe Scott's head impacted with a marble fire surround, and that her alcohol intake could not be ruled out as a factor in her death. Tragically, this event was witnessed by the children. Ben was actually in Zoe Scott's arms. Theo ran to hide behind the sofa, while Scarlet tried unsuccessfully to stop her father.

The Wildes found the hearing of 7 January difficult, and left the building before I could speak to them.

•

'They walked out.' Joseph was sitting at Abigail's kitchen table, a mug of very strong tea and one of her rock buns at his elbow. He felt deafened, as though he'd narrowly made it through the mortar fire of an enemy bombardment. 'Just stormed past my solicitor. There was a social worker waiting to meet us all but he couldn't because they'd gone.'

Richard O'Brien had arrived back in their meeting room looking bemused. 'Well, I'm public enemy number one,' he'd announced, scratching his head.

'You're definitely not,' sighed Joseph. 'That's my honour.'

'Grandma Wilde led the charge. If looks could kill, I'd be dead as a doornail right now.'

When Joseph relayed this conversation to Abigail, she raised her eyebrows. 'I bet she wishes *you* were dead, Joseph Scott.'

'I couldn't even look the Wildes in the eye.' He grimaced ruefully. 'I know what I'd think of any bastard who laid a finger on Scarlet. I'd throttle him with my bare hands. But that judge—it was like he was on my side. It was . . . I felt as though he forgave me.'

'Ah, forgiveness.' Removing her glasses, Abigail rubbed her eyes. 'There's a prize to be treasured.'

And that was true, thought Joseph. It was something he hadn't valued at all, until he himself committed the unforgiveable.

Abigail replaced her glasses and stood up. Joseph watched her moving quietly around the kitchen, gathering ingredients for some concoction. He sat with his palms wrapped around the mug.

'They wanted to tell me,' he said thoughtfully. 'Hannah and Frederick. I really think they did.'

Abigail looked confused. 'Tell you what?'

'About Zoe.'

•

Joseph's first sight of the Wildes was at York Station, waiting side by side under the clock and presenting a graciously intimidating united front. They politely greeted the young teacher their daughter had brought home, but they had eyes only for Zoe.

Frederick would have been about sixty then, with a long, lined face and mud on his trousers from gardening. Joseph immediately felt drawn to him. Hannah was a handsome forty-something: energetic, blue-stocking and distant. She and Joseph disliked one another on sight.

Joseph was too embarrassed even to touch Zoe's hand with her parents around, and was appalled when she came creeping into the spare room during the night. She mocked his protests with her low laughter, peeling her T-shirt over her head in one lithe movement.

'Why are you winding my poor mother up?' she murmured, crawling cat-like onto his bed.

'Ssh! They'll hear you . . . I'm not winding your mother up.'

'You bloody well are! Telling her you've just decked some old enemy in a pub, behaving as though you've got the IQ of a goldfish.'

'She was so patronising.'

'Yep, I can't deny it—but did you have to rise to the bait? Never mind, you can make it up to me right now.' She took his hand and pressed it to her breast.

Later she whispered, 'Tomorrow's the day. Collar him in his study.'

Joseph squirmed at the toe-curling image. 'Can't we both tell him?'

'No! My lovely father's only got one daughter. It's got to be done properly.' She nuzzled his ear. 'He won't eat you.'

Frederick looked surprised when Joseph knocked on his study door the following evening, but hospitably offered his guest a gin and tonic. It was a hell of a mess in there, scripts and letters on every surface. The screensaver on the desktop showed a vivid picture of Zoe, her face brightly lit against a dark stage. Frederick cleared just enough space for them to sit down.

'Zoe and I are engaged,' blurted Joseph, still standing.

Frederick froze in the act of sitting. He sighed, and straightened again. He rubbed his mouth. Then he wandered to the mantelpiece and stood rearranging photographs. He wouldn't look at Joseph. 'You haven't known her very long,' he said quietly.

'Long enough.'

'You think you know her well enough to make this decision?'

'Probably not, but I plan to spend the rest of my life getting to know her.'

'How old are you?'

'I'm twenty-three—the same as Zoe.'

'Look. I think I ought to . . .' Frederick pinched the bridge of his nose, closing his eyes.

This wasn't quite the reaction Joseph had expected. 'I know this is a bit sudden,' he said, 'and we're young, and you're obviously shocked. She isn't pregnant or anything. Frederick, it's as simple as this: I am utterly, hopelessly, helplessly in love with your daughter. I believe she is in love with me too. I never thought I'd marry until I was at least forty, but Zoe has changed all that because I know for certain that she's the right person for me. I can't risk losing her to someone else.' He hesitated. 'You think that sounds brainless, don't you?'

'No. No, not at all. Quite the opposite.' Frederick was silent for another long moment. Perturbed, Joseph watched him. At length the older man seemed to pull himself together. His gentle smile returned, though Joseph could have sworn he detected tears. 'Well, marvellous. Congratulations! Another drink? I think I'll have a large one.'

Hannah's reaction was even less joyous. She actually used the expression 'reckless haste', and asked tight-lipped questions about how well they knew one another. After she'd mentioned their youth for the third time, Zoe's cheeks flushed dangerously.

'For God's sake, Mum, stop it.'

'Stop what?'

'You know very well what you're doing! You weren't much older when you married Dad.'

'That was different,' said Hannah unhappily.

Fifteen years on, Joseph could see exactly what had been in their minds. It must have been a truly hellish dilemma for them—should they keep their fingers crossed and let him stumble into marriage blind, or tell the truth and risk his walking away? Hannah would have been pleased to see the back of him, but Zoe might never have forgiven them.

Abigail turned on the hot tap and began to warm a metal mixing bowl. Neither she nor Joseph had spoken for ten minutes or more. It was one of the things he most appreciated about the old farmer's company: silences weren't awkward, they were peaceable. He always felt his agitation lessen when he was with her.

'They should have told me,' he said. 'But I can see why they didn't.'

'Zoe never dropped a hint?'

'No. Well . . . just oblique references. She said she'd had a bit of depression. I didn't even want to know.' Joseph held out his hands. 'I loved her, Abigail. I was nuts about her. Yes, I noticed things—quite big things, really. The ups and downs, the times when she wouldn't see me, some spectacular spending sprees . . . but it was all part of her personality, the dazzling and most exhilarating part as well as the scariest. She was a white-knuckle ride, and I kept going back for more.'

'What if someone had told you? What if you'd known all about Zoe Wilde, every last secret?'

'I've often asked myself that,' mused Joseph. 'What would I have done? Would I have gone ahead and married her anyway?'

Abigail put down her mixing bowl with a clunk. 'And what do you answer yourself?'

A hopeless smile twisted Joseph's mouth. 'Bloody silly question. Of course I would. I'd marry her again right now.'

Seventeen

Hannah

The Oracle acted faster than we expected. Jane had tried to reassure us that his service was snowed under and it might be weeks before he'd track us down, but violent death creates VIPs. Our phone was ringing when I walked in from work the next day.

'Dr Wilde?' The voice was irritatingly calm. 'Lester Hardy here. Family court adviser.'

'Yes?'

'We weren't able to meet after the hearing yesterday.'

'No.'

I could hear what he was thinking: *difficult woman.* 'The judge has ordered me to prepare a report on Mr Scott's contact application. I need to talk to you and take on board your views.'

'I can give you my views right now,' I declared. 'The answer's a definitive "no". The children don't remotely want to see him. It would do nothing but damage.'

He must have heard it all before; there was no change of inflection in his voice. 'It's very important that I meet you and Mr Wilde.'

'I work twenty hours a week,' I snapped. 'I look after three children. Time is extremely precious.'

'I can fit in with your schedule.'

'And will you also see the children?'

'Together, we can plan how best I might approach them. You know them better than anyone else.'

I ignored his blatant buttering-up. 'I've no choice in this, have I?'

'Well . . . no. Not really.'

•

Sure enough, a week or so later he was at our door: bearded, middle-aged, needed to lose some weight. Frederick showed him into the sitting room. Our cleaner had been the day before, so the place was at least presentable. I'd also picked up a thousand bits of Lego and plumped the cushions. As he shook our hands, I noticed the man's gaze straying to the one photo of Zoe we had on the mantelpiece. He was asking Frederick about her acting career as I went to fetch the coffee. By the time I returned, they'd got out a box file of letters people wrote to us after she died. There were three hundred and nineteen of them, if you counted the cards that came with flowers.

'Here's one from her kindergarten teacher.' Frederick picked up the letter. 'And her first boyfriend . . . and my sister Clara. And dozens and dozens of others. You see? Zoe touched people's lives. So many people.'

We sat around the coffee table, clearing our throats politely as though our visitor was selling life insurance. His beard covered rolls of chin, and he was wearing a purple shirt and a tie. He might have been a bishop.

'How long have you lived here?' he asked, as I poured the coffee.

'Er . . .' Frederick scratched his head, blinked, then glanced anxiously at me. 'Mind's gone blank. How shocking.'

'We moved in when Zoe was a baby,' I said quickly, trying to cover his memory lapse. 'Thirty-six years, or thereabouts.'

'Yes.' Frederick nodded without certainty. He looked bemused. 'Thereabouts.'

'But Zoe and her family were living in Tadcaster when she passed away?'

'You mean when she was killed,' I retorted.

'I'm sorry, Mr Hardy,' said Freddie. 'We both hate euphemisms. Always have. They are dangerous things. *Final solution. Ethnic cleansing.*'

'Passed away!' I cried testily. 'What does that mean, exactly? It's just an illustration of the cowardice of mankind that people can't say the proper words. Zoe was *killed*. She *died*. It's a fact. It doesn't help to wrap it up in airy-fairy language.'

'Point taken. I apologise.'

'They were living in Tadcaster when Joseph Scott killed her. They found a house they liked there, and it was convenient for both York and Leeds.'

Lester—it was embarrassingly easy to slip into first-name terms—asked about Zoe's childhood. We were only too happy to oblige. Frederick dug some photograph albums out of the bookcase and we showed him our daughter as a baby, a toddler, a dramatically lovely teenager, and as a young woman.

'She was striking,' remarked Lester, looking at some professional shots Zoe had taken for her agent. 'Talk about photogenic.'

'Heads turned.' Frederick patted the album. 'Heads turned when this girl walked down the street. It wasn't just how she looked, it was pure charisma. She had it in spades, didn't she, Hannah? From the day she was born. People were drawn to her. We'd pick her up from town when she was a teenager and she'd always be deep in conversation with somebody, man or woman, child or adult, hearing their life story. She was a magnet.'

'I understand she was taken ill.'

Ah, there it was. We'd known it had to come. In the silence that followed, Frederick's hand found mine.

'She was unwell from time to time,' I admitted defensively. 'She didn't deserve to die for it.'

'Of course not.'

'Then why ask?'

'Because it's part of the picture.'

'The subject is not only painful, it's wholly irrelevant to the issue at hand.'

Lester tilted his head. 'I can't agree with you there.'

I snorted and looked away. I had no intention of discussing Zoe's illness with this stranger; no intention of partaking in the sullying of her memory. Lester calmly sipped his coffee.

'Thirteen,' said Frederick quietly.

'No, Freddie,' I whispered.

He stroked my arm, hushing me. 'She was thirteen when it began. Until then, she was an undiluted joy. Lots of friends. Focused on acting, singing, dancing . . . on everything she did. Perhaps too focused, looking back on it.' A little coffee spilled over the edge of Frederick's cup. He lowered it carefully onto a coaster, and it rattled. 'It crept up. People tried to tell us it was adolescence. Hormones. She was our first and only child—we had no experience, no way of knowing why the joy had left her. She'd drag herself home from school, pull the blankets over her head, refuse to come out. The life was gone. One night I went and sat on her bed, and she said she felt so dark inside that she never wanted to wake up again. That scared me silly.'

'Scared us both,' I murmured.

'She started cutting herself. She had scars up her arms but we just didn't know what to do. One day she was upset by a row with her best friend, so she deliberately scalded her own leg with boiling water. We had to rush her to hospital. After that we got help.'

'What help did you get?'

'A beautiful girl.' I heard the tremor in Frederick's voice. He had to pause, to swallow. '*Our* beautiful girl, on antidepressants! Counselling. Psychiatrists. Depression, they said. Depression! We couldn't think what we'd done wrong.'

I bent my head, clutching at Frederick's hand for dear life. I felt him squeezing back ferociously. Then he reached into his pocket and handed me one of his white handkerchiefs.

'It was a waking nightmare,' he continued. 'Her friends began to drift away. She alienated them one by one, fight after fight, crisis after crisis. She'd be singing and laughing, then fly off the handle. Everyone felt as though they were walking on eggshells. Oh, my word! The barneys we had—the slamming of doors and the smashing of ornaments. But she was still our lovely girl underneath. There were times of peace, months when we dared to hope it was all over and she was well again. She still had her charisma. People were still mesmerised. She could be such *fun*. Excuse me.'

Frederick took the hankie back from me and buried his nose in it. I looked up at the fireplace. I seemed to see Zoe standing there: her eyebrows high and arched, her face haggard. Tapered fingers swept along the shelf, smashing our precious things to the floor. *I hate you! I hate my life!*

'I still wonder what we did wrong,' I said.

Lester didn't shower us with platitudes and for that I was grateful. He watched and listened without comment.

'On her sixteenth birthday, she weighed less than seven stone,' Freddie went on. 'She didn't seem to need to eat at all. She wasted away, didn't she, Hannah? Skin and bone. There was nothing of her. We feared she was going to kill herself that way.'

'That must have been hard to watch.'

'Hard to watch. Hard to watch.' The rims of Freddie's eyes looked red and swollen. 'But somehow she got through school and off to drama college in London. We hoped it might be the making of her because she was buzzing when she got in. She absolutely flew there, as well as holding down a job in a café. I asked my sister to keep an eye on her. Clara lives in Wandsworth—very capable woman, made sure Zoe came for a meal at least once a week. That good patch lasted two whole years—we honestly thought we were out of the woods. We had no idea of what was coming. No idea at all.'

'What happened?'

'She came home for the long summer holiday, landed a job in a bar by the river. Something wasn't right. She was drinking too much, sleeping too little. Mood swings, oh my goodness. One night we had a call from the bar manager to say she'd gone wild and smashed the place up before using a piece of broken glass to cut herself. He'd already called the police, and they'd taken her straight to the hospital to get stitched up. She was admitted to the psychiatric unit then and there, sectioned under the Mental Health Act. We had to leave her in that terrible place.'

Zoe's fingers clutching at my arm. *Don't leave me here! Please, Mum, I'm so scared. Don't leave me here with all these mad people.*

'Thank heavens for Jane,' said Frederick.

'Jane?'

'Jane Whistler.'

'Ah, yes.' Lester smiled. 'I know.'

'A dear friend. She guided us through the legal process. It was shattering. Zoe was in the unit for two months, and hated every second of it. All that time they talked about various diagnoses, but we were told nothing definite. She didn't want the doctors speaking to us, which put them in a difficult position.'

'It would,' said Lester.

'After she came out she seemed much better, and we truly believed she was getting the right treatment at last. She headed back to London, completed the drama course—imagine the courage that took!—then lived on acting and waitressing. She even began to get telly work. We weren't naïve to hope, were we? People have episodes of depression and get well again, don't they? They never look back. That's what we hoped for.'

'Prayed for,' I added.

'Which was when she met Joseph Scott.' Frederick emphasised each syllable of the name, as though to highlight the tragic significance. 'And that was a black day indeed. That was . . .' He broke off, shaking his head.

'Newcastle boy,' I continued, wanting to make sure Lester understood about Scott. 'I suppose to Zoe he seemed an intriguing mix of back-street brawler and academic. His ancestors were Lithuanian Jews, apparently.'

Lester nodded. 'Quite likely. Many did settle in that area, I believe.'

'Well, I think it appealed to the romantic in Zoe—though the man's a lapsed Presbyterian himself. She brought him here to meet us, and to us he appeared . . . well, a lout. He had an ugly black eye, and cuts on his knuckles, and was openly proud of the fact that he'd got them in a fight! I immediately recognised an inverted snob, ready to dislike me on sight.'

'He and Hannah didn't hit it off,' admitted Freddie. 'But to be fair, I think he was suffering from nerves.'

'I'd imagined someone so very different for her,' I said, and sighed. 'But they were married within months. We couldn't stop them. We urged Zoe to tell Joseph she'd been sectioned, and she refused point-blank. "It's all in the past," she said. "This is my future." Her wedding dress hung on the back of what is now Scarlet's bedroom door. Seems like yesterday.'

I could clearly see Zoe showing me the dress, a stunning piece of style and simplicity made especially by one of the costume designers she'd met at drama school. Sunshine streamed in through her bedroom window, and the ivory fabric seemed to blaze in a spotlight. I lent her my diamond earrings—something borrowed—and the veil that my own mother wore on her wedding day and I had worn on mine.

'Have a good life,' I said, before I left for the church. She and Freddie were standing in the hall, taking nervous sips of champagne as they waited for their car. He had his speech in his breast pocket. He looked exquisite in his tailcoat, and very proud. Zoe looked simply breathtaking.

'It's like escorting a film star onto the red carpet,' said Freddie.

She smudged her lipstick as she kissed his cheek. 'Thanks, Mum and Dad. Thanks for loving me no matter how awful I've been.'

'Never awful,' I whispered.

Her smile was radiant. 'I'm so happy. I can't believe I'm this happy. I definitely don't deserve to be this happy!'

I'd spilled a drop of coffee on the sofa, and dabbed at it with my sleeve. Then I saw that Lester Hardy was watching, and pulled myself together. 'The next minute, Scarlet was on the way.'

He waited, eyebrows lowered. He looked unhappy, as though he knew what was coming.

'It was disastrous,' said Freddie. 'Hormonal changes, the birth, breastfeeding, lack of sleep . . . it was all too much for Zoe's system. She had a massive breakdown. It was unimaginably terrifying.'

'I'm sure it was,' murmured Lester.

'We were slow to catch on. Joseph was taken unawares and he didn't ask us for help. If he'd only asked! Actually, I don't know what we'd have done if he had. She became psychotic and he found her threatening to drown herself and the baby in a pond. Scarlet was just a few days old.'

'How did he handle that?'

'He called an ambulance. So . . . Zoe was admitted to hospital in London, and we finally got a diagnosis.' Freddie paused to catch his breath. 'Our lovely girl was bipolar. Manic depression, they used to call it.'

My poor husband was overwhelmed by the memory. He slumped with his hands flat on his knees, mouth sagging, staring straight ahead.

'It was a relief,' I said. 'Alongside the grieving. At least we knew it wasn't our fault. There was a physiological explanation, and things that could be done. Lithium, mainly. It was hard to get the cocktail balanced—took a long time—but when she had the right drugs, and did everything else she needed to do to stay well, she was stable. That diagnosis gave her a new lease of life. She had amazing courage.'

'And the marriage survived?'

'She stuck with him,' I conceded bitterly, 'and eventually it led to her death. God knows he made life harder for her—hypercritical, forever undermining and questioning her judgement. They came to Yorkshire, partly to be nearer to us and partly because Joseph got the job at Tetlow. The boys were both born here.'

'I expect you were able to support them more, when they lived locally.'

He'd touched a nerve. Ever since Zoe died, I'd been haunted by the appalling fear that I hadn't done enough. 'She hated living up here,' I said, not quite answering his question. 'She wanted to move back to London, but he refused. He never appreciated how difficult each day was for Zoe. He had no idea. She was worth a thousand of him!'

I sprang to my feet in my agitation and stood with my hands on the back of the sofa, not knowing where to go next, or what to do.

Lester drained his coffee. 'I'd love to see your garden,' he said. 'I caught a glimpse as I was coming in. And I'd also like to hear about the children. Could we combine the two?'

'A good idea,' said Frederick, hauling himself to his feet. 'Let's go.'

It was a device on Lester's part, but I was grateful because I needed time to compose myself. I went up to our bedroom to wash my blotchy face, and for some minutes I sat on the edge of our bed, feeling drained and wishing our visitor would simply leave. By the time I rejoined the men, they'd reached the cast-iron seats in the sheltered spot by the greenhouse, and were talking about religious faith.

'I'm good old C of E, technically.' Frederick's smile was self-deprecating. 'The older I get, the keener I am to believe in a beneficent God; preferably one with a soft spot for ageing luvvies. Hannah's beliefs are rather less self-centred.'

'Oh?' Lester raised his eyebrows at me. 'But you're a scientist.'

'Science isn't incompatible with religious conviction,' I countered hotly, taking a seat. 'The only people who claim it is are extremists from both sides. Creationism is a celebration of ignorance that brings Christianity into disrepute. The idea that the Bible is some sort of divine textbook—ridiculous! On the other hand, those who claim that science disproves the existence of God are equally blinkered. It doesn't, as long as you're prepared to be flexible in your view of Him or Her. Or It.'

'Or Them,' added Lester with a smile.

Frederick sighed. 'The bottom line for me is this: it's impossible to believe that Zoe has simply ceased to exist. She was so massive a personality, in terms of bending the universe around her. A punch, a fall, a bleed in the brain—that wouldn't stop Zoe. She *has* to be somewhere, and I'd rather believe she was happily dancing away in the Elysian Fields than any of the alternatives.'

'That's easy to imagine,' I said, laughing. 'She always seemed to be on the point of dancing, as though her world had a rhythm of its own.'

A blackbird hopped along the garden wall, scattering its wistful song. Even birdsong had seemed melancholy since Zoe died. Beauty was stained with loss.

'I've already made contact with Nanette Marsden,' said Lester, once we'd sat silently for a minute. 'I've met her before. She's excellent.'

'She must be on our side in all this?' Frederick sounded hopeful. 'She saw the mess we were in.'

'She has an open mind.'

We tried so hard to make him understand. We described all that we'd been through over the past three years—ever since the day Zoe died, leaving three shocked, bereft children. Lester listened, nodding sombrely.

'You have to remember that their last memory of him is as Zoe's killer,' I said. 'They were trying to save her.'

'Mm.' Lester glanced down at the table, running a plump finger along the cast-iron tracery. 'Perhaps that is not a good last memory for them to have of their father.'

'Well! He should have thought of that, shouldn't he?'

'All the same, we have to consider what is in their best interests. Now. Today. I don't yet know the answer to that question.'

'I know the answer.' I threw dignity to the wind. 'Please *listen* to us! Please. I'm actually begging you and—believe me—I rarely beg. Don't turn us upside down again. I don't think any of us could cope.'

Our visitor's elbows were resting on the table. He dropped his mouth onto his interlaced fingers, thinking. We held our breath, praying that he'd leave us in peace. The blackbird hopped closer, as though he too wanted to hear the answer.

It was some time before Lester stirred. 'When can I meet the children?' he asked.

•

It is to the Wildes' credit that they have felt able to put aside their unhappiness at Judge Cornwell's decision and engage with me.

Hannah, Frederick and the children live in a three-storey terraced house just inside the city wall. They have a large and well-kept garden and the benefit of a small park with swings and play equipment within a few seconds' walk. They have devoted themselves to their care of the children: this is evidenced in the abundance of toys, children's art on the walls and child-friendly furniture such as beanbags. Hannah Wilde is sixty-four years old. She works part time as a lecturer in physics at York University. Frederick is twelve years her senior. Although he is largely retired from his work in theatre, he tells me that he has one or two directing projects 'on the go'.

I have sincere admiration for this couple who, despite their intense grief at the tragic loss of their only child, have given three grandchildren a nurturing, vibrant and stable home. They are to be congratulated on the superb job they have done and continue to do. They have sacrificed much to achieve this, including their retirement plans. They had been saving for an extended world tour, but accept that this is unlikely ever to happen. Hannah cut her working hours radically in order to care for her grandchildren. Both Frederick and Hannah feel a high degree of mistrust of Joseph Scott. This is perfectly understandable, in the circumstances.

By all accounts, Zoe Scott was a talented and charismatic woman. On this the Wildes and Joseph Scott agree. It is also common ground that she had a diagnosis of bipolar disorder. While this was well managed for long periods of time, there were also episodes when it was not. At such times, her behaviour and moods could be extremely unpredictable.

I am aware of the intense distress exhibited by the children in the months after Zoe's death, which still impacts on the family on a daily basis. The Wildes impressed upon me that the present application is threatening to damage the stability which they have so carefully built up. They insist that the children do not want to see their father.

I have been assisted by a telephone conversation with Gilda Grayson, Scarlet's headmistress at St Mary's College. She expressed concern about the effect of these proceedings on Scarlet, whose previously exemplary behaviour has deteriorated. I have spoken also to Theo's teacher, Nuala Brennan at Fossbridge Junior School. In recent weeks Theo has appeared distracted in class, has withdrawn from his peers and has been involved in violent altercations in the playground. According to school records he exhibited similar behaviour in the year after his mother died.

Ben has only recently begun attending Fossbridge. Staff report that he is a lively boy who has settled in well, and appears to have a warm and loving relationship with his grandparents.

I have had the benefit of speaking to Nanette Marsden, a bereavement counsellor who worked with the family after Zoe's death. She described patterns of behaviour clearly indicative of trauma and bereavement. Scarlet and Theo, through play, expressed profound guilt and helplessness at their inability to protect their mother in her last moments. Even Ben, who was twelve months old, was observed to make dolls attack one another in an enactment of a violent scene. Ms Marsden assisted the children to work through a grieving process while providing channels for their need to nurture memories of their mother.

It is of note that the children's attitude to their father was a significant concern to Ms Marsden. She felt that Scarlet and Theo were extremely conflicted. On the one hand they felt anger towards their father and strong ties of loyalty to their mother and grandparents; however, these emotions clashed with grief for the loss of their father, their old home and their family life.

Ms Marsden described the Wildes as caring and dedicated. However she expressed concern that Joseph Scott was afforded no contact with the family whatsoever after Zoe's death. The grandparents felt unable to accept even indirect contact from him in the form of letters or cards.

I did discuss with Nanette Marsden the possibility of her playing a part in introducing their father into the children's lives. She felt that this would not be appropriate. The work she did with the children was specifically around their bereavement. That work is now over and the family have been assisted to move to another stage. She believes it would be confusing for the children to involve her now.

The Wildes asked me to see Scarlet by herself before meeting her brothers. They were keen that she should have the opportunity to express her feelings openly. Therefore, I arranged to meet Scarlet at her home.

Eighteen

Scarlet

I couldn't believe it when they told me this guy wanted to see me by myself. I was nervous. I was sick-stomach nervous, but I agreed all the same because I actually wanted to speak to him. There were things I needed to say.

I don't know what I expected, but it wasn't a weirdie beardie with a shirt the colour of Ribena, carrying a carpet bag in great big sausagey fingers. He looked a bit like Babar the elephant, all oversized and forced to wear tidy clothes. He shook my hand, and he had this rumbling voice. He said I could call him Lester, but I really didn't want to. I hate calling adults by their first names, unless they're very close to me. Gramps tactfully headed out to the garden while Hannah steered Mr Hardy and me into the sitting room.

'May I stay?' she asked, and plonked herself onto the sofa without waiting for a reply. She'd spent hours tidying up. Poor Hannah. She just can't keep the house tidy; she isn't that sort of person, and she worries that people will think she isn't fit to have us. The fake log fire was flickering away. Mr Hardy started by going on about who he was and why he was there. Then he spent ages asking me about school and my hobbies. I knew he was just softening me up. I could feel myself getting closer and closer to yelling at him. Finally, I had to interrupt.

'Can we please get to the point?' I burst out.

'If you like.'

'I have a message for my father, and I'd like you to pass it on.'

'Go ahead.'

I looked him in the eye. 'Piss off.'

He looked right back at me. 'That's the message?'

'That's the message. Piss off and die.'

'Why do you want to send him that message?'

'Why? I'd have thought that was obvious!'

'Sounds as though you're very angry with your father.'

I waggled my head sarcastically. 'Well, *hello*! I think it's normal to hate the person who kills your mum. I think you'd be pretty effing angry.'

'Scarlet!' warned Hannah, sounding shocked. 'Language.'

Mr Hardy waved at her, probably to show that he didn't care about my language. 'Wouldn't you like to give him the message yourself?'

There was a long silence, and I wasn't going to be the first to break it. I don't know whether Mr Hardy signalled to her somehow, but Hannah got up and started muttering about making tea. He thanked her and let her go.

'Well,' he said, once she'd disappeared, 'since you want to get to the point, would you like to tell me about your mother?'

I shrugged. 'She was my mum.'

'Yes. And what else?'

'I don't really want to say any more.'

'Why not?'

'Because what's the point? Just tell him to piss off. That's all I want to say.'

He fished in his bag before passing some paper and felt tips to me across the coffee table. 'How about you write down three memories of your mother, and three of your father? They can each be very short, just a few words. Or even just one word, if you like.'

He didn't wait to see whether I would do it. He got up and stood at the mantelpiece, looking at our photographs. I was pleased when he bent his head to stare more closely at one of Mum and me. It was a copy of the one in my memories box, the one taken near our caravan with our faces pressed together. I could hear Hannah in the kitchen, filling the kettle.

I picked up the pen. 'Three things?'

'Three.'

It took me ten seconds. 'Finished,' I said in a bored voice, dropping the pen.

He came over and looked at what I'd written.

MUM SCREAMING DEAD CREMATED

DAD BASHING BASHING BASHING

The music had started. The man was singing. His voice filled my whole brain. My head was blowing up bigger and bigger, like a balloon. I jammed my fingers into my mouth.

'Are you okay?' asked Mr Hardy.

'Not really.'

He sat down and waited.

'It never goes away,' I said. My voice sounded like Ben's when he's whining. 'It keeps coming back. This frickin' music.'

'What's the music like?'

'Singing. A man, singing.'

'Your father?'

'No. This man's got a really deep growling voice. I get this freaky feeling . . . I feel scared to death.'

Mr Hardy looked again at what I'd written. 'When you wrote these memories of your dad, did other ones come into your head?'

'I dunno.'

'I think there might be others.'

Dad things were all swirling around me, feelings and smells and pictures of things we did together. I didn't want to let them in. My eyes were stinging. 'No,' I said.

'None at all?'

'Only that he was my hero.'

'In what way was he your hero?'

'Because he was!' I searched for the words. 'He smashed everything in our lives. He never even bothered to come and see us. Not once. He didn't even phone. Why didn't he come? Didn't he care?'

I felt tears welling up in my eyes and sliding down my cheeks. I was furious with myself for crying.

Mr Hardy passed me a tissue out of his big bag. 'Did you ask to see him?'

'We never say his name. Nobody does. We pretend he doesn't exist.'

'Do you think he was allowed to contact you, Scarlet? He was arrested by the police. Maybe he couldn't speak to you. Maybe he wasn't able to send letters from prison, either. Maybe your grandparents felt it would be best.'

I thought about this, with my nose shoved into the tissue. It was as though he'd turned a sand picture upside down. Suddenly, everything looked different. Not better, not worse. Just different. Perhaps Dad wasn't allowed to get in touch. Hannah and Gramps might have thought that because we never mentioned him, we wanted to forget about him.

'He used to look after us,' I said quietly. 'I remember him cooking our supper, bangers and mash. He did that a lot.' I could see Ben in a blue highchair, and Theo and me at the table. I felt happy. Dad had his sleeves rolled up and he was clowning around, pretending to dodge because the sausages were spitting at him. Ben was just a blob with a squashed nose, dressed in a little red hoodie. Dad made faces at him, so he shrieked and banged his tray with a spoon.

'You say you hate your father,' said Mr Hardy.

'Mm.'

'But I'm getting a sense that it's a bit more complicated than that.'

'No, it isn't complicated at all. I don't want to see him again, ever in my life, and neither do my brothers. He'll just have to deal with it.'

Mr Hardy started leafing through one of our photo albums. I didn't feel the subject was closed; I was sure he didn't either.

'Have *you* seen him?' I asked.

'Yes,' he said. 'And I'm planning to see him again very soon. Is there anything you'd like me to ask him?'

I had such a lot of questions. I was wondering whether Dad thought about me very often. I was wondering where he was living, what he was doing. I wanted to know what it was like in prison, whether it was terrible, whether he'd been raped. Some boys at my old shool told me men always get raped in the prison showers. These two boys were smirking, and they said my dad wouldn't even be able to walk properly when he came out, because he'd have been effed up his A-hole every day. I wanted to know whether Dad cried for Mum. I wanted to know why he'd waited outside my school. I wanted to know all these things, but I didn't ask any of them.

'Hannah and Gramps couldn't handle it if we saw him,' I said instead.

'What makes you think that?'

'It's obvious. Have you seen how old Gramps is?'

Mr Hardy smiled. 'In the end it's the judge's decision, Scarlet. You don't have to make a choice, and you don't have to worry about upsetting people. It's all down to the judge.'

I tried to imagine this stranger who had such massive power over my life. I pictured an ancient codger with a wig and robes banging a gavel. 'You'd better tell that judge from me: we won't go.'

'I like this one,' said Mr Hardy, pointing to a photo of me as Puck. 'When was it taken?'

We talked about the play. He was very ignorant about Shakespeare, but he seemed to want to know more—he wasn't doing what most adults do, putting on a fake interested voice which made me feel patronised. He asked me to describe my brothers, and that took me a while. I told him I was worried about Theo because he was wetting his bed again. I talked about how he'd attacked Ben on the way to school.

Mr Hardy asked how did I think he should meet them—should they come to his work, where he had a playroom, or should we all go out somewhere? He suggested maybe a park, but it was winter; and then I had a light bulb moment and came up with the brilliant idea of the Railway Museum.

'It's always a happy place,' I said, 'especially for Theo, who's a railway geek. He'll be less uptight there. Ben's completely off the planet, but if you take him to the platform café and buy him apple juice and a bowl of chips, he might sit still for five minutes.'

'Done,' said Mr Hardy. 'Thank you, Scarlet. And will you come, too?'

I sighed. 'I think I'd better. My brothers are a real handful.'

•

Scarlet struck me as an intelligent and articulate young woman who knows her own mind. She has strong loyalty to her grandparents and is painfully aware of their anguish at the loss of Zoe. She gave me a clear message for her father: loosely translated, this was that he should leave the family alone. Initially she described memories of him that were violent and negative, clearly arising from the last moments in which she saw him; however, I sensed ambivalence. At one stage she wept as she described him cooking for herself and her siblings. She appeared relieved when I reassured her that any decision about contact was out of her hands.

At Scarlet's suggestion, I spent a morning with all three children at the National Railway Museum. This outing proved to be a lively and stimulating event.

•

Oh my God, what a frickin' disaster. I have never been so embarrassed in my life.

Mr Hardy walked with us to the museum. He'd asked Hannah and Gramps to explain to the boys that our dad wanted to see us, and he was there to help the wise people at the court decide what was best. Hannah looked as though she was sucking on a lemon when she said the words 'your father'.

God knows how, but Mr Hardy persuaded her and Gramps to stay at home, which was a very good job because they would have had heart attacks at the way the boys behaved. I don't know what had got into Theo, but he was a monster from start to finish. At first he wouldn't speak to Mr Hardy at all. He dawdled along behind, looking like he hated everything and everyone. I tried kicking him to get him to be polite but he just kicked me back, really hard. He only started talking when we arrived at the Flying Scotsman. It turned out that Mr Hardy was a railway enthusiast too, and he acted like a little kid when it came to old steam engines. Theo didn't smile, but he did at least liven up a bit and even pointed out a few things Mr Hardy hadn't noticed.

All Ben wanted to do was play with wooden models, so we all did that for a while. He kept making the trains crash into each other. I was scared he was going to break them. In the end, Mr Hardy suggested it was time for lunch at the café. Once we'd found a table I went to the toilet, and I was just coming back when I saw Ben grab two empty glasses the last people had left on the table, and smash them together. And—you've guessed it—there was glass and mess all over the place. I tried to sweep it up into a serviette, but by the time a waitress arrived with a cloth and a bucket I was so embarrassed that I went to sit at another table. Mr Hardy was really nice about it. He delivered my toasted sandwich to my table and said it was okay if I wanted a bit of time to myself.

I couldn't hear their conversation, but the three of them seemed to get on better for a while. I'd almost decided it was safe to join them when all hell broke loose—Theo was yelling and pushing Ben onto the floor, and Ben lay there hamming it up like a football player, pretending his leg was broken. When I ran over to help, Theo stuck his middle finger up at me as though he really hated me and snarled, 'You shut your fat mouth, Scarlet.'

Suddenly, it all got on top of me. I very nearly cried. I asked Mr Hardy if we could please go home, and he agreed. As we reached Faith Lane, I took him out of earshot of the boys.

'This is all because of Dad turning up again,' I said. 'All this nastiness. We were doing okay before.'

Mr Hardy looked at me. 'Were you?'

'Yes,' I said firmly. 'We were. Tell him, will you? Tell him to leave us alone.'

•

Theo impresses as a sensitive boy with a keen mind. It was clear that he understood the reason for my visit, and at first he appeared unwilling to engage with me. However, he shares my boyhood interest in locomotives and we were able to spend some time exploring the exhibits.

Ben is a chatty four-year-old with a delightful sense of fun and mischief. He did not appear unduly concerned at being brought on an outing, and I suspect was reassured by the presence of Scarlet, who was most attentive towards him. He enjoyed using wooden model engines in an interactive area of the museum. I noted that a recurrent theme was the enactment of a violent assault by one engine on the other. A third engine then arrived to drag the miscreant to prison. I was struck by this role play, which appeared markedly joyless and angry.

I decided not to raise the subject of their father directly with the boys. For some time, both were happy to chat about their lives and interests. However, Theo abruptly told me that 'My friend's dad wants to bring back the death penalty for murderers.'

I asked him how he felt about this, and he shrugged. He looked extremely uncomfortable. A little later he returned to the subject again: 'My friend's dad says murderers don't deserve to live. They're costing the taxpayer good money. He says they should all fry in boiling oil.' I sensed that this image disturbed Theo very deeply.

Ben did not partake in the discussion and appeared more interested in ensuring that I had ordered chips. However shortly afterwards he began to play out the same violent scene as before, using two glasses. Unfortunately he smashed them together with such force that one broke.

One further incident is of note. Towards the end of our visit, Theo was telling me about his ambition to be a professional footballer. Ben interrupted, describing a football talent scout who had seen Theo playing. I am aware that Joseph Scott recently spoke to the boys in a park. Despite Theo's obvious agitation, Ben refused to stop talking about this man. In the end, Theo angrily pushed Ben onto the floor. I suspect that Theo is well acquainted with the identity of the stranger in the park. It seems likely that he enjoyed the interaction, and is struggling with conflicting feelings. I would hazard a guess that Ben, too, has some inkling that this stranger was significant.

Scarlet behaved with maturity throughout the day. She seemed painfully embarrassed by her brothers at times, which I regard as typical for her age group. She also took charge of them in an adult way, for example trying to clear up the mess when Ben broke a glass and running to comfort him when he was hurt. I felt that she took this responsibility more seriously than I would expect of a girl of her age. She is perhaps mothering them in the absence of her own mother.

My observations bore out Nanette Marsden's view that all three have flourished under the care of their grandparents, but that they are conflicted in their feelings about their father. I fully accept the grandparents' account that Joseph Scott's application has upset and destabilised the entire family. It is to all parties' credit that they have the best interests of the children at heart.

The decision regarding interim contact is finely balanced. I have not found it easy to reach a clear recommendation.

Nineteen

Joseph

In late January, winter gripped the moors. Snow spilled from heavy skies, roads became blocked by drifts several feet deep, and Brandsmoor was cut off from the world.

Joseph spent hours with a shovel each day, digging routes for himself to get to the farmyard and to enable him and Abigail to reach her stock. The sheep had been brought down for the winter, but tending them and the other animals was a daily polar expedition. Their fourth day of imprisonment found him and his two companions—Abigail and Rosie—playing Scrabble at Abigail's kitchen table. Joseph had been up and feeding animals since dawn, and Rosie had dug her way out of her van and come to help him. She'd appeared smiling by the tractor, smothered under a woollen shawl, her nose and cheeks crimson in the sub-zero temperatures. Once the job was done they left their boots in the hall, making ice-melt puddles, and sought refuge by Abigail's range.

The women seemed cheerful about their enforced seclusion, but Joseph was a caged lion. At nine o'clock he asked to use Abigail's museum piece of a telephone. He knew Richard O'Brien's number by heart.

'I'm on my way to court,' said the solicitor. He sounded harassed. 'Any news?'

'Not yet. He's going to write an interim report.'

'How long until we know?'

'Piece of string, Joseph. Piece of string.'

Abigail was winning the game. She always won. Her killer instinct at Scrabble was a delight to Joseph, who knew for a fact that she'd left school at fifteen. By contrast, Rosie seemed to have mild dyslexia, couldn't spell to save her life and always came last. It never dampened her spirits.

Joseph had just picked up the worst set of tiles in history—AAOOIIQ—when the phone jarred their peace.

'Bloomin' thing never stops,' grumbled Abigail. She hobbled over to the cabinet. 'Like Paddington Station in here.'

Rosie cupped her hand around her mouth. 'She means someone rang last year. A wrong number.'

'I heard your cheek, young woman,' chided Abigail, lifting the receiver. 'Button your lip . . . Yes?' She stood, listening. Joseph could faintly hear a male voice.

'Yes,' said Abigail.

More words.

'Yes,' said Abigail.

She carefully laid the receiver on the cabinet, returned to the table, and sat down. 'Does Joseph Scott live here?'

Joseph leaped across the room as though she'd jabbed him with a cattle prod. 'Hello? . . . Oh, hello, Lester. Sorry to keep you waiting . . . No, we're snowed in, I'm afraid . . .'

He listened for a long moment, then slapped his palm onto the cabinet. 'That's fantastic! Thank you! Wednesday? I'll get there if I have to ski from here to York. Thank you, thank you . . . Well, I know you're only doing your job, but all the same. Okay then! See you on Wednesday.'

He rang off and paused, gazing out of the deep windows. He felt stunned. Clouds were breaking apart; sun and shadow raced across the bleak hillside opposite.

'Zoologist!' crowed Abigail, from behind him. 'Triple word score. Eighteen times three, plus . . .'

'I knew a zoologist once,' said Rosie wistfully. 'He was chronically unemployed. He wanted to marry me.'

'And you turned him down?' Joseph heard Abigail sucking on her front teeth, a sure sign of disapproval. 'Daft lass! Hang on—where's my dictionary?'

Dimly, Joseph was aware that Abigail had left the room. Rosie's steps crossed the kitchen towards him. 'Seen a vision?' she asked quietly.

'Maybe.'

'I saw a vision, once.'

Joseph raised one eyebrow. 'What exactly had you been smoking?'

She didn't answer, and he stole a glance at her profile. Her cheeks were rounded, faintly blushing under the wild hair. 'What was it?' he persisted. 'A ghost?'

'Nope.'

'A pink elephant?'

'I don't have visual hallucinations,' she said. 'It isn't insanity that's driven me out of society and into a kombi van.'

'Thought never entered my head.'

'Liar.'

Joseph rubbed the side of his nose. 'Actually, I wondered whether you're escaping an abusive relationship. A man, I mean.'

'A man.'

'Yes.'

'As opposed to . . .?'

'Erm, well, a woman, I suppose.'

The idea seemed to amuse her. 'Oh, I see. Well, no, I'm not escaping . . . no, no I don't think that's the word. I'm taking time out,' she said carefully. 'To think about a relationship that is good and loving.'

'Good and loving? What's the catch?'

'There isn't one. He's offered me everything. He's enriched my life.'

Joseph felt a sudden surge of resentment. What was this—surely not jealousy?

Don't be daft, he scolded. *What rights have you got? You wouldn't wish yourself on a nice girl like Rosie.*

'Sounds perfect,' he said blandly. 'Maybe a tad obsessive.'

'Not at all.'

'What went wrong?'

'I have commitment anxiety. And that's quite a few questions you've asked me, so here's one for you.'

'Fair enough.'

'Who was on the phone?'

Joseph shook his head in disbelief. 'A miracle.'

•

In the overwhelming majority of cases, it in the best interests of children to know both parents. Where one has died, the remaining parent has enhanced significance. There is undoubtedly risk inherent in introducing this father to these children; however, the court has to balance such risk against the negative consequences of their conflicted feelings about him. Furthermore, I believe that Joseph Scott has much to offer his children should he prove able to rebuild a relationship with them. In the medium and long term, his input may be of considerable help to the Wildes in meeting the needs of Scarlet, Theo and Ben.

I suggest that I speak to the children in advance and reassure them that they will be reunited with their father in a safe environment; also that the decision has been made for them by others, so that they do not need to take responsibility for the anxiety of their grandparents. Contact will be brought to an end immediately if any child appears to be unduly distressed.

My recommendation is that there be contact between Joseph Scott and his children, supervised by me, at the CAFCASS office in York. I shall then provide an addendum to this report.

Lester Hardy
Family Court Adviser

Twenty

Hannah

Frederick's hands began to shake on the morning of the funeral. They have shaken ever since.

He was sitting at the kitchen table, trying to write on the card we wanted to put with Zoe's flowers. I was frozen nearby, watching the tremor in those strong fingers. I couldn't help him; I was barely functioning myself. I didn't even remember getting dressed. I had channelled every drop of courage I had into the children over the past ten days, and that had saved me. If it hadn't been for them, I believe I would have lost my mind.

I'd experienced grief before. My sister Eliza died in her fifties, after a lifetime of abusing her liver. My parents—and Frederick's—had all gone over the decades, and several friends, too. It happens as you get older. People begin to die. I thought I was mature and wise about Death.

Losing Zoe was in a different league. The pain took me to a black and lonely place, well beyond tears. It was a place with no hope, and no future.

They'd arrested Scott. They'd interviewed the neighbours and friends and us. Zoe's body had been taken away, to lie alone and cold in a fridge. We read the autopsy report later. I don't think people realise to what butchery their loved ones are subjected.

They'd cut her open and weighed her organs. They'd taken out her brain and cut bits off it. They'd checked the alcohol levels in her blood and found them to be high—one of the reasons Scott got off. They said the cause of death was traumatic subarachnoid haemorrhage, probably caused by a blow to her head when she struck the marble fireplace as she fell. Apparently, alcohol is a risk factor. You can imagine how Scott and his lawyers made hay out of that, making Zoe sound like a raddled old lush. Zoe liked a party, liked to have fun; she wasn't like her Aunt Eliza, who was never sober.

Finally, they put her back together—I imagined them stuffing in her organs like pyjamas into a case—and sewed her up. Only then were we allowed to have her back.

Thankfully, Marie Scott offered to lend a hand with the children, bless her. She quietly came to stay, and kept them upstairs on the morning of the funeral. I could hear the baby crying as though his tiny heart would burst. He'd been looking for his mother all week. Sometimes he could be distracted for a few minutes, but the respite was short-lived. Every time he heard a female voice he'd crawl out with a happy yell, looking for her. As soon as he realised it wasn't Zoe, the little chap would simply sit down on the floor, his face would crumple, and he'd wail inconsolably. Nobody else would do. Nobody could comfort him.

Freddie held the pen suspended, mouthing the words he wanted to say to his daughter. A small card for a million words. His lips were moving. He forced the pen down and managed to write

Precious, beloved

before the pen wobbled, smudged and spoiled the pristine whiteness. He was weeping openly now. His shoulders shuddered, his breath tore from his body. Comfortable, competent women bustled in our kitchen, hired caterers taking care of practicalities. They witnessed my dry-eyed paralysis and Freddie's brokenness. They saw how he suffered while I did nothing to comfort him. One of them couldn't stand it; she dropped to one knee and put her arms around him, and I was so grateful for her humanity.

I took up the pen and the card and leaned them on the draining board.

You were our all, I wrote.

You were our light.

You were our life.

Mum and Dad.

The front doorbell rang. The undertaker waited there, controlled and capable in his dark suit, with a long black car parked behind him. Zoe had arrived. Marie brought the children downstairs, slipping tactfully away while we went out to meet our daughter. Ben howled as though he knew what this was—though surely he was too young to understand. Theo gripped my hand. Scarlet walked right up to the coffin where it lay in the back of the hearse, and rested her cheek on it. Beside her, Freddie wept quietly. Then the five of us were gently ushered into another car, to follow Zoe on her last journey.

Joseph Scott did it, with his flying fist. Joseph Scott made the world stop turning. How could I forgive and forget?

'Try to give them *permission* to see their father,' said Lester Hardy.

'Permission?' I snapped. 'You know perfectly well we don't give permission. The choice has been taken away from us. So let's leave the touchy-feely language for your more gullible victims, shall we?'

Frederick rubbed my forearm with anxious affection. 'Hannah, Hannah,' he murmured. 'Shh.'

'I mean give them tacit permission,' explained Lester, unabashed. 'It's a matter of subtle signals.'

'And must we also permit them to like him—love him?' asked Frederick.

Lester met his eye. 'That would be wonderful. He is their only remaining parent.'

Easy for him to say.

'Have you any idea what you are asking?' I demanded bitterly. 'Lester—think about it! Only a saint or a fool would forgive that man. Which do you think we are?'

'Neither,' said Lester. 'But I know that you love your grandchildren. That's why I know you'll help them through this.'

It was his trump card. We couldn't fault the logic, and anyway we had no choice at all. Frederick and I were obliged to parcel up our grandchildren and deliver them to the only man we had ever hated.

•

Scarlet

The devil was singing. He was bringing death. I tried and tried to scream, filling my lungs and forcing out the sound. Then I was awake, lying in the dark, and my heart was galloping. It was a long, long time before it slowed down.

I was going to see my dad.

Sometimes all our living, all our thoughts, and all the time in the world feel like sand in an hourglass. We swirl around, but eventually we have to fall through the narrow part in the middle. Looking back on it, I know the moment Dad killed Mum was like that. It was always going to happen. Everything that happened before it was heading for that chute. I feel as though that moment is always there, still happening forever and ever, making a current that still tugs at me. It changes everything, and it will always change everything. What happened that day is very heavy. It's so heavy and important that it makes a sort of gravity of its own. Hannah once tried to explain that black holes do that.

Meeting my father again was the same. It was bound to happen eventually. I didn't know it would happen in the playroom at Mr Hardy's office, I didn't know it would happen when I was thirteen years old, but I always knew I would meet him again. Over the past three years I'd tried to pretend that he didn't exist. Actually, I'd tried to pretend that he had *never* existed, which was much harder. If anyone asked me, I'd tell them that I had no father. But in a corner of my mind I knew that one day he would be back. Even though I swam around in my hourglass and tried to become a girl with no father, the current was tugging at me. I was always going to end up falling down the chute at the bottom. So in a way, I didn't have any choice about it—but not because of the judge, or Mr Hardy. It happened because it had to.

At some time in the night, I heard Hannah talking to Gramps in their room. Her voice sounded fast and loud. I heard him reply, just a few peaceful words. I think I might have dropped off around then. I felt as though I'd been asleep about five seconds before Hannah came in to wake me, and I sat up with that Oh-My-God feeling you get when you've got an exam. Or your mum's funeral.

I wanted to be looking my very best when I told my dad to piss off. I had a shower and brushed on blusher and mascara—but not so much that Hannah would notice. She makes narky comments about me wearing makeup. I wore my skinny jeans, crocheted beret and the bright blue jacket I'd persuaded Gramps to buy when we took a trip to Stratford to see *Hamlet*. It was a fantastic production but, to be honest, I thought Hamlet needed a good kick up the backside. I know what it's like to have a parent murdered, and there's no excuse for making everyone's life a total misery. He caused another eight people to die, including himself. And Ophelia behaved like a total drip, though I hope I get to play her one day. I'm good at madness. We were met by some old luvvie mates of Gramps'—invited backstage to meet the cast—and we stayed in a hotel with an ensuite and no squabbling brothers to spoil it all. The next day we went shopping; hence the blue jacket.

I'd asked to see Dad on my own, first. Mr Hardy agreed, so Gramps took me to his office first thing in the morning. In the old days they used to execute people at dawn. I asked Gramps why, and he thought perhaps it was so the poor things wouldn't have time to think about it all day. Mind you, I don't imagine people slept the night before they got executed, any more than I slept the night before they took me to see my dad.

Mr Hardy's office building was made of square sandstone blocks. It had been built into a row of old ones and was obviously trying to look like one of them. As we walked up to the front doors I glanced up at the windows. I was sure my father was looking out at us. I felt his grey eyes on me, bloodshot with those dark eyebrows and round glasses. I pictured him in the long black coat, and then I pictured him in the green-blue sweater he used to love, the one that Mum gave him for Christmas.

We clattered up some smooth concrete stairs to the second floor, through glass doors and into a carpeted lobby. The heels of my ankle boots sank into the carpet. There was a woman behind a desk but before she spoke, Mr Hardy came bustling up to meet us.

'Ah! Hello, Scarlet,' he said. 'Nice jacket. Very chic. Dad's already here.'

I felt Gramps rest his hand on my elbow. 'All right, Scarletta?' he asked. I nodded, but he kept looking at me. 'Are you sure?'

I managed a feeble smile.

'Right.' Gramps straightened his flat cap on his head. 'Right.'

Mr Hardy opened the door for him, which was a hint. 'Thank you, Frederick. You'll bring the boys at ten, unless you hear from us?'

I made a thumbs-up signal to Gramps. He squeezed my arm. Then he was gone, and the glass doors sighed shut behind him.

'Ready?' Mr Hardy asked me.

'Nnnnyes.' I pulled my beret further to the back of my head. I felt weird, as though I was dreaming. Nothing was real. Any minute now I'd be face to face with my dad. We crossed the lobby and walked down a corridor. Then Mr Hardy began to turn the brass handle of a door.

'Hang on,' I whispered.

He stopped. 'D'you need more time?'

'Will you stay?'

His hand was still gripping that handle. 'Yes, but I'll be very much in the background.'

'Promise you'll stay?'

'Promise. Now are you ready?'

I seemed to have lost my voice altogether, so I nodded.

'Well done.' He winked, as though we were conspirators. Then he turned that handle, opened that door, and stood back to let me in.

•

Joseph

He was going to see Scarlet. She was probably on her way here, now, to this building; to this room.

He was going to see Scarlet, and he was terrified.

Lester had asked him to arrive early, to avoid any unscheduled confrontation with the Wildes. Joseph arrived earlier still, knotted with nerves after a night without sleep. He'd refused coffee but accepted a pep talk from Lester. *She'll be angry, allow her to be angry . . . she's not the little girl you remember. Try not to dwell on the lost years. Try to think about the ones you have ahead.*

'What do I do?' Joseph had asked. 'Can I even hug her? What do I talk about? I don't know anything she's been doing for the past three and a half years.'

'Give her space,' Lester replied. 'Let her have her say. She has a mind of her own.'

'Yep, that's Scarlet,' Joseph had agreed with a touch of pride. 'Her mother's daughter.'

So Joseph waited, alone in a silent room with vinyl furniture and crayon scribbles on the paintwork. It smelled of disinfectant. He sat, stood, sat again. The air was slightly too cold for comfort. Someone walked along the corridor outside. He tensed. A door opening, a swell of adult voices. Laughter. A telephone ringing.

He picked a green cast-iron tractor out of a toy box, turning it around in his fingers. Theo used to have one just like it, but this had only three wheels and the funnel was snapped. Perhaps some child had lost his temper and thrown it at the wall. There were dents in the wall. Tractor-sized.

The minutes tiptoed by.

It happened suddenly, in the end. He heard the door handle jolt before it began to turn. He stared at it.

Whispers. The first he recognised as Lester's. Then somebody else; a higher voice that made Joseph's breath catch. When the door swung open he was standing rigidly on the nylon carpet, clutching the tractor in one hand. Lester walked in, gravely meeting Joseph's eye. Then he stepped back for someone else.

She appeared in one resolute movement. Her second step brought her face to face with Joseph. She stood squarely and looked him in the eye, red-gold hair showing under a royal blue beret. She looked somehow more real than he'd imagined over the past years, more real than she'd seemed in the dusk by the Minster. She wasn't wraith-like at all; she was intensely human. And she'd changed so very much; his skinny pixie was gone.

'Scarlet,' he said. 'You're . . . beautiful.' He hadn't intended these to be his first words; they weren't the ones he had rehearsed. The thought simply burst out of him.

Lightness flashed from her mouth to her eyes. Then she seemed to collect herself; she looked away from him: at the wall, at the ceiling. 'Just tell me why you killed my mother. Then I'll go.'

Behind her, Lester Hardy quietly closed the door. He moved to a small table by the window, picked up a biro and appeared to immerse himself in reading notes.

Joseph fiddled with the toy tractor. He made the wheels run over the palm of one hand. 'Things had been . . .'

'You aren't going to blame Mum, are you? God. That's pathetic.'

'No.'

'Sounds like you are.'

'No. I lost my temper. I never . . . I was an idiot. I was an idiot.'

'Pathetic,' Scarlet said again, but without emphasis. She seemed uncertain of what to do next, twining her wrists around one another and shifting her weight from left foot to right. 'Us three kids just want you to piss off.'

'I wrote to you after I saw you in York,' said Joseph, pulling a piece of paper from his pocket. He'd already shown it to Lester, who'd turned a blind eye to this evidence that Joseph had breached his licence conditions. 'I had no way of getting it to you. Here. You could sit down while you read it.'

Scarlet folded her arms, lips pressed together.

'Please?' Joseph was holding out the thin sheet. It shivered in his hand.

With a snort, she snatched it up and plonked herself unceremoniously into a small vinyl armchair. She suddenly looked much younger, jumbled inelegantly with one leg tucked under her.

Joseph watched apprehensively as she unfolded the note. 'I've rewritten it twenty times,' he said. 'Wrote it again this morning. It still doesn't say what I want it to say.'

She frowned at the page, narrowing her eyes. The more he recalled the words he'd written, the more hopelessly inadequate he knew them to be.

Scarlet,

I want to say sorry. I want to say sorry for everything. I want to say that I have never stopped despising myself for what happened, and I never will. I took your mother from you and you must hate me for that. It was complicated, what was going on. She was very unwell and did some things that hurt me very much. I know that sounds as though I am trying to make excuses, but I'm really not. I deserved to get sent to prison. All the same, I don't believe that I am a bad person through and through. I think I can still be your father, even though I can never undo the terrible harm I did.

I have thought about you and the boys every day for the last three years. I have thought about you every hour of every day. Please know that I have never ever stopped loving you and your brothers with every last ounce of me.

With buckets of love,
Dad

P.S. I like your new hairstyle. It looks very striking. For a moment there I didn't recognise you. Sorry again. It was stupid of me to say your mum's name, I wasn't thinking. I miss the lion's mane, of course, but I am probably way behind the times.

A car horn sounded out in the street, followed by a shout. Scarlet seemed to read the letter many times over. She said nothing, though once or twice she shook her head. Lester sat peaceably writing in a notebook, and gave no sign that he was aware of what was happening.

Joseph took a step back and sank onto the brown sofa, the tractor still gripped in one hand. This was his little girl, a person he'd known since the second she was born; so impossibly precious that he would give his life for her without hesitation. Yet over the past three years she had become a new person. It wasn't just that she looked like a young woman; it was that she'd suffered. She'd suffered without him, and because of him. He didn't know her anymore.

She was folding the letter.

'Lovely,' she murmured sarcastically, sliding it into the pocket of her jeans.

'I mean every word, Scarlet.'

'You can't turn back time! You can't make it not have happened just by saying sorry. You'll always be the one who . . .' She covered her face with a hand.

Joseph crossed the carpet and crouched beside her chair. 'Look, I know saying sorry isn't enough, but it's all I've got.'

For a moment she seemed to freeze. Then her hand lashed out and caught him on the chest. 'Piss *off*!' It was both a snarl and a sob. 'We hate you. Piss right off!'

'No.' Joseph felt his own throat tighten. 'I can't, you see.'

She pushed him away. Pressing her hands over her ears, she curled up in the chair. Every muscle seemed taut, as though her entire body was charged. Joseph waited for a moment, then tentatively stretched out a hand and laid it on her head. The blue beret was falling off, and he carefully replaced it.

'We've got so much to catch up on,' he said. 'I don't know what you've been doing all these years.'

She shrugged, so he knew she was listening. Finally, hesitantly, he began to talk. She didn't interrupt. He told her about prison, about the photographs he'd kept of her and the boys. She uncurled a little as he described Akash, and how he'd bored his cellmate with constant bragging about the three best children in the universe. He talked about living in the caravan, and Abigail, and the snowplough he'd followed up the valley yesterday, and how he'd spent a night in the youth hostel in York to be sure of being on time that morning.

When he ran out of words, Scarlet lifted her face. 'I remember a dog called Jessy.' Her voice was flat, and she wasn't looking at him—but at least she had spoken.

Joseph smiled. 'Jessy's still there—an old lady now. She likes to come and snooze by the gas fire in my caravan. She pretends to hunt for rabbits but they laugh and maypole dance around her.'

'Is the tabby cat still there?'

'Digby? Fat as butter! He climbs on my knee and he's so massive he hangs down on each side. Abigail took him to the vet and they had to give him a dog's worm pill because he weighed so much.'

Her mouth curved. The movement was brief, swiftly smothered and utterly glorious. 'You were in our park.'

'I was.'

'You spoke to the boys.'

'I did.'

She nodded to herself. 'You and Theo had a talk about football.'

'Yes.'

'He knew it was you.'

'Did he?'

'Of course he did, you idiot! He's been in a real state ever since. Ben told on you.'

'I know. I got into hot water.'

'Serves you right.'

'Scarlet . . . I'd missed you all, I was so looking forward to seeing you. It wasn't such a crime, was it, to try and catch a glimpse?'

A roll of her emerald eyes, and a world-weary sigh.

'Ben's quite a young man nowadays,' persisted Joseph.

'Drives me up the wall.'

'I bet he worships you, though. What year are you in at school?'

She swivelled around to face him, though she kept her knees drawn up in front of her. 'This is just small talk. I can't believe you really want to know how I'm doing at school.'

'I want to know everything! Must be . . . no, don't tell me, hang on . . . you're year nine. Of course you are. Doing history?'

'Mm-hm.'

'Who's your teacher?'

By a very lucky chance, it turned out that the teacher was a girl Joseph himself had taught, ten years previously. Scarlet was so impressed that she actually deigned to look at him. He felt the thud as his heart flipped over.

'You're kidding!' she cried. 'Miss Four-eyes Faraday? But she's as old as the hills!'

'Well, I'm even older.'

'What was she like?'

'Um . . .' Joseph dredged his memory for anecdotes about a pupil he barely remembered. 'Never got her essays handed in on time, if I remember right.'

'Ha! She goes ballistic if mine's even a nanosecond late.'

Joseph felt emboldened. 'I once saw her outside the school gates, passionately kissing a boy with a dreadlocks and a skateboard.'

'Oh my God, I don't believe this. Miss Faraday was playing tonsil hockey outside school? A guy with dreads? Can't wait to tell Vienna!'

Perhaps unwittingly, Scarlet had made space on the edge of her armchair. Joseph squeezed onto it. 'Vienna?' he asked.

'A friend. A best friend. Sort of.' The next moment, Joseph was being taken on a tour of Vienna's opulent lifestyle—the fur bedspread and the home cinema and the predilection for chocolate that was starting to show on her bum. He listened and smiled, captivated by his daughter. She was so funny, so wry, so vital. She was beyond anything he had imagined.

Children's voices floated from somewhere in the building. A door swung shut. Footsteps, running and thuds.

Scarlet looked at her watch. 'Oops. That'll be the boys.'

'Already? Help!' said Joseph, making an agonised face. 'Will you help me, Scarlet?'

This time it was unmistakeable. A smile: reluctant, wary, cynical; but a smile all the same. It teased the corners of her eyes and flickered unbidden around her mouth. 'You don't need help, Dad. What you need is earplugs.'

Dad. Joseph felt something warm drape itself around him. She'd called him Dad. For now, it was enough.

Twenty-one

Scarlet

So. I finally saw my dad. I finally got to tell him to piss off. But he didn't piss off.

On our way out to Gramps' car after the visit, I warned Ben and Theo to keep their traps shut.

'Why have I got to keep my trap shut?' asked Ben.

'Look, just don't talk about Dad,' I said. 'You'll only upset Hannah and Gramps if they think we've had a nice time. Make out it wasn't a big deal, okay? Make out it was boring.'

For once they listened to me. When we got home, Hannah had lunch ready. She served up crumbed fish and oven fries, which she knows is the way to our hearts. It was a school day but she gave us the rest of the afternoon off. She was as fussy as a mother hen, ruffled and clucking and peering anxiously at us all with beady eyes. I knew she was busting to know how it had gone. I also knew she didn't like to ask.

'Well now,' she began, when she couldn't bear the suspense any longer. 'Um, you saw your . . . um, father?' Her teeth were actually gritted.

I kept eating. 'Yup.'

Theo yawned noisily, which may have been overacting. Ben

clapped both his hands across his mouth and blinked up at her, which was *definitely* overacting.

'How was it?' she asked me.

'Non-event. Do we have any ketchup?'

'Yeah,' chanted Theo dutifully. 'Bo-*ring*.'

'I've got my trap shut,' said Ben.

Gramps stood up. 'I'm unaccountably weary,' he said to Hannah. 'Might go and catch forty winks.'

He did look tired. He was sagging across the back of his chair like washing on a line. That wasn't his usual style.

'Thanks for all the fetching and carrying,' I said. 'Are you okay, Gramps?'

He saluted me like a naval officer on the bridge. 'Never better, ma'am,' he replied smartly. I saluted back.

Soon after he'd gone, I said I had homework to do and sneaked up to my room. I needed space in my head, because I had too much to think about. I felt churned up. Once I'd got the wedge under the door I sat down on the bed, looking at Mum's collection of costume dolls. I imagined her sitting on this same bed at my age. I tried to let my real self sink away, leaving me free to merge with Mum as I had merged with the character of Puck. I tried to *be* her.

It made me feel wrong. I felt as though I was losing myself. So I stopped doing that.

Instead, I dragged my memories box out from under the bed and unpacked it. I arranged everything in a circle, with a space for myself in the middle. I held the photo of me and her at the caravan in both hands. For a long time I sat cross-legged, staring at us. I tried to imagine the smoothness of her cheek pressed next to mine, the smell of sandalwood and the singing brightness of her voice. I tried to bring her back. I strained every muscle in my memory to bring her back to me.

And yet, try as I might, I could hardly remember her at all now.

'Mum,' I said quietly. 'Are you there?'

A muffled bang echoed from the sitting room; Theo's yell, and Ben crying. He was genuinely hurt—I could tell from the noise he was making. Hannah would deal with it. I shut my eyes. I whispered the word *Mum*, over and over.

Mum. Mum. Mummy.

A breath brushed my cheek. Just the lightest, coolest whisper of a breath. My heart began to beat very fast. Perhaps it was a draught from under the door, but to me it was Mum, trying her very best to touch my face with her ghostly hand. I sat absolutely still.

Mum?

There it was again, as though a gossamer veil had been drawn across my skin. I felt the little hairs stand up straight on my arms. The air seemed to crackle with a presence. I *so* wanted it to be Mum.

'Is that you?' I said aloud.

I'd stopped breathing completely. The air seemed much more still than usual. I even imagined—or maybe it wasn't imagination—a hint of sandalwood and coffee and wine.

'I love you,' I said.

Again, a puff of air. Perhaps she was trying to say that she loved me too.

'Help me,' I begged. 'Tell me what to do about Dad.'

A door slammed downstairs. Bloody Theo, in one of his rages. I barely heard it. Every cell in my body was focused on Mum, on this feeling that she was with me. Suddenly the sun went behind a cloud, and the room was drowned in blue-grey shadow.

'Are you sad?' I asked.

As soon as I'd spoken, a feeling hit me—like a punch in the chest that knocked all the breath out of my lungs. Of *course* she was sad—she was dead, banished from the world. How could I have sat and chatted to Dad?

'I'm sorry.' I began to cry. 'I'm sorry, I'm sorry.'

The next moment, she'd gone. It was very sudden. I knew I was on my own. The cardigan that still smelled of her lay folded in my circle of memories. I wrapped it around my face, and breathed it in, and felt the softness. Then I curled up on the floor, and my tears made the cardigan wet. I hoped she wouldn't mind.

•

Hannah

They liked him. I could tell from the way they crept into the house; I could tell by Scarlet and Theo's guilty politeness over lunch, the blank-faced shrugs when we asked them how they'd got on, the way neither of them could quite look me in the eye. Even Ben—our chatterbox—seemed to be keeping secrets.

It didn't make them happy, of course. We'd barely finished lunch when Scarlet took herself off to her bedroom. She claimed to have homework, and I heard her door shut behind her. Freddie went for forty winks in our room because the morning's ferrying had exhausted him. He'd been gone for some time when Ben ran wailing into the kitchen.

'Theo punched me,' he roared, presenting me with his arm. 'Here.'

I rolled up his sleeve to find a cruel flower of bruises blossoming on the soft skin. 'Theo did this?' I asked. He nodded tragically, rubbing his running nose.

'What happened?' I asked, rocking him on my knee as I rubbed in arnica cream.

He was sucking his thumb. The memory made him sniffle again. 'Theo told me to give him my . . . give him my . . . bean bag. And I said I wouldn't because it's mine and I was comfy. Then he picked me up and threw me onto the floor, and then he hit my arm. And it hurt, Hannah, it hurt! And then he said I was a . . . was a stupid little fucker.'

'He said *what*?'

'Stupid little fucker. That's what he called me.'

Enraged, I set Ben on his feet. 'We'll see about that.'

I found Theo lying rebelliously across the boys' two beanbags, watching TV. He pretended to ignore me when I came in, so I marched across the room and switched off the set at the wall.

'Hey!' he yelled indignantly.

'How dare you attack Ben?'

'He's a liar!'

'He has the bruises to prove it.' I was furious. 'How *could* you?'

Theo rolled until he was face down, screaming, 'No, no, no! He's lying!'

'I'm terribly disappointed in you, Theo.'

'He's just trying to get me into trouble—he's a nasty little liar!'

I folded my arms. 'That's no pocket money this week for you, young man. Come and apologise immediately.'

He was up and off the beanbags, his expression livid. 'You always take his side! You always, always do! He's your favourite. You love him most, you always have, you don't love me at all.'

'What *has* got into you, Theo?'

'Piss off, you fat old cow!'

My jaw dropped as he shot from the room. I followed—yelling dark threats—just in time to see him dart out of the kitchen door, and across the lawn. I abandoned the chase. I knew where he was heading; he had a hiding place in the far corner of the garden, behind the shed. I stood at the kitchen window, staring sightlessly at that barren winter garden and feeling as though I was in a war zone.

Ben's voice behind me made me jump. 'Wow. Theo is in *big* trouble this time.'

'Maybe,' I replied absently.

'Can I read you a story, Hannah?'

He had a dozen first reader books clutched in his arms. I couldn't resist such an appeal. We sat on the sofa and read stories to one another, though my mind was elsewhere. Ben's legs stuck straight out in front of him, and he held the books up like a pompous schoolmaster. He could manage the simpler words. I was willing to bet most four-year-olds couldn't do that. I'd taught him to write his own name, too. One of our all-time favourite books had wonderfully quirky illustrations. It was about Boogie the dog, whose appetite was forever leading her astray.

This is Boogie. Boogie is a big brown dog.
What is that good smell? It is sausages in the shop. Boogie likes sausages.
Look! Boogie has a sausage. She is running.
'Stop!' shouts the man from the shop. 'Stop that big brown dog!'
Boogie runs very fast.
The man runs very fast too.
He huffs and puffs, but he cannot catch Boogie.
Boogie runs all the way home. She is very happy.
Greedy Boogie.

The story was far beyond Ben's reading skills, but he'd learned every word by heart. He seemed intrigued by the penultimate picture, in which a florid butcher in a striped apron galloped after a high-tailing, tongue-lolling dog.

'Boogie was naughty,' he remarked thoughtfully.

'Mm, yes, but we like her, don't we?'

'The man is very cross, look at him. His face is red.'

'Well, I expect I would be cross if a big brown dog stole a sausage from my shop.'

Ben smacked his palm down onto the dog in the picture. 'The shop man should bash Boogie with a big stick—whack, whack!—and call the policeman and take her away to jail.'

I was taken aback. 'Really? But she only stole a sausage. That's what dogs do. They like sausages. We wouldn't want anyone to bash poor Boogie, would we?'

Ben's soft features had become pinched. 'Theo bashed me. If you call a policeman he will take Theo away and put him in jail.'

'Sweetie,' I suggested wearily, 'would you like to watch *Fireman Sam*?'

So I settled him down with a biscuit and a cup of hot chocolate beside him. Then I made a pot of tea and took some up to Frederick. He was just rolling off our bed, his narrow feet bare and blue-veined.

'Tea,' I announced. 'Did you get any shut-eye?'

'I can't find my jacket.'

'The children are all churned up.' I put his mug on the bedside table. 'Damn and blast Joseph Scott.'

'Hannah, I can't find my jacket.'

'Your tweed one? Okay—well, where did you leave it?'

He patted the bedspread, looking dismayed. 'I left it here, on the end of the bed. Just here, you see? Now it's gone. Did you take it?'

'Whatever would I want with your jacket?'

He lowered himself painfully onto all fours and peered under the bed. 'Somebody's stolen it. Somebody must have been in here while I was asleep.'

'Of course they haven't.'

'But I left it here on the bed! Who would come in while I was sleeping? Who would do that?'

That dreaded day had taken on a nightmarish quality. To humour him, I searched around the room. I soon spotted his jacket, carefully folded and jammed onto a shelf of the bookcase. 'Here it is!' I cried, shaking out the creases. 'What on earth did you leave it there for?' I held out the garment and he pushed his arms into the sleeves.

'Where was it?'

'In the bookcase. Funny place to put it.'

'What's it doing in the bookcase?'

'Well, you must have put it there. Now drink your tea, for heaven's sake.'

He sat down again. I moved quietly around the room, hanging up clothes and straightening periodicals on the bedside table. 'They're all at sixes and sevens,' I said. 'The children.'

'Are they?'

'One hour with their father, and they've unravelled. Scarlet's shut herself in her room. Theo's walloped seven bells out of poor little Ben.' I began to hang a pile of Freddie's cotton shirts in the cupboard: pale blue stripes, smelling of soap. Smelling of Freddie. 'Everything we've worked for. It's all coming apart at the seams.'

When he still didn't answer me, I looked around. He was sitting on the edge of the bed with his hands clasped in his lap. His gaze was fixed blankly on the wardrobe doors in front of him. He looked terrifyingly old.

'Freddie?' I said sharply. 'Are you still with me?'

He turned his eyes up to mine. His seemed to have faded in the past hour, as though some light had dimmed. Those same eyes had bowled me over forty years ago, bright with humour and understanding. Now I saw only a horrible emptiness.

'Frederick?' I persisted. 'For God's sake, say something.'

'Hmm?'

I came closer, staring into his face. It was happening. It was happening. My mother had predicted this when first we became engaged. 'He'll be an old man when you're still young.'

At twenty-four, such horrors seemed so absurdly distant as to be irrelevant. I distinctly recall laughing.

'I love him,' I told her. 'I am going to marry him and be happy until death do us part.'

She sniffed. 'You'll end up acting as a private nurse till death do you part.'

As the years passed, and mortality began to leer through aching joints and fading eyesight, I'd remembered her words. Fear had begun to gather in the dark corners of my mind.

'Freddie?' I said now. 'Knock-knock, anyone home?'

A sudden smile transformed him; a sunrise of a smile. I breathed again, as light returned to his face. 'Sorry, my darling,' he said. 'Still half asleep, silly old fellow.'

'All right?'

'I just need to drink this lovely witch's brew.' He reached for the mug.

'Are you sure?'

'Stop fussing, woman.'

Sitting there, sipping quietly at his tea, he became Frederick again. Some quality fluttered down, landed on him and made my man himself once more—what was it? The set of his shoulders, the gleam in his eyes, the strength in his voice. He watched me folding clothes and opening and shutting drawers.

'Don't fret, Hannah,' he said. 'It's just the lost sleep making me a bit slow.'

'Hmph. And I know why you're not sleeping. That man.'

'I used to work and party for seventy-two hours straight, and still function. Ha!' It was a classic Frederick Wilde laugh: a sudden bark, sharp and dry. 'Can't do twelve anymore.'

'Come on downstairs. I need you to have a man-to-man talk with Theo about his behaviour. He's beyond the pale.'

Freddie tutted when I described Ben's injuries, but when I got to the part about Theo calling me a fat old cow before fleeing behind the shed, he began to shake with laughter.

'It's not funny!' I raged indignantly. 'How *can* you laugh, Freddie Wilde?'

He wound his arm around my waist and leaned his head against mine, still chuckling weakly. 'Oh, my darling. You aren't fat, you aren't old, and you certainly aren't a cow. It really isn't amusing at all and I will have a very stern word with him. It's just that I remember calling my mother precisely the same thing. The exact same words. I was seven years old and I was furious! It was the most cutting insult I could muster. Then I ran like hell, straight into the arms of my father who'd just strolled in from work. I got the slipper.'

'Well deserved,' I pronounced sourly. 'Horrid little boy.'

As he followed me downstairs, I persuaded myself that my Freddie was all right; just stressed and sleep-deprived. God knows, we both were. Raising three young children was a challenge at the best of times but Scott's return had stretched us to our limits. Life goes on: washing to fold, mouths to feed, assignments to mark. The kitchen was chaotic and my pot plants wilting for lack of water. With a sigh, I began to empty the dishwasher.

Freddie helped. He'd stopped laughing. I knew he was about to say something I wouldn't like. I knew it from the pattern of his breathing—a series of deep inhalations, as though he was rehearsing lines. I knew every inch of him, every nuance of his body and breath. I think I knew him better than I knew myself.

'Spit it out,' I ordered.

He lifted those elegant shoulders. 'Look, Hannah, I think we may have to let this thing with Scott unfold. We can kick and scream, or we can help the children through it. Do we have a choice?'

I knew we hadn't, and the knowledge left me tight-lipped.

'What would Zoe want us to do in this situation?' asked Freddie.

'She'd want revenge.'

'Really? Was she so unforgiving? Look at it like this.' He ticked the numbers off on his hand. 'One—Scott's back in our lives, whether we like it or not.'

'More's the pity.'

'Two—you and I are not getting any younger.'

'Speak for yourself!'

'I *am* speaking for myself. I'm a real old codger. You're a young codger. The world's changing so fast that we can't keep up. We don't speak the same language. We don't know about apps and iTunes.'

'I'm hip! I have a Facebook profile.'

'Which Scarlet set up for you. You have never posted anything, ever. You don't know how. And you have a grand total of three Facebook friends.'

'Hmph. So what's your point?'

'We can't give them parenting. We can only give them grandparenting.'

'It's all I have to offer,' I muttered, and tipped the cutlery haphazardly into its drawer.

'We're not doing badly—don't be cross, Hannah—we're doing very well. *You* are doing a simply marvellous job and everyone admires you. But the fact of the matter is that we need all the help we can get.'

I clattered plates into a pile, one by one. 'Not from Joseph . . . bloody . . . Scott, we don't.' Slamming the dishwasher shut, I stood with my eyes closed. I was jangling.

Freddie's voice; Freddie's beloved calm: 'You may be right. You generally are.' He sat down at the table and bent his head over the paper. I turned the radio on and tried to distract myself with the evening's news while I chopped vegetables.

'Gerry Mac's gone, I see,' murmured Freddie, who derived a smug satisfaction from reading the obituaries. 'Says here he was a captain of industry and a respected philanthropist.' He laughed shortly. 'Bloody fraud. He's a grubby little oik of a schoolboy at heart, just like me. Inky fingers and socks at half-mast.'

A sigh of wind flicked spots of rain against the window. 'It's getting dark,' I said. 'Could you pop out and see Theo now?'

Frederick looked up from his paper. 'Mm? Theo?'

'Yes, please. It's raining and the wind's getting up. I'd really like him back inside soon, before he catches his death.'

'What's he doing outside?'

'He ran behind the shed after our battle.'

Freddie looked mystified. 'Battle?'

'I told you,' I whispered. 'Don't you remember?'

My poor Freddie. I could see it all in his face. Incomprehension as he struggled to drag the memory out of hiding; terror at the appalling blank space where it should have been.

'He called me a fat old cow,' I prompted. 'You must remember that!'

'Ah, yes.' Freddie sounded doubtful. 'Of course. Ha! Fat cow, eh? Little so-and-so.' He got up. 'Where is he?'

'Behind the shed.'

'Where? Oh, right. Well, if I'm not back by tomorrow, send out a search party.'

I watched through the window as his spare figure crossed the lawn; then I shook myself, and began to rinse some rice.

Zoe smiled affectionately down at me from her photo on the shelf. She looked mellow this evening. I longed to talk to her—I *needed* to talk to her. She so adored her father. She would have understood. She would have cared. She would have grieved with me, stood beside me as we faced what was coming.

But Zoe was gone forever. I worked and worried alone. And if I shed a few tears, there was nobody there to witness them.

Twenty-two

Scarlet

The next time we met up with Dad, the sun was bright and piercing. We strolled through York, slip-sliding on frozen patches of pavement. Ben swung on Dad's hand as though he'd known him for years—which he had, in a way. Mr Hardy tagged along behind.

I barely spoke. It was hard, really hard—but I did it. Poor Dad made a mammoth effort to chat about school, about my week, about the violin, but I gave him one-word answers. I could see he was puzzled, and I felt so sorry for him, but I was determined not to be disloyal to Mum again. She had to come first.

There was a fair on in the town centre. Ben pestered until Dad let him ride on the merry-go-round. My silly little brother sat grinning like a Cheshire cat on a big white horse, waving every time he came around and making us wave back at him. As soon as he got off, he chucked up all down his front. Dad bought him a new T-shirt and cleaned him up in the public toilets.

I went to the toilet at the same time, and when I came out Dad and Ben were waiting for me. Ben was holding Dad's hand and twittering away.

'You're not in jail after all,' he was saying.

Dad caught my eye, and smiled. He had a lovely smile. 'Not anymore.'

'Can we call you on the phone?' Ben had only just learned to use a telephone, and he was obsessed. He wanted to do it all the time.

'Um, I don't think your granny would like that,' said Dad nervously.

'She wouldn't mind.'

Dad was obviously trying to think up excuses. 'I live on the moors, so my phone doesn't work very well.'

'Well . . . can we have your number anyway?'

Dad gave in. He reached into his pocket and scribbled a number on a serviette. 'Scarlet can look after this,' he said, handing it to me. 'But you'd better not phone me. You could try sending a text, and I'll get it in the end.'

I shoved the bit of paper into my pocket, hoping Ben would forget we had it.

We bought baked potatoes from a stall and ate them sitting on a bench, watching the world go by. The potatoes were steaming, and the smell of melted cheese mingled with the winter air. There were no leaves on the trees. When I looked up, I saw pale blue sky through a mass of twigs and branches. Pigeons flew down to share our lunch, strutting with straight legs like clowns on a catwalk, flaunting their tail feathers and making gentle cooing noises. I love pigeons.

That night, the singing man visited. He stood close to my bed, growling secrets into my ear. I couldn't see him but I knew he was going to kill me. I wanted to scream but the only sound I could make was that little-bird squeak. I woke up gasping, staring around the dark room. The telephone rang, and I jumped up and ran down to the kitchen. The floor felt icy cold on my feet as I dashed across and snatched at the phone.

'Hello?' I panted.

'Scarlet.' Mum's voice. It was a very bad line though, crackling and fading in and out. I knew we wouldn't be able to talk for long.

'Mum!' I cried, overjoyed. 'Are you coming home?'

'You have to listen to me.' She sounded angry. I missed her next words. I just heard *don't ever forget that.*

'Are you happy?' I asked.

'Happy?' She laughed bitterly. 'I'm so homesick, Scarlet. I just want to come home to you, and—' Then the man's singing started up, echoing down the line, drowning out her voice.

'Mum!' I screamed. 'What? I can't hear you.'

I knew I was losing her. This was my last chance.

'I love you,' I yelled. Tears were running down my face. 'Can you hear me? I love you.'

'. . . can't forgive.'

Then a terrible noise came down the receiver; a roaring, blaring blast of sound. The line went dead.

My alarm clock was going off. Hannah was in my room, drawing the curtains. She used to have smile lines around her eyes, but lately they'd been more like worry lines. There was a new crease on her forehead. It was vertical.

'What's the matter?' she asked, when she looked into my face. 'You're not crying? You *are* crying!'

'I had a bad dream.'

The vertical line got deeper. 'What was it about?'

'Can't remember.'

She sat down on the bed and tousled my hair. 'What sort of thing? Tell me all about it. Then you'll feel better.'

'Violin lessons,' I said.

•

Mr Hardy took me out to a café after school on the Wednesday. He'd phoned and arranged it with Gramps. We reached Micklegate just as a last ray of sunshine was touching the upstairs windows, golden flashes on wobbly old glass. Rush-hour traffic had already begun to build up, and all those exhaust pipes made clouds in the cold air. I hate to think what York's rush hour does to the environment.

'Another lovely winter's day,' said Mr Hardy, holding open the café door.

I was pretty sure he hadn't brought me here to talk about the weather. Still, I was happy enough to be bought hot chocolate with marshmallows and sit in the window. There was a big group of mothers in the café, with their toddlers in highchairs and babies in buggies. Most of them wore puffer jackets and looked as though they went skiing a lot.

'My mum used to bring us into a place like this,' I said. 'She was forever having coffee with her friends. She used to say caffeine was her fix.'

Mr Hardy smiled as he stirred sugar into his mochaccino. 'I can relate to that.'

I looked out of the window. Shadows were creeping along the cobbled street outside. Since Dad had reappeared, I couldn't seem to talk about Mum without tears coming into my eyes and my face going puffy. I was always teetering on the edge of crying or shouting.

'So,' began Mr Hardy. 'How do you feel about seeing your dad?'

Two slim women in smart suits and little trench coats came striding past. They looked stylish and professional. One of them had short hair, bright green earrings and a long neck. For a second—just a crazy flash of a second—I thought she might be Mum. Then she turned her head to look in through our window, and I saw she was nothing like Mum. She wasn't even pretty, when you saw her face full on.

'Scarlet?' said Mr Hardy.

'Fine,' I said.

'Um, any chance of a bit more detail?'

'It's hurting too many people,' I said. 'And it has to stop.'

'Tell me who it's hurting.'

'Hannah. Gramps.'

'Mm-hm.' He sat back in his chair, stirring his coffee again. That had to be the best-stirred mochaccino in Yorkshire. 'And who else?'

'Mum,' I blurted miserably. 'It's hurting Mum.'

He didn't look at all surprised. In fact, I could have sworn I saw him nod to himself. 'Tell me about how it's hurting your mum.'

'She's so sad! I can feel her . . . she's lonely. She's homesick. How can we like him again after what he did to her? How *can* we?'

The mothers at the next table were glancing at us. I dropped my voice. 'I can't make a friend of my dad. None of us can.'

'It isn't your choice, Scarlet.'

I shook my head. 'Yes it is. I know it is, Mr Hardy, and so do you. I understood what you said about the judge making the decision, but in the end it's my choice. I can choose whether to talk to Dad, whether to be his friend, whether to make it work. The boys will do what I tell them. So in the end it's all down to me.'

Mr Hardy took a sip of his drink. When he put the cup back onto the saucer, some of the foam had stuck on his upper lip.

'You have a moustache on your moustache,' I told him.

He grinned, a bit embarrassed, and wiped it away with a serviette. 'Thank you. What makes you so sure that this is hurting your mother?'

And it all came out. I told him how I sat in a circle of memories in my room and called her up with the power of my imagination. I described how I felt something stroke my cheek, and how I felt darkness. Mum's darkness. I told him about how she'd phoned me in a dream.

'She was trying to communicate,' I explained. 'She had something extremely important to say, but I couldn't hear her. I said . . .'

I couldn't get the words out. I really wanted to tell the story but by now I was crying so much that my voice wouldn't work. I held my hand over my face because I knew it looked red and ugly. Mr Hardy passed me a tissue. He seemed to have a never-ending supply. I suppose he needed them in his job.

'Sorry,' I gulped.

'Don't be.'

'Well, anyway . . . I couldn't hear Mum, but I hoped she could hear me. So I said . . . um, this sounds really mushy.'

'I can do mushy.'

'Okay, well . . . I said, "I love you. I love you." I told her again and again but the line went dead and I don't think she heard. I never got to tell her that I love her, you see, when she died. She died not knowing.'

For the first time since I'd met him, Mr Hardy looked upset. 'She knows you love her, Scarlet. She will always have known that.'

'What if she doesn't, though? What if she thinks I could have saved her? Maybe if I'd said something, their argument wouldn't have got out of hand. I didn't manage to stop Dad from hitting her, did I? I didn't have the strength. I didn't shout loud enough. I was so frigging useless.'

'You were ten years old. You called the ambulance, and you relayed CPR instructions to your father. That was what you did. That was the best thing you could have done.'

'Too late.'

He thought for a long moment, crumpling a serviette in his big hand. 'Scarlet, do you know what actually killed your mum?'

'Yes. Dad hit her and it made her brain bleed.'

'Hm.' He hesitated for another moment and then seemed to come to a decision. 'Actually as she fell, she knocked her head on the fire surround. It was tragic, because if she'd fallen the other way she might not have been very badly hurt. It was the marble fire surround that caused the bleed.'

I stared at him in suspicion. 'How d'you know all this stuff?'

'I've read the medical evidence from the trial.'

'She wouldn't have been badly . . .?' I mouthed the words, letting them sink in. 'Are you saying . . . Oh my God. I think you're trying to tell me it was an accident.' And then it came back to me: something Vienna's bitch of an aunt had said. 'Was she drunk?' I asked. I saw Mr Hardy blink, and he pulled back his head as though I'd tried to bite him. I had to know. 'Was she totally rat-arsed, like I've heard?'

'Who's said this, Scarlet?'

'I hear things. People tell me things. I'm not deaf, and I'm not stupid. I also know that she'd been in a loony bin before.'

'You mean a mental health unit.'

'Whatever. So is it true, about her being drunk?'

'I think it's more appropriate if you ask your grandparents those sorts of questions.'

I was going to get to the bottom of this once and for all. I'd had enough of being kept in the dark. 'Yeah, right, like that's going to happen! If you won't tell me, I'll have no choice but to listen to the gossip.'

Poor Mr Hardy drummed his fingers on the table. 'All right. I don't believe she was very drunk, though it seems she wasn't quite sober either. But whether she had or hadn't been drinking isn't really the point.'

'I think it's pretty important.'

'No, no. The point is that she was your mother. She was a gorgeous mum, a gorgeous person. You loved her. Gramps and Hannah loved her. Your dad loved her too, and he didn't mean to kill her. That's why they didn't try him for murder.'

It was all quite a lot to take in. Until that afternoon, I hadn't talked to anyone about what actually happened the day Mum died. Gramps and Hannah avoided the subject—it was absolutely taboo. Nanette gave me as much paper as I wanted and got me to paint pictures. I'm rubbish at art but I covered sheets of her paper: angry figures and a mouth with dark pink lipstick and blood coming out of it. I drew an ambulance. I drew a gravestone even though Mum didn't have a grave. I drew myself, in the dark, with tears shaped like balls on my cheeks and an enormous open mouth. Nanette never gave me any details about what happened, though.

'Your mum chose your father,' said Mr Hardy. 'I believe they loved one another very much indeed. Together, they had you three children. There were good times as well as sad ones.'

My drink was waiting with its sprinkling of cocoa powder on the top. They'd put it in a tall glass. Evening had floated into the world outside, and all the carbon-spewing cars had their headlights on. People scurried home from work with their hands in their pockets and scarves around their faces. I could tell it was freezing cold by the dull glint on the pavement.

I wondered whether Mum ever felt cold anymore. Perhaps she felt cold all the time. Perhaps being dead meant being cold.

'Where is she?' I asked.

'Where do you think she is?'

'I'm asking you, Mr Hardy.'

He smiled, shaking his head. 'You know her best.'

'She can't have just stopped being. It's not possible. Her soul is somewhere—in heaven, I suppose. But I don't know what a soul is, really. I don't know what heaven is, either.'

'Neither do I.'

'Nobody does,' I said. I had a theory about this. 'Bishops don't. Muslims and Buddhists and Jews and atheists don't. Even the Pope doesn't actually know. They all just hope for the best. That's all any of us can do.'

'How about Hannah? She believes in God, doesn't she? And she's very clever.'

'Hannah is the first to admit she doesn't know. She's much too smart to pretend she has the answers.' I dipped my head and drank half the hot chocolate at once. 'In a way,' I said, 'I want it to be Mum who I felt in my room. I want it to be her I heard in my dream . . . because that would mean she still exists—you know? But in another way I want it not to be, because she was miserable and angry. I want her to be happy. I want her to rest in peace. RIP, Mum.'

'Maybe it was you that was feeling miserable and angry, not her.'

I thought about this idea, and knew he was probably right. The mothers at the next table were standing up, unhooking their puffer jackets from the backs of their seats and fussing around the babies. One of them bumped into me and said sorry.

'That's all right,' I replied automatically. She smiled at Mr Hardy.

'Nice manners,' she said. 'Credit to you.'

I waited for him to tell her that he wasn't my dad. He didn't. He just thanked her and looked proud.

'Fraud,' I mouthed at him, and he giggled in a Mr Hardyish sort of way.

We both watched as the mothers pushed their buggies out into the street, letting in the chilly night.

'Have you got a mother?' I asked Mr Hardy.

'She died a little while ago.'

'Me and my big mouth.'

'You are a very kind, thoughtful person,' he said. 'Please don't worry. She was almost ninety, and she had been ill for a long time.'

'She was still your mum.'

'She was.'

We left soon after that, dodging between the revving cars before hurrying down Faith Lane. The sky was velvety orange, not black, because of the city lights. I looked up at the dark walls as they loomed above us.

'They're so old,' I said. 'They have been here for hundreds and hundreds of years.'

'True.'

'The people who built them are all dead now.'

'Yes, I think we can confidently make that assumption.'

'Funny to think of, isn't it? All dead. They must be wondering why the hell they bothered. And where are they now, I wonder? Is my mum sitting in a café in heaven, gossiping over a latte with a hunky Roman soldier in a metal skirt, Elvis Presley and a couple of dazzling angels? Is she having a giggle with Dick Turpin?'

'Dick Turpin got to heaven?'

We'd arrived back at our house. I unzipped my shoulder bag to fish out the front door key. 'Thank you for the hot chocolate, and thank you for listening to me.'

'Nice manners,' he said. His beard twitched. 'Credit to me.'

Twenty-three

Joseph

Just as the first snowdrops began to hint that spring was on its way, February sank sharp teeth into North Yorkshire. Each night Joseph crouched with Jessy by the heater as sleet and ice whipped against the caravan's windows. He read into the early hours, staving off the moment when Zoe would lie bleeding on the rug.

Each morning his alarm clock clattered through the nightmare. In each indigo pre-dawn, he felt despair. He would never escape from Zoe's death. He would never be whole. Sometimes, as he forced his steps towards the farmyard, he had an impulse to turn the other way; to cross the stream and trudge onto the open moors. If he lay down up there, exposure would kill him long before anyone noticed he was gone.

Jessy refused to get up for these earliest sorties. She woke long enough to watch sleepily as he pulled on layers of clothes—most of them borrowed from Abigail—then gave a smug grunt before resting her nose back onto her paws.

'All right for some, you dozy tart,' sniped Joseph, one morning. He stepped out, teeth gritted against the blasts. As he climbed the slope, he felt oddly cheered by the flicker of a candle in Rosie's kombi. She was an early bird, that woman.

Struggling to start the tractor, his mind was on the children. Theo and Ben seemed to like him. He didn't imagine that they had forgiven him, but he felt more of a father with each outing. Scarlet worried him, though; she seemed terribly troubled. Sometimes she'd forget herself and smile at something he had said, but each thaw was followed by a freeze. Lester insisted that she was 'conflicted'. Good old touchy-feely speak, that. Conflicted.

As he handled the final bale, crimson light unfurled like a glowing flag on the horizon. He cut the engine, fascinated by this dawn spectacle.

Abigail plodded across, carrying the pig bucket. She followed Joseph's gaze. 'Red sky in the morning, shepherd's warning.'

'There is something a bit sinister about it. Looks feverish, don't you think?'

'I expect you wish you were in a nice warm classroom, teaching a load of pimply teenagers.'

'Believe it or not, I don't.' Joseph hopped off the tractor, blowing on his gloved hands. Abigail was wearing the usual khaki trousers, held up with nylon baling twine. She blinked at him through her glasses. 'Message for you on the phone.'

'Who is it?'

'Some bloke. Must have called when I was out yesterday.'

Joseph trotted inside, peeling off outer layers in the narrow hall. Heat and comfort enveloped him as he stepped into the kitchen. The cat lay curled on a cushion by the range.

'Morning, you great lummox.' Joseph stooped to tickle him. 'Why aren't you out there catching rats?'

Digby stretched and stuck out his claws, shivering with delicious comfort. Joseph strode to the phone and pressed *play* on the answering machine. He smiled as he recognised Lester's rumbling tones.

Ah, hello. It's Lester Hardy here, calling for Joseph Scott. Um, Joseph, could you please phone me? I'd like to talk about the way forward. In case you've lost my number it's . . .

Joseph glanced up at the clock. Dammit, far too early to call back.

Behind him, the kettle hit the range with a clatter. He spun around to see Rosie composedly making tea. All her movements were unhurried. She wasn't ethereal or elfin; nor was she plump. She was . . . well, opulent.

'Christ!' he gasped, though he was pleased. 'You crept up on me.'

'I certainly did *not*. I walked in, like any normal person.' She was wearing jeans underneath a russet skirt, her figure obscured by a baggy sweater. She looked like a rag doll, with bright cheeks and gypsy hair. There were ice crystals on her lashes.

'I saw your candle,' said Joseph, moving close to her. 'Still dark, it was. Why d'you always get up at the crack of dawn?'

'Habit,' she replied, smiling placidly.

'Habit?'

Her smile widened, made more mischievous by the crooked teeth, and he realised with a jolt that he'd come to delight in it.

'Yes, actually. Habit. That is the perfect word for it. Are you going to break the rules and ask more questions? Because if you are, I warn you: I have plenty for you, and they won't be pretty.'

He grinned back at her. 'I'll take that risk. What do you do at that time of the morning? Why don't you come and help me feed those bloody animals?'

'I sit.'

'Sit and what?'

'I just sit. That's the truthful answer.'

Her skin glowed, smooth planes beneath a spray of curls. On impulse, he pressed the back of his hand against her cheek.

'Warm,' he said quietly. 'How do you manage to feel so warm, when the world's so cold?'

She met his gaze, and for a moment neither moved. Then, still smiling, she took a step away from him.

He dropped his hand and turned away, mortified, fumbling with mugs and coffee as he berated himself. *What the hell are you doing, Scott? You don't deserve to flirt with this woman, or any woman. Ever again.* The glass jar slipped from his fingers and smashed, sending coffee granules and broken glass across the floor.

'Hell,' he muttered.

'Joseph,' said Rosie, 'it's okay.'

'Look at the mess. Clumsy idiot, everything I touch turns to shit! Everything.'

'I know who you are.'

He heard the words, but wanted them to be unsaid. 'Where does Abigail keep her dustpan and brush?' he asked desperately.

'I know who you are,' she repeated, putting a hand on his shoulder. 'I went to visit Gus yesterday. His mother was all agog to tell me.'

Rosie knew who he was. She knew *what* he was: a man who couldn't control his rage. A man who beat women to death. He needed to be out of the house, away from her. He strode into the hallway but was forced to pause there, pulling on his boots.

She followed him. 'Are you running away from me?'

'Yes.' He tugged at the heavy door.

'How much further do you think you can run?'

He hesitated in the old doorway, its stones worn smooth by the feet of centuries of farmers. A gust whipped into his face.

Rosie joined him, lacing her boots and pulling a shawl around her shoulders. Then she took his arm. 'Walk up the lane with me? It's always more sheltered there, between the walls.'

He allowed himself to be propelled towards the gate, past the bare-limbed sentinel tree with its lopsided sign. The farmyard puddles were solid ice. Even the stream had frozen over, rippled glass under a frosty rime. They negotiated the ford, stepping carefully along the band of cement that served as a bridge.

'I shouldn't have let Gus's mother gossip,' said Rosie. 'I couldn't resist. I'm sorry. Nosy Rosie they used to call me at school. That and Fatso.'

'Nosy Rosie.' Joseph almost smiled.

'Well, I've lived up to my name. Mind you, she was busting to tell. Thought I needed warning, since I might be in danger from the psycho. She's always taken a ghoulish interest, because of Gus knowing you and your wife. Your story wasn't at all what I expected.'

'No.'

'I had you down as a broken-hearted guy . . . Maybe the wife got the house, and you had to live in a caravan. I even wondered whether your ex was a total bitch who was using your children as pawns. I assumed that was what your phone calls were about.'

'Yes.'

'In fact, you're the bloke who divided this fair county. According to all the newspaper cuttings Gus's mother has stashed away—and she's got quite a collection—half of Yorkshire thinks you snapped under intolerable provocation and any red-blooded man would have done the same.'

'And the other half?'

'Um, the other half want to chop off your balls.'

Joseph sighed. 'You can count my sister among the ball-choppers.'

Rosie fumbled in a pocket somewhere beneath her layers of clothing, found a pair of oversized mittens and shoved her hands into them. 'Look up there,' she said, using her teeth to pull the mittens up her wrists. 'A patch of blue sky.'

'Where?'

'There.' She pointed with her chin.

Joseph squinted critically. 'That's not really a *patch*, is it? That's a tiny little dot. My mother would say it's not enough to make a pair of sailor's pants.'

Rosie considered this. 'Yeah, well. I've known a few sailors, and believe me they wear big pants.'

They walked for a time in silence. As they breasted the crest of the hill, Rosie inhaled sharply. 'What's your sister's problem? Why the ball-chopping?'

'Marie.' Joseph blew out his cheeks. 'Marie, Marie. Ah, well . . . That's a long story. Look, can we turn back? This has been very bracing and all that, but I actually can't feel my feet anymore.'

'Nancy boy,' she scoffed. 'Okay, about turn.'

They picked their way down the slope, crunching over ruts of frozen mud. 'We used to be close,' Joseph said finally. 'Marie and I.'

'Not anymore, obviously.'

'She's my big sister by three years. When she was nineteen she had a boyfriend called Jared. She was at college studying physiotherapy; dunno about him. I never liked his attitude to my sister. His teasing had a nasty edge to it. She was part of a big group of girlfriends who lived in each other's pockets. They used to go out clubbing, do the whole dance-around-the-handbag thing. He made her dump them.'

'She went along with this control freak?' Rosie sounded disgusted.

'Seems weak, doesn't it? But Marie wasn't a weak person—she was bloody-minded and nobody's fool. Mum and I couldn't understand it. Then she found out she was pregnant and moved in with him. His idea. Pretty soon she stopped seeing us. He bought her a state-of-the-art phone, took hers off her and monitored her phone calls. He even made her give up her course—said it was too physical, all that lifting might harm his baby. *His* baby, mark you.'

'Your poor parents.'

'Dad was too lazy to care, but Mum made him get off his backside and go round there with her. Jared stood in the doorway with his arms folded and told them both to fuck off and stop meddling. A week later we got the news that Marie had lost the baby. Mum waited for Jared to go out, then shouted through the letterbox until Marie opened the door.'

'Was she hurt?'

'Hell of a mess, face all swollen. She made up a story about falling over in the shower. That afternoon, after I got home from school, I went round and confronted Jared. He laughed in my face, and I hit him. I was in the boxing club, you see, so I thought I was a decent match for a weasel like him.'

'But you weren't.'

'Nope. I ended up with a broken nose, a split lip and my pride in tatters.'

'Didn't you tell the police?'

Joseph shrugged. 'It was me who'd gone round to his place, wasn't it? I thought they'd just nick me for throwing the first punch.'

'So what happened?'

'For three years, we hardly saw her. Nobody did. Mum and I kept up a campaign to get her to leave, but it was us that ended up being rejected. What we didn't understand was that Jared had reprogrammed Marie. She believed she didn't deserve anything better. He'd belt her for no reason—one time he broke her jaw—and then he'd feed her crumbs of affection. She was a bit like a dog, just grateful for anything he tossed in her direction. She thought they'd be happy if only she could be good enough.'

Rosie was shaking her head. 'I'm *hating* this guy.'

'My sister was a tough cookie before Jared came on the scene. She wasn't the sort to get pushed around. He turned her into a colourless, lifeless person.'

Rosie picked up a stone and spun it across a frozen puddle. 'How did she escape?'

'One night he said the fish she'd cooked was off. He decided she was trying to kill him, and worked himself up into a frenzy. Made her run a bath and get in, then held her head under the water. Her life was saved by a knock on the front door, which for some reason he answered. It was mates of his, come to collect him to go out to the local pub quiz. He just grabbed his jacket and left. Marie was only half-conscious, but somehow she got herself out into the street. She was a gibbering mess in a bath towel. Luckily, a passing taxi driver spotted her. Nice guy. He brought her home.'

'I hope you called the police?'

'Yes. Yes, we did. They were great. They arrested him. He lied, his friends lied, even his bloody mother lied. They all made out Marie was fixated on him. They said he'd broken off their relationship and she was a bunny-boiler.'

'Medical records?'

Joseph shrugged gloomily. 'She'd hardly ever been to the doctor—he wouldn't let her, except during the pregnancy. When she did go she made up excuses for any injuries. So the doctor's notes didn't corroborate what she was telling the police. Still, they took it all the way to trial. I'll never forget Jared smirking at me and Mum, in the public gallery. When Marie gave her evidence the judge put him behind a screen, but she was still so scared that she threw up into a wastepaper bin.'

'Oh, poor girl. But he was found guilty?'

'He got off.'

'No! I just can't understand that.' Rosie sounded stunned. 'It beggars belief.'

'The jury were out for hours, but in the end they let him off on a majority. Seriously, Rosie, Jared was a hell of a good liar. He had this sort of reptilian charisma. He played his part to a tee—the decent bloke, hounded by a she-devil. It came down to her word against his, and I guess they wondered why the hell she'd stay in that relationship for three years if it was as bad as she claimed.'

'Mm. They will have wondered that. Actually, *I'm* wondering that.'

'We all did. She was so screwed up by him, so ashamed of being screwed up.'

'He's probably torturing some other poor girl at this moment.'

'Probably. Years later, I came across him playing pool in a pub. I was an adult by then. I was sober, and he wasn't. I managed to get in a good one-two before his mates knocked me down. This time it was *his* nose that was bleeding! We both got thrown out of the pub, but it was . . . um, anyway.' Joseph tailed off as he realised how all this must sound to Rosie. Here he was, a man whose fists had killed, bragging about his prowess in a brawl.

'It was well worth it,' she said, finishing his sentence firmly. 'I wish you'd given him more than a bleeding nose. I wish you'd given him a real hiding.'

'Nothing to be proud of,' he muttered.

'Ooh, I don't know.'

'I still had the bruises when I met Hannah and Freddie for the first time. Hannah looked as though she'd swallowed a wasp when I told her I'd been fighting in a bar.'

'Oh dear, that was *not* a good start. How is Marie now?'

'She's forty, never had kids. After two years of counselling, her personality came back—bits of it, anyway. She did a degree in social work and ended up managing a women's refuge. She's dedicated her entire life to fighting domestic violence, so she hates me with a passion.'

'Why would she hate you?'

Joseph flung out his arms. 'Come *on*.'

'She doesn't understand?'

'What is there to understand, from her point of view—a woman with her history?' Joseph smiled grimly. 'The word *understand* implies that there might be some excuse for killing a defenceless human being, and how can there ever be an excuse? No, no, I am *way* beyond forgiveness.'

'But you're her brother.'

'That just makes it worse.'

They'd arrived on the bank of the ford, and halted for a moment. The river whispered as it slid secretly under the ice.

'When the snow melts, this will be a torrent,' said Rosie. She seemed to glide across the ford, stepping on the thickest stretches of the concrete bar that spanned it. Joseph was halfway across when his foot cracked through the ice with a dull splash.

'Blast,' he muttered, as freezing water engulfed his ankle. 'Wet sock. Gotta go and change. Coffee? My place?'

They stopped at the camp kitchen to collect Rosie's milk before trudging down the slope towards Joseph's caravan.

'Your sister's wrong,' said Rosie suddenly.

He sensed compassion, and flicked it away. 'Maybe after ten years of being Abigail's farm labourer I'll get back my citizenship of the human race. But I doubt it. Look, it doesn't matter. I'm alive, I'm seeing my children. That's enough for now. Come on in.'

He held the door of the caravan. Rosie stamped snow off her boots before stooping to untie the laces. She had a natural grace, he thought, despite the bulkiness of her clothes. He wondered about the man she'd left behind: the man who had offered her everything. Perhaps he was pining after her. Perhaps he was searching for her, stalking jealously as Jared once had.

It wasn't much warmer inside the caravan than out, though Joseph had left a radiator turned low. Jessy got up, arched her back with a groan and tottered down the steps.

'Yellow patches,' sighed Joseph, lifting his kettle onto the gas ring. 'All around my little palace. Lucozade-coloured snow, thanks to that old girl.'

Jessy was soon back, slipping on each step and forcing the door open with her head. She seemed to be muttering *Jeepers! It's cold out there!* as she bustled back to the radiator, leaving a trail of wet paw marks. Rosie patted the dog's soft face while her eyes strayed to a faded book that lay on one of the squabs. The cover was cinnamon and gold.

'Aha!' she cried, reaching for it with a smile of recognition. '*The Prophet*.'

There was no way to stop her. He watched her open the book and read the flyleaf with its flamboyant handwriting. He watched her smile falter.

He turned away, stooping to squint out of the window. 'That patch of blue is more than a sailor's pants now. Look—it's a whole mainsail.'

'I feel like a peeping Tom.'

'Hardly.'

He heard her close the book and put it down. 'What was she like?'

What was she like? Joseph tugged off his beanie, running a hand through his hair. 'She was like a whirlpool.'

'Why a whirlpool?'

'Because she was an irresistible force. Impelling. Dizzying.' His movements automatic, Joseph made coffee in a plunger. 'One of the psychotherapists had this mantra: *I am not my condition. I am not my condition.* Zoe was meant to remember it whenever things got wild. But the fact is that bipolar *was* a part of Zoe. It was an element of her beauty. It was also her personal demon and torturer. Both. It took her to places nobody could follow.'

'All the time?'

'No. No, she was stable for months, years . . . When I first met her she was so well that she could hold down two jobs, acting and waitressing. Acting was in her blood. Her father's a theatre director, the sort who can look forward to an obituary in *The Times*.'

'Mm. Gus's mother saw him on telly when you were sentenced. Apparently the parents were very dignified outside court.'

'Really? I didn't know that.' Joseph carried two mugs of coffee to the table, and Rosie joined him there. 'The problem is that acting is quite dangerous for someone like Zoe. She'd think herself into the characters, leave reality up on the surface and sink into their emotions. If she was playing a tragic role, she'd come off the stage in floods of tears. It wasn't good for her grip on reality.'

'No, I can imagine it wasn't.'

'Eccentricities and ups and downs were a part of the deal. At first, I was happy to ride on her rollercoaster. She showed me a way of thinking that was infinitely more exciting than my own family's.'

'Really?'

'Infinitely! If you met my father, for instance . . . He's like a zombie compared to Zoe. Before we knew it, Scarlet was on the way. That's when things got out of hand. It wasn't fun anymore, it was crazy. Zoe started spending, throwing impromptu parties for total strangers, talking at a thousand miles an hour. Then down she'd crash—couldn't even get out of bed, didn't want to live. I was faced with carnage: the friends she'd insulted, the credit card bills, the reorganisation of the house—every cupboard, every shelf emptied, everything piled on the floor. People said it was her nesting instinct, and I wanted to believe them. I didn't know how pregnant women were meant to behave.' He stared into his mug, remembering. 'Scarlet's birth was shattering, in so many ways. When I first held that brand new human being . . . my baby girl . . . my world completely changed. I hadn't imagined love on such a scale was even possible.'

'You're blessed,' said Rosie gently.

'Yes, I am. I am. But Zoe got worse—mania and depression, cycling wildly. I didn't use those terms then because I didn't know what the hell was going on. I found her in the garden one night, wearing a party dress. She was on another planet. It was surreal because she reminded me of herself, acting Ophelia—you know that scene when she's gone mad?'

'Mm. Vaguely.'

'I'm sure Shakespeare had seen a woman in the throes of psychosis. Zoe . . .' He swallowed. 'She was on her way to drown Scarlet and herself in the pond on Tooting Bec Common.'

Rosie recoiled. 'No! What did you do?'

'I got her back inside and called an ambulance. They knew how to manage her and I didn't, I just didn't, I . . .' He bit his knuckles as he fought for control. 'She was admitted to a psychiatric unit—not for the first time, I discovered.'

'She'd been in before?'

'Yep. Sectioned in Yorkshire—which was a closely guarded secret to which I wasn't privy. This time, though, the shrinks came up with a diagnosis. The thing is . . . The thing is, the thing is . . . she was still the love of my life. So we vowed we'd get through it together. And we did. We moved up here. We had Theo, and it was fine—she didn't breastfeed, and got plenty of rest. I gave up playing football, turned down promotions, brought work home.'

'You were a teacher, right?'

'Right. For a long time, the drugs more or less worked. It wasn't always easy, but lots of marriages aren't. Zoe was an amazing mother when she was well; an amazing lover and friend, too. Loving, fun, inspiring. I thought we'd manage to walk the tightrope.'

'Did she mind taking medication?'

'She said she missed the golden trumpets when she was on her way up, but it was worth it to avoid the depression. We did okay. Really, we did. Years passed, years with lots of joy and some bloody awful rows—especially when she wanted to go back to London and I refused.'

'You didn't want to move back?'

'We needed my income, and I had a decent job; anyway, the stress of life down there would have been too much for her. Everything exploded when . . .' Joseph took a sip of coffee, and grimaced. 'This is gnat's pee. Sorry.'

'I'll make some more.' Rosie slid out from behind the table. 'What happened?'

'Um . . . Ben happened. I'm sure that was the trigger. From then on we were in Wonderland. She wanted a birthday party for Theo, said it would be fit for a prince. And it was. Zoe knew how to throw a party. She hired a hall and decorated it to look like an underwater palace. Fifty children.'

'Fifty!'

'With a clown and a birthday cake so massive that one of your father's lap dancers could have burst out of it. The kids had a ball.'

'The kids had a ball, and you had the bill?'

'Too right. Then she bought ten litres of bright orange emulsion and painted half the house before she lost interest. She threw out all her clothes, bought a whole new wardrobe for herself and Scarlet. I had to use the children's savings to pay for that spree. I managed to cancel the holidays she booked—three of them, in the Bahamas. Next, the brand-new BMW arrived, the one she'd bought on hire purchase, the one we could never afford. I begged her to get help. She said, Why? She was fine, she'd never felt better. Those words made my blood run cold. If Zoe had never felt better, we'd never been in more trouble.'

Rosie placed a fresh mug of coffee in front of him. Steam spiralled up in the thin light. He felt her hand rest lightly on his. It was a fleeting moment of comfort. Then she was slipping behind the table again.

Joseph looked out of the window. 'You forget. You forget what's normal. Like Marie did . . . She no longer knew that normal men don't break their girlfriend's jaws. Life for me and the kids felt like being trapped in a washing machine, with Zoe controlling the spin speed. We just had to hold on tight and grit our teeth as it spun faster and faster. And Zoe . . .' Joseph squinted at the pain of memory. 'Sang. Zoe laughed. And the more she sang and laughed the more desperate she became—she was terrified, my poor girl. She did everything to excess. Booze. Rage. Sex. Sex with me, the old flame she bumped into, the hitchhiker she picked up on the A19.'

'But you didn't leave her?'

'No, I didn't leave her. You start to behave like the White Rabbit when you live in Wonderland. Of course I called her mental health team and they did what they could, but I didn't want her sectioned even if they'd have done it. Zoe decided she loathed my job, I wasn't appreciated and I must get another one. She kept ringing people up and making appointments for me to go for interviews. It was disastrous. I ended up before the management at my school, demanding to know what the hell I was playing at. So Zoe called the headmaster to tell him I despised him.'

'Ouch. Did he understand?'

'He tried.'

Joseph was coming to the end of his story, to the awful end. He wanted to tell it—needed to tell it, dreaded telling it. Jessy rolled, stretched, sighed. Melting snow wept from the roof.

'I used to do exam marking,' he said. 'A levels. We needed every penny we could get. The courier would bring them and there were deadlines. One day . . .' He took several long breaths. 'The second I walked in the door I knew there'd be trouble. Zoe was already halfway through a bottle of wine, excited because they'd had a bonfire—talking nineteen to the dozen—dancing around the sitting room, cheeks flushed, eyes glazed. My heart just sank. I went into my workroom to drop my bag and saw that the latest pile of exam scripts had gone from my table. It was . . . Christ. I knew. I just knew.'

Rosie was staring at him, mesmerised.

'I sprinted into the garden.' Joseph shook his head, denying the moment. 'She'd burned the lot. I found charred paper ground into the ash, bits fluttering away, and I felt my *own* sanity tearing. I barged back inside, yelling. I called her a bitch. I called her . . . God knows what else I called her. I said I'd have her sectioned. I screamed about those poor teenagers who'd sweated over their exams. I said I'd have to resign, I'd be lucky if I wasn't sued, how the hell would we pay for her fucking craziness? And she stood there and laughed, as though it was all hilarious. Ben was wriggling on her hip, wanting to get down, but she didn't seem to notice. She was a total stranger, she wasn't Zoe. I can't describe how that made me feel. I can't . . . Christ.'

'You don't have to go on,' said Rosie. 'I shouldn't have asked.'

He held up a hand, asking for time. 'I lost my . . . like, *really*, lost control. I hit her, and I was shouting and then she was shouting. I couldn't hear anything, couldn't hear my poor kids screaming and crying. I hit her again, even harder—why did I do that? *Why?* What the hell did I think I was doing? Jesus . . .'

He stopped with a gasp, ducking his head low. Rosie reached across the table and took his hands.

He had to tell it all. He had to pass it on, somehow. He gulped, forcing out the words. 'I heard it as she went down. This sickening crack. Next thing she's lying there on the rug. Her eyes are wide open and she's glaring right at me but there's this blankness where she used to be. And there's blood coming from her ear. And I'm crying out, I'm crying out for her to be all right, I'm on my knees beside her and I'm begging her, Jesus Zoe Jesus come back, come back, but she never did, not even for a few seconds—though she's haunted me every . . . single . . . bloody . . . night from that day to this, staring at me like I'm . . . like she can't believe I'd do such a thing. And I can't believe it either because she was my life.'

Ben had fallen when she fell. He sat in his nappy and tiny T-shirt, wailing. Joseph ignored him. He must save Zoe. He yelled to Scarlet to phone for an ambulance. He tried CPR—how many pumps was it, at what speed? He tilted back Zoe's head, tried to breathe his life into hers. After all, her eyes were open. Perhaps if he filled her lungs with air, she'd breathe for herself. She had to. She had to.

But Zoe never breathed again.

A shaft of sunlight found its way through the clouds, throwing cold brilliance onto the scratched table. Joseph dropped his head onto his arms, and felt the steady pressure of Rosie's fingers on his. But she wasn't real.

Zoe was real. Zoe was staring at him from the mat, and his life was over.

Twenty-four

Hannah

Freddie and I sat side by side in Jane's office, staring aghast at Lester Hardy's latest ramblings. Apparently he'd visited Scott's caravan and thought it a perfectly safe place for our grandchildren to visit. The final paragraphs made my hair stand on end.

> *I recommend a pattern of increasing contact. As a guideline I suggest visits of no less than two hours' duration, rapidly increasing to overnight visits. I see no pressing need for contact to be supervised into the future.*
>
> *It is in the best interests of all children for the adults in their life to work together; therefore I hope that the parties will now feel able to meet. It is important that they build mutual trust and agreement regarding the way forward. I am prepared to facilitate such a meeting.*

'Mutual trust!' I exclaimed. 'The man's in la-la land. Trust a person who battered Zoe to death? He's off his head—isn't he, Freddie?'

Freddie sat deep in thought, his chin on his hand. He didn't seem to hear me.

Jane glanced at him, then back at me. 'If you want to keep the moral high ground—' she began.

'Stop.' I waved her away. 'Stop, Jane. I know exactly where you're going. You're about to advise us to negotiate in order to avoid being seen as intransigent.'

'Mm. That just about sums it up.'

'We don't need the moral high ground, thanks. We need to be rid of Scott. Where is this pestering going to end? What will satisfy him—disrupting our lives once a month? Once a fortnight?'

Jane pursed her lips unhappily. 'I'm not sure.'

'You don't think . . .' I stared at her, feeling a shiver of fear. 'Good God. You think he wants to take them away from us! Perhaps that's been his agenda all along.'

'There's no residence application.'

'*Yet!*'

'There may never be.'

I sprang to my feet and began pacing the carpet. I was terrified. 'This is insane. We could lose them altogether. For God's sake, *do* something, Jane!'

'If you really can't bear the idea of more contact, we'll have to bring the matter back to court.'

'That isn't going to work, is it? Not if we get the same judge.'

'Look, wouldn't you agree to a—'

'No,' I interrupted, before she'd finished the sentence. 'I wouldn't agree to a meeting.' Terribly distressed, I reached for the comfort of Frederick's hand. 'We won't talk to him, will we, Freddie?'

He looked down at our entwined fingers. 'Talk, my darling? To whom?'

'Freddie! Joseph Scott, of course.'

'Talk to . . . ? Oh, no. No. I really don't think we want to do that, do we?' Freddie shook his head too many times before blinking sadly at Jane. 'He killed Zoe, you know.'

For a second, shock tightened her features; but she was professional enough to control herself. 'Quite,' she murmured. 'I understand.'

The heavens had opened by the time Jane walked us downstairs.

'We're going to get wet,' fretted Freddie, looking out at the downpour. 'I'll run home and get the car, shall I?'

'Or I could lend you our spare umbrella,' suggested Jane. 'It's big enough for both of you. Hannah, come with me—it's in the ladies'.' She led me into a staffroom at the back of the building, where she handed me a large black umbrella.

'What's up with Freddie?' she whispered anxiously.

'Nothing's up.'

'You know very well there is.'

'It's the stress,' I suggested. 'He's not sleeping.'

'Has he seen anyone about his memory lapses?'

'No. And he isn't going to. Have you any idea how much strain this is putting on our household? Freddie will be absolutely fine as soon as we get rid of Joseph Scott.'

My dear friend. I stalked away, and she trailed after me to the street door. Freddie was waiting patiently, his figure a thin question mark against the muted light. I handed him the umbrella as we stepped outside. He opened it with a flourish, holding it gallantly over my head as I took his arm and we sallied forth into the wet city.

Jane stood at the door, letting the rain throw diagonal streaks across her linen dress. At the corner, I glanced back. She was still watching us. I had never seen her look so sad.

•

We arrived home at five o'clock, to chaos. Scarlet was meant to be babysitting but the only sign of her was tuneless music booming from the direction of her bedroom. I found Ben and Theo lying like two indolent piglets in front of the television, munching packets of crisps and Penguin bars while watching *The Simpsons*.

They were surrounded by a mountain—wrappers, mugs, socks, K'Nex and about fifty other assorted toys. Sighing, I began to collect up the strewn debris. It all seemed futile. The mess would be back tomorrow, after all. It was beyond me. It was a rising tide. It would drown us all one day.

'Where's Scarlet?' I asked wearily.

'In her room.' Theo didn't take his eyes off the telly. 'Gettin' ready.'

'Getting ready? For what?'

'Um . . .' He dragged his attention away from Homer Simpson. 'The social's tonight. You know, when they all go kissy-kissy snoggy-snoggy with the boys from the choir school.'

Ben giggled luxuriously and made smacking lip noises before beginning to chant:

'Zac and Scarlet sitting in a tree,
K-I-S-S-I-N-G!'

I was flummoxed as I watched both boys dissolve into hysterical laughter. '*Who* and Scarlet?'

'Zac,' gasped Theo, still chortling.

'Whoever is Zac?'

'He goes to the choir school and he fancies Scarlet.'

'How do you know all this?'

'His sister told me. She's in my class. She says tonight's the night.'

This was yet one more thing to worry about. Should I be having some kind of a talk with Scarlet about the facts of life? Surely not. She'd be mortified. *I'd* be mortified.

Lethargically lobbing bits of plastic into the toy box, I came to a decision about Joseph Scott. In that, at least, I could be proactive. Lester thought the children shouldn't be questioned directly about their views—but to hell with Lester! They weren't his children. How was I supposed to know what they wanted unless I asked them?

When *The Simpsons* ended, I switched off the television—howls from Theo—and sat down in an armchair, facing the pair of them.

'Listen,' I said seriously. 'I want to ask you something.'

Ben's nose was deep in a crisp packet as he licked out the last few crumbs. Theo glowered suspiciously. 'What?'

'It's about your father.'

He turned his back on me and buried his face in a beanbag. Meanwhile, Ben began blowing air into the empty packet, making it into a silver and blue balloon.

'Theo,' I said, 'would you please take your head out of that beanbag and talk to me?'

'No.'

I jumped as Ben smacked his hand into the crisp packet, shrieking '*Bang!*' at the top of his voice. Salt sprayed across the carpet. Theo didn't take his head out of the beanbag but he did manage to swing one leg across and kick Ben, who bellowed and kicked back. For the first time since I could remember, I felt like smacking the pair of them. My palm itched.

'Come on, boys! Gramps and I have to make decisions. I need you to tell me the truth. Do you like seeing your father?'

Ben grabbed a model Tardis and flew it around the room, humming the *Dr Who* theme tune. I leaned down and pulled Theo upright by his shoulders.

'That's enough,' I growled. 'You're making me cross.'

'I don't like seeing him,' he said flatly. 'It's boring. But we have to go, so that's that.'

'Well, have you told Mr Hardy you don't like going?'

'Yeah. Sort of.'

'Well "sort of" isn't good enough. If you don't want to go, you have to say so very clearly.'

He flushed. 'Okay, okay.'

'Mr Hardy is suggesting you go more often, maybe even stay overnight.'

I saw it then, though Theo tried to cover it with a yawn. Interest. Excitement. I felt a sickening jolt. 'A sleepover?' he asked. 'In a caravan?'

'You never do sleepovers.'

'That's 'cos he pees in the bed,' crowed Ben.

Theo ignored him. 'I don't wanna go for sleepovers,' he said. 'But maybe, if the judge says I have to go, I'd better. 'Cos the judge says. Ow, Ben!'

The Tardis had crash-landed on his head. I confiscated it, then reached out and drew my smaller grandson onto my knee. 'What about you, Benji? Do you want to see your father anymore, or should I try to make him go away?'

He looked away from me. 'Can we have the telly back on?'

Neither of them had any intention of answering sensibly. I left them arguing over which channel to watch, and made my way up to Scarlet's room. I winced at her music as I climbed the stairs: a female caterwauler, and Scarlet singing along. I knocked—quietly—before pushing open her door. There she was, sashaying around the room. I could smell nail polish.

She stopped dancing. She was wearing a short, floating dress with one of her mother's brilliant green bands around her hair. The broad cloth looked stylish, and it matched her eyes. The effect was startling. 'You might have knocked!' she squawked accusingly.

She looked so sophisticated, that was what alarmed me. Her dress was almost non-existent; her legs were bare and long and I was pretty sure she'd shaved them. She'd done something to her eyes and her mouth; they seemed defined and . . . well, sexy. My granddaughter, barely in her teens, and she was going out looking sexy.

I had to shout over the music. 'Are you wearing makeup?'

'A bit.'

'Too much, Scarlet.'

'Nah! You should see Vienna when she goes out.'

'That dress isn't decent. You've grown since we bought it. I can almost see your knickers.'

She smiled. It was patronising, as though I was the child. Perhaps I was, in some ways.

'It's fine, Hannah. Other girls wear much sluttier stuff.'

'*Please* will you do something about that racket?'

She shook her head in despair at my lack of taste, but turned the music down.

'We have to talk about your father,' I said, sitting on the bed. 'He's got the thin end of the wedge through the crack, and we have to decide whether to take a stand. So I need to know what you want.'

She turned her back, staring critically into the long mirror. I could see her face in the reflection. She looked serious now: an artist observing her model. 'Does this headband work? It was Mum's.'

'Definitely. Look, Scarlet, what about this thing with your father?'

'Not my choice.' She began to fossick through a drawer. 'Where's that pesky bracelet?'

'But it *is* your choice,' I persisted. 'I'm asking you because I need to decide. Wouldn't you be frightened to go and stay with him?'

'Yes. I *would* be frightened.'

'The boys would be terribly unsettled.'

'Mm, it would be a big thing for the boys.'

'All right.' I felt a surge of relief. 'I'll tell them we refuse.'

'We can't just refuse.'

'Of course we can.'

'It's complicated.'

'Why? I should have thought it was very simple.'

She slammed the drawer shut. Then she sat on the bed beside me. 'Hannah, could we please not talk about this?'

The years dissipated. I was there with Zoe again, in that room, sitting on that same bed. I touched the vivid cloth on her head, and remembered Zoe wearing it. I'd been so proud.

'This looks lovely,' I told her truthfully. 'Are you meeting anyone, er, special at the school social?'

'Just Vienna. Some other girls.' The answer came much too quickly.

'Is Zac going to be there?'

She was all wide-eyed innocence. 'Who?'

'He'll be knocked off his feet,' I said meaningfully. 'Just make sure you stay on yours.'

Twenty-five

Scarlet

I thought Hannah was going to have a hernia when she caught me getting dolled up for the school social. I was just layering on some super-lash-lengthening mascara when she walked in. Bad timing. She stood there looking as though she'd just had her lip pierced. I found this extremely hypocritical, because she's always happy enough to slap on the warpaint herself—especially red lippy—but when it comes to me it's a different matter. If it was up to her I'd be wearing pigtails and a pink gingham dress down to my ankles.

She'd heard about Zac. Walls have ears, obviously. And little brothers have big mouths.

Luckily her mind was on my father and his application, so she didn't want a fight with me. In the end, she even got into the spirit of the thing. She gave me two little gold safety pins, to attach my dress to my bra straps, and she managed to smile as she waved me off.

Gramps drove me to the party. He opened the car door like a chauffeur, bowing and murmuring 'milady,' as he handed me in. When he dropped me off at school, he called out: 'Dance with all those lucky young men, but only kiss one.'

That was good advice. I danced with a lot of blokes but in the end I didn't even kiss the one. Zac had been too full of himself since he was on the radio on Christmas Day, singing the solo in 'Once in Royal David's City'. He turned up at the social like a strutting cockerel, and he'd used a ton of hair gel which is a real turn-off. Once he realised I wasn't going to get it on with him, he started chasing Vienna. Proves how much he cares about me.

The next day was a Saturday. Gramps always collected me after my drama lesson on a Saturday morning, and we'd do the weekly trip to the supermarket. This particular day, Hannah had taken the boys out with some colleague of hers whose children were similar ages. Gramps and I decided to go for lunch in York after our supermarket shop.

Sainsbury's was hyper-crowded that day. I pushed the trolley while Gramps and I walked along. He carried the list Hannah had given us.

'Pitta bread, crumpets . . . check!' he muttered, as we found everything. 'So how was the party last night?'

'Great.'

'Did you dance all night?'

'Yep. Taught everyone my new moves.' I demonstrated a couple of them in the supermarket aisle.

'Dancing's come a long way since I was a callow youth. What kind of washing powder should we get? Hannah thinks Theo might be allergic to the usual stuff.'

We filled the trolley, queued and paid, and got everything stashed in the car. I was shivering because I'd left my coat in the passenger seat. The sky looked like cotton wool after you've used it to take off your makeup, and it was leaking drops of dirty cotton-wool rain. Even the air felt soggy, but as we drove back into York I felt cheered by thousands of daffodils covering the banks of the city walls. They made me think of Mum and Dad's wedding. I wondered when their anniversary was.

We parked near the river and climbed a set of billion-year-old steps towards street level. We were halfway up when Gramps stopped dead.

'Ah! Zoe, look at this,' he said.

Zoe.

'Scarlet,' I reminded him.

'Mm?'

'I'm Scarlet.'

I don't think he even heard me. He was going a bit deaf. 'See this lichen?' he said. 'This small patch, just the size of a saucer?'

I squinted over his shoulder as he talked.

'It might be as old as this piece of wall. Medieval. It grows very, very slowly—but it lives an unimaginably long time. Unlike people. Did you know that lichen can survive in outer space?'

I didn't know that. He'd put his glasses onto his nose, and was peering at the patch of grey-green on the stonework. People were edging around us on the narrow stairs, and the cold was starting to trickle in through the seams of my coat. 'It's actually made of two organisms,' he said.

I gave him a subtle tug. Too subtle, apparently, because he didn't budge.

'A fungus and an alga.' He seemed to be lost in wonder about a patch of stuff that most people would clean away with bleach. That's Gramps all over. The tiniest things—aphids, caterpillars, algae, people—are magical to him. That's one of the reasons I love him so much. He sees beauty everywhere and in everybody.

Eventually we walked on, with him talking about how they can use lichen to date things. I was still feeling a bit funny about him calling me by my mother's name. Once we were in the restaurant he took off his cap and smoothed down his hair. We ordered some lunch at the counter, and then he pulled out a chair for me as though I was a duchess. He's always done that, ever since I can remember.

A bus rattled the bay window. It had an advert for some holiday on the side, with a picture of a woman in a white bikini, sipping a cocktail by a glittering sea.

'Vienna's going to Thailand soon,' I said.

'How is young Vienna nowadays—still a chocaholic?'

I told him about Vienna's latest addiction, which was Crunchie bars, and we gossiped until the waitress brought our drinks.

'Lovely,' sighed Gramps ecstatically, lifting his coffee cup. 'Nothing like that first shot of caffeine.'

'That's exactly what Mum used to say.'

'Is it? I didn't know. I suppose there are many things about your mother that you remember well, and which I know nothing about. Those are your own precious treasures, those memories. Hold on to them.'

'I've never thought of memories as treasures before.'

'Oh, yes!' Gramps' whole face became a gentle smile. 'Good memories are treasures to be hoarded. They bring light when life seems dark.'

I used my teaspoon to dig out froth from the hot chocolate. The bubbles dissolved into sweetness on my tongue. 'Gramps?'

'Present and correct.'

'Can I ask you something?'

'Fire away.'

'Promise you won't be upset?'

'I'll do my best.'

I looked down at the froth in my cup. 'Do you think we should start staying over with . . . um . . . our dad? Or is now the time to put our foot down?'

The silence went on for a long time. I stole a glance at him. He was staring out of the window, and there were valleys running from his nose to his mouth. I'd never noticed them before. 'Sorry,' I said. 'Silly question.'

'Not at all. A good question.'

I let him think for a minute. We both watched the traffic pass by.

'I've experienced many wonderful things in my life,' he said in the end. His voice was hoarse. 'I've travelled, made mistakes, learned from people better than myself. I've been in love with beautiful women. I've married Hannah and shared forty years with her. It has been my privilege to work with many brilliant individuals, but the most extraordinary magic of all was your mother. The fact of her existence gave meaning to mine. She was, quite literally, the light of my life.'

I felt so guilty. I was kicking myself for even mentioning Dad when the waitress came by with our order. She seemed to sense something was up. 'Everything all right?' she asked. 'Like some ketchup?'

'No thanks!' I gushed, sticking up both my thumbs like a prize geek.

After she'd moved on, Gramps gave a great heaving sigh that seemed to shake his body. 'That radiant light went out.'

'I'm so stupid,' I muttered. 'I shouldn't have asked you.'

'No, no.' He turned away from the window and looked at me. 'I didn't mean . . . I am not trying to tell you what to do, Scarlet. I was merely trying to explain why Hannah and I are finding this so very difficult. We mustn't make decisions out of bitterness, though. We must think about what's best for you children.'

'But what *is* best for us? Hannah was asking me last night and the truthful answer is I don't know. I don't want to be disloyal to you and Hannah. I don't want to be disloyal to Mum. But he's the only dad we'll ever have. I don't know what to do.'

Gramps' eyes looked saggy, as though weights were pulling down the skin below them. 'What do you want to do?'

'I want to *not* hurt anybody's feelings.'

'You three have suffered the greatest loss. If you can forgive, then surely so can we.'

'It isn't about forgiving our father,' I said, choosing my words carefully. 'It's about living with *not* forgiving him.'

Gramps reached across the table and took both my hands in both of his.

'Come on,' he said. 'Let's eat up. Your wedges are getting cold, and there's nothing worse than a cold potato wedge.'

We didn't mention Dad again, but the subject was so massive that it didn't go away. It hung around, making everything else we talked about seem false and twittery-shallow. Dad was what

Hannah would have called the Elephant in the Room. Actually, he was fast becoming the Elephant in my Life, and that wasn't a good feeling.

'Shall we take a constitutional along the walls?' asked Gramps, as he paid the bill. 'There's nobody at home, after all.'

I didn't feel like going home yet either. Gramps wrapped his scarf around his neck. He dropped his cap and seemed to have trouble picking it up, so I did it for him. As we stepped outside, dark dishcloth clouds were scudding across the roofs of York. The air felt refreshing after the hot café. Feeling happier, I put my arm through Gramps' and we headed along the pavement towards Bootham Bar.

'The air must be very cold,' said Gramps, shaking his free arm in the air. 'Gone numb.'

'I don't think it's cold. Just damp.'

Those old walls take you to secret places. You climb the steep staircases, and then you walk along the narrow path and feel as though you're invisible. Gramps and I were soon suspended high among the trees, spying on back gardens. Leaves were starting to unfurl, and birds nested at eye level. A pair of neat little squirrels ran along a branch right beside us. We could hear them chattering.

'Theo and Ben,' chuckled Gramps. 'Squabbling over an acorn.'

Four young men in stripy pyjamas and old-fashioned dressing gowns were walking towards us.

'Hi,' they said, one after the other, like wind-up dolls—hi, hi, hi, hi!

Once they'd passed, I turned to take another look. '*Pyjamas?* At lunchtime?'

'Students,' replied Gramps peacefully, as though that explained everything.

From our lofty height we looked down upon compost heaps, garden sheds and lawns. There was the ruined pillar that Gramps always said was Roman—a Roman pillar, in someone's back garden! In the yard of a restaurant, two chefs sat smoking in white jackets. We spied on them for a while, making up stories about what they were saying. Gramps thought perhaps they were planning on putting a laxative in the soup.

'Shall we take a breather?' he suggested, as we came to a corner with a seat. 'I feel a little worn out.'

He did sound puffed. As we sat down, a family came past. There was a mum and a dad holding hands, and a yelling little boy who ran ahead. The mum carried a baby in a sling. I could just see its red bobble cap and matching red bobble nose.

'Excuse me,' the mother asked us. 'Do you have the time?'

I looked at my watch. 'Exactly two fifteen.'

'Thanks,' she said. 'Don't want to get a parking ticket.' A minute later, they'd disappeared around the corner.

I felt a spot of rain, and then another. I held out my hand. 'Uh-oh,' I said. 'I think we're going to get wet.'

No reply from Gramps.

The raindrops grew heavier. After a while, I stood up. 'D'you want to go back?'

'Mm.' He pushed his hands onto the wooden slats of the seat, as though he was planning to stand up, but then his arms gave way and he fell sideways so he was slumped with his face pressed onto the back of the bench. The wood was digging into his cheek as he looked up at me. It distorted his whole face.

At first, I laughed. I can't believe that now. I actually laughed. I thought he was play-acting, being a clown. You never quite knew with Gramps. But suddenly it seemed as though the joke was going on too long. There was something not at all funny about it.

'Gramps?' I asked. 'Are you okay?'

He made a weird gabbling sound, and one leg pedalled as though he was trying to put it on the ground. I grabbed his arm and helped him up. He leaned on me.

'Okay?' I asked.

'Dunno,' he mumbled. 'Where we . . .?'

'On the walls, Gramps.'

'Paris?'

I felt really scared then. It was like a terrible dream. 'No! The York city walls, Gramps. Look, there's the Minster. See?'

He didn't see at all. He didn't even look. He slumped down all the way to the ground, and I shrieked in fright. He lay there, crumpled and helpless with half of his body in a puddle. His coat was wet.

'Oleer,' he moaned. It was sad, as though he was a scared child. He couldn't say the words *oh dear*, and tried again. 'Odurr.'

'It's all right!' My voice was a squeak of fright. 'I'll get help. Um . . .' I didn't have my phone—it was plugged into the charger in my bedroom—so I leaned over the wall and screamed: 'Hello? Anybody . . . somebody . . . I need help!' But we were above a garden and there was nobody around to hear. On the other side there was only the inner ring road, with traffic and those useless bloody daffodils. No people.

'Zoe,' mumbled Gramps. He tried to say something else, but it came out like no words I have ever heard. It could have been a foreign language. It was what Hannah might have called gobblydegook.

'I don't understand you, Gramps,' I wailed. 'Don't worry, I'll find someone. Just lie still.'

I tried to move him from the puddle but he was too heavy, so I took off my coat and put it under his head. *Oh God, Oh God.* I was sobbing in my mind, but without any tears. This was no time for tears. *Mum, are you there? Please help me!*

I don't know whether God heard me, or maybe Mum, or perhaps both. All I know is that I have never in my life been so pleased to see a party of Japanese tourists. They burst around the corner like a chattering flock of birds, taking photographs and exclaiming about the view. They were led by a beautiful guide in a rain mac. She had a tiny waist, a rosebud mouth and black hair rolled into a tight bun. She looked at Gramps as he lay across the path.

'There seems to be a problem. Can I help?' she asked, in perfect English.

It turned out that there were two doctors in her party. Two! It was a miracle. They didn't need her to tell them what to do. Both of them dropped down beside Gramps and spoke to him. They did things with his arms, and they took his pulse. They moved him into a different position, muttering to each other. Then they called something to the guide and she got out her phone.

'Ambulance,' she said. At the sound of that word, I almost burst into tears. I knew what an ambulance meant. I'd called one before. It meant Gramps might be dying.

Those people stayed with us until help arrived. I will never, ever complain about tourists in York again because they were so kind. I sat on the ground beside Gramps, and one of the women put her jacket over him, which soaked it. I kept saying thank you, and they shook their heads and clicked their tongues to show that they cared. One of the doctors suggested I talk to Gramps, so I held his hand and babbled rubbish about the weather and how he was probably just getting a cold. The pretty guide let me use her phone to call home. I spent a minute listening to our answer machine message (Gramps' voice, so calm and lovely) before it hit me—of course! Hannah and the boys were out to lunch. How could I have forgotten? She'd be gone for at least another hour. I didn't know her mobile number. It was stored in my contacts, so I'd never bothered to learn it.

I wondered whether it would be the same ambulance crew who came when Mum died, but it wasn't. First a man arrived by himself; then two more, carrying a kind of chair. One of them—a woman—crouched close beside Gramps.

'What's your name, Sir?' she asked.

Gramps pursed his mouth as though he was trying to force it to work. 'While.'

'While?'

'My . . .' he said, pointing at me.

'Granddaughter,' I said. 'His name is Frederick Wilde.'

She looked down at him again. 'Can you hear me, Frederick?'

''Es.' muttered Gramps, with a big effort. He was dribbling from the corner of his mouth. It was horrible. I looked away. He must have realised about the dribbling, because I heard him desperately trying to say 'sorry'. It broke my heart. He was such a gentleman, even at a time like that.

'Don't be sorry, Gramps,' I whispered. 'There's nothing to be sorry for.'

One of the doctors leaned towards the ambulance lady and murmured a word. He said it in a Japanese accent, but I knew what it meant. Oh yes, I knew.

'Stloke,' he said.

•

Apparently, if you get someone who's had a stroke to the hospital really fast, they sometimes give them this stuff that dissolves the clot. I looked it up later, because I wanted to understand. Two million brain cells a minute can die during a stroke. Two million. That's a lot. I'm glad I didn't know about that when it happened.

I rode in the back of the ambulance with Gramps. He was frightened, that was the saddest part. I could see his eyes rolling around, trying to focus, trying to understand. The side of his face had collapsed. I held his hand and murmured, 'It's all right, Gramps.' But I knew it wasn't all right, not at all.

'Nearly there, sweetheart,' said the woman.

The hospital wasn't far away but it seemed to take a year to reach it, even with the sirens and lights. Our driver pulled into an ambulance bay where more people met us. They transferred Gramps onto a trolley and wheeled him in, with me tagging along. One of the doctors was a woman. She was quite pretty, and she said her name was Jenny. She asked if I knew what time Gramps was taken ill.

'Just after two fifteen,' I said promptly.

'Sure?'

'I'm certain. I'd looked at my watch just before. Look, he'll want Hannah,' I explained anxiously. 'My grandmother. I need to try and phone her again.'

Someone took me to a telephone behind a long desk and showed me how to get an outside line. Hannah was still out. I left a message for her to phone the hospital, which was all I could think of to do.

I felt completely alone. I stood and looked around the ward, at all the coming and going, and I knew nobody had time for me. I thought desperately about who I could phone, who would want to help me. The fact was, I couldn't think of anyone.

Then I remembered. I was wearing my jeans, and in my pocket was . . . I dug deep into the pocket and pulled it out. Yes, the bit of serviette with Dad's phone number scribbled on it. Worth a try.

Please God, please Mum, I whispered to myself. *Please God, please Mum.*

I lifted the hospital phone again. My fingers kept missing the numbers. At the fourth try, I managed to dial.

It rang three times, and then I heard the best sound in the world. Dad's voice.

•

Joseph

Akash was on fine form. As soon as they'd met in the Prince Albert, Joseph sensed momentous news.

'Got a date tonight,' the young man announced coyly, once they were propping up the bar.

'Female?'

Akash ignored the remark. 'She's an architect.'

'How did you meet her?'

'At my uncle's place. She's even got the seal of approval from The Mob. This is our third date. She's dragging me along to some arty French film.'

'*Third* date? This is getting out of hand!'

'Mate,' declared Akash, without a hint of levity, 'I'm in love.'

'Those are three words I never expected to hear from you. Well, I hope she . . . hang on.' Joseph reached into his pocket as his phone trilled. He peered at the screen, but it wasn't a number he recognised. 'I'd better just answer this.'

'Go ahead,' said Akash, sinking his nose into his glass.

'Hello?' Joseph could make out background sounds, but nobody spoke. 'Hello? Joseph Scott here.'

A young voice, high with distress. 'Dad?'

'Scarlet!'

'Where are . . .' The words dissolved. 'Where are you?'

'In Leeds. What's up?'

'Um . . .'

Concerned, Joseph walked away from Akash, pressing his hand to his other ear. 'Are you okay? What's happening?'

'I'm in York Hospital. Could you please come? I really need you.'

•

Joseph burst through the doors of the ward. The lonely figure was waiting for him, young and vulnerable in jeans and a sweatshirt. She hurled herself down the corridor and clung to him, her arms around his neck. Joseph suppressed his joy. Only a heartless bastard would take pleasure in Frederick's tragedy.

'Any news?' he asked.

'They're scanning his brain.'

'But they think it's a stroke?'

'They're sure it's a stroke. They just want to know more about it, and they're probably going to give him some special treatment.'

Father and daughter sat close together on a lumpy sofa in the relatives' room. Scarlet's clothes were damp, and she shivered. Joseph took off his heavy overcoat and scarf and bundled her into them. He held her close to him while she told and retold her terrible story. He pictured her and Frederick consulting Hannah's shopping list in the supermarket; saw them companionably eating wedges before wandering together along the slippery stones of the wall. He saw poor Scarlet, frightened and alone, shouting for help.

'You managed brilliantly,' he assured her. 'Brilliantly. I'm really proud of you.'

'He was trying to talk. It was so sad. D'you think he's going to be all right?'

'I don't know. But what I do know is that it was lucky he had you with him.'

'What exactly is a stroke?'

Joseph dredged his memory and was doing his best to explain when a figure appeared in the doorway. A stethoscope hung around her neck, and she wore scrubs. Joseph's overall impression was of extreme youthfulness—like policemen, he thought wryly, as he stood up to meet her; even hospital doctors seemed to be getting younger.

'Hello again!' she said amiably to Scarlet.

Scarlet too had got to her feet, Joseph's overcoat trailing on the ground. 'Hi. This is my dad,' she murmured. 'Dad, this is . . . um, a doctor. I think.'

The newcomer smiled. 'Jenny Jones, medical registrar.'

'Any news?' asked Joseph.

'He's stable—asleep at the moment. A CT scan has established that there's been at least one stroke. He's been given thrombolysis to break down the clot, which we're hoping will limit the damage. We'll do another scan in about twenty-four hours. We'll keep him in, obviously. He may be with us for some time.'

Joseph put his arm around Scarlet. 'How d'you think he'll do long term?'

Dr Jones shook her head noncommittally. 'It's very hard to say at this stage. It looks like this isn't his first stroke; there may have been a series of small ones.'

Scarlet interrupted, 'Can we please see him? I don't want him to wake up and be alone.'

The doctor was about to reply when she was distracted by some conversation further down the ward. 'Relative of Frederick Wilde?' she called to someone Joseph couldn't see. 'Come this way—there are other family members in here.'

Joseph heard the tap-tap of female footsteps, and knew whose they must be. He couldn't escape. He was trapped. A second later Hannah had rushed blindly into the room, her face death-white and taut with shock. At the sight of her enemy, she halted as though she'd run into a brick wall.

'What the *hell* are you doing here?' she demanded icily.

'Scarlet phoned me.' Joseph fought to keep his voice neutral. 'She needed somebody. I wasn't too far away, so of course I came.'

'It's true, I did!' cried Scarlet.

Hannah's gaze took in the fact that her granddaughter was swathed in a man's overcoat. Joseph's overcoat. She seemed ready to faint. 'Did you honestly think Frederick would want you anywhere near him?'

'No, but Scarlet did.'

'How dare you show your face here? You caused this!'

'Hannah, I—'

She stepped closer. 'How much more damage will you do, before you're satisfied? Will you never leave us in peace?'

'I've never intended to cause any damage.'

'Get out!'

Scarlet ran across to Hannah and took her arm. 'I asked him to come. Don't be angry.'

But Hannah wasn't listening. 'You have thirty seconds to get out of this building. After that, I call the police.'

Anger flared in Joseph. 'For Christ's sake, Hannah, why do you have to be so unreasonable? I came here because I care about my daughter.'

'Really! Just as you cared for mine?'

'Yes—which is more than can be said for you.' Joseph's self-control was in tatters now, his voice low and furious. 'You know

Zoe made my life a misery at the end. You know that damn well. And I got no help from you. I wish you—'

'Excuse me!' Dr Jones held up a warning hand.

'—could admit that to yourself, for all our sakes.'

'*Excuse me!*' The doctor had a surprisingly loud voice. 'Stop right there! I don't know what's gone on here, and frankly I don't care. You'll have to sort this out somewhere else, because we don't have time or space for family spats. The pair of you might like to think about the effect you're having on Scarlet.'

Ashamed, Joseph looked at his daughter. The poor child was trying to block her ears, and her eyes were screwed shut.

'Leave,' said Hannah. 'Now.'

Joseph saw that he had no choice. He laid his hand briefly on Scarlet's head as he passed her. He was halfway down the ward when he heard Hannah's voice behind him.

'You forgot this.' She was holding his overcoat at arm's length, as though it was contaminated. He reached to take it from her, but she thrust it into his arms.

'Listen to me,' she hissed. 'If you care at all, you'll disappear and let them get on with their childhoods. It'll be the most decent thing you've ever done.'

Twenty-six

Hannah

They had him walking—though it wasn't quite in a straight line; they had him talking—though he sounded drunk, more so when he was tired. They got him to perform silly little tasks, like a monkey. He was an old man in a hospital bed, pyjamas rumpled on a shrinking body, clinging to the memory of himself. He slept. He lay and stared with empty eyes and sagging mouth at mindless morning television. He slept again.

When the children visited, he made a supreme effort.

'Scarletta!' he'd cry, struggling to his feet as she appeared in his doorway with her elf-hair and pale watchfulness. 'Theo! And my little . . .' I could see him smiling fearfully at Ben, trying different names on his tongue.

'Ben,' I said quickly, 'take your shoes off before you climb on the bed.'

He was in the rehabilitation ward when Scarlet turned fourteen. I'm afraid she didn't get much of a birthday; I'd spent the past weeks rushing between home and hospital, and was feeling thoroughly institutionalised. I threw money at the problem and paid for her and Vienna to go to the cinema. Instead of a party, the five of us sat in Freddie's ward, eating shop-bought cake and trying to be jolly.

'Fourteen,' Freddie kept murmuring. 'Fourteen.'

Scarlet grinned at him. 'I know!' she said. 'Ancient.'

When it's somebody else's husband—or parent—whose brain has been decimated, it's blissfully easy to be wise. 'It would be so much kinder if he just slipped away,' we say blithely. Or, 'He wouldn't want to live like that. Can't anything be done to end it?' We who have grey hairs think we know all about these things. It's a form of arrogance. When Freddie's mother's ninety-four-year-old heart began to falter—years after dementia destroyed her personality and dignity—I remember telling a group of colleagues that I hoped she wouldn't be resuscitated next time she collapsed.

'They should let her go,' I said. They all agreed. Of course they did. We sipped our morning coffee kindly, actively wishing that another human being would die and stop cluttering the place up with her dicky heart and her incontinence pads and her soft brown eyes. We told ourselves that we were only thinking of her; but that wasn't true. The truth was that she unsettled us. She reminded us. She made us look along our own roads, where we saw the convergence of parallel lines.

Now it was my turn. Freddie's turn. And by God, I wasn't letting him go. I sat beside him with my laptop, intending to get on with a backlog of work but more often researching *stroke*. I became a lay expert. I terrorised the ward, buttonholing every doctor who came within range. I'm sure they thought me a harridan—and a hard one, because I didn't shed a single tear in public. I shed plenty at night, after the children were asleep.

Freddie came home in early April, a month after he and Scarlet set off to do the grocery shopping.

Or perhaps he never came home.

When did I lose him, really? I don't know which part of my beloved's mind made him Frederick. I don't know, precisely, when that part died. He left me by degrees, so there was never a right time to say goodbye. I lost my soulmate inch by inch. I watched him suffer, diminish and shrivel away. I wonder what he or I had done to deserve that.

Sometimes I run time through my hands like rosary beads, and try to touch the moment of loss with my fingertips. I recall mislaid jackets and tea caddies and strange conversations long before the Big Stroke; a slack-jawed bafflement that I tried to deny. Yet a vital part of Freddie was still intact, even after he came home from hospital with his shattered memory, even when the occupational therapist said it wasn't safe for him to drive. According to her he shouldn't even make a cup of coffee by himself. She treated him like a child. Bossy girl! What did *she* know of Frederick Wilde—magnificent theatre director, witty raconteur, polymath? What did *she* know about how it feels to lose your youth and health? Nothing.

Freddie knew what was happening. He'd known for a long time. I see that now. He felt the sly slipping of his personality—his intellect, his *self*—down the vortex and into oblivion. He knew that Freddie Wilde was leaving the building. He tried to cling to his mind with sheer force of will. It must have been terrifying.

Meanwhile, Joseph Scott lay in wait on his web, biding his time like a hunting spider. The children continued to see him every couple of weeks and came home with their lips firmly buttoned. Freddie hadn't been home five minutes before Scott was pushing the issue about the children staying overnight. His solicitor said we had to get some arrangement sorted out before the summer holidays.

'No,' I said to Jane. 'We gave him an inch and he's trying to take a mile. I've made my decision. It's no.'

She sighed. 'Well, in that case they'll have it listed as soon as possible.'

She was right; we were back in court by the end of April. I couldn't let Freddie be exposed to those gazes, not in the state he was in. I went alone, and sat behind Jane.

The Siberian husky was as brisk and pitiless as ever. 'There's no reason why they shouldn't have contact overnight with their father,' he said to Jane. 'They've been seeing him regularly. It's a natural progression.'

Jane argued valiantly. She put forward every possible argument, and he listened with obvious impatience. Finally he rubbed his forehead.

'Oh dear, Mrs Whistler. Well, Dr Wilde may give evidence if you think that will help me. Step into the witness box, Dr Wilde.'

It really was like stepping into a box, an upright coffin with dead-looking wood and a reek of polish and unhappiness. Scott sat slumped in his seat, his face turned towards Dick Turpin's grave; the man they dissolved.

I took the oath before Jane led me through everything we'd discussed. I said all I could think of to say. I described bed-wetting and angry outbursts, night-time wandering and slammed doors; I talked about Nuala Brennan and her concerns for Theo, and Gilda Grayson and hers for Scarlet. Nobody interrupted. Nobody listened.

The judge sat with his pale eyes fixed on me. He nodded gravely from time to time, brow creased into lines of compassion. He took copious notes. It wasn't until later that I understood: he was going through the motions, letting me have my say. He'd already made up his mind.

'We've coped,' I said. 'Frederick and I. We picked up the pieces—three children who'd seen their mother die. We made a home for them.'

Compassionate nod. Scribble.

'Tell us about Frederick's health,' suggested Jane.

'Frederick is ill because of all this,' I said. 'He was fine before Scott came out of prison. He will be fine again, if only this stress could end.'

Nod. Scribble.

'And what do you fear?' asked Jane. 'If they go to stay in a caravan with Joseph Scott, unsupervised?'

'A dozen things! He doesn't know them. The younger two are a handful. They squabble, and Ben can be hyperactive. Scott may lose his temper. He may get drunk. He may say something to upset them. They may be frightened and homesick.'

Nod. Scribble.

'Anything you'd like to add?' asked Jane.

'Yes. They feel safe in their home. They feel loved. Staying with a half-stranger, with a man they've feared for years, in some remote caravan site is just too much for them. It isn't putting them first. It's putting Scott's demands first, at their expense.'

The judge laid down his pen and pinched the bridge of his nose. 'Mrs Wilde,' he said slowly. 'Sorry, Dr Wilde . . . Forgive me if my question sounds insensitive, but have you thought about your husband's future?'

'Of course! With the right input, he will recover. People frequently do.'

Again, the furrows in that brow. I was beginning to loathe them. 'Conversely, he may need increasing care. That would mean you'd be harder pressed than ever. In any event, it looks as though he will be less active in family life. Driving, and so on.'

'I'm ready for that. I have taken indefinite leave from work. The children are older now, and Scarlet is a great help. Many families manage illness. We're hardly unique in that way.'

'You don't think it might be a blessing for them to stay with their father from time to time?'

I laughed incredulously at the idea. 'Joseph Scott, a blessing? Hardly.'

Then I went off script. I thought it was my only chance—I didn't yet understand that I had no chance at all. I could have put on a red nose and done the hokey cokey in the upright coffin; the outcome would have been exactly the same.

'I'm not an intransigent battleaxe, Your Honour,' I said, turning to face him properly.

'Nobody's suggesting—'

'Oh, yes. I think they are. But I'm not. It's just that the risks of letting those children go to stay with that man are far too high. Please believe me. I *know*. My daughter married him, and look where she is now.'

He thanked me warmly, and waved Scott's solicitor away. 'No, Mr O'Brien. You don't need to ask any questions.'

When he gave his judgment, it was brief and to the point. It was in the best interests of the children to build a relationship with their father, which meant staying with him every fortnight, starting from . . . he consulted a calendar on his desk . . . Saturday week. And he expected that during the summer holidays, ten days would be on offer. Minimum. After all, what was ten days in such a long holiday? Understood? Good. Excellent. Well, Mr O'Brien and Mrs Whistler, perhaps you'd draw up an order? Lovely. Now, I think there's another case waiting to come in.

Thank you. Thank you. Goodbye.

Twenty-seven

Scarlet

You know, there were times over that first weekend when I forgot about Dad killing Mum. He became an ordinary dad again. Just a dad. My dad.

He picked us up in a blue rust bucket of a car, which he called his 'chariot'. He looked as excited as a big kid, but I thought he was nervous as well. When we pulled away down Faith Lane, I turned back to wave at Hannah and Gramps. They'd already gone in. That surprised me. It worried me, too.

It was May. The sunlight looked soft and dewy, as though it was shining through gauze. As we passed the shopping centre on the ring road, Ben spotted McDonald's.

'Can we go to McDoodle's?' he asked hopefully.

Dad grinned. 'With all the other McFathers having their weekly McContact visits? No, my friend, not today. I've brought us a picnic.'

After a long drive through the countryside he turned the car up a bumpy track, finally parking at the edge of a wood. We sat for a moment, in that extra quiet silence you get when a car's engine has been turned off.

'Is this the moors?' asked Theo.

'Not quite. Hop out.' Dad went around to the boot and lifted out a cardboard box, and then we followed him into the trees. Ben and Theo grabbed sticks and began to play fight, sliding on mud and last year's leaves.

'Careful!' Dad took Ben's left hand with his right. I looked at those big fingers, wrapped around Ben's little ones. I couldn't help it. I remembered what those fingers had done—I could almost see the blood on them. The last human contact my mum had was that hand smashing into her face. How could I spend twenty-four hours with someone whose hand did that? I stumbled over a tree root and Dad said, 'Careful, champ.'

Suddenly, Ben was pointing and shouting. 'Look, Scarlet! Water!'

We all stopped walking, and stared. I forgot about Dad's hand.

There was a lake in the woods. It was a magical mirror, full of sky and spring-leafed trees. Two swans were drifting on the surface, each gliding upon a reflection of itself.

'Wow,' I breathed.

Dad chuckled. 'I thought it would be fun to have our picnic here. It's not my home, and it's not yours.'

'Neutral ground?'

'Exactly.'

He led us along one edge of the lake until we came to a wooden jetty. We followed him onto it, through reeds and bulrushes—clump, clump, went our feet, echoing across the stillness—until he put down his cardboard box. A family of black moorhens came paddling out of some reeds close by. Tiny ripples spread from them in a V shape, and every ripple flashed with jewels of light.

'Where are we?' I asked, looking around in amazement. 'This is the most beautiful place I've ever seen.'

'We're in the grounds of an abbey—the monks' back garden!'

'Holy woods, then,' said Theo. He was taking off his shoes and socks, and plonked himself down on the edge of the jetty with his toes dangling in the water. 'Brrr! Holy water is freezing.'

'Well, it has holes in it,' said Dad. 'Also very large holy pike, apparently.'

I imitated the music from *Jaws*—duh *dum*, duh *dum*, and Theo jerked his feet out of the water.

Dad had tried really, really hard. It was sweet. He'd been to a baker's and got sausage rolls and buns with Smarties on them. He'd got cans of juice. He had crisps, apples and cheese sandwiches he'd made in the caravan—'In case anyone's still hungry,' he said anxiously, as though he wasn't quite sure how much his children might eat. Poor Dad.

'This is a great picnic,' I said, watching Ben stuff an entire sausage roll into his mouth. 'How did you know all our favourite treats?'

'How did I . . . ? You don't remember? I used to take you out for picnics, when . . . ' He stopped short, and looked away. After a minute, he reached out and ruffled Theo's haystack hair. 'Should we bring a fishing rod next time, Captain Theo?'

Theo rolled onto his tummy and edged his head and shoulders out across the water, like a plank. 'I can see hundreds of tiny fish,' he said. 'No pikes at all. Oh—look, Dad!'

He was pointing at a dragonfly that skimmed and darted near the surface. It moved so fast that I couldn't follow it with my eyes.

'Amazing fellow,' breathed Dad. 'He looks like an electric blue helicopter.'

'Gramps would know exactly what that's called,' I said, without thinking. The words weren't out of my mouth before I wished I hadn't mentioned Gramps. Dad on one side, Gramps and Hannah on the other.

Zipping my lips, I lay on my back. I looked through the depths of the sky and into outer space. There were dark dots, zillions of them, speckling the blue. I knew it was just my eyes playing tricks, but I imagined they were the blackness showing through.

The boards of the jetty felt warm. I could smell rotting leaves and mushrooms and damp earth.

'Can I have another bun?' asked Ben. Dad said he could, and then I heard the two of them wandering away to explore among the trees, chatting like old friends. I could hear Theo's feet swishing in the water. Somewhere very close by, a bird called. I don't know what it was (Gramps would have, though), but its cry was thin and reedy, ringing across the still water.

I closed my eyes. Just being by that lake seemed to calm everyone down. I can't explain it. It was the most tranquil place you can imagine, as though we were taking in peace with every breath. I felt myself sinking down, down through the boards of the jetty. I suppose I was tired, because I hadn't slept properly the night before—I'd woken up in the bathroom again. Gradually, the swishing of water and calls of birds seemed to fade away.

I was dozing when Theo splashed water on my face. It was cold and wet and not funny at all. I shrieked blue murder.

'You freak!' I yelped. 'Effing tosspot! Look at my top, it's soaked.'

Then I saw that he was laughing himself silly. Solemn Theo who wet his bed, sad Theo with the serious face, savage Theo who attacked his brother in the street. His eyes were crescents, with tears of laughter squeezing out. He looked normal. He looked happy.

So I giggled, and stuck up my middle finger, and called him a butt-hole.

'Ladylike,' remarked Dad, who was striding back. Ben trotted at his heels like a terrier dog.

Theo looked disgusted. 'Scarlet's not a lady!'

'She is to me,' said Dad firmly.

Back in the car, we talked about the caravan. Ben claimed to remember being there before, which was rubbish as he was a baby back then. I really did remember it, and so did Theo. We talked about things that didn't hurt anyone—the stepping stones and the rope swing. Dad told us about lambing at the farm, and how he'd actually delivered quite a few, and he'd introduce us to them. Nobody mentioned the fact that last time we'd been at the caravan, Mum was there with us.

But we were all thinking it.

So Mum was the Elephant in the Car.

•

Joseph

'Here we are,' he announced, swinging into Abigail's rutted yard. 'Welcome to Chez Dad. And here's old Jessy, come to meet us.'

The children piled out of the car, and he showed them the way through the kissing gate. Ben and Theo galloped ahead, rushing in circles among the buttercups that carpeted the margins of the campsite.

'Pretty!' said Scarlet, shielding her eyes.

'There's nowhere lovelier at this time of year.' Joseph picked a golden flower and held it under her chin. 'Apparently, you like butter.'

She smiled politely. Her composure was unsettling; he had no idea what she was thinking. 'Can we go down to the caravan?'

The place rocked to the thudding of children's feet, exploring, throwing open doors, exclaiming at the fun smallness of everything. Joseph quickly saw that someone had been into the caravan while he was away. They'd aired the towels and bedding and left a bunch of wildflowers. A plate of Abigail's rock buns lay on the table. He suspected Rosie.

'Let's paddle in the beck!' demanded Ben.

'Good idea.'

'Right now?'

Joseph hesitated with his hand on the kettle. He'd been looking forward to a mug of coffee, but he couldn't bring himself to refuse any request. Not today.

'I'll go with them,' offered Scarlet. She was ushering her brothers out of the door when she ducked back inside, whispering, 'Um . . . look, don't say anything . . . but you'll need to get Theo up in the night.'

'Oh.' Joseph blinked.

'Better safe than sorry. If you don't, he might wet his bed and he'd be mortified. About midnight, okay? He won't even remember it.'

'Okay.'

'Thanks,' she said, and disappeared outside.

Joseph was gripped by an odd sensation as he followed her. It was a mellow evening, and the hedgerows were bursting into life. The breeze carried a trace of bracken. Three children dashed around beside the beck, absorbed in some game. Two boys lugged a rock between them—one, two, three . . . splash!—into the water. Laughter. High voices, resounding up the valley. Two boys, and a girl with fiery hair. His children.

The odd sensation swelled. He wanted to shout, to let it out.

'Beautiful kids,' said Rosie's voice. She stood a little apart from him, looking at the scene.

'They are.'

They watched for another minute. Scarlet was stooping to roll up Ben's trousers, and he was tipping water on her head.

'Thanks for the flowers and everything,' said Joseph. 'I assume that was you.'

'Yes, but Abigail donated the rock buns. I'll give you all a wide berth this weekend. This is precious time with their dad.'

'You're always welcome.'

'How do you feel?'

He hesitated. 'Like I've got an airbag inflating in my chest. I'm blowing up like a massive balloon.'

'Sounds to me like joy,' she said quietly.

•

Abigail had invited them for supper. Darkness was gathering when they set off for the farmhouse, so Joseph opened the box of glow sticks.

'I remember these!' Scarlet exclaimed, as Joseph handed them out. 'Mum totally loved them. She always—' She broke off in confusion. 'Never mind.'

There was a ghastly pause. Scarlet and Theo exchanged unreadable glances. Even Ben looked wary.

'She did,' said Joseph evenly. 'She did love them. She bought these very ones, that you're holding. So you can think of them as a present from her.' He tried to smile at the three, but they didn't smile back. They stared down at their coloured lights, mesmerised, as though they held the memory of their mother in their hands.

It was Ben who spoke first. 'Thanks, Mum.'

'Yeah,' agreed Theo, nodding. 'Thanks, Mum.'

They set off up the hill, the children twirling their luminous wands on strings like spinning Catherine wheels. Blossoming hawthorns were pale smudges in the gloaming. As they neared the top of the hill, a van door slid shut. It sounded harsh in the stillness.

'Who's that?' whispered Scarlet.

'Someone called Rosie.'

'Oh, yes. I met her in the toilets. She was cleaning. We got chatting.'

'Oh? What did you chat about?'

'Digby. She said he'd just caught a giant rat in the barn. She actually saw him pounce.' They were negotiating the kissing gate when she added blandly, 'I think Rosie's pretty. She looks like a wildflower. Gypsy Rose.'

'She's just a neighbour,' said Joseph firmly, feeling the need to make the position very clear. 'I hardly know her.'

He heard a suppressed giggle. 'That's funny.'

'Funny?'

'She said exactly the same thing about you.'

Abigail served up a stew, followed by upside-down pudding. Digby was ecstatic to have company, rubbing against the children's ankles and basking in their admiration.

'We should have brought Flotsam and Jetsam,' said Ben. 'They could be friends with Digby.'

Scarlet laughed. 'Gosh, they're much too toffee-nosed to mix with a farm cat. They'd think he was frightfully rough.'

'He's as big as a tiger,' said Ben.

They did the washing-up (Theo and Ben squabbled over who should do which job) and were back at the caravan in time for a game of Twister before bed (*Not left hand on red, Ben! You bloody cheat, I saw you, did you see that, Scarlet? Left hand on blue . . . ow! You did that on purpose*).

At bedtime Joseph took them across to the shower block. They'd asked for another night-time expedition, and in any case the caravan's miniature bathroom was a squash.

'I like camping,' declared Ben, standing on a wooden chair to use the basin. 'It's fun.'

Joseph squeezed a blob of toothpaste onto the brush and handed it to Ben. He was determined to make a good job of these practicalities, because he bloody well wasn't going to give Hannah any ammunition.

'At home,' said Ben, 'we have a special rack where we keep our toothbrushes.'

Joseph felt as though he'd been slapped. The child had said the word so comfortably, so instinctively. *Home*. Home was with Hannah and Frederick. It was a simple fact. They were Ben's people.

'Don't forget your inhaler, Theo,' bossed Scarlet, taking it out of the sponge bag.

'I didn't know you had asthma,' said Joseph. 'How could I not have known that?'

Theo seemed embarrassed. 'No big deal. I hardly ever get ill anymore. I don't even need to use this every day; the doctor says I can stop soon.'

The three went to bed at intervals, in order of age. Scarlet explained that this was what happened at *home*, and Joseph tried not to wince. Ben and Theo had a squab each in the sitting room, but Scarlet was in the lap of luxury—a double bed that was made by removing the table and pulling a sliding panel from underneath the seats.

Joseph read stories for an hour, choosing them at random from the bookshelf. He could not stop thinking about the slender fingers that had last turned those pages. He heard the water-clear voice, lilting and laughing at Roald Dahl's foul-mouthed Goldilocks.

Finally, he put the books away. For a time he strolled around, picking up toys and clothes. He had the radio playing by the sink as he made his last round, bending to kiss each child. Ben was asleep at last, his round cheek sinking into the pillow and long eyelashes fluttering. Joseph lingered, savouring his son's warmth. The radio station had begun playing back-to-back classic hits. Abba was merrily crooning a sad song about Chiquitita. Joseph hummed along for a few bars.

'You have a nice voice,' called Scarlet from her bed by the kitchen, 'but that song's as old as the hills.'

''Night, Dad,' murmured Theo.

Joseph felt the airbag swelling in his chest. 'It's nice to have you here, Theo,' he whispered. '*Much* more than nice.'

'I'll get out my football tomorrow.'

'Great!'

Theo snuggled under his cover. 'Maybe we could have a bit of a game.'

'It's a fixture.'

Abba finished their song, and another merged into its closing bars. Leonard Cohen's gravelly depth, this time. Ah, yes. 'Hallelujah'. Zoe would have approved. She'd been a fan of Leonard Cohen, and this song was her favourite. Joseph could see her now, swaying to the slow rhythm, reaching out for his hands with the smile he could never resist. He watched her longingly for a moment. Then he ruffled Theo's hair.

'Sleep well,' he said. 'I'll just be through that door if you need me.'

As he straightened, he heard a muffled scream from Scarlet's bed. He was beside her in less than a second. She was curled under the duvet, gasping for breath.

'Scarlet!' he cried, horrified. 'What is it?'

'Make it stop, make it stop!' she shrieked, covering her ears.

'Stop what?' Joseph felt helpless. She was obviously acutely ill, having some kind of fit. Epilepsy? Meningitis? Psychosis, like her mother? Please God, no.

'Stop him!' She was panicking, really panicking, her face and hair wet with tears. This was a different girl altogether from the composed young adult who'd helped him make the beds and handed her brother his inhaler. This poor child knew terror. Joseph reached out to touch her head, but she jerked away as though he'd electrocuted her.

'I don't understand,' he cried helplessly. 'What do I do?'

Suddenly she was on her feet. She lunged at the radio, snatching it, frantically pressing every button. When this failed to stop the music, she hurled it onto the floor. Joseph swiftly picked it up and twisted the volume dial.

Leonard Cohen was silenced.

Theo was sitting up in bed, looking frightened. Scarlet stood rocking, a thin figure in the middle of the floor, her arms wrapped around her chest.

'Oh my God,' she sobbed. 'Oh my God, oh my . . . It was the man. The devil man.'

'What man?' Joseph asked. 'Who? I don't understand.'

Then it came to him, in a rush of icy memory. Leonard Cohen, singing 'Hallelujah'. A beautiful song. Zoe's favourite.

She often played it. She often danced to it.

She even died to it.

•

The caravan was submerged in darkness. Inside, the two boys slept soundly under bedding that their mother drove all the way to York to buy, on one of her last ever spending sprees. The duvets were goose down, and their covers matched the pillowcases: birds of paradise in a hundred vibrant colours. Zoe knew how to make life look beautiful.

There was no moon. No stars, either. The clear evening had given way to rain so fine and light that it was almost a mist, pattering its wet fingers dully on the roof and trickling in the guttering. Father and daughter sat on the top step of the caravan, under the awning. She was wearing his heavy overcoat, boyish hair half-hidden beneath the collar. Mugs steamed on the step beside them: chocolate in hers, tea in his. They each fidgeted with garish wands of light.

Joseph found his voice. 'I'm so sorry.'

She turned her stick this way and that, watching the trail of mauve.

'That was the soundtrack to my nightmare,' she said. 'My ultimate, oh-my-God nightmare.'

'I think I know why.'

She held out the palm of her hand, and he saw tiny droplets settle there. 'It's the music that was playing when it happened, wasn't it?'

'It was.'

'She was singing that same song. I remember now. Before you came in—*when* you came in—she was singing. She knew all the words. She was dancing around with Ben on her hip.'

Joseph remembered too. Zoe was dancing. Zoe was singing. Zoe was laughing and flushed. *What d'you mean, burned the exam scripts? What exam scripts? Hallelujah . . . Hallelujah.*

'It was still playing when I called the ambulance,' said Scarlet. 'I think I remember that . . . do I? Yes, I remember. The lady asked me to turn it down.'

Raindrops ran like glass beads along the edge of the awning, gathering in one corner before falling to the steps.

'Her last song,' said Scarlet bleakly. '"Hallelujah".'

Joseph put his arm around her shoulders, and she rested her head against him.

'At least I know what it is now,' she said. 'The nightmare soundtrack. Funny, really. It's just a song. In fact, now I know what it is, I recognise the tune. They used it in *Shrek*, didn't they, though it sounds a lot different?'

'I think they did.'

He felt her nod. 'That must be why I avoid watching that film. All these years, it's haunted me . . . I couldn't remember the words, couldn't remember the tune; just that deep voice, and how it made me feel. So dark, so cold, so scared . . . Turns out it's just a man, singing a beautiful song. A real-life man.'

'He's real, all right.'

'I used to think it might be the devil himself.'

'Not sure how he'd feel about that. He's Jewish, and he's a Buddhist monk, and a poet. Among a lot of other things.'

Scarlet pondered this. 'I bet he still hasn't got the answer, though. He still doesn't know where they go when they die.' She picked up her mug and sipped absently. Joseph could hear the stream chattering to itself in the black shadows.

'I have to ask you something,' said Scarlet.

'Okay.'

'You have to answer truthfully.'

'Um . . . let's hear the question.'

'*Why* did you hit her? I mean, what actually made you do it at that particular moment? You'd never done it before, had you?'

'Scarlet. That's . . .' Joseph fumbled for the safest way to answer. 'That doesn't matter.'

'It does to me.'

'Nothing excuses what I did. Nothing could.'

'All the same.' She turned her head to look at him. 'I'd like to know.'

Joseph thought for a time. 'Okay. I'd been marking A-level papers. Mum burned them all on the bonfire. I lost my temper.'

'On the bonfire?'

'Yes.'

A long pause. 'Out by the playhouse?'

'Yes.'

Scarlet's voice had become breathy. 'That day? She'd burned them all that day?'

'Yes—but it doesn't matter. It's irrelevant.'

'It wasn't her that burned them,' said Scarlet. 'It was me and Theo.'

Joseph had been over those last moments a thousand times, as though by some effort of will he might divert the flow of history and give the story some different ending. He'd stood stunned in the garden, staring down at the smoking embers of his marriage. There were still sparks in the cinders, still smouldering twigs. He turned the dying fire with his foot in the vain hope that by some miracle he was wrong; that the scripts were safely parcelled up and waiting in his study, ready for him to mark them and send them off with the courier. His shoe was caked in grey ash. He felt the crackle of paper, stooped, and picked up a forlorn little fragment. It lay charred in his fingers, edged in black, a teenager's anxious exam handwriting:

> *be argued that the fact that there are so many conspiracy theories surrounding the assassination of President Kennedy is a symptom of the paranoia and*

Joseph felt sickening grief for the young person, whose hopes and dreams and university places rested on this exam.

The pain of months—years—had caught light in that one moment. He'd been caught, spun and dizzied but never lost sight of his love for Zoe, and yet she seemed hell-bent on destroying everything they had. Grief flared and exploded, engulfing Joseph in a fire-red rage.

It was too much. It was too much. He crammed the charred fragment into his pocket. Later, it became an exhibit in the case of *Regina v Scott.* Then he strode back into the house, deafened by the roar of flames.

Scarlet was speaking hesitantly, as though recounting a half-remembered dream.

'We raked everything into a big heap. Leaves. Branches. Mum got it started with firelighters, and . . . and a massive pile of paper. She said it was the recycling and we had to burn it all because the bin was full. She gave us each a wodge to chuck in. She said we were people from some lost tribe, dancing around our campfire . . . It was fun. We scrumpled our paper and chucked it on. We burned it all. Then we toasted marshmallows.'

'Marshmallows.' Joseph sighed. The rage was long gone. It had flared with searing heat during the three terrible minutes between his leaving the bonfire and Zoe's head hitting the fender. Then it had been doused. Permanently.

'I'm sorry we burned the exams,' said Scarlet.

'Don't be sorry. You didn't know.'

'Dad?' He felt her fingers, warm as they clambered over his cheek. 'Don't cry.'

'I love her,' spluttered Joseph.

'Me too.'

The beck was trying to cheer them up, giggling and gurgling around the stepping stones.

'Do you think she's still here?' asked Scarlet.

'Do you?'

'Um . . .' She turned up her face, as though trying to read something in the blanketed sky. 'No. I think she's gone. I think she left us right then and there, in our sitting room. She isn't coming back. And you know what else I think?'

'What else?'

'I think we'll manage.'

Twenty-eight

Scarlet

Ben and Hannah were making biscuits in the kitchen. I recognised the smell of baking as I arrived home after violin on Monday—a warm butteriness that made my nose crinkle. Ben was wearing his red shorts and kneeling on a chair at the table, using a biscuit cutter to cut out gingerbread men. He was working extremely carefully, pressing down with all his might—until his eyes just about popped—and peeling each man shape off the board. When Hannah wasn't looking, he shoved a bit into his mouth. Then he smiled naughtily at me.

Hannah was standing at the table too, wearing an apron and rolling out the dough for him. She did air kisses and waved floury hands at me. 'Hello there!' she said gaily. 'Cottage industry going on here.'

I stopped to look at a very messy picture on the dresser, obviously one of Ben's from school. Hannah claims he's good at art for an almost five-year-old, but I can't see it myself. He uses gallons of water and oodles of black. The paper gets so wet his brush goes right through it, and his pictures always consist of messy black puddles and black sticks that he swears are people.

This particular picture was different from normal, though,

because it actually had some colour. In fact, there were lots of colours and an enormous purple swirl in the middle.

'Hey, Ben,' I said, and whistled. 'Nice.'

'My best ever,' he boasted, doing his chest-puffing thing.

Hannah's rolling suddenly seemed a lot more vigorous. 'Good day at school?' she asked.

'It was okay.'

'Learn anything?'

'Nope.'

Her fingernails were like pink seashells, coated in mother-of-pearl. She had them done at the hairdresser. It was what she called her 'naked self-indulgence'. I watched her hands, gripping that rolling pin as though she was trying to throttle it.

'Did you get your marks for the science test?' she asked.

'Nope . . . Those biscuits smell lovely. What's your picture about, Ben?'

Bang! Hannah's rolling pin came down like she'd seen a scorpion scuttling across the dough. Not so stupid as you'd think, my little brother. His eyes flickered across to her. He froze for a moment—a mischievous tongue came out and reached halfway to his nose while he pondered. Then he dropped the biscuit cutter, hopped off his chair and came over to show me.

'Here's the sky,' he announced, jabbing his forefinger at a wobbly blue strip along the top.

'Mm-hm. I thought so. Love the colour.'

'Grass.' Jab. 'Flowers.'

'And these white things?'

He blew a loud raspberry to show how dim he thought I was. 'Lambs, silly!'

'Of course . . . and, er, this blue box? A Tardis?'

Hannah was rolling that poor old biscuit mixture to within an inch of its life. By now of course I realised the picture was a sore point, but it was too late to turn back.

'Dad's caravan,' explained Ben. 'And here are you, me, Theo and Dad. We're smiling, see? And—' he pointed at two smaller messes—'Jessy the dog and Digby the fat cat.'

'And this?' I touched the swirl.

'That's a great . . . big . . . purple . . . *sun*!' Ben yelped joyously. He began to rocket around the kitchen. 'A great big massive GINORMOUS purple sun! Because it was . . . because it was purple when it was going down and we played in the beck.'

I watched him running in crazy figures-of-eight, bashing into chairs and walls. He was going totally loco and I thought I understood why. He had all this pent-up excitement, and he wanted to talk about everything, but instinct told him he couldn't. It had been hard for me to sound bored and unenthusiastic after our weekend with Dad. It was such a big thing, such an important thing, but we couldn't say so.

Hannah's lips were tight. 'Ben,' she snapped. 'Stop running around! It's going to end in tears.'

But Ben's legs just wouldn't let him stop. He began another circuit of the table and this time he was unleashing his Red Indian yodel. Unfortunately, Gramps came wandering through the door at that moment.

Hannah shrieked a warning—*Freddie!*—but it was too late. Ben ran straight into him at top speed. Gramps' mouth opened in shock. 'Oof!' he gasped, staggering against the kitchen drawers. One foot shot out from under him. He tried to clutch at a shelf with both hands, but missed and hit the ground. It was awful.

Ben stood there looking horrified. 'Sorry,' he said, in a very small voice.

Well. Hannah lost it. I have *never* seen Hannah lose it like that before. Never, ever, in all my life. The rolling pin rattled across the table and onto the floor. She flew across the room, grabbed Ben by one arm, swung him around and smacked him on the bare leg. I heard the sound of it—*thwack!*

'I told you!' she shouted, and smacked him again. 'I *told* you! Look what you've done!'

Ben was a stunned mullet. His mouth opened a good twenty seconds before he started to howl. By then, Hannah was kneeling down beside Gramps, gazing anxiously into his face and asking if he was all right.

Gramps looked totally bewildered. 'Just mis . . . mis . . . mislaid my feet.'

Ben's hullaballoo drowned out whatever Hannah said next as she helped Gramps up and across to a chair. I went over and picked Ben up, and he wound his arms around my neck. His face was slippery with snot and tears and he was wailing like his heart would break. I thought perhaps his heart actually had broken. I wouldn't have been surprised, because he loved Hannah so much and she was so angry.

'Hush, hush,' I whispered. 'C'mon.' I carried him out and up the stairs to the bathroom. Then I sat on the toilet seat, rocking and shushing him while he sobbed. The more I replayed it in my mind, the more I knew Hannah had lost her temper because she was terrified for Gramps. I was scared for him too. He hadn't been the same man since the stroke. I heard one of his friends say it had 'knocked the stuffing out of him', and I thought that was about right.

'Hannah w-w-whacked me,' moaned Ben, and just saying those words set him off wailing again.

'She didn't mean to. You gave her a big fright.'

'She whacked me really hard!' He pointed at a bright pink patch on his thigh. 'It's sore.'

I thought it was his feelings that were hurt really, but I rubbed the place until his sobs turned into hiccups.

'Would Terry and Sue like a nice bath?' I asked, once he'd calmed down. He nodded, so I sat him on the toilet seat while I turned on the taps. Then I rummaged in the cupboard for his bath toys: a pterodactyl (Terry Ducktill) and a blue whale he'd named Sue Blue. I have no idea why he loved this pair so much, but to him they had big personalities and adventures all of their own.

'How about bubbles?' I asked, pouring in some pink gooey stuff Vienna gave me for my birthday. It smelled of fake strawberries. Then I turned back to him. 'Skin a rabbit,' I ordered, meaning that I wanted him to hold up his arms while I peeled off his top. That's something Mum used to say to us. Skin a rabbit. I remember her grinning as she said that, and I remember giggling as I held up my arms. I knew what was coming next. She always tickled me in the armpits.

Ben held up his arms. I tickled him, and he laughed feebly. Then I peeled off his T-shirt and jersey all in one before leaning down to kiss his nose.

'It's okay, poppet,' I said. 'Gramps wasn't hurt, and Hannah will have forgiven you by now.'

He pulled off his own jeans and pants and stepped into the bath. The bubbles were forming a great white continent, and he slid among them. Then he grabbed Sue Blue.

'Swosh,' he said quietly, making her dive.

'Has she gone exploring?' I asked.

'Glug glug glug.'

I dropped his not-very-clean undies—*euw*—into the washing basket, and tried to fold his other clothes. I'm not very good at folding. I was thinking it was a shame Hannah hadn't liked his picture, and even more of a shame that she'd smacked him.

'Ben?' I said.

'Ker-splash! Oh, hello, Terry Ducktill. Shall we go fishing?'

'It was a good picture. Honestly. It reminded me of all the things we did at the caravan.'

A smile spread across his face. 'I liked going to the caravan.'

'Me too.'

'Will we go again?'

'I hope so.'

Ben played for a long time. I sat back down on the toilet seat and thought about Dad. About Hannah. Gramps. Mum. I thought about what a mess everything was. Steam rose out of the bath in a plastic-strawberry cloud, and gathered like a plastic-strawberry veil on the window. I wrote italics in it with my fingernail. *Scarlet Scott. Scarletta Scott. Scarlet Scott Rox!!!* The glass was covered in swirling letters when I heard a knock on the door.

'Scarlet?' It was Hannah's voice. Ben began to cry again.

I jumped up and opened the door. She stood there in her apron, with flour on her cheek and a deep gully between her eyebrows. 'The gingerbread men are ready,' she said brightly. 'They smell lovely! Come and have some, you two.'

I knew what she really meant, and Ben knew, and she knew that we knew. She was trying to say sorry.

'Yum! We'll be right down,' I told her. 'Ben's in the bath.'

She gave me a tight little smile and darted away.

'It was a nice time in the caravan,' said Ben, once I'd pulled out the plug, 'but I don't think we should go back very soon.' He rescued Sue Blue and Terry from the plughole and laid them on the edge of the bath. Then he stood up and waited like a naked Lord Muck for me to wrap him in a towel.

'Why shouldn't we go back soon?' I asked, as I hauled him out of the water. He smelled of pink strawberry bubbles.

'Whoa!' He staggered dramatically as I rubbed his hair with a towel. 'I nearly fell over!'

'Why shouldn't we go back soon?' I persisted.

'Because I like being in my house.'

'Perhaps you could have two homes. A Hannah–Gramps house and a Dad house.'

'No, because you can only have one house.' He picked up Sue and Terry and demanded that I dry behind their ears, too. So I did, which was ridiculous, as pterodactyls and whales don't have ears to speak of. Then we went along to his bedroom—which was complete chaos as usual—and I found his pyjamas scrumpled up inside the duvet cover. He was in too much of a hurry, and tried to force his head down one of the sleeves. I had to rescue him before he suffocated. Finally we got the top on, though it was inside out.

I expected him to go galloping downstairs at that stage, since there were gingerbread biscuits on offer. He didn't. He hung back and reached for my hand as we left his bedroom. His own hand was soft and still a bit damp. He tugged on my arm until I stopped and leaned my head down to his. His breath tickled my ear. Then he spoke in a sad, little-mouse whisper.

'I don't think Hannah likes my picture,' he said.

Twenty-nine

Joseph

'So.' Rosie unscrewed the cap on a bottle of red. 'You're busy being a real father again.'

'I think I am.' Joseph chuckled, incredulous.

'Judging by the happy sounds I heard this weekend, you've all had a riot.'

'Yes. No. Well, yes. What about Scarlet, though? If you'd seen her, so terrified . . . It made me realise how I've destroyed her childhood. And Theo wet his bed.'

'So did my brother Tom, until he was eighteen. He's running a chain of hotels now. Very happily civil-unionised, with his lovely Ivan.' Rosie tilted the bottle over Joseph's almost-empty glass. 'From where I'm sitting, your weekend went brilliantly. You pulled it off.'

He watched as the liquid crept higher. 'Whoa. That'll do—thanks.'

Rosie wiggled her head, mouthed the word *puritan* and topped up her own glass.

'I miss them already,' said Joseph, smiling in self-deprecation. 'Miss them like buggery. I only dropped them off three hours ago and I feel as though I'm in an empty waiting room, just sitting there until they come back. And it's a pretty boring waiting room.'

Rosie feigned indignation. 'Thanks!'

'No, no. I didn't mean . . . I just mean I've got used to them. Without those three clowns, I'm sort of pointless. Like an empty cake tin or something.'

'That's pathetic,' Rosie retorted. 'You are just as much of a human being as you were before you became a father. You have the same brain.'

'I don't know . . . Once you've been a parent, everything else seems a bit facile. Children do that to you.' He caught her eye, and could have bitten his tongue. 'Sorry. I don't mean that people who don't have children are facile. I just meant—'

'That only the fertile and partnered can be fulfilled? That only child-rearing is valuable?'

'No, just that having them is . . . oh God, um, I mean obviously not having them is—'

'Joseph Scott.' Rosie's dimples were back in place. 'When you're in a hole, stop digging.'

'Sorry.'

It was almost nine o'clock, but evening was only now drifting into the valley. Rabbits ventured onto the far bank of the beck and began nibbling at the turf. The landscape seemed like a Japanese painting, sweeping ink strokes in the silk-thin light of dusk.

'I'm always happier when the days begin to lengthen,' said Rosie, turning her face towards the window. 'It feels as though darkness and death are losing the battle.'

Joseph looked at her, surprised. He'd rarely heard his friend speak about her own fears and insecurities, though she calmly soaked up his. They were on to their second bottle of the evening; perhaps that explained this burst of honesty.

'*Are* they losing the battle?' he asked seriously. 'Death and darkness?'

'Yes. Tonight, at least.'

'I'm glad to hear it.' He took a breath, summoning his courage. 'I'm going to start looking for somewhere to rent. A house. Maybe in Helmsley.'

'Oh? What about the cost?'

'We're not talking Buckingham Palace.' He swirled the wine in his glass, considering. 'If the children come to live with me one day, they'll need something more than a caravan. And they'll need to be able to get to school easily.'

She blinked in surprise. 'You mean live with you permanently?'

'Well, we'll see.'

'Your in-laws aren't going to take that lying down.'

'Nope, they're not.' Joseph sighed. 'They've declared war and used every possible weapon, every step of the way. I can't see that attitude changing—can you?'

'Maybe not.'

'So the only way to end all the battles is for the children to live with me.'

'You think that will end the battles?'

'Yes, because I won't fight. I'll be ultra-reasonable. I'm worried about them. From what Scarlet's let slip, I reckon poor old Frederick is struggling now. How much longer? Scarlet's fourteen and the boys are getting bigger, stronger, more complicated . . . Ben isn't a baby anymore, even though everybody treats him like one. He's a schoolboy. How is Hannah going to manage all that as well as Freddie?'

Rosie's eyes narrowed in thought. 'There's no right answer.'

He almost always felt calmer for talking things through with Rosie. As the weather warmed, she'd gradually emerged from the shapeless layers of knitwear. They had been replaced by cheesecloth blouses and summer frocks. Joseph heartily approved of the change. This evening she was wearing a flimsy button-up affair, with quite a plunging neckline. Looking at the effect, Joseph thought fleetingly of Nell Gwynn, then mentally slapped his own wrist.

'Um, look.' He rubbed his nose with his forefinger. 'Please don't take what I'm about to suggest the wrong way.'

She waited, eyebrows raised, ready to burst into laughter.

'This cottage in Helmsley,' said Joseph. 'Or wherever. You're welcome to come too, if you like. Help with the rent. It might be a squeeze, but I expect there'll be a damn sight more room than there is in that sardine tin you call home.'

'Just a cotton-picking *minute*.' Rosie smile was wide and startled. 'You're asking me to move in with you?'

'No strings,' Joseph insisted, holding up his hands.

'And what are the children supposed to make of this arrangement?'

'We'd just be flatmates.'

She snorted cynically. 'Nobody's going to believe that, even though it would be absolutely true.'

'So? Who cares?'

'I love you, Joseph Scott,' she declared artlessly, stretching out her hand to touch the back of his. 'And I thank you for that gallant offer. But my answer is no.'

'Oh.' Joseph felt crestfallen. 'Why? Is this because of . . . that man you were with?'

'Yes. It's because of him.'

'Who is he?'

'Who is he?' Rosie regarded Joseph with clear, candid eyes. 'Promise you won't laugh.'

'I promise.'

'Seriously. Please don't laugh.'

'Scout's honour.'

'Okay, here goes.' She screwed up her face, as though about to bungee jump. 'I'm a nun.'

'A *what*?'

'You heard.'

Joseph gaped at her. 'You're not serious! You *are* serious? I . . . bloody hell.'

'Indeed.'

Joseph held up his hands, baffled. 'How am I supposed to react?'

'That's up to you. But if you start humming *How d'you solve a problem like Maria?* I shall have no option but to sock you.'

He let the information sink in, recalling the things about her that had intrigued him over these past months: her air of self-containment, the pre-dawn candle in her kombi; the odd fact of such a woman staying here, in this isolation.

'I began living with the community over six years ago,' she said. 'Though I still have to take my permanent vows.'

'For Pete's sake—what on earth made you do a thing like that?'

'I was contracted to work on the vineyard at an abbey in Cornwall. The vines hadn't been managed in years, they were in a real mess; but I gradually got them under control. My parents are Catholics—very nominally. I've always had a faith of sorts. It was pretty dormant, but I found myself spending longer and longer with the community, joining in with their life. They became my friends. One day, I realised I had a calling. It just hit me, really, that this was the right place for me. *This* was my family. I spent months thinking about it all. Then I joined as a postulant. Three years ago, I took my temporary vows.'

'So much sacrifice,' said Joseph. 'Too much. I don't understand why you'd choose to . . . I mean . . . well, you seem like a . . . you know—a normal woman.'

'I *am* a normal woman.' Rosie rubbed her face tiredly. 'Oh dear. Et tu, Joseph? I knew this would be your reaction. It's everyone's reaction. People are incredibly judgemental, incredibly negative. This is why I didn't want to tell you.'

'I'm not being judgemental,' protested Joseph. 'I'm trying to get my head around it. I dunno. You're intelligent, you're independent. Why would you want to do something so bloody medieval?'

'It isn't remotely medieval. I expect you think a modern woman would want to marry and have a career and a family and a car and a mortgage and a super-duper divorce complete with wall-to-wall bitterness?'

'No, but—'

'Or maybe a modern, un-medieval, liberated woman would prefer to be like one of the girls in my father's club—bung on a thong and sell herself. Lovely!'

'There are other choices.'

'I didn't choose the life. It chose me.'

'Jesus.' Joseph stood up. 'I'd better not use that word anymore though, had I? *Jesus.* You must have been shocked on a daily basis by my profanities.'

'Where are you off to?'

'For a walk.'

'Why are you so offended?'

'I'm not in the least offended! I'm just surprised.'

She smiled. 'Well, being surprised appears to have offended you.'

Moodily, Joseph shoved his feet into his boots. 'It's just . . . all these months, you've been somebody totally different to the person I thought you were. Your beliefs, your outlook, your future—everything. I feel cheated.'

'I am still the same person, Joseph. As are you, despite your past.'

'That's a fair point,' admitted Joseph, pulling himself together. 'I'm sorry. I'll just have to imagine a wimple from now on. You're awfully fond of red wine, aren't you, for a woman who's taking the veil?'

'It's not forbidden. Lots of abbeys have vineyards.'

Joseph jerked his head towards the fields. 'Coming?'

Several families were still packing up after their weekends, and Joseph was flagged down by a couple who wanted to extend their stay. Rosie waited patiently while he talked to them; then she helped him push a caravan out of the mud. It was almost dark when they climbed the gate into a small, sloping field with frothing white hedgerows. A posse of lambs galloped past. Their mothers bleated, but without anxiety.

'So why are you here?' asked Joseph, as he and Rosie crossed the field. 'Wobbling faith?'

'Not wobbling. My problem is that I'm not sure what to do with it. I was coming to the point of no return and I found I wasn't absolutely sure. So I ran away. Well, I didn't actually run. I had permission. I keep in touch by email. *He* certainly knows where I am.'

'He? Ah, the celestial bridegroom.'

'Don't be crass.'

'Well, if I were you I'd make a break for it while you still can.'

As if by mutual agreement, they crossed a stile into the next field, and then followed the line of a dry stone wall. Rosie's face seemed translucent in the half-light.

'My dad says joining the community *was* making a break for it. *Spineless*, he calls it. Running from the real world. Reckons I'm just afraid to get my hands dirty.'

'I s'pose he's not afraid to do that, given his line of business.'

'So true. What really gets up my parents' nose is the vow of poverty. They think it's immoral. They're kind-hearted people, but they measure success by the flashiest car and the biggest house. Life is all to do with amassing as many status symbols as possible, and the person with the most toys at the end wins.'

'Like Monopoly.'

'Exactly like Monopoly. To die without owning anything—really, nothing at all—is to come last in the great game of life. And I will die with nothing. I can't own anything to speak of. That's why I'm dressed courtesy of the Oxfam shop. Tom and Ivan lent me some money for the kombi.'

'So is that why you've got cold feet? Your family?'

'Once I take the permanent vows, that'll be it. I will have promised to stay in that same community forever. I found I was struggling with the permanence. And the obedience.'

'Yeah,' said Joseph, allowing himself a small chortle. 'I don't see you as the obedient type. How about chastity?'

'Ha! Everyone wants to know about that, but most people aren't cheeky enough to ask. Not as big a deal as you'd think. I was thirty-something by the time I became a postulant, and I'd spent many debauched years living like a true bachelorette.' Rosie giggled unrepentantly. 'Probably indulged in enough wickedness to last me the rest of my life. I got close to a lot of men, but never one I wanted to hold on to. Two were keen to marry me, for some bizarre reason, but it would have been a disaster. I had no direction, no plan. Feeling that call was the first time I'd seen a point to my life.'

Joseph stopped. A memory niggled at him; something she'd said during the heavy snow, as they looked out of Abigail's kitchen window.

'What?' she asked, turning to peer at him through the gathering dark.

'You once told me you'd seen a vision.'

'Yes. Well, that's a long story . . . Hey, if we turn up here and through the gate at the top, we'll come out on the lane. Might be a good plan, unless we want to fall down a rabbit hole in the dark.'

Joseph found he didn't want to go back to the caravan. He wanted to be here with Rosie, in the fragrant twilight. Spotting a fallen log, he sat down on it. 'We've no telly,' he said. 'No mates. No nothing. Might as well sit here and hear a long story.'

'If you snigger, I shall put a rat in your bed,' warned Rosie, settling beside him.

He elbowed her. 'Get *on* with it!'

'Okay . . . here goes. I was ten years old, so Tom must have been about eight. We were on a beach in Devon, messing about in the waves, which wasn't a good idea because there was a big sea. It all went horribly wrong. Tom got rolled by a series of massive waves, held under, had the breath knocked out of him, and suddenly he was way out beyond his depth. *Way* out. Mum was running into the surf, screaming. She's a terrible swimmer. She got nowhere.'

'How ghastly,' said Joseph.

'I remember all these holidaymakers on the beach, watching in horror as my brother was literally drowning in front of us.

I was screeching *Tom! Tom!* as though shouting might save him. People were trying to get to him but the waves kept throwing them back in. The sea is such an implacable enemy. Tom kept going under, coming up, going under . . . and one time he didn't come back up. I was hysterical.' Rosie blinked hard, as though clearing salty water from her vision. 'Then I saw someone far out there in the water. Not one of the guys from the beach, they were still battling to get through the surf. *Someone else.* It was a man, a young man, and he was obviously an amazing swimmer. I thought perhaps he was a surfer because they do go way, way out. He'd got hold of Tom, who seemed to be exhausted. He was holding him up so that his head was above the water. I remember it all quite distinctly, because that was my brother he held in his arms. He seemed utterly serene, this man. He looked right at me, and he smiled. And I stopped feeling frightened.'

A copper-green blush on the horizon was all that remained of the day. Joseph watched the colours drain away. He imagined the young man, the amazing swimmer, holding a drowning child.

'Someone got hold of a surfboard and used it to push through the waves. They managed to get Tom onto it and back to the beach, where he threw up a gallon of water. I looked around for my surfer, and he wasn't there. I asked everyone in the crowd, but they just looked blank. And later I asked Tom, "Who was the guy beside you in the water?" And he said—'

Joseph finished the sentence for her. 'And he said, "What guy?"'

'Yes,' said Rosie quietly. 'Those were his exact words.'

'Did you tell anyone about this man?'

'I tried. Dad thought if he existed at all, he was a surfer who hadn't wanted to be a hero so slipped away. Mum said I must have imagined him because nobody else had noticed him. But I knew what I'd seen, and I knew how I felt when he smiled at me. I believe I looked into the face of an angel that day—and you can take that look off your face.'

'What look?'

'Like I belong on the funny farm.'

'You can't even see my face,' Joseph objected. 'It's too dark.'

'I don't need to see it. I can sense that pitying look.'

Joseph took the look off his face. 'So is that the real reason you wanted to be a nun?'

'Possibly. Partly. Though for many years I forgot my poor angel. I was a good-time girl, Joseph. My life's been far less worthy than yours. I travelled, I partied, I worked, but I was never content. What finally gave me some kind of peace was when I discovered how to shut up; when I gave myself time to sit with God and listen. I felt as though I'd met my young man again.'

Joseph was stumped. What the hell was the correct response to all this? Obviously the mysterious rescuer was a shy surfer who saw what was happening and acted fast; a young hero who went unnoticed in the waves and chaos. It seemed a perfectly reasonable explanation. However, he had more sense than to say so.

'Blimey,' he murmured faintly.

'I can tell you've got more to say than *blimey*.'

'Um . . . well. All right. Why *your* brother? Kids drown every year. Millions starve to death. Too many get tortured or turned into child soldiers or run over by cars. Nobody saves them. Why would an eight-year-old called Tom Sutton get the Rolls-Royce Guardian Angel treatment?'

'I've no idea. I love Tom dearly, but there's nothing saintly about him. Look—let's assume for a moment that this was in fact a surfer. Let's assume he was a fantastic swimmer who just happened to be in the right place at the right time. Okay?'

'Okay.'

'How come nobody else saw him? Nobody! Not even Tom.'

'Who'd probably lost consciousness.'

'*Nobody* saw him. All those people, and not one of them saw him except me.'

'Okay, I believe you,' said Joseph, wishing he actually did.

'You don't.' She sounded unruffled. 'Still, at least you didn't laugh.'

The moon was rising as they climbed over the gate and made their way home along the lane. 'You don't have to go back to Cornwall yet, do you?' asked Joseph.

'I can take my time. They've been very understanding.'

'Will I see you again, if you decide to go back?'

'No.'

'Not at all?'

'We're allowed family visitors, but you aren't family. And . . . well, I don't think it would be such a good idea.' She leaped a puddle, her skirt swirling. 'I'd be tempted.'

Joseph stopped dead. He felt forlorn. 'So this is why you were so nice about my past. You were busy being all Christian.'

'Idiot! I was *nice*—as you put it—because I liked you very much from the day I met you; also because it isn't for me to judge what mistakes you've made. Goodness knows I'm not Persil-white. I told you that—and my father's a jumped-up version of a pimp! My posh education was paid for by a club that sold booze and tits. And more.'

They turned into the farmyard. Joseph reached instinctively for her hand, and her fingers curled around his. The contact felt utterly right. It struck him that he hadn't thought about Zoe for over an hour. Not once. It had to be a record.

'So finally we know one another's secrets,' he said. 'We know what we're both doing here in the middle of nowhere.'

'We do. The mysteries are solved. You're a killer, and I'm a religious fanatic.'

'So can we sleep together now?'

'Oh Lordy, another one with a nun fetish.' Rosie chuckled, gently removing her hand. 'What is it with you people? The wimple? The habit?'

'Thanks,' he said.

'For what?'

'For being here in the middle of nowhere. For being a fantastic swimmer. In the right place, at the right time.'

Thirty

Hannah

It became a hellish sort of routine. Every other weekend, the blue car pulled up in Faith Lane. The children said goodbye, gathered their things and walked away across no-man's-land. I dreaded it each and every time.

One Saturday we awoke to the dreary applause of summer rain. I thought Scott might have the sense to cancel, but of course he didn't. Ben—who was always more forthcoming than the other two—later told me they'd had to huddle indoors and play board games all that weekend ('I was bored of board games,' he said dejectedly). The caravan leaked, so Scott put out buckets. I'd like to pretend I was sorry, but that would be dishonest. I did wonder whether the damp had done Theo's asthma any good.

Eventually, Ben rebelled. It was June, soon after his fifth birthday, and it was raining yet again. Scarlet and Theo stood at the sitting-room window like vigilant meerkats, watching for the dreaded car. Theo was cradling his football. I realised I'd forgotten to give Freddie his morning pills, and rushed into the kitchen to get them lined up for him. There was a plethora of the wretched things; made him feel like an invalid. I was popping them out of their blister pack—two red, three yellow, and the big horse tablet—when Ben came trotting in, moaning. He had his hand pressed onto his stomach and exquisite suffering etched into his features.

'Got a tummy ache,' he declared tragically.

I squatted down to his level and put my hand on his forehead. He didn't feel warm. 'Where does it hurt?'

He lifted up his shirt, regarded his potbellied torso for a moment, then poked himself just above the navel. 'There.'

'There?'

'And there, and there,' he added, jabbing himself at random. 'It's really, really sore.'

'Do you want to snuggle down in bed?'

He nodded dumbly and began to suck his thumb. Who can resist a just-turned five-year-old with round eyes and a sucked thumb? So I made him a hot-water bottle and he crawled under the duvet in all his clothes. There he lay, smugly, with a very healthy smile on his face.

'Dad's two minutes away,' announced Scarlet, hurrying into the room. Her eyes glinted like shards of green glass. 'He sent me a text.'

'A text!'

'He doesn't usually,' she added quickly. 'It's just in case we don't see him out of the window.'

I didn't like the sound of that. It was a breach of the contact order, surely? If he could text her, she'd never be free of his influence. He could pester her in the middle of the night, or at school. I decided to ask Jane about whether we could stop him.

She'd spotted Ben. 'Hey, mister! What are you doing in bed? C'mon, chop-chop. Where's your bag?'

'Ben isn't coming this weekend,' I said firmly.

'Really?' She looked at her brother, who wisely wiped the smile off his face and replaced it with a mask of anguish. 'Why not?'

'He has a stomach upset. Could you please tell your father?'

Her phone whistled, and she glanced at it. 'He's outside.'

Freddie and I stood at the sitting-room window and watched Scarlet and Theo running through pelting rain. We saw them get into the blue car, to be driven away by my son-in-law. I feared for them.

'Well,' I said briskly to Freddie, once the car had disappeared. 'Cup of tea?'

'Where . . .?' Freddie asked, pointing out of the window.

'Up on the moors, remember?'

He looked shaken. 'Long way.'

Ben miraculously rallied, leaping from his sick bed the minute his siblings were safely out of sight. We all had a lovely time. He and I baked a sponge together, decorating it with icing and Smarties. Then he got out his plasticine, and he and Freddie made snakes on the kitchen table. Ben chattered away, unperturbed by Freddie's oddness.

That afternoon, the heavens seemed to run out of rain at last. Clouds parted like curtains to reveal a spring-cleaned sky. The sun had a special brilliance, as though it had just come back from holiday. Ben helped me to hang out the washing. Freddie also made a sortie into the garden, inhaling the scents of flowers and lush growth. He looked much perkier. I even dared to hope that he might be coming back to us, little by little.

Or perhaps it was I who was growing used to the new half-Freddie.

Scarlet and Theo were dropped home on Sunday afternoon, as usual. They looked poker-faced, as usual. And as usual, I longed to hear them say they'd had a vile weekend.

'Nice time?' I asked.

Shrugs. 'Mm-hm.'

'Do anything fun?'

'Just stuff.'

'Did you explain to your father that Ben was ill?' I asked Scarlet.

''Course.'

'Did he say anything?'

Another shrug. I didn't press her.

The next time they were due to go, Ben announced that he'd been invited to a schoolmate's house.

'Alexander is allowed a friend today, because his sister is having one. You have to phone his mum,' he said, pulling a scruffy bit of paper from the depths of his school bag. On it was a telephone number penned in very childish handwriting.

I felt torn. 'But you're supposed to be spending this weekend with your father. He'll be here soon.'

'Alexander has a flying fox in his garden,' Ben persisted doggedly. 'And Alexander's my best friend.'

We both knew Alexander wasn't anything of the kind.

'Why didn't you mention this before?' I asked.

'I forgot. Then I remembered. I said I'd go, so I have to go. Alexander is waiting for me to go. *Please?*' Ben ran to the phone, picked up the receiver and held it out for me. So there it was: a cast-iron invitation from a new best friend. It seemed abundantly clear that Ben was trying to avoid going to Brandsmoor. I called the number, and Alexander's mother sounded charming. Yes, she said, Ben was very welcome. Yes, Alexander had mentioned it—though she'd assumed it was one of those hit-and-miss arrangements children make.

When Scott arrived, I gave Scarlet a note to pass on to him:

Ben has been invited to a friend's house today. He is very keen. It's vitally important that he maintains his social interactions. I am sure you will understand and respect this.

H.W.

The following Monday, Jane had an email from Scott's solicitor. She forwarded it on to me.

Dear Mrs Whistler,

I understand that Scarlet and Theo have been attending fortnightly contact with their father as ordered by His

Honour Judge Cornwell. However, Mr Scott instructs me that Ben has missed the last two such visits. This is an unhappy state of affairs.

May I have your clients' assurance that all three children will attend contact visits from now on? If not, I am instructed to have the matter relisted without further notice.

I phoned Jane.

'Ben simply doesn't want to go,' I told her. 'He'll come up with a new excuse next time, for sure. I wonder what's going on? Why is he trying to avoid his father?'

'Maybe he just likes having you and Frederick all to yourselves.'

'No, no. It's more than that.'

'He's bound to be picking up on your unhappiness, Hannah. You're very close. Perhaps he worries about how you'll cope without him.'

'I'm sure he doesn't,' I snorted. 'I hide my emotions. I don't burden the children.'

'Send him next time,' said Jane firmly.

'What—force him?'

'Persuade him. Use bribery if necessary. I'm sure he doesn't always want to go to school, but you put your foot down, don't you?'

'That's *completely* different.' I was indignant. 'Come on, Jane. We're talking about staying in a strange bed, in a strange place. He met this man for the first time just a few months ago. It's simply not comparable to a familiar school, ten minutes' walk from home.'

'Try,' she said. 'Please, Hannah. I don't want this to end up back in court.'

So I did try, and it was awful. Ben and I packed his coloured satchel with his favourite clothes. He seemed chirpy, even ran to fetch his toothbrush; but as the time to leave drew nearer, he clambered onto a chair at the kitchen table and announced that he wanted to bake a cake with me. He said *please* could he bake a cake with me, and *please* could Gramps tell him a story after that? When Scott arrived, I had to prise that poor child away from the kitchen table and force him—wailing—out of the front door. He was getting rather heavy for me, but I carried him all the way to the hated blue car.

Scott must have seen me in his wing mirror, because he leaped out.

'Hannah,' he muttered coldly. 'Hello.'

'An unhappy boy,' I snapped, setting Ben down on the ground.

Scott forced an unconvincing smile. 'How're you doing, Superman?'

Superman clung miserably to my waist, and I leaned down to cuddle him. 'See?' I said, glaring at Scott. 'See what you're doing? Does this make you happy?'

I don't know what would have happened if Scarlet hadn't intervened. I really don't.

'C'mon, Ben,' she called brightly, clapping her hands. 'Fatcat Digby's waiting for you! If you hop in quick, you can sit by the window.' Ben let go of me and clambered into the car. She organised his seatbelt, chatting all the time. I didn't speak to Scott again, nor he to me. Seconds later, he'd started the engine and driven off.

That was the pattern for the rest of the summer. Every other weekend, my grandchildren would be taken away in a pale blue car whether they liked it or not. It was terribly invasive. It dominated their lives. They missed sleepovers and birthday parties; they missed school plays and gymnastics competitions.

They missed us.

We missed them.

In August, Scott took them for ten days. Jane was adamant that we had to allow this. The judge had made his views clear, and we'd be in contempt of court if we didn't cooperate. I hated getting them ready for such a long stretch away. We packed a lot of clothes, and I hid little treats in their bags. I tried to reassure them, especially Ben, but I felt tortured by anxiety—would Theo wet his bed, and if so would Scott be angry? Would they be able to eat the food he cooked? If Ben was homesick, would Scott let him phone us?

Once we'd seen them go, Freddie and I trudged back into a house that seemed eerily silent. The children's absence hung in heavy layers. For us, they seemed to stave off the ageing process. We had to gallop around at their pace, talking their talk and telling their stories. Life was vibrant and real. Without them, I felt like a husk.

I found Frederick in the garden on that first barren afternoon. He wasn't gardening. The truth—never spoken—was that he couldn't any longer, he hadn't the balance or the stamina, so I'd quietly employed a man to do it for us. Freddie was wandering along the edge of the flowerbed, sometimes stooping—very, very carefully—to pull out a weed. He'd collected a trowel from the shed as though he meant business, but it hung unused in one hand.

'Your roses are a triumph this year,' I prattled brightly as I joined him. 'They'll be glorious well into autumn, I should think.'

He was tired; it took him a long time to form his reply. I'd become used to that, and I waited. When the words finally arrived, it was as though he'd compressed them into a tight, not-quite-sense bundle. 'Unlesh the aphidsgetem.'

'Unless . . .? Oh, unless the aphids get them. No, they're very healthy. It's your marvellous compost we've to thank.'

He managed a wink. 'My sheeklet recipe.'

The charade of jollity was suddenly too much to bear. 'I miss them,' I gasped, sinking into a chair at the cast-iron table. I felt my voice give way.

My darling. He understood. He understood perfectly, because he knew me so very well. Somewhere inside that shambling wreck was the man I'd loved for forty years; the man with whom I'd chosen to share this one life I'd been given. Shuffling closer, he laid his hand on my arm. I could feel the gentle weight of his fingers. They calmed me as they always had, always did.

'Me too,' he said, absolutely clearly. 'Me too.'

Thirty-one

Scarlet

School sucks. Then again, when you're at school you know what to expect. There's a bell that rings bang on time—rush rush rush—and a timetable set in stone. I could tell you exactly where I'd be on, say, a Wednesday at eleven am. I could tell you exactly who'd be teaching us, and what subject.

Boring. But at least you know where you are.

Home life wasn't like that anymore. Nobody said it, but Gramps wasn't going to get any better. He was still somewhere inside that handsome old head, still loving and interested, but he just couldn't keep up with the goings-on. His thoughts and his words didn't seem to work together as they should. As for poor Hannah . . . well. There were shadows on her face that never used to be there.

The day we left for our long stay at the caravan, she was as tense as a tightrope.

'What will you do while we're gone?' Ben asked dramatically.

'Ooh,' murmured Hannah, playing with his hair. She does that when she needs time to think. Her nail polish was chipped. 'We'll be flat tacks! Lots to do. And you'll be home before we know it.'

'I could stay here.' There was the hint of a whine in Ben's voice. 'I could just stay . . . just stay here with you.'

'What will you be busy doing, Hannah?' I asked quickly, before the little toad could wind himself up and make a scene. He could be naughty about going to Dad's, pretending he didn't want to go when really he did. It had caused all sorts of dramas. I suppose he felt torn, like the rest of us.

She rolled her eyes around, thinking. The skin on her face looked dry, her hair wasn't quite clean, and she hadn't bothered to put on lipstick. 'Well, we need to visit a garden centre and get some seedlings—don't we, Freddie? You said you wanted some seedlings? I have things for the university, just finishing off and handing over. Oh, and Gramps has to decide whether to direct that play for the amateur dramatic society.'

I glanced at Gramps. He looked dignified as he stood holding on to the Aga rail, but his sweater was inside out. I could see the big label sticking up behind his neck. I thought it would be lovely if he could still direct a play, but I had my doubts. Serious doubts.

'Do him a power of good,' said Hannah, as though she'd read my mind. 'Wouldn't it, Freddie? You need a challenge.'

He smiled at her. His mouth began to form the words a couple of seconds before the sound came out. 'Mmaybe.'

'Look at you!' she cried, setting Ben on his feet as she jumped up. 'You've got that sweater on inside out. Isn't it uncomfortable? Dear oh dear. Let's put it right.'

I watched as she fussed over him. I don't think she realised she was doing it, but she spoke to him as she would to Theo. Even to Ben. She almost said 'skin a rabbit'.

When Dad arrived, our grandparents saw us out as far as the pavement. Dad always parked a little way down Faith Lane—Hannah's stipulation—so they didn't have to speak to one another. We all hugged Gramps and Hannah (Ben made a meal of it, of course), but the moment came when the three of us had to turn around and walk away from them towards Dad's car. I always hated that part.

I wasn't in a cheerful mood as we drove away. Far from it. I looked back as we turned out of Faith Lane, and I could see two lost souls standing on the pavement. They were holding hands, which was something they *never* used to do in public. I felt so guilty. I wanted Dad to turn the car around and take us back.

'Ten days might be a bit too long,' I burst out.

Dad looked at me as he changed gear. 'Really? You think you'll be homesick?'

I just shrugged.

'Let's see how we go.' He seemed disappointed, and I knew I'd hurt his feelings. So then I felt guilty about him too.

It wasn't a great start to the holiday, but Dad tried very hard to be jolly and it was always fun to be back at the caravan site. It was crowded with campervans and tents now, and there were children everywhere. It was all looking much smarter than it had the first time we came. Dad kept the grass perfectly mown, and he'd repainted the ablution block. He said he'd be starting on the kitchens next.

Abigail suggested we make a campfire, and pointed out a ring of stones down by the stream. We gathered wood from fallen trees along the beck. I chose a massive log that was covered in a squidgy forest of white toadstools. After I'd carried it all the way to the fireplace, I could smell mould on my clothes. It reminded me of Gramps and the medieval lichen that day we walked on the walls. I wished I'd listened properly, instead of hurrying him along. It was our last real conversation.

We used newspaper to get the fire going.

'An inferno,' said Dad happily, surveying our handiwork. 'Remember, guys—nobody is to step inside the ring of stones. That's the house rule.'

Theo and Ben got down on all fours, spitting on a hot rock and watching their spit balls sizzling into nothing. They're strictly forbidden to play this game on Hannah's Aga. Actually, it's easy to make your spit sizzle on the right-hand hotplate of the Aga. I know this for a fact, because Vienna and I have mastered the art. I didn't broadcast that fact.

'Disgusting,' I said.

'Have a go, Scarlet!' Theo was grinning from ear to ear. 'It's cool. It bubbles. Look!'

'Marvellous,' I declared sarcastically. 'You've made a boiling gob.'

'So, Captain Theo,' said Dad, settling himself down on a tree stump. He was holding a mug of tea between his palms. 'How did the gym club gala go?'

'I got a gold medal for my back handsprings. I'll show you.' Theo found a flattish bit of grass and then he was off, a flick-flacking little acrobat.

Dad whooped and clapped madly. 'What a champ! Ten, ten and ten from the judges.'

Ben couldn't abide seeing Theo get all the limelight. He started doing forward rolls, squeaking, 'Look at me, Dad!' Big mistake. He rolled over a sharp rock and collapsed in a wailing heap. 'I broke my back!' he howled.

Dad didn't look too worried. He strolled across and lifted him onto his knee. 'Let's see, does it hurt here? Or here?'

Theo met my eye, and we both made lying-little-sod faces.

'He's Hollywooding, Dad,' advised Theo. 'He does it all the time. Ignore him.'

Dad winked at him over Ben's head. 'But it's a good excuse for a cuddle, isn't it?'

Soon, Theo set off to see a family who were camping at the top of the hill. They had a boy about his age who was another football nerd. Once he'd gone, Dad, Ben and I played I-Spy. I think it's an unbelievably boring game, but I was happy to be sitting by the fire with Dad.

'Something beginning with L,' said Ben. 'Ellyellyelly.'

Dad and I racked our brains. 'Light?'

'No!'

'Loos?'

'Nooo!'

'Elephant? No? We give up.'

'Lady!' crowed Ben, pointing. 'And she's coming here right now!'

'By Jove!' Dad laughed. 'You're absolutely right.'

I spun around, and by Jove he *was* right. It was that woman I'd talked to on our first day, the one I'd nicknamed Gypsy Rose. I'd seen her from time to time around the campsite, but she'd seemed to be avoiding us.

Dad was sitting on a lump of wood, with Ben cuddled against his chest. He smiled up at her as she approached. Well! It was as plain as the nose on your face that something was going on there. He carried on looking at her far longer than he needed to, as though just the sight of her made him happy. I got the feeling they'd shared something important, like a secret. I hoped it didn't involve . . . Euw. The very thought made me want to throw up.

'Coming to join our sausage sizzle?' I asked her. I spoke loudly—rudely, probably—in order to make it clear that I had my eye on them.

She looked uncertain. 'Um . . . well, I don't like to intrude. Abigail made some flapjacks and sent me down with them. I'm afraid I ate two on the way. Couldn't resist.'

'Have a cup of tea,' offered Dad. 'And do stay. We're going to put a grill across the fire in a minute. Think they'll cook all right?'

'I've no idea, Joseph. I wasn't a girl guide.'

He got to his feet, still holding Ben. Gramps couldn't hold Ben at all nowadays but Dad easily jumped up, throwing him onto his shoulders. 'I'll just grab a few things, and we'll get on with our culinary masterpiece.'

After he'd gone, there was an awkward silence. Rosie sat on a stone, poking the fire. Her clothes were a fashion disaster, even for an older woman like her, but I have to admit they suited her. She was wearing a white cheesecloth shirt with a round neck and embroidered flowers. It looked old-fashioned but pretty, and it showed off her tan. Her skirt looked as though it was made of curtains. A long plait hung over one shoulder. Actually, she had hair to die for—dark brown, with little wisps curling around her face. She needed to dye out the grey strands, though, and maybe use some serious product to get it under control.

'School holidays?' she asked, after a minute of fire-poking.

'Thank goodness. I hate school.'

'I didn't think much of it either.'

I wondered what she'd been like as a teenager. She looked as though she might have been a bit of a rebel.

She scuffed her foot in the fire. 'Some people claim their school days were the happiest days of their lives. I think they should all be sent straight back there. It would serve them right for talking such utter . . . um, rubbish.'

She'd been going to say *shit*. I was sure of it. I liked her already, despite the vomit-inducing way Dad had smiled at her.

'Digby caught any rats lately?' I asked.

'Rats? Oh yes—last time we met he'd got one, hadn't he? As a matter of fact he's caught plenty. It's like a massacre up there in the barn. You wouldn't believe such a hefty animal could move so fast.'

'He needs to go to Weight Watchers.'

She had a mischievous smile, as though she hadn't quite grown up. 'Or join a gym. He could run on the treadmill.'

The question just popped out of my mouth. I didn't even know it was coming. 'Do you fancy my dad?'

Rosie pulled back her head as though I'd spat in her face. Her cheeks turned pink, and I felt mine doing the same. 'I'm sooo sorry,' I gasped, pressing both hands over my face. 'Can't believe I asked you that.'

'Don't worry.'

'My big mouth!'

'I've got a fairly sizeable one myself. In fact, I can fit my foot in it.' She put her hands on her hips, looking straight at me. 'Look, I really, *really* like your dad. I do. I could count my real friends on one hand, and I hope he's one of them. But there is not, and there never will be, anything more between us.'

'Why not?'

'Because there can't be. It isn't possible. And anyway, just at the moment he's got you three to think about. So you don't need to worry.'

I was relieved. Well, sort of. I didn't want anyone to take over as my mother, and I certainly didn't want Dad to love any other girl more than he did me. Then again, for some reason I felt a little disappointed.

'But why—' I began, but I buttoned my lip when Dad came bounding out of the caravan with a steaming mug and a big grin. He looked years younger when Rosie was around. Ben followed close behind him, talking loudly as he negotiated the steps. He was carrying a plate of raw sausages, made out of one of Abigail's poor pigs.

'The finest Earl Grey, Reverend Mother,' said Dad, holding out the mug.

Rosie thanked him as she took it. 'Scarlet and I have agreed that Digby should join a fitness club,' she said.

'Leave that cat alone!' protested Dad. 'He's happy with his weight. Don't you go imposing your body-image obsessions on him.'

I loved the smell of that evening: mushroomy wood smoke mingled with the soft air of the moor, and mud and water from the beck. Theo dribbled his ball back just as the sausages were turning brown. We sat around the fire and ate them wrapped in bread, with ketchup. The wind must have changed because smoke drifted all around me, and made my eyes water. I didn't want to move, though. I got out my phone and took some pictures.

Every now and again I'd wonder how Hannah and Gramps were doing. I told myself they'd be fine—probably loving the peace. I didn't believe it, though.

We played charades. My idea. Though I do say so myself, I am pretty darn good at charades. Rosie claimed not to have played for years but she caught on fast. She collapsed into giggles when it came to miming *Moby Dick*. I was amazed at how good an actor Dad was. I'd always assumed all of that came from Mum's side of the family, but his *Fireman Sam* was what Gramps would have called a 'thespian masterpiece'. I told him so, though without mentioning Gramps.

We played until long after our usual bedtimes, and then we lazed around and talked as the fire died down. Our voices were peaceful; even the beck sounded as though it was sleep-gurgling. A column of tiny ants discovered our dropped bread and carried it away, crumb by crumb. Rosie sat cross-legged like Buddha, while Dad sprawled near her with his head propped up on one hand. Ben fell asleep with his head on my leg, but still Dad didn't pack us off to bed. 'It's so light,' he said. 'And it's the first day of your visit. Doesn't seem fair to make everyone go indoors.'

We talked about all sorts of things, from bitchy schoolgirls to pop concerts to whether dolphins have a language as complicated as ours. Rosie and I thought they did. I offered to paint her toenails during our visit, and she wiggled her toes and said she'd love that and please could I paint little masterpieces on each one? Then the conversation moved on to Flotsam and Jetsam. Dad said when they were kittens, they used to go missing all the time.

'One time they totally vanished. We ransacked the house, searching. Mum found them both together—curled up and fast asleep in a cut-glass fruit bowl.'

We all said *Aw*. Theo hugged himself with the cuteness of it all. 'They must have been so *small*.'

'Just dots with miaows,' agreed Dad. He looked sad for a few seconds. I'm sure he was thinking about Mum.

A blackbird sang to us, hopping about in the hedgerow. He looked like a man in a black tailcoat. That bright-eyed, orange-beaked bird understood music and feelings more deeply than Mrs Hag ever will. The sky looked like the ceiling of a gigantic, lavender silk marquee.

'A summer's evening,' said Rosie dreamily. 'And to cap it all, the moon's rising.'

She was right. The moon gleamed above the moor, with the evening star at her heels. It looked as though someone had cut a fingernail-clipping hole in the lavender silk, and a spotlight was shining through.

After a while Rosie rolled to her feet, picking up Dad's mug and her own. 'One more for the road?' she suggested. As she was heading for the caravan, she glanced back at our fire. 'It's burned right down to the embers. Now's the perfect time.'

'Perfect for what?' asked Dad.

'Toasting marshmallows. Haven't you got any?

•

The next day, Dad drove us all to Helmsley. Rosie came too; she said she wanted to do some emailing. He stood close to her just before she headed for the library. I flapped my ears, desperate to overhear. I caught the words, but their meaning was a mystery.

'Tell them not yet,' he said. 'In fact, tell them not ever.'

She just smiled before swinging away across the square.

Helmsley in the sunshine looked like a picture in a jigsaw puzzle, with its humped-back bridge and jumbled stone buildings. I took more photos. The market was on, so Dad bought vegetables and a few other things he said we needed. We went into Thomas the Baker and got sausage rolls and Smartie buns, which we ate sitting on the steps of the market cross. Dad explained that the cross was medieval, and that's why the stones were worn into bottom shapes, from all the bottoms that had sat on them over the centuries. Ben made friends with a girl in pigtails whose parents were having a picnic too, and the pair of them played with her slinky.

While we were sitting there, a load of motorcyclists roared into town and parked in the square. They looked threatening until they took their helmets off. Their average age was about sixty. I'm not kidding—I've never seen so many grey heads and wrinkles in one place, apart from at Christmas when my school choir went to sing in a rest home.

'Heavens Angels,' said Dad. 'They used to be Hells Angels. Then they became accountants. Then they grew old.'

I spread my hands on the warm stone step. 'They've probably got Zimmer frames at home.'

Dad stood up, brushing pastry crumbs off his jeans. 'Ready to move on? There's a place I want to show you.' He managed to get Ben to disengage from his girlfriend, took his hand and led us across the road and down an alleyway.

'Where are we going?' asked Theo.

Dad smiled up at the sky. He seemed a bit nervous. 'I'll explain when we get there.'

Soon, we were walking along a lane. It had a strip of grass running down the middle, where the cars' wheels hadn't squashed it. On one side there were fields with sheep, and also the backs of some big warehouses; on the other there were five-barred gates leading into long gardens. We saw a bald man mowing his lawn. Next door to him, some toddlers played on plastic motorbikes (*Hells Cherubs*, I whispered to Dad, and heard him chuckle). A massive dog lay in the shade of a lilac tree with its tongue hanging out.

The next gate was a wooden one, wide enough for a car to get through. Dad stopped. 'Here we are!' he announced.

We were looking down a long, narrow garden. It was a hell of a mess. There were rolls of barbed wire, oil drums and tumbledown sheds with corrugated-iron roofs. The nettles were about four feet high in some places. At the end we could see a brick house, joined to the one next door.

'Who lives here?' asked Ben.

'Nobody, at the moment. It's been empty for a while. Actually, I was thinking of living here myself. Shall we take a closer look?' Dad unhitched the gate and swung it open—not easily, because grass had grown up all around. In the garden, Ben found a rusted swing and demanded that someone push him. Dad obliged, while Theo and I shinned up a big apple tree. There was a fork halfway up, and we both sat there surveying the place.

'You can see the moors from here,' I called to Dad. There they were, rolling away beyond the tiled roofs. The heather wasn't in bloom yet, but there was just a shimmer of purple.

From our vantage point we could see the whole garden. Brick walls ran down both sides. Under all the weeds and mess, you could tell it had once been cared for. There was an orchard and a paved circle with some wooden chairs and a table. Someone had built a trellis over that, and it was covered in white climbing roses.

'We're allowed to look in through the windows,' said Dad. 'But I haven't got a key.'

So we climbed down from our tree and pushed through the long grass to the back of the house. Dad carried Ben on his shoulders. The windows were covered in cobwebs and dust and smears, but we cupped our hands to the glass and squinted in at an old-fashioned kitchen with its own fireplace. A flock of sparrows scolded us from the chimney-pot; they seemed to be telling us that this was their garden.

'It's like something in a fairytale,' I said. 'A little lost house. Where's the witch? Where's the gingerbread?'

'Are you really going to live here, Dad?' Theo moved to the next window. 'You haven't got any beds. Or chairs. Or . . . anything.'

'Well, yes. I think I might. D'you like it?'

'Nn . . . yes. But I like the caravan.'

Ben wasn't listening. He was sitting up there on Dad's shoulders, making clip-clop hoof noises. 'Giddy-up, horsey,' he yelped, kicking Dad's chest with his heels. 'Giddy-up and off we go!'

'You shouldn't put up with that,' I told Dad. 'It's naughty.'

'He's just having fun.'

'He's being a monster. You shouldn't let him get away with it.'

Dad ruffled my hair. 'Don't worry. He'll grow out of it.'

We spent quite a while exploring the garden and looking in through the windows of the cottage. Gradually, a suspicion came sneaking up and bit me on the behind. Once it had taken a bite,

I couldn't forget it. I sat down on the back step and tried to get my thoughts together.

From next door we could hear the shouts of the Hells Cherubs. Ben climbed onto the wall and had a long and very silly conversation about their enormous dog whose name, apparently, was Yoda. Theo was lying with his stomach across the swing, turning himself around and around until the chains creaked. Then he let go and spun like a top. Meanwhile, Dad was poking about among the sheds. He'd hung his jacket up on the lowest branch of an apple tree, and rolled up his sleeves. He was wearing a pale blue shirt with no collar. I thought it looked romantic. He smiled as I walked up.

'They've had chickens in here. Geese as well, judging by these feathers.'

'Oh,' I said.

'And pigs, I think.'

'Oh.'

'Fancy keeping pigs? I'm sure Abigail would help us. Might be fun.'

When he got no reply, he straightened and looked enquiringly at me. His eyes were battleship coloured, grey-blue. A heavy lock of his hair had flopped in front of his face. He was definitely Mum's Russian prince today; a lost Russian prince, who might even keep pigs. He seemed as though he was doing his very best to be happy.

'You're showing us this house for a reason, aren't you?' I asked.

He looked wide-eyed and innocent, like Ben when he's been into the biscuit mix.

'Aren't you, Dad?' I persisted.

'I just wondered whether you'd like it. *Do* you like it?'

'You wondered that because you want us to come and live here. With you. All the time.'

He leaned against the chicken hut. Sunlight flickered through the apple tree and made water patterns on his face. 'Would that be a terrible thing?'

I pictured Hannah and Gramps with nobody to wake them up in the mornings, nobody to kiss goodnight. I pictured them eating supper. Just the two of them. Quietly. Sadly. Alone.

I imagined growing up with a real dad. *My* dad. I imagined living in this house with its apple trees, having him to take care of us and being there when things went wrong for us. I wouldn't have to worry about Ben and Theo anymore; Dad would do the worrying.

And all the time Leonard Cohen sang 'Hallelujah', and Dad's fist smacked into Mum's face, and she hit the ground with that final clunking sound.

It was just too much. It meant too much. I felt as though the earth was moving under my feet, and I was losing my balance. I was going to fall.

So I said nothing at all.

Thirty-two

Joseph

The children's last day at Brandsmoor was a masterstroke. Joseph didn't want them to spend it thinking about how they'd be leaving that evening. He didn't want that for himself, or for them. Together, he and Scarlet planned the ultimate day out for a railway enthusiast like Theo—a journey to Whitby on the North Yorkshire Moors Railway. Rosie refused to come at first, insisting that she shouldn't intrude, but the children nagged so desperately that she dived into the car at the last minute, wearing sandals to display the lurid patterns Scarlet had painted on her toenails.

Theo was struck completely dumb when he saw the massive shining dragon, snorting and hissing by the platform at Pickering Station. He stood transfixed. Scarlet took a picture of him with her phone.

'Oh my God, Dad,' she breathed, as they settled into a wood-panelled carriage. 'This is amazing. It's the Hogwarts Express.'

For that one day, their family seemed almost normal. The steam-powered journey across the moors landscape was an adventure (though Ben and Theo came to blows over who would look out of which window); Whitby awaited them with a sandy beach and fish and chips (though Ben bit his tongue and cried);

and the five of them were singing at the tops of their voices as they drove home. Rosie was conducting.

She'll be coming round the mountain when she comes (WHEN SHE COMES!).

She'll be coming round the mountain when she comes.

Joseph turned into the farmyard, ducking his head to avoid the blast of Ben bellowing in his ear: *WHEN! SHE! COMES!* As he parked, Abigail was emerging purposefully from the house.

She'll be wearing pink pyjamas when she comes! sang Rosie.

Theo giggled. 'I bet Abigail wears pink pyjamas.'

'Now, now. Show a bit of respect,' said Joseph mildly, and pulled on the handbrake. 'Last station,' he called, in the nasal voice of the guard who'd been in charge on the train. 'All change, please. We'll have to leave for York in an hour, if I'm to get you home in time.'

Rosie, Theo and Scarlet set off through the kissing gate, but Joseph waited as Abigail approached. Ben was holding his hand.

'Afternoon,' called Joseph. 'All well with the happy campers?'

'One of the toasters blew up and set off the fire alarm. Then a toilet got blocked. Don't fret, it's all been taken care of. You've got a message.'

'A message?'

'Your sister.'

'Marie—really?' Joseph whistled in surprise.

'Says to contact her. Urgent.'

•

The phone rang only once before it was answered. Marie's voice, her accent stronger than ever. 'Hello, Joe.'

'Marie! What's happened?'

'You've continued to wreak havoc, that's what's happened. Frederick Wilde had another stroke today.'

'Oh no,' groaned Joseph, and meant it. 'How bad?'

'They're at the hospital.'

'He's conscious?'

'Apparently. It's often drip-drip-drip with strokes, isn't it?'

Joseph looked down at Ben, who lay by the range with Digby in his arms. 'You wouldn't wish it on your worst enemy.'

'Frederick's your worst enemy? Well, anyway. Hannah asked me to ask you to keep the children another night. Naturally, she hates the idea, but she's got no choice. I'd come and get them from you but I'm on duty at the refuge.'

The line crackled with animosity. Joseph almost felt the heat on his ear. 'Why did she phone you?' he asked. 'How come you're the go-between?'

'Who else is prepared to talk to you?'

'I'll keep them forever, if she wants.'

Marie's voice sharpened. 'Don't you dare even suggest such a thing.'

'Maybe it would be better for everybody. Freddie's going to need a lot of nursing care soon, if he doesn't already.'

'Back off, Joe!' Marie sounded ready to explode. 'I'm warning you. Back off. You hear me? You bloody well take them home tomorrow. Then you back right off and give them all some space. Jesus, man, have you no compassion?'

It was useless to argue. 'Ask Hannah to text me,' sighed Joseph. 'You've got my number. I'll climb the hill and check my messages last thing tonight. Ask her please to send a progress report on Frederick, for the kids' sake. Could you do that?'

'Okay.'

Unspoken words hung drearily between them. Neither brother nor sister seemed keen to end the conversation. 'So,' began Joseph, 'how are you?'

'I'm fine, Joe. Just fine. Now, if you'll excuse me—'

'Still busy at the refuge?'

'Very. There's plenty of abused women out there. Plenty of men who never grew up.'

He ignored the jibe. 'Are you . . .? You know. With somebody?'

'Are you?'

'No.'

There was a long pause while Joseph racked his brains for some way to prolong the conversation. Marie wasn't gushing with warmth, but at least she was talking. It was a breakthrough of sorts.

'Did you hear about Gus?' he asked. 'He's left.'

'Abigail tells me you're Gus now. She says you've been sprucing everything up and it's all running like clockwork. No bad thing—the place was looking scruffy last time I was there.'

'I've had to do a bit of DIY on our own caravan. The roof was leaking.'

Marie laughed shortly. 'It always did. Mum used to put saucepans out.'

'Did she? I'd forgotten. That would explain the smell of damp. Anyway, I think I've plugged all the holes. Um . . . have you heard from Dad at all?'

'I phone him once a month. He never bothers to return the favour.'

'Any news?'

Marie snorted. 'Nothing but moaning. From what I can make out, he spends his life drinking rum with other losers.'

'So after all that dreaming, money didn't make him happy?'

'Nope. Bored to tears.'

'Poor old Dad.'

'He's a fool.'

Marie might think their father a fool, reflected Joseph, but she phoned once a month to check up on him. It was more than he'd ever done. 'Anyway. Thanks for letting me know about Frederick,' he said.

'Yeah . . . well. Bye.'

The call ended with a curt little snap.

'Whooo was that?' asked Ben, imitating an owl from his prone position by the range. 'Whoo? Whoo?'

'Your Aunty Marie.' Joseph replaced the receiver. 'Let's go and find the others.'

They crossed the farmyard, Ben swinging from his father's arm while he long-jumped the cowpats. He kept up a running commentary—*three two one take off! Ooh, that's a slushy one, I think that cow had a runny tum . . . Oops, stepped in it.*

Joseph barely paid attention. His mind rattled with thoughts of Frederick, and how he should tell the children. Scarlet met him halfway up the hill, her hair shining like copper wire in the sunshine.

'They've built a new rope swing while we were out,' she announced. 'D'you want to come and see it? Do we have to go yet?' She looked more closely at his face. 'What's up?'

'Gramps was taken ill today,' he said, and saw fear widen her eyes. Poor Scarlet. She seemed always to be shrinking from the next blow.

•

Late that evening, once the three children were in bed, he sat on the caravan steps beside Rosie.

'What a way to go,' he said heavily.

'You like him very much, don't you?'

'A gentleman. Bloody clever. Bloody nice.' Joseph blew out his cheeks, picturing the angular figure who'd greeted him with such courtesy at York Station a lifetime ago; the father who loved Zoe with a passion that never faltered. That man was changing. He was leaving. 'He's been the best thing in the children's lives since their mother died. He's wise and affectionate and . . . God knows how they'd manage without him.'

'But there's Grandma.'

'She's a snob. An intellectual snob, at least. My God, she can be cold!' Joseph shuddered.

'So Freddie's the peacemaker?'

'Yes. The peacemaker. Just by being there.'

'It's vile,' said Rosie bitterly. 'Death by a hundred strokes—I'd rather go under a bus.'

Bats zipped overhead as quick as thoughts, hunting insects in the moonlight. Inside the caravan, all was quiet. Joseph had left Theo and Ben sleeping with their faces pressed into the birds-of-paradise pillows that their mother chose, their fingers tight around the glow sticks she'd left in the drawer. Scarlet lay awake, staring at the ceiling, no doubt fretting about her grandfather.

Joseph began to plan for their future.

Thirty-three

Dear Mrs Whistler,

Your clients will be aware that Joseph Scott has recently moved into Flawith Cottage, Back Lane, Helmsley, from where he will continue to work for Miss Abigail Gilmour. He intends to rent this property in the long term and is in the process of redecorating it. I am sure you will agree that he has taken all possible steps to provide a stable home for the children to visit.

I understand that Frederick Wilde suffered a further stroke in August of this year, and Mr Scott asks me to extend his deep concern and sympathy to both your clients. He is aware that Mr Wilde spent two nights in hospital and that his speech has deteriorated somewhat. Clearly this state of affairs must be putting a great deal of strain on both grandparents.

Mr Scott is keen to acknowledge the excellent care the Wildes have given the children. However, he suggests that the time has now come for the children to live with him permanently. Flawith Cottage has four bedrooms and a large garden, and is close to excellent schools. Your clients are welcome to visit, to assure themselves that it is an appropriate home. The September term is now underway, and Mr Scott suggests that it might be easiest if all parties work towards making this move during the Christmas school holidays. He is more than happy for the children to visit their grandparents regularly, and will actively facilitate such contact.

I look forward to hearing your clients' response as soon as possible.

•

Dear Mr O'Brien,

Thank you for your letter of 10th September.

I feel obliged to express my astonishment at your client's using a difficult event as an occasion to question the children's residence with their grandparents. I would remind you that the Wildes have now been primary carers for over four years; indeed, Ben has no memory whatsoever of living with any other carer. Really, your client's cavalier and opportunistic attitude beggars belief.

The Wildes have facilitated contact between the children and their father for the past eight months in an exemplary fashion and will continue to do so. Yet at every step he appears to want more, and they question whether he will ever be satisfied.

Let me make it absolutely clear that there will be no agreed change of residence for these children. Their needs are being well met, and it cannot be in their best interests to change the status quo. Please advise your client accordingly.

On another note, my clients understand that the house at Back Lane is damp, and Theo complains that this exacerbates his asthma. In addition, when Ben came home after the last contact visit he was wearing the same clothes he had left in the day before, and did not appear to have washed all weekend. Please address these matters with your client.

•

Dear Mrs Whistler,

Thank you for your letter of 20th September.

Mr Scott's suggestion was motivated entirely by concern for his children. Frankly, I find your description of him as 'cavalier' and 'opportunistic' both unwarranted and unhelpful.

It is clear to Mr Scott that Frederick Wilde's condition is worsening. He is extremely saddened by this on a personal level, as he had at one time a close relationship with Mr Wilde. He wishes me to reiterate that he only wants what is best for the children.

Please reply by return. If your clients continue to be intransigent, Mr Scott will have no option but to apply for a residence order without further reference to you.

•

Scarlet

Mr Hardy met me and Theo after school, and we went for a walk beside the river. Autumn was in the air; stillness and smoke. There were rowers sliding along the water. Nine men above it, nine in the underwater world of their reflection. Eight oars moved in perfect unison, as though the boat was an eight-legged creature. That was more than could be said for my family.

'I'm like a bad penny,' said Mr Hardy. 'I keep turning up.'

I smiled politely, wishing he didn't.

'Do you know why I'm here again?' he asked.

'Yep.'

'Can you tell me, then?'

Theo pretended he wasn't listening, and turned his back to watch the rowers. I felt like doing the same thing. The fact was that we didn't want to answer any more questions about our future. We didn't want to think about it. We didn't want to have this conversation.

'We walked up those steps,' I said sadly, pointing to a bridge nearby. 'Gramps and me. It was a few minutes before the Big Stroke.'

'He's not been so well, has he?'

'Not so well. Mum died in one second—*bam!* My last memory of her alive is dancing and singing. But Gramps is changing slowly. I still love him as much as ever, perhaps even more in a way, but . . .'

'But?' prompted Mr Hardy.

'But he used to be strong. Old, but strong. He drove me around and winked when Hannah was having an eppy, and told stories and . . . made everything all right. He was a good friend. I mean, he still is a good friend, but now I feel I have to care for him. Not the other way around.'

'Hmm. That must be a big change.'

'He can't talk properly,' Theo said angrily. He was looking a bit peaky, but then he often did nowadays.

'It's true,' I agreed. 'He can't. Sometimes he can't seem to think of any words, or the wrong words come out of his mouth. It's like there are big crevasses and his words fall down them. So he tries to do all his talking with smiles. Some days he seems better, some days worse, and on the worse days I'm not sure he's even thinking straight. Yesterday he got himself shut in the downstairs loo and he couldn't get the door open.'

'He was . . .' Theo beat frantically at an imaginary door. 'Bang bang bang! And yelling.'

'Hannah nearly had a heart attack,' I said. 'She thought we'd have to get in a neighbour to break the door down—but you know what? It wasn't even locked.'

Mr Hardy tutted. 'Oh dear.'

'It was sad,' said Theo, and kicked a pebble with his foot.

It *was* sad. When we finally got Gramps out he tried to laugh at himself, but there were tears in his eyes. I think he'd been really frightened.

'Have you talked to your father about this?' asked Mr Hardy.

We both shook our heads. I felt like crying. 'We never mention them to him. We never mention him to them, either. When I'm with them I feel ashamed for even seeing my dad.'

'They don't speak to each other at all, your father and your grandparents?'

'Speak? Ha! They won't even *look* at each other!'

'That's true,' said Theo glumly. 'Dad parks down the street and we have to walk to his car. It's like being on both sides of a war at once.'

The path was wide in the place where we were walking. People on skateboards and bicycles were shooting past. A plump woman bustled along with three yappy little dogs on leads. She nodded at Mr Hardy.

'Afternoon, Lester,' she said. 'There's a nip in the air.' Then she tappity-tapped off in her high heels, talking baby language to the dogs.

'Do you know her?' I asked.

Mr Hardy tilted his head to one side, as though trying to decide whether he'd ever clapped eyes on the woman. 'Clerk, down at the court. I meet a lot of people in this job. What do you think of your dad's new house?'

'It's lovely—isn't it, Theo? Well, it will be once he's finished painting it. We chose the colours. There's more space than in the caravan. We've got our own bedrooms.'

Theo made a face. 'Yeah, but it's not so fun. I've got friends at the campsite, and there's Abigail. And the animals. And Rosie.'

'Rosie?' asked Mr Hardy.

I rolled my eyes. 'Dad's *not* girlfriend. Dad's *just-good-friend*.'

'Oh?'

'I really think she is a just-good-friend, but she and Dad are always laughing when they're together. She lives in a van at Brandsmoor and does a bit of work for Abigail, cleaning the site kitchen and stuff. She looks like a gypsy.'

'Wish we had some bread,' said Theo. A duck was swimming alongside us, gabbling hopefully.

'I should have thought to bring some,' said Mr Hardy. He started asking me about schools and whether I knew anyone at Ryedale, the school I'd go to if we moved to Dad's. I did, actually, because one of the girls I'd met at the campsite went there. Theo and I told him about the rope swing, and the dams we'd built, and our trip on the steam railway. I realised later that between us we'd done quite a lot of talking, but he never once asked us where we wanted to live. That was very sensible, because I think I'd have nutted him if he had.

We turned around after half an hour and strolled back along the river towards Mr Hardy's car. There were some chestnut trees near the car park. The leaves were piled up, swishing dryly under our feet. They had that slightly rotting smell that makes you think of warm firesides and crumpets. Theo began to search for conkers beneath the trees. He ferreted out spiny pods and crushed them with his heel, to get at the conker inside. Some were a disappointment but one of them was as big as a mouse, shining red-brown in its perfectly smooth, perfectly white case. He showed it to us.

'That's a beauty,' said Mr Hardy admiringly.

Theo stuffed it into his pocket—which was already bulging—and carried on with the treasure hunt.

'If I was a genie, popping out of a bottle and offering to grant you one wish,' Mr Hardy asked me quietly, 'what would it be?'

'To have Mum back. That's a no-brainer.'

'What about this dispute between your father and grandparents, though? What's your top-of-the-list wish there?'

I watched Theo as he rootled around among the leaves. 'I wish they'd just sort it out without getting their solicitors to write stupid letters all the time.'

Theo paused, with his foot raised over a conker case. 'I wish they could be friends,' he said. Then he smashed down his heel.

•

Joseph

'There's no point at all,' said Joseph.

Lester Hardy's office faced onto the Foss River. Joseph stood at the window, watching people fishing in those sluggish waters.

They crouched under umbrellas and ate their sandwiches. There wasn't a fish in sight.

'Someone has to set the ball rolling,' reasoned Lester.

'There isn't a ball, though, is there? Even if I agreed to see them, they wouldn't turn up. There's no *way* Hannah will ever speak to me, and they make every decision together. United they stand!' Joseph took off his glasses and polished them perfunctorily on his shirtfront. 'Boy, those two are nothing if not united—whether it's concealing their daughter's mental health problems or reviling their prodigal son-in-law. Actually, son-outlaw.'

'It's a long shot, I accept. But if you could extend the olive branch, it's just possible they'd meet you halfway. Have you ever apologised to their faces?'

'I've written letters,' said Joseph, replacing his glasses and pushing them up his nose. 'They've never bothered to reply. It doesn't matter what I do—Hannah will always think of me as Old Nick himself. I've given up.'

'But what have you got to lose?'

Joseph turned away from the window. 'Look, they wouldn't turn up. If by some miracle they did, there would be an unholy dogfight. Hannah and I almost got ourselves thrown out of York District Hospital when we found ourselves within shouting distance of one another.'

'Yes, I heard about that from her. She took a dim view of your being there at all—and, to be fair, she'd just had news of Frederick's major stroke. She was profoundly stressed.'

'As was poor Scarlet!' protested Joseph. 'I've had a gutful of that woman. She's never approved of me, never thought I was good enough for Zoe. She's constantly needling: encouraging Ben to stay away, complaining the house is damp, fussing about Theo's asthma—which, incidentally, appears to be non-existent. Give her the smallest excuse and she piles in. She's a bloody nightmare!'

Lester chuckled under his beard. 'She's a mother-in-law.'

'God. They can't all be like that, can they?'

'Wanna bet? The point is that your children would like the adults in their lives to work together. I asked Theo what he'd ask for if I could grant only one wish, and he said *I wish they could be friends.*'

Joseph crossed moodily to a chair and dropped into it, legs stretched out. He sat for a time with his hands in his pockets, regarding his feet.

'Theo said that?'

Lester nodded gravely. 'And Scarlet agreed.'

'Not gonna happen. Over Hannah's dead body . . . Okay.' Wearily, Joseph rubbed his hands down his face. 'Okay, okay. If they agree to meet me, I'll cooperate. But I'll bet you a tenner it won't happen.'

•

Hannah

Freddie was playing the harpsichord. It was transformative, an escape from the imprisonment of his dementia. As soon as he sat down to play, vocabulary became irrelevant; even arthritis was conquered. He could still express himself with those mathematical progressions. He could still reveal his inner self and be the man I loved and admired.

Theo was at gym club. Scarlet was shopping for bikinis with Vienna (just off to Thailand, poor spoiled child) but would be dropped home soon to entertain Ben while we talked to Lester. Ben was sprawled underneath the harpsichord, doing his homework—which consisted of drawing a picture.

And me? Ah well. As usual, I was trying to tidy up. As usual, I was failing. The clutter was winning. They'll put that on my gravestone: *The clutter won.* I moved ineffectually around the mess, arranging piles of detritus into bigger piles. Pencil cases, newspapers, toys, letters, envelopes, crumpled paper bags from school lunchboxes. Ben and I had been baking biscuits the previous evening, and the mess was lightly dusted with flour.

Scarlet had forgotten her phone. I found it under a mound of flour-dusted bills. Keen for a distraction from the chaos, I stopped cleaning and clumsily navigated my way through her pictures. Nosy of me, in hindsight, but I was sure she wouldn't mind. She often showed me her photos and they were always such fun. Sure enough, many of them I'd seen already. Several were of the school dance: girls wearing obscenely short dresses, and gawky teenage boys. There were some lovely ones of Freddie in the garden. *Ouch*—there was me. I winced. I wished she'd delete that picture; it made me look like a plump cross-dressing wolf.

Then there were a whole batch that I didn't recognise at all. Ben, cuddling a collie. Three lambs. My grandsons with some children I didn't know, all of them knee-deep in a stream and waving at the camera. Theo in mid-swing on a rope, mouth wide open and turned up in cartoonish delight, as though he was yelling. Such a solemn child, generally; I'd rarely seen him look so animated.

This, then, was their other life.

With sick fascination, I scrolled on through the photographs. It was foolish masochism because I knew I'd see him in the end.

Yes. Oh, yes. There he was: Joseph Scott in blue shirtsleeves, the image glamorously blurred by speed, kicking a ball. He'd obviously taken a tumble because his clothes were muddied. Dark hair was flying at all angles; it made him look young. Those irritating round-rimmed glasses were sliding down his nose. Ben and Theo seemed to be tackling him, heads down as they concentrated on the ball.

A duvet, covered in colourful birds. Scott was lounging on the bed with Roald Dahl in one hand. Ben—my little Ben—was kneeling up beside his father. They didn't seem to know they were being photographed. My grandson's arm was hooked around Scott's neck, and they gazed into the book, absorbed. Their heads were close together.

Another must have been taken by Scarlet with her arm outstretched. It was an unflattering image, fisheyed, distorted by the proximity of its subjects. She was sticking out her tongue at the camera; Scott was smiling at her. They looked like friends.

I spied on this alternative universe, and I felt lonely. The quiet undulations of the harpsichord seemed to thread and twine around it all. One image after another; snapshots of a life in which I could never take part.

The doorbell made me jump.

I let Lester Hardy in quietly. I wanted him to hear Freddie playing. He followed me into the sitting room and stood smiling benignly at Ben, who was still lying at his grandfather's feet.

'Lovely,' he murmured. 'What perfect companionship.'

Freddie didn't hear us, but Ben looked up and instantly his face took on a wary, closed look. He slid out from under the instrument and ran to bury his head in my skirt.

'Benji!' I exclaimed, half laughing. 'You're not shy!'

'Hi Ben,' said Lester, but the little boy slid around the back of me.

The music had stopped. Freddie was getting up from the piano stool, holding on to the top of the instrument as he slowly turned himself around. His balance had suffered after the most recent stroke.

'Ah!' he cried. His tone was as hospitable and cheerful as ever, but that one syllable was all he uttered. I could tell he wanted to add more, was searching his brain for more, but the words had fallen down a bottomless well. So he smiled broadly, and let Lester shake his hand.

'Frederick,' said Lester, with what sounded like real affection. 'Good to see you again.'

'I've got a pot of tea half-made,' I said, and dashed to get it. I was as fast as possible because I didn't like to think of poor Freddie left struggling to talk. Ben ran beside me like a baby elephant with its mother, his hand skimming my skirt.

'Why are you being all shy with Mr Hardy?' I asked him, though I knew the answer. Ben had worked out why Lester was there. He knew his dad wanted to take him away from us. Clinginess was to be expected.

Back in the sitting room, Lester bent to look at Ben's school book. 'What's this picture all about?' he asked.

Ben's natural gregariousness won the battle. 'A seed growing in a pot,' he replied promptly. 'We planted them. My one has two leaves—see?'

They talked amiably as I poured the tea. Freddie sat in an armchair, watching his grandson with a lopsided smile.

'And what is the best thing about school?' asked Lester.

Ben considered this question. 'Lunch,' he decided in the end. 'Hannah puts cake in my lunch.'

'Aha! Good for her. And I bet she makes marvellous cake.'

'I'm her 'prentice,' declared Ben proudly.

It wasn't until later, after Scarlet had arrived home and taken Ben off to the park, that Lester mentioned Scott's name.

'Despicable,' I said furiously. 'Kicking us when we're down.'

'What do you think is motivating him?'

I looked to Freddie for guidance, and he nodded encouragingly back at me before his mouth began to form words. 'Nnn . . . not-conshrijun,' he mumbled.

I stared at his mouth, trying to interpret, replaying the sounds. It was no good.

'Sorry, Freddie? I didn't get that.'

He took a deep breath and tried again. 'Not . . . conshishun.'

'Not contrition?' I queried, and he slapped a hand on his knee.

'Freddie's hit the mark,' I said to Lester. 'Whatever is motivating that man, it certainly isn't contrition! If he was genuinely contrite—had any remorse at all—he wouldn't be putting us through this. Lord! If I'd killed somebody, I wouldn't think myself worthy to tie their parents' shoelaces, let alone drag them to court.'

Lester sat holding his cup, the porcelain delicate in those heavy hands. He was wearing the purple shirt and yellow tie. 'It would really help if you could open a line of communication,' he ventured.

'No.'

'In my office. I would be there.'

'No.'

'The children would benefit immensely. If you could just meet him halfway, he—'

'I said *no!*'

I must have startled Freddie because he spilled tea down his trousers. I saw him carefully resting his cup on the saucer before reaching for a handkerchief in his jacket pocket. His struggle for dignity was unbearable.

'The answer is no, Lester! Please don't ask again. I will not sit in a room with Joseph Scott and that is final. I won't do it now, next week, next year—never. He has destroyed both my daughter and my husband and I will not—under any circumstances—meet him *halfway!*'

I realised I'd unwittingly spat. A pulse was throbbing away in my temples and I felt dizzy—I'm sure it was the rage, pumping me full of adrenaline. I was ready to fight to the death, then and there.

Freddie leaned across and patted my arm. Lester looked at him expectantly.

'Th . . . th . . . they're . . .' Freddie took breath, gathering his strength for a supreme effort. Then he spoke each word separately. 'They're . . . all . . . we have leff.' He swallowed painfully, as though there was a pebble stuck in his throat. 'All we have leff. Of Zoe.'

•

What emerged very clearly from my conversation with Scarlet and Theo is that they feel sharply divided loyalties. Theo described himself as 'on both sides of a war at once.' Whilst this is not a dispute punctuated by violence, it is one of enormous hostility and tension. It is a cold war.

The Wildes have been primary carers for over four years, and share a close bond with these children. Ben in particular remembers no other parenting. I have observed him to cling to Hannah when uncertain. To change the status quo would have a considerable impact on all the children but perhaps especially on Ben.

Joseph Scott made the point to me that that the Wildes are grandparents, not parents. While this is undeniable, it is only one factor among many. Frederick Wilde's health is another such factor. Despite his aphasia, he made a number of perceptive remarks when I visited and was as personable as ever. It is clear that he has the needs of the children firmly to heart. Yet he struggles to express himself and I understand that on occasion he can become confused. The Wildes' ability to provide care is likely to be tested increasingly as time passes. This of course is true in any family where one carer has health difficulties, and if handled sensitively it can even be an enriching experience.

I regret that I am unable to make a firm recommendation in this case. Whatever decision is made, these parties must set aside their personal feelings if the children's wellbeing is to be preserved. What matters is not where the children have primary residence; what matters is whether or not the adults in their lives are able and willing to work together.

•

Scarlet

'Yeah,' I said, when Mr Hardy told me he was going to put that in his report. 'But it's not going to happen.'

He'd come to visit us at Dad's house in Helmsley, and asked me to show him around the garden. Bees zigzagged over the lavender bushes.

'Maybe one day things will change,' he said.

'That would take a miracle.'

'Sorry. Can't do miracles.'

'So you're not a genie, then?'

He patted his belly. 'Too plump to fit in a lamp.'

The rubber band in my stomach had started twisting again. It began the moment I learned that Dad had applied to have us live with him.

'When are they going to court?' I asked.

'Next Wednesday.'

'Maybe we could shove them all into a lift,' I suggested, breaking a dead stick off an apple tree. 'We could make it jam. After three hours trapped together in a tiny space, they might start to talk.'

'Nice idea.'

'Then again, they'd probably just throttle each other.' I beheaded a clump of weeds with my stick. *Swish-thwack*. 'Perhaps it would help if us children died.'

'If you *what*?'

'Died.' *Swish-thwack*. 'If we were all three killed in a car crash, they'd have to talk to each other . . . No, even that wouldn't help. They'd have separate visiting times at the cemetery. We'd have to have two lots of funerals. Maybe they'd cut us in half and have two graves each.'

He pointed across the orchard. 'Is that a chicken house?'

'Sure is! We've got four pullets. They'll be around here somewhere.'

'So they're free range?'

'Mm-hm. They dig up everything we've planted and make a mess on the doorstep, but they're really fun. We just put them away in the evenings so a fox doesn't get them.'

The hens were at the far end of the garden, mooching about. They came racing down the grass when they saw us, hoping we had food. They looked like four red and brown ladies, holding up their skirts and screaming insults at one another. I went over to the metal bin beside their house, grabbed a cupful of grain and scattered it for them.

'It's an idea, isn't it?' I mused, as we watched them pecking in fast motion. 'Us three dying. Then they'd have nothing left to fight about.'

'These are rather dark thoughts for you to be having.'

'That's how I feel,' I said simply. 'Dark.'

'Tell me about feeling dark.' He was still looking at the hens. 'What do you mean by that?'

The rubber band was twisting. It made me feel as though my whole self was about to snap. It seemed to squeeze the fury out of my mouth. 'I can't do it. I can't do it anymore.'

'Can't do what?'

'I can't keep everyone happy. I can't pretend to Hannah that I don't care about Dad, or make Dad feel that we don't really love Hannah and Gramps. I have to be two people all the time, living two lives, always pretending and covering up and watching what I say . . . Everyone's upset, and I feel as though it's my fault.'

'How can it be your fault?'

'Because I exist.' I slammed the metal lid back onto the bin. 'Whatever happens in court, it's going to be a disaster. Whatever happens, everyone is still going to be upset. This is never going to end. Never, ever.'

•

I didn't sleep that night. Not until three in the morning, anyway. I didn't sleep the next night either, or the one after that, or any night in the days leading up to the court hearing. I felt more and more tired, but at the same time twitchy and tangled up. I tried to act normally, but I must have failed because Hannah asked me if I was feeling ill. I said it was that time of the month, which did the trick. She gets embarrassed by that kind of thing.

The singing man was back. Every night he came and stood by my bedside like some kind of nightwatchman, siphoning terror into my head with his beautiful song. I knew I would never escape him.

Thirty-four

Joseph

When he drove to York for the final hearing, Rosie came too.

'Could I hitch a lift?' she'd asked the night before. 'I've some birthday gift vouchers I never spent. They're about to expire.'

Joseph was fairly sure she had nothing of the kind. Akash had driven across from Leeds during the previous weekend, and the three of them had spent the evening in a tiny moorland pub. He'd overheard his two friends having a hurried conference about how best they could support him if things turned nasty in court.

They set out early, to beat the traffic. A silver-fringed mist hung over Helmsley's marketplace.

'How beautiful,' said Rosie. There was a wistful edge to her tone.

Their route south plunged through ploughed fields and russet woodland. Rosie wound down her window, closed her eyes and let the wind play havoc with her hair. Joseph found himself glancing sideways, watching her. She seemed so still, physically and emotionally; so very different from Zoe.

'How are you feeling?' she asked.

'Cat on a hot tin roof.'

'Scared of facing the in-laws?'

'Always.' Joseph slowed to a crawl behind a tractor.

'Because Zoe's mother hates you?'

'Yes; and because I feel so bloody guilty every time I see them; and because a selfish kid in me thinks they might've given me a bit more support when Zoe was ill and we were struggling. Maybe that's unfair, though. You know, they seem to think she was absolutely perfect—they just don't understand the incredible power she had. They don't know what it was like to be spun in that whirlpool, year after year.'

'Maybe they understand more than you think,' suggested Rosie. 'After all, they were with her when she went through her teens. She must have hurt them too.'

'If so, they've never acknowledged it. They seem to think being widowed and losing my children and spending three years in prison was all part of my cunning plan.'

It had been a bad night for Joseph. Time and again he'd heard the crack of impact and looked into wide green eyes.

'Am I making a mistake?' he asked now. 'Is this the most selfish thing I've ever done?'

'Not selfish,' she said thoughtfully. 'I don't think you're motivated by selfishness.'

'Stupid, then?'

'Hmm . . . not that, either. No. Look, anyone who sees you and those kids together would know that you're absolutely devoted to them. Then again, it's a really big thing to move them permanently.'

'You think I don't know that?'

They lapsed into silence. Rosie broke it.

'Do you want me to wait with you at the court?'

He glanced at her, touched by the offer. 'That would be so . . . but no, you do your errands. Spend your vouchers. We could meet up at lunchtime, maybe?'

'Maybe.'

Their road meandered through sandstone villages, past pubs with window boxes, past sleeping churches. The sun twined its rays through the mist. Joseph wished the day was over; wished he knew his children's fate, either way. He felt as though he'd joined in battle only to discover that he feared winning.

Rosie wound up her window. 'I'm out of time,' she said suddenly.

'Out of time?'

'I've stayed far too long already.'

'Rosie, no.'

'I'm going back next week. I've already told them.'

Joseph didn't trust himself to speak.

'You'll either have the children by then, or you won't,' she said. 'We're not even neighbours nowadays. There's nothing more I can do to help.'

'Help! Is that why you've stayed so long? Out of charity—to *help* me?'

'Partly.'

'Bullshit.'

She shrugged. Their easy camaraderie had been obliterated. Joseph drove mechanically, thinking about life without Rosie. Finally, he exploded.

'No, I'm not buying that! You stayed because you're happy. You love Brandsmoor and that scruffy kombi. You are your own person, not some black-veiled expendable with your hair and body and . . . personality all covered up!'

'You really don't know me, Joseph.'

'For God's sake!'

'Precisely. For God's sake. I've promised to stay in that community. Those women are my sisters. I found meaning there, and I must go back now. And you're far too close to that car in front. I don't want to die just yet.'

Gritting his teeth, Joseph eased his foot off the accelerator. He realised that he was hunched over the wheel, and forced his shoulders to relax. He knew he had no right, no claim upon Rosie; yet he felt as though she'd kneed him in the stomach.

Neither spoke again until they were in York. They pressed through an increasing sludge of traffic, around the ring road and into the city itself. Joseph sulkily asked where she'd like to be dropped, and she sulkily told him. The castle car park suited them both. Joseph squeezed into a space right beside the mound of Clifford's Tower, and switched off the engine.

'We're here,' he said.

'Yep.'

'Far too early.'

'Mm-hm.'

'I suppose you're going to beetle along to an internet café and start emailing your fellow sisters. Tell them to sweep your cell.'

'Childish, Joseph.'

'Starch your wimple.'

Rosie sighed exaggeratedly.

Neither made a move to get out of the car. Tourists toiled up and down the steps of the tower, and they watched in an unhappy silence.

'In 1190,' said Joseph, 'one hundred and fifty Jews took refuge in that tower. Families with children. The mob was baying for their blood. When a fire broke out, they realised they were facing horrible deaths. So they committed mass suicide. Husbands killed their children and wives, and then the men killed each other.'

A group of schoolchildren rolled down the mound, pushing one another with shrieks and giggles. Their teachers took photographs.

'Did anyone survive?' asked Rosie.

'The survivors were tricked into coming out, then butchered. All of them.'

'I've never heard that story.'

The morning's mist had burned away. The tower looked tidy and snug in the sunlight, its mound manicured. Joseph had never been able to look at it without imagining one hundred and fifty terrified ghosts. He closed his eyes.

'Stay,' he said. 'Please stay.'

She made a sound of exasperation, reaching to pick up her handbag from the floor.

'Sorry,' said Joseph. 'I've no right to ask. Forget it.' Abruptly, he got out and walked across to the ticket machine. When he returned she was waiting by the car, shielding her face from the sunshine.

'Your phone went off,' she said, handing it to him.

It was a text from Akash.

Gd lk scott. Lt me know if u up 4 a pint 2nite.

'He's a good lad, Akash,' remarked Joseph, as he wrote a short reply. 'Always thinking about other people, even though he'd rather die than admit it. He collected me from Armley, looked after me, made sure I didn't make a dick of myself. I owe him.'

Rosie's bag matched her clothes. It was large and vaguely 1970s, made of a rich crimson cloth. As she hitched it onto her shoulder, the strap tangled in the mass of her hair. Joseph stepped closer, lifted the strap and freed her curls. She looked up at him.

'Sure you don't want me to keep you company this morning?' she asked.

'No, no. Thanks. Better not. They might assume you're . . . you know.'

'Quite.'

'Don't want them thinking I've got myself a fancy piece already.'

'Do I look like a fancy piece? Well, good luck. Text me.' She kissed his cheek before turning to walk away. Joseph watched her with a rising feeling of loneliness.

'Um,' he muttered.

She turned back, eyebrows raised enquiringly. '*Um?*'

'On second thoughts,' said Joseph.

•

Hannah

Back in that wretched little room. Waiting. Waiting.

Freddie was at his best in the mornings, and today he seemed far calmer than I felt. He'd dressed himself and knotted his own tie—not too badly, either. He and I saw the children off at the door, waving as Scarlet led her brothers up Faith Lane. They were all subdued, but Scarlet looked terrible—pale and pinched, forcing every word. When I asked her, she said she'd slept badly. I wondered how Scott could do this to her.

Once they'd gone, Freddie did the washing-up in his shirt-sleeves, listening to Radio 4. It took him a long time, but he did it. When he discovered me compulsively tidying the sitting room—as though I had one last chance to be a good grandmother—he clicked his tongue and gently took the wooden trains from my hands.

'Don'orry,' he said. I was getting better at understanding him. 'Not . . . tide that matters.'

'I feel as though it is,' I replied bitterly. I could always be honest with Freddie; perhaps more honest than I could be with myself. 'I feel as though I have made my whole life untidy. I've never achieved order, as other women seem to do.'

'Other women . . .' He ran out of steam, and finished the sentence by looking theatrically sickened. Then he wrapped his arms right around me. I shed a tear or two, while he shushed and rocked.

My phone rang as we were leaving. I scrambled to find it in my handbag, and was surprised to hear Marie Scott's voice.

'Hannah,' she said. 'The hearing's today, isn't it?'

'We're just off to court.'

'My bloody brother.' She sounded agitated. 'Heck, I'm sorry.'

'It's not your fault.'

'All the same, I'm sorry. I can't believe he's doing this to you. D'you need anything? Should I come down and collect the kids from school?'

I was touched by her kindness. 'No,' I said. 'But thank you so much.'

'Good luck.'

I turned my phone off after that. I was afraid I'd forget and leave it on, and it would ring while I was in the witness box. Freddie had reached my coat down from the stand and was holding it for me to shrug into—right arm, left arm. Before shutting the front door behind us, I glanced back into the house. I had a sense of things ending.

I drove the car, but it was Freddie who steered us in the real sense of the word. When we arrived at the court building, he walked in steadily with his hat tucked under his arm. He nodded courteously to Malcolm at the desk. This time, we took the lift.

We sat in the little room. And sat. And sat. Both courts had busy lists. We hadn't managed to settle our case, and as retribution they put us last. By ten fifteen we'd run through our statements, discussed every angle. We were already exhausted, though the day's fight had not yet begun. Frederick stood ramrod-backed by his usual window, blinking at the traffic.

'Children at school?' asked Jane.

'Yes.'

'I did show you the reports from both schools, didn't I?' she asked, extracting some papers from her file. 'They were accepted by the other side at the last minute, so we haven't needed to call the teachers.'

'That's good,' I said. 'I'm sure teachers have better things to do than wait around at court all day.'

I have never been good at small talk; Freddie used to be infinitely more competent, in his heyday. To think of anything at all to say—in that airless room, on that airless day—was impossible. Nothing was sensible. Nothing was relevant. At ten forty I rushed to the ladies'. I was afraid I might be sick, as I'd once been in Leeds Crown Court. I felt that same clutch of doom. My breakfast stayed down, but I emerged feeling ghastly.

As I washed my hands at the basin I caught sight of an old woman in the mirror. She had crêpe-paper cheeks and half-moons beneath her eyes. Even her hands were unkempt. I tried to smile at her, but she just bared her teeth in a grim rictus. She looked downright sinister. I combed her hair and brushed colour onto her lined mouth, but all I achieved was to turn her into a sad old clown.

I stopped by the drinks machine in the lobby. We had the same kind at work, and I usually avoided them like the plague, but I thought a cup of sweet tea might help Freddie—and the crone in the mirror—to look less pallid. The lobby was dimly lit as ever, and the usual platoons of desperate combatants waited to join battle. I caught a distant glimpse of Scott's solicitor, looking cuboid and sober.

A woman was stooped beside the machine, watching mud-coloured liquid trickling into a mud-coloured plastic cup. Not old, not young. Fortyish and hippyish, with a purple midi skirt and a mop of long hair. I assumed she was there to divorce her husband and take him for every last penny; or possibly she was a battered girlfriend, hoping for an injunction. She caught my eye as I approached.

'Sorry,' she said cordially. 'I'm holding you up. I've just pressed the button for one more.'

'I'm in no hurry.' I dropped into a nearby chair and fished in my purse for change. We both watched as another cup dropped out of the machine, to be filled by a frothing brown fountain. The whole operation looked faintly obscene.

'Do you think it's going to taste anything like coffee?' the woman asked curiously.

'I can assure you that it won't.'

'Mm.' She grimaced. 'I was afraid of that.'

'I'd go for the tea next time,' I advised her.

Her smile was so friendly and open that I found myself returning it. She was apple-cheeked, her face rather rotund for beauty. In that awful place, on that awful day, kindness was particularly welcome. I decided she couldn't possibly be a divorcing wife. She was far too tranquil for the role; there was no bitterness. Perhaps she was a social worker.

She looked more keenly at me, and I'm fairly sure she saw the white-faced crone I'd met in the powder-room mirror. 'Actually, are you all right?'

'Certainly not!' I tried to smile. 'Isn't this a place people come to when things are all wrong?'

'Can I help? Should I call someone?'

'No, no,' I assured her. 'Thank you. I'm absolutely fine. I have people waiting in one of these rooms.'

The plastic cup was full. She had two more stacked on a small shelf, and somehow managed to pick them all up. 'Betcha I'll drop the lot,' she predicted, as she moved away. 'I hope your morning goes well.'

'You too,' I murmured automatically. Then I turned my attention to the machine, which seemed determined to give me soup instead of tea.

'Shouldn't be too much longer,' said Jane, as I entered the room with my plastic cups. Over at the window, Freddie lost his footing and clutched the sill.

'Freddie,' I snapped. 'For God's sake, sit down before you fall down.'

He turned his head to look at me, hurt stretching his eyes. 'All right, all right,' he murmured gently, and made his way towards a chair.

'Sorry,' I said.

A tap on the door made us all swing around. The blonde court clerk was poking her head into the room. 'He has risen!' she announced breathlessly.

I overcame an inclination to enquire whether she was referring to the judge, or to Jesus Christ. Funny how the most inappropriate and puerile ideas pop into one's head in times of crisis.

'Thank you, Vera,' said Jane.

'Five minutes. He wants to crack on.'

Jane glanced from Freddie to me. 'Phones turned off? Good. Let's go.'

•

Joseph

'Five minutes,' said Vera.

Joseph and Richard O'Brien both stood up, while Rosie reached into her handbag and lifted out a heavy book.

Joseph stooped to squint at it. 'What the hell is that?'

She showed him the cover: *Pruning the Vine: A History of Medieval Viticulture.* Despite his dry-mouthed tension, Joseph chuckled incredulously. 'Light bedtime reading?'

'No. Heavy, waiting-for-my-friend-in-court reading. If I get bored I'll nip out and spend those vouchers. Maybe I'll even treat myself to some real coffee.'

'Wish me luck.'

'Good luck.'

Still, he hesitated. He didn't want to leave her. 'Will you be praying for me?'

'Should I be?'

He gestured helplessly.

She smiled. 'You lot have taken up a fair bit of airtime lately. You, the children and the Wildes. Now off you go.'

Joseph forced himself to follow O'Brien out the door and across the lobby. He was pushing open one of the double courtroom doors when he glanced over his shoulder. To his horror, he realised that the Wilde contingent was hot on his heels. Hannah had hold of Frederick's arm, either to give or receive support; possibly both. Joseph felt a rush of shock at the change in Frederick. He seemed diminished, his cheeks sunken, his tweed suit hanging as though from a tall skeleton. He'd lost his casual confidence. Each step was taken carefully, the polished shoe testing the ground before he transferred his weight, as though the lobby was mined.

Joseph had no choice but to wait for them. If he let the heavy door go it would swing shut in their faces, which would seem deliberately offensive. He was forced to stand with an expression of awkward blankness, holding the door open as they approached.

Mrs Whistler was first, sailing into the courtroom with a genteel nod. As the Wildes came closer, Hannah's face was firmly averted. Her mouth looked as though it was set in concrete, downturned and grim. They were level with Joseph when Frederick stopped and faced his son-in-law.

'Come *on*, Freddie,' muttered Hannah, through her teeth.

Freddie didn't come on. He spoke with an effort, deliberately but intelligibly. 'Good mm . . . morning, Joseph.'

Joseph ransacked his mind for perfect words: words that might heal wounds, or at least do justice to the old man's bereavement. 'Freddie,' he stammered in the end. 'I'm . . . sorry.'

Hannah looked stony. 'If you were sorry, you wouldn't be doing this.'

Joseph was left to close the door behind them, like a schoolboy. Lester Hardy sat at the back of the room, his head bent over a sheaf of papers. Vera busied herself at her desk.

And there they all were, yet again. In that explosive silence. Waiting.

The clock said it was eleven twenty.

A bluebottle buzzed up and down the double glazing, anxious to escape into air so cold that it would be dead by lunchtime. Joseph heard tiny snaps as the kamikaze crashed against the glass. He was acutely aware of Hannah and Frederick, just a few feet away from him. This was his last chance. He gathered his courage.

'Freddie,' he said out loud. 'Hannah. Can we talk? I really want to—'

Too late. Knuckles sounded on the door of the inner sanctum. 'All rise!' roared Vera, leaping to her feet as the judge strode in and took his seat. The show had begun.

'Mr O'Brien,' began the judge without preamble. 'I've read your chronology and the agreed statement of issues. You can open briefly.'

O'Brien didn't seem very brief to Joseph. He told the story all over again: the ages of the children, the dates of various applications, the involvement of Lester Hardy. That poor bluebottle's buzz became frenzied; Joseph wondered whether he could somehow let it out. Gradually, he became aware that O'Brien had stopped speaking.

'Joseph,' the solicitor hissed. 'C'mon! I've called you.'

Later, Joseph couldn't remember getting into the witness box or taking the oath. He heard his own voice, and felt a vague surprise at how unwavering it sounded. O'Brien took him through his statements, and he did his best to explain why he felt the children would benefit from the change. The bluebottle was walking along the windowsill. It seemed resigned.

Mrs Whistler had got up and was smiling sunnily at him. Joseph thought of the smile on the face of the tiger, and watched her warily.

'Mr Scott,' she began graciously, 'after your wife . . . er *died*, you were on bail for how long?'

'About six months.'

'Yes. And in that time you didn't once see your children?'

'I wasn't allowed to.'

'Quite. And then you were incarcerated for three years?'

'Yes.'

'So that made a total of three and half years that these children had no contact with you whatsoever.'

'I didn't want them to see the inside of a prison. I didn't want them being searched, and herded like cattle, and to hear those doors clanging. Anyway, I knew the Wildes wouldn't bring them. I wasn't even allowed to send them letters.'

'Do you accept that three and half years is a very long time in the life of any child?'

'Yes.'

'And for Ben, who couldn't remember you at all, it was effectively *all* his life?'

'Of course, but . . .' Joseph sighed. 'Yes. It's a long time.'

'And you also accept that their last sight of you—on the day Zoe died—was extremely disturbing?'

Someone scurried quietly into the room, easing the doors shut; a youngish man in a too-tight suit. He glanced at Joseph in the witness box before tiptoeing to whisper to the clerk. Joseph was distracted.

'Mr Scott!' Jane Whistler glared at him. 'Their last sight of you was disturbing—surely you aren't going to argue with me about that?'

'No, I won't argue. Of course it was disturbing.'

Vera and the young man were agog about something. She asked a question, and he gave a sibilant reply before hurrying away. Then Vera turned around and began to whisper to the judge. Mrs Whistler had noticed all this activity, and suspended her barrage of questions. The judge sat, head down, fingers tapping as though gathering his thoughts.

'Mrs Whistler,' he said finally, 'I am going to stop you there for the time being.'

'So be it, Your Honour.'

'Yes. In fact I'm going to rise for a while.'

The solicitor lifted an eyebrow, and Joseph supressed a smile. Clearly, she wasn't best pleased at the interruption.

'The court office has just received a telephone call from St Mary's College,' continued the judge. 'They've been trying to contact the grandparents. It seems that there has been some kind of incident involving Scarlet, and they would like Dr Wilde to call them immediately. So I suggest—'

'*What?*' Hannah was on her feet, squeezing past Frederick, scrabbling in her handbag as the judge quietly left.

Joseph strode out of the witness box, fists clenched. An *incident*. The very word triggered a flood of adrenaline. To him it was police double-speak, a euphemism for horrors. In their early reports, Zoe's death had been described as an *incident*.

'Messages,' shouted Hannah from the back of the court. 'Freddie, there're three messages on my phone!' Her voice shook. Joseph had never heard his mother-in-law sound truly frightened before; not even in the hospital after Freddie's stroke. In fact, he'd never seen any real chink in her rigid self-control. She seemed a different person now. She pressed buttons and waited with the phone to her ear, eyes wide as she strained to listen. Joseph moved several steps closer, his gaze fixed on her face. Even the bluebottle stood still.

'Oh God,' breathed Hannah. She dropped her handbag. Keys and a wallet spilled across the blue carpet. 'Oh dear God.'

'What's happened?' asked Joseph.

Her eyes swivelled to Frederick. 'Scarlet's been hurt.'

Thirty-five

Scarlet

They tried to pretend it was just another day. That was the worst thing. How could they do that? I wanted Hannah to say something real. I wanted her to show she knew how awful this was for us. But she was so busy trying to hide her own feelings that she hadn't the time to notice ours.

I'd spent the whole night blocking my ears against the singing. Theo had wet his bed, of course, and tried to cover up by bundling all his sheets into the basket and sneaking into the shower. Even Ben was in a state. I just about had to drag him down the street.

'I don't want to go to school,' he moaned.

'You do,' I reminded him. 'They need you in the play, remember?'

That cheered him up. He was the wolf in the reception class production of 'Three Little Pigs', and was really throwing himself into the role. He huffed and he puffed all the way to school. Theo didn't say a word, though.

'You okay?' I asked him, when we got to their entrance.

He shrugged. 'I wish today was over.'

He was clamping his lips, trying not to cry. I hugged him furiously. Then I hugged Ben. I was almost in tears myself as I pushed them towards the door.

'Bye,' I said quickly. 'Love you both.'

By the time I reached my own school my eyes felt dry and aching, and the rubber band was twisted all around my guts. I was afraid I was going to throw up during assembly. They were dishing out awards that day. Everyone else seemed to care so much—as though it mattered who had the highest marks in biology, while three of the people I loved most were fighting and hating. I thought perhaps it would be easier not to exist at all.

I got through maths somehow, checking my phone under the desk every two minutes to see if there were any messages. Second period was chemistry, taught by bald Mr Hicks. He's about to retire, and is a good teacher except that he has absolutely no control over the class. He had us working in pairs with Bunsen burners, testing for glucose. Vienna doesn't do chemistry, so my lab partner that day was a girl called Livvi, one of the cool crowd. She's the kind of total bitch who straightens her hair every day—hair that's a different colour every week, incidentally—and pretends to be all friendly, then openly giggles about you with her mates. Hannah reckons they're jealous, but that doesn't help. Livvi left all the work to me, of course, because she was far too cool to make any effort herself. I felt weird from not sleeping, and my hands were shaking. I accidentally tipped too much Benedict's solution into the test tube.

Livvi was delighted that I'd cocked up. 'Scar-*let*!' she yelled, for everyone to hear. People stopped to look. 'Now we'll have to start all over again.'

Mr Hicks was in the storeroom, so he wasn't there to calm things down. One of Livvi's friends chimed in from another bench. 'Oh, Scaaaar-let!' she sang. 'Poor you, Livvi, I feel so sorry for you. D'you want to come and join me and Brianna?'

I was holding the test tube over the Bunsen burner using tongs, waiting for the solution to turn orange; but with all the distraction I burned my hand and that made me drop the tongs. The next moment there was shattered glass and chemicals all over the bench, and Livvi was going ballistic.

'What did you do *that* for?' she shrieked.

'Shut up,' I said.

'Oh my God, you've ruined this jersey!'

That was when the rubber band snapped, big-time.

'I said shut up, you frigging bitch!' I screeched. I grabbed the nearest test tube rack and smashed it onto the floor, which caused pandemonium as glass shot out in all directions. Then I did it again, with another rack. There were girls screaming and running away. I felt as though I had to do this—I had to break things, I had to smash everything up. Mr Hicks came belting out of the storeroom. By then I was crying hysterically. I picked up a piece of glass and sliced it across my forearm, near the elbow. It didn't hurt so I did it again, making a big X.

Immediately, blood gushed out. Livvi wailed and pretended to faint, but Mr Hicks ignored her. He was actually a lot more sensible in a crisis than I would have expected. I vaguely remember him sending one girl to fetch the teacher from next door and another to get the lab technician. Then he marched me into the storeroom, snapped open the first-aid kit and pressed a pad onto my arm. I was still crying, and he didn't try to talk to me. Suddenly, I realised that the classroom had fallen silent. I heard the tap-tapping of a pair of heels.

'Scarlet went mental, Miss!' That was Livvi's voice.

Whoever had come in obviously wasn't interested in talking to Livvi. Seconds later, Miss Grayson looked into the storeroom.

'Hello, Scarlet,' she said calmly. 'I hear you've had an accident?'

I nodded, still sobbing.

She cast an eye over the damage. 'Not nearly as bad as it looks. Think you can walk to my office? Good girl. I'll take over, Mr Hicks, thank you.'

I don't remember much about getting to her room; I was beside myself. I wasn't even worried about all the trouble I'd be in for trashing the science lab. The outside world had stopped mattering—the girls, the teachers, Miss Grayson's secretary: they all seemed to be fictional, like people you see on television. Or perhaps it was the other way around. I was fictional. I didn't matter. As Miss Grayson settled me into an armchair in the corner of her office, I noticed a streak of blood on her silky blouse.

'I've bled on you,' I gasped, getting control of the tears. 'Sorry.'

'Worse things happen at sea. Now, I think you're going to need a few stitches. We've tried your home number, and your grandmother's mobile, and got no answer.'

'They're all in court.' I felt very sick all of a sudden, and damp on my forehead. 'They're arguing over where we should live.'

'Ah. That was today, was it?

'Mm. Excuse me, I think I'm going to be—'

She didn't hang about. She bundled me through a door and into a tiny room with a toilet and basin. I made it just in time. It's horrible, being sick. It burned my throat. Eventually I managed to stop long enough to wash my face and rinse my mouth in the miniature basin. The room was painted in pale lilac; even the air seemed to be pale lilac. I sat on the floor and leaned against the wall, which felt cool, and shut my eyes. I could see pale lilac behind my eyelids. My arm had started to throb. It really hurt.

Mrs Grayson came in with a glass of water. She had a new wound pad too, and this time she taped it onto my arm. The cuts had nearly stopped bleeding.

'Thanks.' I said, and drank all the water. 'Sorry.' The pale lilac was like a mist. I couldn't see very well. It was frightening to be half-blind, so I shut my eyes again.

'I suppose I'll be expelled,' I said.

'I doubt it.'

'Say sorry to Mr Hicks from me.'

She got to her feet. 'We still can't raise your grandparents; nor your aunt, who we have down as an emergency contact. So I'll drive you to casualty and just ask whether you'd be best to have some stitches. All right?'

I felt knackered, but I managed to stand up and together we walked out to her car. It was a very flashy soft-top. Any other time, I'd have been happy to ride in it.

'I'm sorry to give you all this trouble,' I said, as she checked my seatbelt.

'Never mind. You've got me out of two meetings, both of them exceedingly tedious.' She started the car. 'So today's a big day, is it?'

'Mm-hm. The fight to the death.'

'That must be hard.'

'It is,' I said, and burst into tears yet again. I just didn't seem able to stop crying. It was pathetic. 'I just wish this wasn't happening. It doesn't matter where we live, does it? Why the hell does that matter so much?'

Miss Grayson didn't answer, but she made a sympathetic sound. She reached into her handbag and handed me a little packet of tissues, and I sobbed into one of those. The traffic was gridlocked that day so I had time to tell her all about Dad and my grandparents. I was still talking when we turned into the hospital car park.

'It's a miracle,' she said. 'There's a parking space for us.' She manoeuvred the car, and turned off the engine. We sat for a minute. Raindrops began to speckle the windscreen.

'Do you have parents?' I asked. It sounded like a silly question—of course she had parents. It's physically impossible not to have parents, even if you've never met them. But Miss Grayson knew exactly what I was getting at.

'They divorced when I was ten,' she replied, her voice matter-of-fact. 'My father was in the diplomatic service and my mother fell in love with an Egyptian businessman. She ran away with him. You could say it was romantic, though it caused quite a scandal.'

'But what happened to you? Did she take you with her?'

Miss Grayson smiled. 'She wasn't that sort of woman. I was at boarding school at the time, so I stayed on there. In the holidays I shuttled around between parents, aunts, friends of aunts . . . anyone who would have me. I got to travel the world.'

I tried to imagine a girl of about Theo's age, suddenly finding she had no home.

'That's awful,' I said.

'It was awful, at times. But bad times do not last forever, Scarlet. There are other moments.'

I hoped she was right.

The casualty department seemed busy. There were rows of plastic seats, and quite a few people sitting in them. Miss Grayson said that was 'par for the course'. She got me a cup of sweet hot chocolate from a machine, and then a nurse arrived. After she left, another woman turned up. Miss Grayson walked away with her and they had a long conversation; I was pretty sure it was about the fact that I'd cut myself.

We were being taken in to see a doctor when Miss Grayson's mobile phone rang. She flipped it open.

'Aha,' she said, looking at the number. 'At last.'

Thirty-six

Hannah

We were back in that ghastly little room, sitting round the same table, but this time we had a still more immediate terror.

'Scarlet was cut by some glass,' said the school secretary who'd answered the phone. 'On the arm.'

'On the arm? Has she damaged an artery?'

'I doubt it. Miss Grayson didn't call an ambulance. She drove her in her own car, didn't seem to be rushing at all. I think she's got a soft spot for Scarlet.'

She gave me Gilda Grayson's mobile number, and I called it. The headmistress sounded relieved to hear from me.

'Dr Wilde? Just a moment while I find a quiet spot.'

'How is she?'

'Now, the first thing to say is that Scarlet is all right. We've seen a triage nurse, and she thinks stitches are necessary so we need your permission for that. Scarlet has two quite deep cuts on the upper part of her forearm, but she's in no immediate physical danger.'

'Thank God,' I breathed. I passed on the good news to Jane and Freddie. Jane immediately set off to tell the opposition, who were waiting in their own little hellhole.

'I said no *physical* danger,' added Gilda Grayson meaningfully.

'What d'you mean?'

She hesitated. 'How are things going in court?'

'We've hardly started. Look, I'll come straight round to the hospital and—'

'Hang on. Don't do anything until you've heard me out. Dr Wilde, what happened to Scarlet today was caused by an emotional overload. She screamed, she threw glass objects onto the floor. Then she cut herself with a broken test tube.'

I was silenced. I could actually feel the hairs rising to attention on the back of my neck, because the person she was describing was Zoe. It couldn't be happening all over again. It just couldn't. That would be too cruel. Frederick must have seen my horror, because he took my hand.

'Her mother,' I whispered. 'She was diagnosed . . .' I couldn't say it.

'I know about the family history.' Gilda Grayson dropped her voice. 'But as I have just told the hospital social worker, I really don't think Scarlet's outburst was caused by mental illness. I think she's overwhelmed.'

'Overwhelmed?'

'Stressed. She's been trying to please everyone, trying to keep you all from being hurt.'

'I see.'

'Do you? I wonder. You know what she told me in the car? She said she feels she and her brothers are the rope in a tug-of-war, and they're being stretched.'

'I'm coming to the hospital,' I said flatly. 'I'm on my way. I must be with her.'

'Yes, you could do that—but I am here, and I will deliver her home later, if necessary. Why don't you stay right where you are? If you would only talk to Scarlet's father and agree on a plan for her future, you could spare her further distress. She doesn't care where anyone lives! She just wants the anger to stop.'

'Can I talk to her?'

'She's actually with a doctor at the moment. She'll call you when she's free.'

'How does she seem?'

'Upset, crying from time to time, but calm in herself. I've seen girls her age have meltdowns before. Given the appalling stress she's under, this one isn't so surprising.'

I thanked her numbly and said I'd call back. I needed time to think. Jane had returned, so I relayed the whole conversation to her and Freddie. He seemed to retreat into his own mind, blinking slowly as he pulled his handkerchief from his waistcoat pocket and blew his nose. I could tell he was terribly disturbed, as I was. Jane hurried away to put everyone else in the picture.

'I don't know what to do,' I moaned in bewilderment.

Freddie's arm crept around me, and I leaned against him. He was still my strength and shield. When Jane returned, I went to splash water over my face and commiserate with the crone in the mirror. She didn't even try to smile. She looked as though she'd never smiled in her life.

'You were so taken up by your own pain,' I told her accusingly. 'Did you fail to notice hers?'

There was nowhere for me to hide while I gathered my thoughts. No haven; though it was at least quiet in the lobby. We were the last case standing. All other battles had been lost or won, or perhaps the bloodshed had been adjourned to another day. I found myself a corner, half-obscured beside the humming drinks machine. Behind me, a door opened and closed. I heard footsteps, but didn't glance around. If it was Scott, I certainly didn't want to catch his eye.

Then a swirl of purple skirt swam into the periphery of my vision.

'I didn't introduce myself before.' I recognised the voice. Steady, but warm. 'Rosemary Sutton. I'm a friend of Joseph's. I've met your grandchildren.'

I looked at the skirt, not at the face. 'I didn't realise.'

'Me neither.' I heard her sitting in a chair near to mine.

'Do you know about his past?' I asked, with genuine curiosity.

'I do.'

'Then why are you his friend?'

She hesitated. 'I hear Scarlet's harmed herself,' she said. 'I'm so sorry.'

The machine hummed at us both.

I heard myself sigh. 'Her headmistress wants us all to talk—but she doesn't understand.'

'What doesn't she understand?'

The loss, I thought. *The fear.* 'Joseph Scott has forfeited his role as father,' I said bitterly. 'He doesn't deserve to be loved.'

There was no response from my companion; she didn't even move. It's rare to meet someone who doesn't need to have the last word—or the nastier word—or the cleverest word. Very rare. I used to listen to conversations among my colleagues, or students as they sat waiting for tutorials to begin. Everyone is permanently standing on their own imaginary stage, playing to an imaginary audience. It doesn't matter what any of us say; nobody is ever listening. Every minute, around the world, a billion words are swatted away to make room for a billion more.

This woman did no swatting. My words were left unmolested to take to the air, to swoop and holler like savage children. *He doesn't deserve to be loved*. I didn't like them, seen so close up. They unsettled me. They were too brutal.

Images spun beside the words. A man caked in mud, letting two laughing sons tackle him. A bedtime story, and a small boy's thin arm casually slipped around his father's neck. Joseph Scott was loved. Whether or not he deserved to be, he was. I knew that. I had always known that.

I rubbed my cheeks. I felt impossibly tired. 'The truth is that I simply can't afford to lose anything else.'

'No.'

'Neither can my husband. He has already lost his only daughter. He's lost his health. I think perhaps he's even lost his future.'

'I know. I'm sorry.'

'Are you Scott's girlfriend?'

'No. Not.' She shifted in her chair; clasped her hands in her lap. 'I haven't befriended him out of ghoulish prurience, if that's what you're thinking. I met and liked him before I knew his past, though it seemed to me that he was someone who . . . well, there was obviously some appalling sadness there.'

'Huh.'

My enemy's friend leaned a little closer. 'He was in love with your daughter, you know. He still loves her. He thinks about her all the time. I don't get a look-in.'

'Do you want a look-in?'

A wry smile. 'I'm not free.'

'I warn you, he doesn't know what love is,' I said. 'He's far too selfish. He wouldn't let Zoe express herself. He didn't appreciate her brilliance. He wouldn't even move back to London—though she was desperate to live there again—because his career was more important than her happiness.'

Once again, my companion didn't argue with me. She didn't need to. I knew very well that uprooting the family and returning to London had been out of the question. Zoe's stability became more fragile once her children arrived; she was balanced on a knife-edge. We were keen for her to stay in Yorkshire, close to us.

My phone made its text noise. It was Gilda Grayson.

Scarlet doing well, being stitched now. She wonders if you are talking yet?

'Look.' I held up the message. 'Apparently, Scarlet wants to know if we're talking.'

My companion's lips twitched. 'And what will you tell her?'

Vera chose that moment to barge through the courtroom doors. The clerk seemed pathologically noisy; she was a maelstrom even when walking on soft carpet. 'Judge is thinking of adjourning until two. Wants to know what's happening. What shall I tell him?'

I shut my eyes. I had never felt so tired. Never.

'Tell him we're talking,' I said.

•

They filed wordlessly into the family court adviser's room, a sparsely furnished space accessed through a keycoded door. The room must have adjoined the court, because its windows looked out towards Dick Turpin's grave.

It struck Joseph that for three people who had gathered with the specific and stated intention of talking, they seemed remarkably tongue-tied. They'd been forced together by the shock of Scarlet's desperation, and by their collective culpability; that didn't mean they'd be able to overcome the bitterness of years.

'She's no dragon,' Rosie had said, after speaking to Hannah.

'Oh yes she is,' protested Joseph. 'On a good day she actually breathes fire.'

'I think she's exhausted. I think she's frightened of losing the children forever, because they're all she has left. Fear makes her defensive. But she's a good, thoughtful woman at heart. I like her.'

Joseph didn't want to think about Hannah. In his mind's eye, he watched Scarlet using a piece of glass to mutilate her young arm. The image horrified him. It was with him still as he followed Hannah and Freddie into Lester's room.

Lester gestured to chairs around a cheap wooden table. He seemed utterly relaxed, as though chairing a meeting of the steering sub-committee on court upholstery. 'Take a seat,' he invited.

Joseph obeyed. Hannah demurred.

'I'd rather stand,' she maintained stiffly. Joseph stole a sideways glance at his mother-in-law. Her chin was haughtily tilted, but he thought he glimpsed vulnerability through the cracks.

'Free country.' Lester sank into a chair. 'Forgive me if I give in to middle age and mild obesity? If I stand for too long, my knees complain. I think Freddie, too, might like to take the weight off his feet.'

Clever, thought Joseph. Lester knew damned well that Freddie would never sit while Hannah was standing. Hannah looked exasperated, but she sat down.

'You're manipulative, Lester,' she huffed. 'Don't think I haven't noticed.'

Freddie didn't sit, however. He took up a post behind his wife with one hand on her shoulder. They looked like Victorian missionaries, highbrow and stiff-collared, posing for a photograph. Joseph sighed inwardly. This was never going to work. It was hopelessly artificial to force himself and the Wildes to gather around a table, especially when all any of them wanted to do was rush away to be with Scarlet.

'Who's going to start us off?' rumbled Lester. 'Joseph? I heard you trying to say something this morning, just as the judge was coming in.'

Joseph stared down at the plywood table. He wondered what scenes it had witnessed over the years; how many men and women had sat around it and hated one another. Or loved one another. Or both. 'I wanted to say a couple of things. First, I . . . No Hannah, don't. Just don't.'

'Don't what?' demanded Hannah.

'Explode. I know you're gearing up to explode. I can feel it. I don't mean sorry as in "I'm sorry I tore your dress," or, "Sorry, I reversed into your car."'

Hannah muffled her explosion and turned to look out of the window.

'It lives with me,' said Joseph. 'It always will. The unforgiveable thing I did. It's driven me half-crazy. I don't know whether you will ever be able to forgive me but I do know that I'll never forgive myself. There isn't a day, there isn't an hour goes by when I don't wish I could put the clock back. It's unbearable. It's . . .' He shook his head, finishing in a whisper. 'Sorry.'

'So you've said,' snapped Hannah.

'I'm not making this application just to upset you.'

'Oh, come on! We weren't born yesterday.'

'I'm really not. I admire you both.'

'Don't bother to pull that humble-boy-from-the-wrong-side-of-the-tracks charm out of your tool box, Scott. It doesn't disarm me.'

'For God's sake! I know you've never liked me, Hannah, but—'

'I tolerated you, until you murdered my child.'

Joseph was losing his cool. 'If you'd been less critical of me and more honest about Zoe's illness, we might not even be here! I needed support from you, desperately needed it, and all I got was endless negativity.'

Hannah had leaped to her feet, face flaming, and was making for the door. 'How dare you! I'm not staying to hear any more abuse from a man I absolutely despise.'

'All right,' said Lester evenly. 'Let's just pause there.'

The protagonists subsided, though their fury didn't. Hannah folded her arms, still standing. Freddie moved close to her; he was blinking at Joseph, trying to speak. When his words arrived, they were slurred.

'Sh'was our . . . light.'

Joseph winced. It took him a moment to find his voice. 'I know, Freddie. I know she was. I'm sorry.'

Frederick clearly wanted to add something, but his thoughts emerged as meaningless strings of vowels. He tried twice, three times, with increasing frustration.

Eventually, Hannah squeezed his arm. 'Shh. All right, I know what you're saying. I'll tell him.' With a visible effort, she turned her head to look straight at Joseph. 'He says . . .' She cleared her throat. 'He says she was your light, too.'

Perhaps it was the generosity of the thought that did it; perhaps it was his father-in-law's grief-stricken dignity. Joseph felt something inside himself give way, some last barrier of pride and anger. 'She was,' he whispered. 'Thank you.'

Frederick seemed utterly spent. He limped to a chair and dropped into it, ashen-faced, breathing a little too fast. Hannah followed, watching him anxiously.

'Yes indeed, thank you,' said Lester. He looked around at the three of them, rolling his fingers in an over-to-you gesture. 'Okay. What's clear is that the children want—*need*—their most important adults to agree upon their future. Scarlet has acted out her emotional pain in the most graphic way this morning. Do you all accept that?'

Hannah and Joseph nodded unhappily.

'So how shall we move forward? Who's prepared to make concessions?'

The question was met by a charged silence. Joseph was battling with himself; he hated to give up now—he knew exactly what Akash's view would be—but he was no longer sure what a good father would do.

Freddie had rested his elbows on his knees and his face in his hands. If he'd been the man he used to be, thought Joseph, he might have steered them all towards some new understanding. The family couldn't function without Freddie.

Lester raised an encouraging eyebrow. 'Any thoughts?'

More silence.

And more.

Suddenly, Joseph made his decision. 'Okay,' he said, holding up his hands. 'Okay, okay. I surrender. Someone's got to. Ending this is all that matters, so I'll drop my application.'

If Lester felt any surprise, he hid it. 'All right. That's progress. Hannah, Frederick, what are your thoughts now?'

Freddie had straightened in his seat. A tear roamed down his thin cheek, and his hand crept out and took Hannah's. He smiled tenderly at her, even as his mind and his muscles battled to form words. She looked into his eyes.

They're still in love, thought Joseph, with a painful jolt of envy. *A love affair that's lasted forty years.*

When Frederick finally spoke, it was as though there was nobody else in the room but Hannah and himself; nobody else in the universe.

'Let 'em go, my love,' he said.

Thirty-seven

Scarlet

It hurt like billy-o when they injected the local anaesthetic, and I almost swore at the nurse. Once I'd gone numb, having the actual stitches wasn't nearly as bad as I'd expected. The main problem was that everyone made a fuss about me cutting myself, and various people came to talk to Miss Grayson. She was brilliant, and swung into full headmistress mode. It was pretty reassuring to have Maggie batting on my side. She was bullying some doctor when I had a text from Hannah:

We are on our way.

What's happened? I replied.

There in fifteen mins xx

Sure enough, it wasn't long before she and Gramps came hurrying through the main doors, looking all around the department with worried faces. When she spotted us, Hannah left Gramps behind, charging across to throw her arms around me and stand there rocking. She'd hardly ever done that before; Gramps, yes—he's an old softie—but Hannah generally uses words more than touch. It started me blubbing again. I felt as though I'd turned on the tears tap in the lab that morning, and it was stuck in the *on* position. Gramps followed her with one of his bear hugs. He didn't even try to speak.

I realised he was crying too, though very quietly and without many tears.

Miss Grayson spent a few minutes putting Hannah in the picture, and handed over the papers the hospital had given us. She said they'd write to my own doctor, and we needed to go and see him. Hannah thanked her about fifty times. Then Miss Grayson laid her hand on my upper arm.

'I'm going to bow out now, Scarlet,' she said. 'I've promised to have a word with Mr Hicks and his lab technician.'

'Sorry to Mr Hicks,' I gulped.

She looked mystified. 'For what? Accidentally breaking some test tubes and then falling on one?'

I looked at her, not understanding. She winked. 'The good thing about being Maggie Thatcher is that you have *power*,' she declared, widening her eyes dramatically. Then she gave me a very quick hug—the first and last time she ever did—and strode away in her boring shoes.

I was desperate to know what had happened in court. I tried asking Hannah, but she made a zipping motion across her lips. 'I think it's best if we tell you and your brothers all together.'

'The boys!' I yelped in dismay. 'The poor things—what time is it? They'll be waiting for me.'

'It's all right,' said Hannah. 'Someone's collecting them from school. I've arranged it all.'

I felt exhausted in the car on the way home. The local anaesthetic was wearing off and my arm was throbbing, but I think some painkilling tablets they'd given me took away the worst of it. Once we were home Gramps waited for me to get out, and we walked up to the house together. We were just going in when I heard another car turn into Faith Lane. I looked casually over my shoulder to see who it was.

Then I did a double take.

'I don't believe it,' I said. 'Um, Hannah . . . Dad's here, and he has the boys in the car.'

Gramps laughed in delight. Hannah glanced out through

the doorway. 'Ah yes,' she said nonchalantly. 'That's right. He's collected them for me.'

I felt as though the genie had popped out of his lamp and granted my wish. '*Seriously?*' I gasped.

She nodded. I looked at her, trying to read her expression. She was working hard to hide it, but I could see the strain in her face. She looked very pale, and her mouth was quivering.

Gramps tapped me urgently, and pointed out the door. 'Gwonthen,' he said.

Still, I hesitated. I couldn't believe he and Hannah wouldn't mind if I ran out to meet Dad.

'Go *on* then!' cried Hannah, echoing Gramps. 'You father's been very worried about you. Tell him to come in.'

So I pelted out to the car, and found myself being lifted almost off my feet by Dad. Ben was squeaking away like a mouse with cheese—I suppose it was the surprise of finding his black sheep of a father at his school. Theo stood unsmilingly nearby, rigid as a board, hands hanging by his sides. I knew he was worried that there was going to be a row. To put his mind at rest I cleared my throat importantly—because these next few words were truly momentous—and announced, 'Hannah says you're to come in!'

'She does?' Dad rubbed his hands rapidly and straightened his shoulders, as though he was playing the part of a soldier in a war film. 'Wish me luck, boys. I'm goin' in.'

I'm not going to pretend the three adults did hugs and had a fuzzy Kodak moment. They didn't. To be honest, none of us quite knew how to behave. Gramps was waiting at the door and he shook Dad's hand. Hannah couldn't quite manage a handshake but she did force a very stiff smile, and showed him into the sitting room where he sat awkwardly in an armchair while she gave him tea and biscuits.

'Who's going to do the talking?' she asked.

He inclined his head towards her. 'I think that had better be you, Hannah.'

'All right,' she said, taking a seat on the sofa with Ben snuggled up close. My little brother had gone all clingy again, and was holding on to her skirt. 'I think it's time we explained what we've organised for you all.'

The three of us looked at her.

'The first thing you should know,' she said firmly, 'is that Gramps and I and your father have all come up with this plan together. The next thing is that you are *not* going to lose a home. You'll have two homes and you will always be welcome at both of them. And let me tell you something else—I'm not having my grandchildren living out of suitcases like little lost refugees, so you'll keep clothes and things in both places. You won't have to pack every time.'

'I'll have to pack Bigwig,' said Theo.

'Yes, well maybe Bigwig, poppet,' agreed Hannah. 'And maybe . . .'

She stopped. I looked at her more closely, and realised she'd choked up. Gramps was gazing sadly at her and trying to speak. I didn't know how to help them. Dad obviously understood what had happened, because after a few seconds he took over.

'What we've decided is that in the long run it's best if you, um . . .' He looked enquiringly at Hannah, but she just flapped her hand, telling him to go on. 'We all think it's best if you are based with me at Flawith Cottage from the start of next year. You'll be going to new schools. But don't worry—you'll still spend a lot of time here, you can phone every day, and I hope Hannah and Gramps will often visit us in Helmsley.'

Ben had climbed right onto Hannah's lap and was cuddling close to her. His thumb was in his mouth and his eyes were round. He whimpered, just once and very quietly. Dad heard, and hesitated.

'Go on, Dad,' I said. 'It's okay.'

He looked from Ben, to Theo, to me. 'Really?'

'Mmm,' said Gramps, nodding vigorously.

Dad smiled at him gratefully. 'So until then, you'll spend all the weekends with me. You can visit your new schools, and I need all hands on deck to get Flawith Cottage ready for when you move in. My friend Akash has already agreed to come over with a team of cleaners and some industrial gear, and we'll help them to scrub the place from top to bottom.'

'But what about Flotsam and Jetsam?' asked Theo in a trembling, almost-crying voice.

Dad held out his hands, palms up. 'Well, what do you think? It's for all of us to decide together.'

Theo looked grave, and his brow lowered as he pondered this question. 'I think they should stay here,' he decided. 'They can keep Hannah and Gramps company when we can't.'

'I agree,' I said.

At this, Ben's thumb came out of his mouth. I could see the old gleam in his eye, and from that moment I knew he was going to be all right. 'Can we get a kitten, Dad?' he asked. 'I'd like a new little tabby cat.'

•

The following Sunday, Dad took us over to Brandsmoor. The boys charged off to find their friends but Dad said that Rosie particularly wanted to see me, so I went to look for her. I found her cleaning the big campsite kitchen. I thought she looked a bit depressed at first, because her shoulders were down and so were the corners of her mouth, but she broke into a smile as soon as she spotted me.

'Scarlet!' she cried. 'I'm really glad you're here.'

She didn't say why she especially wanted to see me, and I thought it must just be that we hadn't had any time together for a while. I spent an hour helping her with the cleaning. There was a sticky mess on the stove top. We took bets on what exactly had been baked onto the electric rings (I thought marmalade, she thought beans), and I took a Brillo pad to it.

While we worked, we chatted. She asked about what had happened in the science lab. I gave her a blow-by-blow account, with all the gruesome details. She listened and said 'oh no' and 'ouch' in the right places.

'You must have felt like a pressure cooker,' she said. 'Ready to explode.'

'I did . . . yes, that's right. I feel silly about it now, though.'

'Don't—there was nothing silly about it. But I want you to promise me you'll never, ever do it again. Will you promise? Once is enough, Scarlet.'

I promised. 'It was bloody agony when they gave me the injection,' I assured her. 'I'm never doing that again.'

'Your poor father was beside himself when he heard. He almost burst out of his clothes, like the Incredible Hulk.'

I giggled. 'Did he turn green?'

'He did actually.' She was smiling to herself, as though even thinking about Dad made her happy. 'Livvi and the cool girls,' she said, wrinkling her nose. 'Funny how there's a trio of those little madams in every single class. There were in my school, too. I hope they're ashamed of themselves now?'

'They seem a bit scared of me, actually.'

We carried on with our cleaning. I could hear the boys outside, playing a rowdy tag game with their gang.

'So,' said Rosie, as she tugged out the grill pan. 'You're going to be . . . Ugh, look at this! There's a mouldy sausage stuck to the bottom . . . You're going to be living with your father from after Christmas. Have you forgiven him?'

That was Rosie's style. She asked the hard questions. She didn't mess about.

'Um. . .' I thought long and hard, sloshing water across the floor with a grey string mop. 'It's complicated.'

'I bet it is.'

'Forgiveness is a funny thing. You know when you've swotted for a science exam?'

'That was a long time ago, in my case.'

'Well, use your imagination! You think you've got the hang of . . . let's say photosynthesis. You're sure you've cracked it and you'll get one hundred per cent in that section; but when it comes to actually writing the answer, you find there's far more to it than you realised. Well, that's like forgiveness. One minute I'm absolutely sure I've forgiven Dad.' I squeezed out my mop in the big metal bucket. The water was filthy.

'And the next minute?' she prompted.

'The next minute the man has started singing *that* song—I used to call him the devil man, but I Googled him and it seems he's an iconic musician. Absolutely brilliant. When I hear him singing in my head, I feel as though Mum is dying all over again.'

'Poor Scarlet.'

'It's always there, what Dad did. It always will be. I can never forget it.'

'But you love him.'

'But I love him.'

'Yes. Well, that part is easy to understand.' She was wiping the grill pan when she added quietly, 'I'm moving on tomorrow. That's the main reason I was hoping to see you.'

'Oh?' I said casually. 'When will you be back?'

'I'm not coming back.'

I dropped the mop, staring. 'You're kidding me!'

She'd started polishing that stupid grill pan, lots of elbow grease, making it shine like the crown jewels. 'It's time for me to go home. You dad's kindly agreed to sell my van for me.'

'This *is* your home, isn't it?'

'No.'

'You and Dad . . .'

'There is no me and Dad.'

'Well, there should be! He likes you. You like him. What's the problem?'

She sighed, peeling off her rubber gloves and draping them over the taps. 'Here's the problem,' she said. 'Now, this is going to sound a bit surprising . . .'

And she began to tell me. As she talked, I gave up on my mopping and sat on one of the tables, with my feet on a wooden bench. The more she talked, the more bewildered I felt.

'You aren't a nun!' I protested.

'I'm going to be, though.'

'No, you can't. Look at you—just look at you!'

She glanced down at herself. 'Mm-hm? I'm looking.'

'You've got long messy hair, and you wear bright clothes, and you like to drink a glass of wine. And I love you.'

'Oh . . .' She came rushing across the kitchen to hug me. 'And I love you too, so much! But still, I can't stay here. Scarlet, you've only just got your father back. That's enough to be going on with.'

'He won't want you to leave,' I argued.

'Oh, I think you're wrong there. Your mother is still *very* much in occupation in his head. And from all I've heard, she'd be a hard act to follow.'

That was true. Dad did still have Mum in his head, and I was sure he always would. I remembered him saying *Gotcha*, and the pair of them dancing together like film stars before he kissed her.

'So what?' I asked, shrugging. 'Don't try to follow her! Start up your own show, instead. The Rosie show. I can see your name in lights.'

She climbed up and sat close beside me on the table. She looked beautiful that evening. Her eyelashes seemed very dark, and her hair curled around her face. The day had faded outside; there wasn't much of it left.

'We have to leave soon,' I said. 'Hannah's expecting us back for supper.' I felt terribly unhappy, because I was losing my good friend.

She put her arm around me.

'Please don't go,' I said miserably.

'Scarlet, your life's complicated enough without . . . complications.'

At that moment, Dad walked into the kitchen. He was wearing a baggy white shirt—he'd bought it in Oxfam—and he'd got really tanned from working out of doors all summer. He was a Russian prince today, and he certainly looked lost. He stood on my freshly mopped floor, staring at Rosie with a smile that really wasn't a smile. She stared back at him. As the moments passed, I found I was holding my breath.

'You're not a complication,' he said quietly.

'Well, you are,' she cried. Then she jumped down from the table, hugged me fiercely, and ran out. I thought I heard a sob before the door banged shut.

She wasn't in her van later, when we all went to say goodbye.

'Couldn't you make her stay?' I asked Dad as he drove us back to York that evening.

'I can't make her do anything she doesn't want to.'

'But you'll try?'

He sighed. 'I have already tried.'

'She's in love with you, Dad. Anyone can see that. But she thinks you're out of bounds. She told me you still have Mum in your head.'

His eyebrows shot up. 'Rosie said that?'

'Rosie's nice,' snivelled Ben, from the back seat.

Dad scratched behind his ear, staring at the road ahead. I knew him well enough to understand that he was trying to come up with the right words. 'She's very different to your mother,' he said. 'Different in almost every possible way.'

'Mum was no gypsy, that's for sure. I can't imagine her for one second in the rags Rosie calls clothes, or with that mop of hair,' I chuckled. 'Not to mention Rosie's glam-girl bust!'

'It wouldn't be gentlemanly for me to comment on *that*,' said Dad, grinning. 'But I know what you mean. The first time I saw Zoe, it was like a bolt of lightning. I was head over heels . . . but we didn't become real friends for a while. We were in love, and friendship evolved from that.'

'Mm . . . but with Rosie it's been the other way around, hasn't it?'

He didn't answer.

I gazed out of the window. The hills seemed grey and white, like an old film. 'I wonder whether we'll ever see her again,' I said.

Thirty-eight

Joseph

They had just one more hour together, and they were wasting it.

Her few remaining clothes and possessions were in a small rucksack on the back seat; everything else she had given away. The keys to her kombi were in Joseph's trouser pocket. He would sell it for her, and pay the money into her brother's bank account. From now on, she would have nothing of her own. She was sitting beside him, but soon she'd be gone forever. He felt profoundly miserable.

Joseph's first thought, as he woke, had been that she was leaving today. The knowledge hit him even before he opened his eyes. It ached painfully, like homesickness or bereavement. He hadn't wanted the day to begin at all, because Rosie was leaving. They hadn't talked the previous night; he'd driven back to Brandsmoor after taking the children to York, but she had already gone to bed. He suspected that was because she wanted to avoid him. And now he was driving her to the railway station, and they would say goodbye, and he would never see her again.

'How long's your journey?' he asked now, desperate to start some kind of conversation.

'Hours and hours. Gotta change in Plymouth. I won't get to St Ives until after eight.'

'And will someone meet you at the other end?'

She tucked her hair behind her ear, though it immediately sprang out again. 'Of course.'

Joseph drove on. Time was running out.

'Thanks for the lift,' she said.

He turned his head to look at her. 'Are we reduced to this, Rosie? Polite chitchat?'

Her eyes met his before she looked away. Hers were hypnotic. He saw that now: dark and unerringly clear. He'd come to love the swell of her cheek, framed by its thicket of curls; he'd come to love the way she moved, the way she talked, the way she was. He wanted to swerve onto the verge, cut the engine and pull her into his arms; but it was too late for that. She had made up her mind and he must respect her decision.

Neither of them risked conversation for the rest of the journey. Silence seemed more bearable than pleasantries. With every mile travelled, Joseph felt the ache of loss intensify. They'd allowed extra time, and he was turning into the short-stay car park long before her train was due.

'Don't hang about,' she said, opening her door. 'I'll be fine, and I hate drawn-out goodbyes.'

'Don't be so bloody noble,' growled Joseph, also getting out. He lifted her bag, and then dropped it again. 'Bugger! Got any change for the ticket machine?'

They bought takeaway coffee and sat on a stainless-steel seat on the platform, looking out across the tracks to where some pigeons battled over a dropped sandwich. The ache was drilling into Joseph. It felt raw. He dreaded her absence.

'Funny how railway stations are always cold,' she said, huddling into her shawl.

'It's the shape, I think. Funnels the wind.'

Overhead, a tannoy echoingly reminded passengers not to leave their belongings unattended. Joseph looked at his watch, and felt a sudden clutch of panic. There were four minutes left.

Four minutes.

'Please don't do this,' he said urgently.

She leaned away from him, throwing her cup into a nearby bin. 'My family are there, in the community. Yours are here.'

'My family are yours, too.'

She sounded exasperated. 'They aren't, Joseph! That's the point.'

'The children need you.'

'No.' She shook her head vehemently. 'They need you—just *you*—not distracted, not thinking about anything else. And if I don't go back to Cornwall now, I never can.'

His own cup crumpled under his fingers. 'If you think I've had trouble forgetting Zoe, you're right. I can't forget her, and I never will. But life with her was terrifying and destructive. I don't know how much longer I could have gone on.'

Rosie had become very still. He knew she was listening.

'You're my best friend,' he urged desperately. 'No—far more than that. I feel as though some vital part of me is about to be torn away and get on that bloody train. And you expect me to stand here and merrily wave you off!'

The tannoy blasted again, smashing through his last few words, announcing the imminent arrival of the Plymouth service. He felt a stirring of cold air as it approached, and something close to terror.

'Life without you is going to be bloody awful,' he yelled, above the screech and roar as carriages rolled past, slowed and stopped. Rosie leaped to her feet, threw her rucksack onto her back and headed for the platform edge, furiously wiping her eyes. Joseph followed. Doors opened. People got out, and others began to file on board.

'Give my love to the children,' she said quickly. 'Tell them thanks for everything. I have to go now, because I'm about to start crying and that will be messy.'

He took both her hands in his, drawing in the warmth of her as the crowd jostled and pressed around them. She was wearing walking boots and a full skirt, just as she had when she first knocked on his door, and they played cards on Christmas night. He felt an appalling urgency. In a few seconds she'd be gone. A guard walked along the platform, slamming the heavy doors. Bang. Bang. Bang.

'Okay. I'll let you go,' he said. 'But know that I love you.'

The guard blew his whistle.

Thirty-nine

Hannah

The children left Faith Lane on 27 December. We'd had time to get used to the idea, and I imagine that helped, but at first their absence was a harrowing sadness.

Freddie never directed another play. In theory, he and I were now free to savour our retirement as we'd always planned. In reality, of course, there was no voyage to Alaska; no intrepid expedition on the Trans-Siberian railway. If it was new experiences I was after, I got my wish when I found myself cast in the role of carer for an elderly man; for better or for worse, in sickness and in health. There was no question of my returning to the university—I felt uneasy about leaving Freddie alone in the house—but Scarlet nagged until I signed up for a weekly watercolour class. I was supremely inept at painting but it was something I could do while sitting with Freddie, and it certainly taught me to observe the world with new eyes.

The children came to stay often, at first, but as they settled into their new home it became disruptive for them to have to travel to York at weekends. Instead, Joseph urged us to visit Helmsley. I didn't want to become his guest—we maintained a civil relationship, and that was all—but Freddie overruled me. Our first visit was during the Easter holidays, and Joseph took us to see Brandsmoor. We made small forays around the farm while the children played in the stream, occasionally showing us a spindly-legged lamb or a bunch of daffodils. Joseph worked hard to make the trip a success. Freddie smiled all day, and I realised that his happiness must come before my pride.

So from then on we became regular visitors at Flawith Cottage. Freddie loved to sit in a striped deckchair in the long garden, quietly inhaling the life of the place. His grandchildren took it in turns to hang around beside him, nattering about their schools and friends, perhaps pointing out a butterfly or chuckling with him at the antics of the tabby kitten they'd brought home from the RSPCA. The children were our joy—more importantly, they were our hope.

One autumn evening, Freddie and I were sitting side by side as the sky deepened. He was exclaiming at the aerobatics of a swift, while I made a hash of painting a blush-pink rose. Scarlet had plumped herself down on an upturned bucket with a chicken in her arms, and was chatting merrily to us both. The scars on her arms were barely visible now. The air was starting to feel chilly, but I didn't want to go inside. I was thinking about fetching a sweater for Freddie when Joseph strode out through the back door, carrying two tartan rugs.

'Here we are,' he said, and spread one each across our knees.

'Good God, Scott!' I protested. 'D'you think we're two old codgers?'

He grinned. 'Can I take the fifth on that?'

It was kind of him, but I felt awkward. I still found it difficult not to bristle in his presence, no matter how affable he tried to be. At that moment Rosie appeared at the back door with a bottle and some glasses, and her calm and warmth set everything to rights. Freddie's face lit up, and he lifted a thin hand in salute. She smiled, crossing to him with her easy gait.

'Can you smell the heather?' she asked, inhaling deeply as she took his hand. 'It's in bloom. *So* beautiful. Tomorrow we must go for a drive across the moors.' She poured us each a glass of wine, and lowered herself into the last empty deckchair.

'Hello, Stepmother,' said Scarlet cheekily, as she set her chicken down.

Rosie stuck out her tongue at her. 'The next time you call me that, I'll tan your hide. Makes me sound like a witch with an evil cackle and poisoned apples.'

'Whereas,' retorted Scarlet, rushing to throw her long arms around Rosie's neck, 'you're actually the tart who snogged my father at York railway station—right by the door so they couldn't close it—providing free entertainment for the entire Plymouth train.'

The newspapers had a field day when Joseph and Rosie married. They tried to make it a hush-hush affair at a registry office: just the two of them and the children, and Rosie's brother Tom and his partner, with Abigail and young Akash for witnesses. I am sure none of those people were indiscreet but the story got out somehow. You wouldn't believe the appalling rubbish that was printed.

WIFE-SLAYER WEDS EX-NUN! shrieked one member of the gutter press.

PROBATION, CHASTITY AND OBEDIENCE? asked another.

BLACK VEIL TO WHITE: WHY SISTER ROSEMARY GAVE UP HER CALLING FOR A KILLER.

We coped. We're used to it in our family; we know all about being in the paper for the wrong reasons.

As we sat in the garden of Flawith Cottage, the sky became streaked with red fire. Rosie and I began to talk about the research I'd been involved in over the years; she had a good mind and she grasped ideas very quickly. After a time, the scents of evening began to call to us and she and I took a stroll down the garden, enjoying the stillness. Joseph and Freddie were listening to Scarlet telling a long and apparently hilarious anecdote—complete with funny voices, gesticulations and dramatic tosses of her head. Rosie watched the three for a moment before turning her steady gaze on me.

'Do you still think he doesn't deserve to be loved?' she asked.

I wasn't ready for the question. 'I think . . .' I looked again at Joseph. He sat leaning forward in his chair, his forearms on his knees, delighting with Freddie in Scarlet's monologue. 'I think that he *is* loved.'

'I'm not sure you've answered my question.'

I picked a fallen apple from the ground, turning it around in my hand. There was something that had to be said; something I'd never openly expressed before, even to myself. 'We didn't do enough.'

'When didn't you?'

'Freddie and I knew in our hearts that Zoe was ill again. We had the knowledge and experience, we'd seen it all before—and we could feel the storm clouds gathering. I did try to talk to her about it, but she became angry and I didn't want that. We told ourselves we'd end up alienating ourselves if we interfered. Perhaps . . . if I'm really going to be honest, perhaps I even felt it was Joseph's turn to go through the mill. So we stuck our heads into the sand, and went along with her life view.'

'Joseph didn't ask you for help?'

'No, he didn't. But we should have offered it. To that degree, at least, we too are culpable.'

'Nobody could have seen it coming,' said Rosie gently. 'What happened, I mean. Zoe's death.'

I straightened my arm, holding up the apple. It made a circular hole in the fiery sky. 'I'm not sure,' I said. 'I think I did see it coming. I always felt that her life wouldn't run its natural course.'

Scarlet was still entertaining her father and grandfather. She'd stood right on top of the bucket now, and had begun declaiming.

'Of course Joseph deserves to be loved,' I said. 'But Zoe died at his hand. Please don't ask me to forget that.'

Suddenly, Freddie levered himself out of the chair. He stared around confusedly, probably looking for me. Then he began to stumble off into the darkness, towards the hen house. Joseph leaped to his feet.

'Can I help, Gramps?' called Scarlet. 'Where are you going?'

'It's all right,' I said quickly, running to take his arm. I turned him around and led him towards the back door of the cottage, staying close beside him right into the bathroom. It wasn't something I'd ever imagined I'd be doing, but I really didn't mind. It was both my horror and my privilege—and yes, sometimes my drudgery—to walk beside my soulmate as his body, his dignity and his mind crumbled.

I hate to admit this—really, I hate to—but perhaps it was a good thing our grandchildren weren't living with us towards the end of Freddie's life. Dying isn't a cheerful business. Even Freddie couldn't make it so, though heaven knows he tried.

They weren't there the night he fell heavily between the loo and the bath and dislocated his shoulder, and I simply couldn't lift him up, and he was in such terrible pain. They weren't there when he asked where Zoe was, and wept inconsolably when he remembered. They didn't see him wandering off along Faith Lane, demanding to 'go home' (go where? The home of his childhood? Demolished in the 1970s, to make way for a motorway). They didn't catch me crying when, for the first time, he asked me who I was.

Those last days weren't the most glamorous he and I ever had together; they weren't the sexiest, that's for sure. Yet I treasured them. Just Freddie Wilde and me, living in our shambolic home, somehow finding a path through each moment. Together.

The children had been gone for over a year when—kneeling carefully to examine a ladybird among our spring flowers—Freddie suffered that final stroke. The one that blew out the candle.

Epilogue

Scarlet

It was only the second funeral I'd ever been to. They persuaded Hannah to hold it in the Minster, because Gramps was distinguished and adored, and so many people wanted to be there to give him a send-off. He had glowing obituaries in both *The Times* and the *Guardian*. Beat that.

Ben and Theo were wearing brand-new suits, bought for the occasion. Ben looked cute in his. I'm sure he'll always be cute. He'll always trade on it, too, because he is a spoiled little brat and we all dote on him. Theo's still a miniature version of Dad—except he has that lanky, slightly spotty look boys get when they're about to have their growth spurt. His nose isn't a button anymore; it's starting to be more of a hooter. He'll be hot one day soon, and I plan to vet his girlfriends. Bitches and bimbos need not apply. Ditto the cool gang.

Hannah had been like a tissue-dispensing machine for days, because we three grandchildren had been bawling our eyes out. She was totally dignified but she looked wrong without Gramps at her elbow. She looked like a half-person. He had always, always been there, even when he was slow and jumbled; and now suddenly he wasn't. All that week, besieged by undertakers and vicars and relatives and weeping friends, Hannah must just have wanted him back, but I hadn't seen her shed a single tear. I don't know how she did it.

Hundreds of people turned up for the funeral, including a crowd of what Gramps used to call 'luvvies'. To them it was obviously a giant reunion, and they were delighted to meet up with old friends. I have never seen so many air kisses on one day. Jane Whistler was there, looking fashionable but sad. Mr Hardy was too, and I'm pleased to report that he'd given the purple shirt a miss. Aunt Marie came along, of course, though there still wasn't much love lost between her and Dad. Rosie sat with our family, in the front row of seats. She and Dad looked lovely together. They fitted.

Gramps planned his funeral not long before he died, in one of those precious moments when the mist of his confusion seemed to part for an hour. He wasn't a revered theatre director for nothing, and it was the most glorious service. He especially wanted to choose the six people who would carry him out of the Minster at the end. He asked Hannah to write down the names of these honoured pallbearers, and got her to promise that she would invite them all. Four were very dear friends of his, all from the theatre world. The fifth was me. The last one was Dad.

As we lifted the coffin from its stand, the organ struck up so loudly that Ben covered his ears. The music made me feel as though I could fly, as though I could take off and soar as high as the vaulted ceiling. It was like a thousand trumpets sounding. They were sounding for Frederick Wilde: brilliant director, funny storyteller, kind listener, lover of lichen and tiny things. Frederick Wilde, who adored my mum and forgave my dad.

The coffin was heavier than I expected. Hannah had someone lined up and ready to take over if I couldn't manage, but I was almost sixteen, and practically as tall as some of the men, and I was bloody well going to do this last thing for my grandfather. We walked slowly, pacing down the long aisle of the Minster while the choir joined in with the organ and sang the most beautiful music I have ever heard. There were tears streaming down my face, my nose was running and my tissue was in the pocket I couldn't reach, so I must have looked a sight. Dad was walking in front of me with his strong hand curled around the handle. I'm pretty sure he was trying to take on extra weight so as to make my job easier.

Breezy sunshine met us outside, and the pavement was strewn with pink blossom. It made me think of confetti at a wedding. We carefully laid Gramps in the back of a car, and the undertaker began to replace the wreaths. People in dark funeral clothes were streaming out of the Minster, while tourists in anoraks queued to get in.

Theo nudged me. 'D'you think Mum's here?' he gulped miserably.

I tried to imagine Mum standing beside us, green eyes in a laughing face.

'I'm sure she is,' I fibbed. 'And Gramps as well. I can feel them.'

'Really?'

'Really.'

Hannah had drawn a little apart from everybody. Endless people kept stopping to say kind words and she replied graciously to each one, but she seemed utterly alone. Nobody stayed with her for long; they moved on to jollier companions. She was wearing her special emerald earrings, the ones that Gramps had given to her. As I watched, she rested her hand on the coffin. I knew exactly what she was doing.

The next moment, Dad was beside her. He didn't say anything at all, and neither did she. I don't think either of them needed to. He put his arm around her shoulders. They stood side by side, quietly saying goodbye. I hoped Gramps could see them; he'd be turning cartwheels. I imagined him and Mum, and Dick Turpin, and Elvis Presley, and a metal-skirted Roman soldier and a couple of dazzling angels, all drinking a toast in their heavenly café.

'To absent friends!' they yelled, and tossed back their glasses of nectar.

It was a blue and gold morning, and a million daffodils rippled beneath the city walls.

About the author

Charity Norman was born in Uganda and brought up in successive draughty vicarages in Yorkshire and Birmingham. After several years' travel she became a barrister, specialising in crime and family law in the northeast of England. Also a mediator, she is passionate about the power of communication to slice through the knots. In 2002, realising that her three children had barely met her, she took a break from the law and moved with her family to New Zealand. Her first novel, *Freeing Grace*, was published in 2010 and her second, *After the Fall* (published in Australia as *Second Chances*) was published in 2013 and was selected for the Richard & Judy Book Club.